Mr. and Miss Anonymous

Books by Fern Michaels

Published by Kensington Publishing Corporation

FERN MICHAELS

Mr. and Miss Anonymous

ZEBRA BOOKS
KENSINGTON PUBLISHING CORP.
http://www.kensingtonbooks.com

Prologue

University of California
Berkeley Campus, 1986

Peter Aaron Kelly stared out of his grungy apartment window not caring that he was running late. His roommates had gone home for the Christmas holiday, so he had the sparsely furnished apartment to himself. Maybe he should just blow off his appointment at the clinic and go straight to his job at the café, where he worked as a waiter for the three-hour lunch period. But, he needed the last payment from the clinic. Needed it desperately to pay the final installment on his tuition for his last semester. In the end, what the hell difference did it make one way or the other? He shrugged his shoulders, reached for his Windbreaker and baseball cap.

* * *

Thirty-five minutes later, Pak, as he was known to his friends, entered the Berkeley Sperm Bank thirteen minutes late. The unlucky number didn't go unnoticed by him. For one crazy moment he wanted to bolt, but the last reminder from the billing office told him he had no other choice. He signed in using his donor number of 8446. He turned his baseball cap around so the bill could tickle his neck as he sat down and picked up a magazine. Like he was really going to read *Field & Stream.*

His eyes glued to the glossy magazine cover, he didn't look up when a steady stream of guys paraded past him, some leaving, some entering. He'd done this gig eleven times. Everyone entered and exited this place with eyes downcast just the way he did. No one spoke, no one made eye contact. All they wanted was to get the hell out of there so they could try to exorcise their personal shame and spend the guilt money. He should know because he was one of them. He took a moment to wonder how many of the donors walking through the clinic's doors went to the counseling sessions that were so strongly recommended each time a donor signed a contract. He took another moment to wonder who owned the place. Probably some very rich person. More guilt piled up on his shoulders as he waited patiently for his number to be called.

Pete shifted his mind to a neutral zone and closed his eyes. He thought about his family back at the farm in Idaho where they grew potatoes. They'd all be getting ready for Christmas.

One of his brothers had probably cut down the tree by now, and it was sitting in the living room just waiting to be decorated. His nieces and nephews were probably driving everyone crazy to decorate the tree, but his mother would make them wait for the branches to settle themselves so, as she put it, her heirloom decorations wouldn't fall off. He wondered what his mother would serve for Christmas Eve dinner. A turkey or a ham. Maybe even both. Five different pies. Well, probably just the turkey or just the ham, but not both. And maybe only two pies this year, he thought, remembering his father had told him it'd been a bad year with a blight that had hit the plants midseason. His mouth started to water at the thought of what he was missing. Oh, well, five more months and he could go home for a week or so before he started job hunting.

Pete's thoughts shifted to his three-and-a-half-year struggle to get through college. He thought of the lean meals, the long days of work followed by all-night study sessions, and getting by on only a few hours' sleep. So many times he wanted to call it quits, but something deep inside him wouldn't allow it because he was determined to be a self-made millionaire by the age of forty.

The day he made his first million he was going to do two things. The first thing he was going to do was send his family to Hawaii and set them up in a nice house right on the ocean. The second thing he was going to do was buy this goddamn place, and the minute the ink was dry on the contract, he was going to burn it to the ground.

A chunky woman in a nurse's uniform appeared in the doorway. "Number 8446. You're up next. You're late this morning, 8446." Not bothering to wait to see if he would offer up an explanation, the woman said, "Room 5. You know what to do."

Yeah, I know what to do, Pete thought as he brushed past the woman. He knew she didn't approve of what went on there behind the numbered doors, but she worked there anyway, collected a paycheck. As hard as he tried, he couldn't make it compute in his head. At one point he decided she was a hypocrite and let it go at that. He didn't give a good rat's ass if she approved of what he and hundreds of other guys were doing or not. He always stared her down when she handed him the envelope at the end of the session.

Pete entered Room 5. The setup was always the same. Small TV. Porno movie in the VCR. Dozens of what his father would call "girlie magazines." *Equipment.* He argued with himself for a full five minutes. *I don't want to do this again. I can't do this anymore. You have to do it. If you don't, the next semester is gone. Just close your eyes and do it. No. Yes.* In the end, he lost the argument. He unzipped and turned on the VCR.

In the building next to the sperm bank, Lily Madison entered the egg donor clinic for her last session. She looked at her watch, knowing she had only an hour. She hoped that today's session would go as quickly as her others had. She closed her eyes, trying to imagine what she was going to feel when she picked up her last check for $6,000. Relief? Guilt? Satisfaction that her last semester was going to be paid for? Maybe all three. When she left after graduation, she would never, ever come back to this place. Never, ever.

Lily adjusted her homemade denim hat with the big sunflower on it as she walked through the swinging doors. For some reason, wearing a hat gave her confidence and courage. She'd tried to explain it to her roommates, but they just laughed at her. They said she wore hats because she hated her kinky, curly hair. Maybe it was both. Her head up, she marched up to the desk and signed in as Donor 1114. Within minutes she was whisked into an examining room.

When it was all over, Lily dressed and sighed with relief. She could leave the place and never come back. Her eyes filled with tears. How weird was that? She swiped them away as she walked toward the payment window. She handed the clerk the slip the doctor had given her and waited. She almost swooned when the check was in her hand. She thought about buying a bottle of wine and drinking it all, by way of celebrating the end of this . . . this . . . experience in her life. It was such a stupid thought, she chased it out of her mind. From here on, what had transpired over the past months was a memory. A memory she could think about or forget about.

It's no big deal, she told herself as she walked out into the late-afternoon sunshine.

Her thoughts all over the map, she didn't see him until she landed on the ground, and a hand was outstretched to help her up. "You knocked me down," Lily said inanely.

"I know, I know, I'm sorry. I mean it, I'm really sorry. Are you all right? Can I do anything for you?"

He smiled, and Lily was charmed.

"I like your hat!"

"I made it."

"Wow! Are you sure you're okay?"

He sounds like he cares if I'm all right or not. She nodded and held out her hand. "Lily."

"Pak," Pete said, electing to go with his initials instead of his real name. "Are you . . . what I mean is . . . did you?"

Lily nodded again. "I guess you did the . . . uh . . ."

"Yeah, it was my last session."

"Mine, too."

"This is embarrassing," Pete said, offering up his megawatt smile.

"Yes, it is. Are you a student? Do you suppose that when we meet up at one of our reunions, we'll remember this moment?" Lily asked as she jammed her hat more firmly on her head. Like she was ever going to go to a reunion.

"Yeah. I'm studying to be a teacher. I bet we do. Well, I'm really sorry. If you're sure you're okay, I have to get going or I'll be late for work."

"I'm okay. I have to get going myself. Good luck."

Pete turned to walk away, then walked back. "Do you mind if I ask you a personal question?"

Lily shrugged. "Try me."

"Did you . . . uh . . . did you go to any of the counseling sessions?"

The expression on Pak's face told her he was serious. "No. I wanted to go, but my schedule . . . No, I didn't. Did you?"

"No. I hope neither one of us regrets it."

"You sound like you regret it already. It's not too late if you feel like that." Lily wondered if what she was saying was true or not. "Hey, wait a minute. Let me ask you a question. That concrete building that runs across the back of the sperm bank and the donor clinic . . . what is it, do you know? Did you ever hear who owns this place?"

Pete shook his head. "I asked one time, and they more or less told me that it was none of my business. I walked around the block after . . . well, after, and thought it a little strange that the building doesn't have doors or windows. Is there a reason why you're asking? Some rich guy with tons of money probably owns it. Isn't that the way of the world, the rich get richer, and the poor get poorer?"

"The first time I went to the clinic, I sort of got lost and wandered down·the wrong hallway and you would have thought I was going to plant a bomb. An Amazon of a woman shooed me away. I guess the building belongs to the sperm bank and donor center. I'm just curious by nature. Like you said, no windows or doors. I find that strange."

"So, are you thinking something *sinister* is going on? That's what I thought at first. Now I couldn't care less. I'm outta here." Pete narrowed his gaze as he waited for her reply.

Lily laughed, but it was an uneasy sound even to her own ears. "No. Just my womanly curiosity." But she knew that it was not just "womanly curiosity" at all.

He didn't know anything about "womanly curiosity." It was Pete's turn to shrug. "See ya," he said, waving airily in her direction.

"Yeah, see you."

A brisk afternoon wind whipped up. Lily clutched at her hat as she headed for her car, a rusty Nissan with over 150,000 miles on it. Before unlocking the door, she said a prayer, as she always did, that the car would start. To her delight, the engine turned over on the first try.

Lily drove aimlessly, up one street, down another, seeing Christmas shoppers out in full force. It was going to be her first holiday alone. Since her grandmother's death earlier in the year, there was no reason to go back home to South Carolina. Her parents had abandoned her at the age of four to be raised by her grandmother, then left the country. She didn't know where they were or even if they were alive. There had been no way to notify her mother when her grandmother passed away. Her eyes filled with tears. She was so alone.

Lily continued to drive and finally decided to

stop at a café for a late lunch. She parked the Nissan, climbed out, and entered the cheerful-looking little restaurant, where she settled herself in a far corner. She was shocked out of her wits when she saw the guy with the beaming smile walk toward her table. She gasped. He stopped in his tracks to stare at her.

Pete took the initiative. "I'm not intuitive or anything like that, but do you suppose our meeting like this means something?"

Lily felt her face grow warm. "That we're both embarrassed? How's the tuna?"

"Too much mayo. Try the corned beef."

"Okay. So you work here, huh?"

"Yep. Just the lunch hour. Three hours, actually. Then I pack groceries for three more hours. The jobs work with my schedule, but since we're on Christmas break I log all the hours I can. How about you?"

"Okay, I'll take a corned beef on rye. I waitress and tutor. I owe a ton of money on my student loans," she blurted.

"Yeah, me, too. Coffee or soda?"

"Coffee."

"I'm about done here, so I'll bring your order and have coffee with you if you don't mind. I get to eat here for free, that's why I keep this job. That's probably more than you wanted to know."

Lily shook her head and smiled. Suddenly, she wanted to know everything there was to know about the guy standing next to her.

While she waited for her food, Lily looked around. Crisp black-and-white-check curtains hung on the windows. There was nothing fly-specked about this eatery. The floors were tile and exceptionally clean. The chairs had seat cushions with the same black-and-white-check pattern. Green plants were on the windowsills. On closer examination, Lily decided they were herbs and not plants. She wasn't sure, but she rather thought the special of the day was meat loaf. The aromas were just like the ones she remembered from her grandmother's kitchen.

"This is a nice place," Lily said, when Pete joined her with his coffee.

"Two sisters own it, and they do all their own cooking and baking. Once in a while they try out new recipes on me." He laughed.

Lily loved his laugh, his smile. An awkward silence followed.

Pete stopped drinking his coffee long enough to ask, "So, do you want to talk about *it*, or do you want to talk about . . . stuff?"

"By *it*, I guess you mean our donations at the clinic. I'd just as soon forget it. It's no big deal, you know."

Pete rolled the words around in his head. *No big deal.* He looked at her. Her eyes were telling him it *was* a big deal. "Yeah, right, no big deal. Well, I have to run. It was nice to meet you, Lily. Maybe we'll run into each other again someplace."

He wasn't interested in her. For some reason she thought he was going to ask for her phone number or her address. "Yeah, right," she said flatly before she bit into her sandwich.

At the door, Pete turned and waved. He didn't

think he'd ever forget the young girl with the sad eyes and the sunflower hat. *I should have asked her for her phone number.*

The minute the door closed behind Pete, Lily placed some bills on the table and left the café. *It's no big deal, it's no big deal,* she told herself over and over as she slid into the Nissan. *Five more months, and I can put this all behind me. Just five months.*

Tears rolled down her cheeks as she drove away from the café.

Little did she know how wrong she was.

Chapter 1

Peter Aaron Kelly looked around his suite of offices and grinned. He'd done it. He'd made it happen. And he'd pulled it off right on schedule. He patted himself on the back as he made his way into the private lavatory that was as big as his family's living room back in Idaho.

Pete, as he liked to be called, stared at his reflection in the huge plate glass mirror that took up one entire wall of his private bathroom. He straightened the knot in his tie. Not just any knot but a Windsor knot. He loved Windsor knots because they looked so neat and finished. The suit wasn't half-bad either. Custom-made Armani that draped his lanky frame to perfection. Not that he normally wore such attire, but it was a special day, and he owed it to his people to look his best. If he showed up in his jeans, a washed-out, ragged Berkeley T-shirt, and his tattered baseball cap, no one would take him seriously. The power suit and the Windsor knot shrieked: *PAY ATTENTION*.

The eight-hundred-pound gorilla and founder of PAK Industries continued to study himself in the mirror. No one would ever call him handsome. Nor would they say he was cute. Articles, and there were hundreds of them, said he was "interesting." One even said he was "chameleon-like," whatever the hell that meant. Those same articles then fast-forwarded to his financials and more or less said he could be ugly as sin because no one cared, and with all that money in the bank, he was the CIC. His secretary had to translate that for him. CIC, she said, meant Cat in Charge. If he wanted to, he could start purring right then. He laughed at the thought.

"Hey, Pete, you in here somewhere?" his long-time motherly secretary shouted from the doorway.

Pete ran a loose ship, and as long as the work got done, he didn't care who wore what or who said what. Familiarity in the workplace worked for everyone's comfort zone.

"Just checking my tie, Millie. Do you need me for something?"

Hands on her plump hips, Millie stared at her boss. "Well, would you look at you! You want some advice?"

"No, but that isn't going to stop you. Spit it out."

"You look silly. Ditch the duds and go back to being you. You only get dressed up like that when you go to funerals. Did someone die, and you forgot to tell me? We always send flowers or a fruit basket. By the way, some personal mail just came for you. I put it on your desk earlier while you were getting dressed. I think it's the third request for your RSVP in regard to your alma mater's fund-raiser. You might want to take care of that."

Pete walked over to his desk to see a large, cream-colored square envelope with the return address of his alma mater. Millie was right, he needed to get on the stick and make a decision one way or the other.

"Well? So, who died?"

He was off-balance. Just the sight of the cream-colored envelope and the return address rushed him back to another part of his life. A part of his life he didn't want to deal with just then. "No one died. I'm dressed like this for the ten o'clock meeting. Then I have that photo op with Senator what's-his-name. I still don't know how I got roped into that."

His voice was so cool, so curt, Millie drew back and closed the door. She rushed around the floor warning everyone that the boss had his knickers in a twist and was all dressed up. Something was going on. The entire floor huddled as they tried to understand why the boss would attend a meeting in a suit and tie even though he was going to have his picture taken later. Peter Aaron Kelly didn't give a damn about suiting up for photo ops. Everyone in the whole world knew that.

"And," Millie said importantly, "the boss is wearing Armani and not his regular hand-stitched HUGO BOSS funeral attire. Something is definitely going down this morning. He's chipper, though, so it must be a good thing.

Well, he was chipper until the mail came," Millie muttered as an afterthought.

While Pete's staff whispered among themselves, he was busy ripping open the envelope Millie had left for him. She was right, he had twenty-four hours to say yea or nay. Even at that late date they were still willing to have him as their guest speaker if he would commit. "Well, boys and girls, I don't see that happening anytime soon. I'll send you a check, and we'll call it square." To make himself feel better, he scribbled off a sizable check and tossed it in the top drawer along with the two previous invitations. Millie would take care of it. He'd have her send off an e-mail or overnight letter nixing the speaking gig.

Screw it all. Now he was in a cranky mood. He flopped down on his custom-made chair, whose leather was butter soft, and propped his feet on the desk. He had fifteen minutes to, as his mother used to put it, woolgather. He made a mental note to ask her if she still used that expression.

Pete opened the drawer again and reached for the invitation. He twirled the cream-colored square in his hands. Maybe he should go back. So what if he'd made a promise to himself *never* to do so. People broke promises all the time, especially when the person made the promise to himself.

As the minute hand on his watch crawled forward, Pete slid the invitation back into the drawer. Maybe he'd think about it later. Not too much later, he cautioned himself. The reunion was across the country in two days.

What the hell, he had a corporate jet. But getting that baby all fired up with a pilot was a whole other ball game, especially on short notice. Then again, maybe he wouldn't think about it. He blinked when a vision of a young girl in a floppy hat with a big sunflower on it appeared behind his eyelids. Lily. Lily something. He took a minute to wonder where she was and what she was doing. She was probably married with four or five kids and a doting husband. He corrected that thought immediately when he remembered the last time he'd seen her and the sad look in her eyes. No, he'd bet PAK Industries that Lily something-or-other wasn't married with kids.

Pete looked down at the calendar on his desk. He had a busy day. After the photo op with the senator, he had an appointment with his shrink. Maybe after his appointment he would be in a better frame of mind to make a decision about attending the fund-raiser.

The pricey TAG Heuer watch on his wrist chirped. Time to head for the boardroom so he could make his announcement. Fifteen minutes, tops. Five minutes to get downstairs to meet the senator and smile pretty for the cameras. What the hell *was* the senator's name? Then off to the shrink. After that, he was on his own time. The thought left him light-headed.

Precisely three minutes later, Pete entered the conference room. For some reason, the room always amazed him. It was half the size of a football field, with wraparound windows for light, and was dominated by a long teak table whose shine was so bright he could see his reflection. Twelve leather chairs surrounded the table. Off to all four sides of the large room were private groupings of chairs, small sofas, tables, and tons of greenery. In the center of the teak table was a magnificent silver coffee urn, with fine china cups and a crystal decanter of orange juice as well as four trays of assorted pastries.

"Hi, people," Pete said, taking his seat at the head of the table. He looked around at all the people who had worked at his side for years and years to make it all happen. He owed them all big-time. He nodded to Millie, who was trotting around the long table, placing in front of each person a snow-white envelope with the PAK logo in the corner.

"A show of my appreciation. Look, there's no easy way to say this other than to come right out and say it. I'm taking some time off. A year at the least. Maybe longer. You can run this place without me. There are some things I need to do. Personal things. So, having said that"—Pete tossed a set of keys to his second-in-command, Marty Bronson—"the keys to everything, Marty, and you get my parking space. Before you can ask, no, I am not sick, no, I am not getting married."

Pete pushed back his chair and stood up. "Oh, there is one other thing. Every one of you in this room has my cell phone number. If you call me, you're fired. I'll check in from time to time so you can hear my cheery voice. I want to walk out of here knowing I didn't make a mistake when I hired you all. Just make me proud and let me get out of here before I start blubbering. Don't get up. Sit there and plan how you're going to spend those checks I just gave you. See ya!"

Outside in the hallway, Millie stared at him, tears rolling down her cheeks. "That was a really shitty thing you just did in there, Peter Aaron Kelly. You should have prepared us, given some kind of warning. Everyone's in shock. What are you going to do now, watch television?"

It was the worst thing Millie could have said to her boss. Pete never watched television; he hated it with a passion. Every day his staff tormented him with what they'd seen on the tube that he'd missed. Pete turned away, too choked up to reply right away. When he finally got his tongue to work, he said, "Call Berkeley and tell them I might or might not attend. There's a check in my top drawer you can forward by overnight mail. Give my regrets about not being their guest speaker, say I was flattered, yada, yada, yada. I'm going to forget that crack you just made about me watching television. C'mere, give me a big hug so I can go meet that senator. What the hell *is* his name?"

Millie wiped at her eyes. "His name is Hudson Preston, the senior senator from California. You didn't mean me, did you, when you said you didn't want any calls from here? I'm sorry about my television comment. I was upset. I am still upset, Pete."

Pete squared his shoulders. "Sorry, Millie, it means you, too. I need time and space. I'll call you. I promise."

"Go on, get out of here, you big *schmuck.* Shame on you for making an old lady cry," Millie said, wiping at her eyes. She did her best to summon up a smile to send Pete on his way.

"I love you, Millie. Keep your eye on things. I'll be back, I just don't know when." Pete waved airily as he headed for the elevator. He was glad no one was looking at him when he swiped at his own eyes with the back of his hand.

Pete stepped out of the elevator to see the senator and his entourage milling about the spacious lobby of his building. He realized in that one second that he did not like the senator, had never liked him.

An aide approached him, a young guy with his share of zits and spiky hair. "It would be so much better if we could do the photo op in your corporate offices, Mr. Kelly. This lobby is so cold and sterile-looking. It really isn't the kind of warm and fuzzy image the senator wants to convey. This," he said, waving his arm about, "is so . . . corporate."

"Sorry, rules are rules," Pete said briskly. "Can we get on with it? I have a meeting, and I don't want to be late."

The aide looked horrified at Pete's words. He started to sputter. "But . . . but the senator cleared his calendar for an hour. We came all the way from Washington."

"It's a forty-five-minute shuttle ride. A letter went out to your offices explaining all this. Now, let's get on with it, or I'll leave you all standing here to suck your thumbs."

Before the aide could reply, the senator approached Pete, his personal camera crew right behind him. "Ah, Peter, nice seeing you again."

Pete extended his hand and gave the senator a bone-crushing handshake. "Guess it's that time of year again. I hate to rush you, but I have a meeting I can't be late for."

The senator's eyes narrowed, but he didn't lose his affability. He smiled, knowing he was being captured on film. "I understand, we allotted only fifteen minutes ourselves. I appreciate your agreeing to the op at all. I know how busy you corporate types are."

Pete bared his teeth in what he hoped was a smile. "Good, that means we're on the same page."

When the allotted fifteen minutes were up, Pete looked pointedly at his watch.

Senator Preston threw his arm around Pete's shoulders. "I have a limo out front. Can we drop you off somewhere?"

Pete shrugged off the senator's arm, and replied, "Thanks, but I'm walking." He was through the revolving door within seconds and on his way down the winding walkway. He had a bad taste in his mouth. Later he would think about the fact that he didn't like Senator Preston. He wondered if it had anything to do with the few visits he'd made to the shrink. The last thing Dr. Myers had said last week when Peter was leaving his office was to think about the "why" of everything. Why didn't he like Senator Preston? Peter didn't have a clue.

The trees were dressed for spring early that year. As he exited the PAK Industries campus and walked on out to the boulevard, Pete started shedding his clothing. He yanked at the power tie and stuffed it in his pocket. The only reason he knew it was a power tie was because Millie had bought it and told him so. Next came the Armani jacket. He slung it over his shoulder as he maintained his easy gait while at the same time rolling up the cuffs of his pristine white shirt. Ah, now he could breathe. He wished he'd had the foresight to jam his baseball cap into his hip pocket. He always felt undressed without it.

Thirty minutes later, Pete arrived at a six-suite brick medical building with ivy growing up the bricks, all the way to the top of the second floor. He liked the look because there was something homey about it. The plaques attached to the brick weren't the standard polished brass but chunks of driftwood that were sanded, then shellacked. Dr. Harvey Myers was on the first floor.

Pete looked at his watch. He was one minute early. He felt proud of himself when he opened the door to the waiting room to find Harvey Myers waiting for him with a cup of coffee. Harvey handed it over. Pete laughed. "You're spoiling me, Harvey."

The easy familiarity between doctor and patient went back years and years. Harvey had once coached the PAK Industries softball team until the demands of his practice required cutting back on his outside activities. They made small talk, Pete sipping the strong black brew and Harvey drinking decaffeinated herbal tea.

Together, the two men moved toward the doctor's private office. As always, Pete eyed the chaise lounge, then moved to a recliner that tilted backward and had a footrest.

Harvey set aside his herbal tea and picked up a pad and pen, but not before he turned on the portable recording machine. Pete sipped his coffee as the doctor recorded the date, the time, and the patient's name.

"So, how's it going, Pete? You sleeping any better?"

"No. I prowl all night long. No, I don't want any sleep help. You know how I feel about pills of any kind. When my body is tired, I'll sleep."

"Did you do it?"

Pete didn't ask for clarification. He knew exactly what Harvey was referring to. "As a matter of fact, I did, about an hour ago. I thought it went well. I'm a free agent. Nice feeling. Well, I think it's going to be a nice feeling once I get used to the idea."

"Any plans?"

"No, not really. I haven't decided if I'm going to California or not."

Harvey put down the pen and pad and leaned forward. "Let's cut the bullshit right here, Pete. You've been coming here three times a week for a month. I can't help you if you won't open up to me. Whatever past relationship we had, inside this room, we're doctor and patient. The fact that you actually decided to make an appointment—and kept it—tells me something is bothering you. Having said that, I want you either to tell me what's bothering you or get the hell out of here so I can help someone who needs and wants my help."

Pete looked around the comfortable office. For the first time he could hear soft music coming from somewhere. He thought he heard water trickling in the far corner. He wondered if it was something new. He asked and blinked when Harvey said the music was always on, and the trickling water went into a fish tank. "Am I that obvious?"

"Well, yeah. I am a psychiatrist, Pete. You came here to unload, so will you get on with it?"

Pete jerked at the handle on the recliner and bounced upright. He, too, leaned forward. "I made a promise to myself, and I didn't keep it. Well, I kept the first part but not the second part. I want to know if that kind of promise counts. You know, when you make it to yourself. I didn't even make an effort to keep it. I think I know why I didn't, but I'm not sure. By the way, no one knows about it. Well, that's not really true, someone does know. A girl I told way back when. At least I think I told her. It was a lifetime ago, Harvey."

"Tell me about it, Pete. Everything you can remember. I'm not going to judge you."

Pete was up off the recliner and pacing. From time to time he would smack one balled fist into the palm of his other hand. He gulped for air. "It was a long time ago. The summer months, right before my senior year. I was working around the clock for tuition money. My dad told me there wasn't enough money to send me for the last year because of some blight to the potatoes. I was on my own. I tried skimping on food, then I got sick. I was just about to drop out and look for full-time work when one of the summer guys told me about this clinic where I could sell my sperm. Man, I was off like a rocket. I signed up for . . . I did it twelve times. That's how I got the money to finish up on time.

"In the beginning, it didn't seem important. I'd go, *do it*, leave, and get on with my day. Then it started bothering me. Then it started bothering me even more. I hated it, yet I had to finish what I started—I needed the goddamn money.

"You know my story, Harvey. I made a promise to myself that when I made my first million, I was going to relocate my parents to Hawaii. Of course, that went up in smoke because they refused to go. I told you that a few times already. What I never told you was there was a second part to the promise. I promised myself I was going to go back to California and buy the damn sperm bank, then burn it down. They weren't just words. I meant it. I never did it. I need to find out why I didn't do it. I could have, Harvey. I could have paid whatever the owner wanted. I didn't even try. I should have tried, Harvey. It haunts me."

"Why?" Harvey asked.

"Haven't you been listening to me, Harvey? That's why I'm here. I want you to tell me why I didn't do it. I think there was something fishy going on there. It's easy to say now, but it wasn't so easy to say back then. Then there's the girl who was donating her eggs at the same place. We bumped into each other on the last day. She looked so damn sad. We both had trouble looking at one another because we both knew why we were there, and it was embarrassing."

"Go on, Pete." The pen and pad were back in Harvey's hands.

"She . . . her name was Lily . . . she said, maybe I said, damn, I don't know, but one of us said there was something *sinister* about the place."

"What made you think that?"

"Lily said it was because of the big, long building that ran across the back of the sperm bank and the egg donor clinic. She said it didn't have windows or doors, yet it was attached to the egg donor clinic and the sperm bank. She also said she tried getting into it, but an Amazon of a woman stopped her. She damn well spooked me, Harvey, and I've been spooked ever since."

"Is this why you can't sleep?"

"Damn straight. Plus, every time I see a teenage kid, I think it's one of mine. Am I losing it, Harvey?" Pete asked in a tormented voice. "For all I know I could have twelve kids out there walking around. Before you can ask, yes, they tried to get me to go to counseling sessions, but I blew them off. Look, I was young and stupid. Back then the only thing I was thinking about was how I was going to make it through the last year so I could make my first million by the time I turned forty. Did I know I was going to be a *billionaire* at forty instead of a millionaire? It just snowballed and happened. It's not like I was counting the dollars on a daily basis. Lily whatever-her-name-was didn't go to the counseling sessions either. The way she put it was, 'It's no big deal.' I think back then it *was* a big deal for her, more so than me, but that's how I'm seeing it now."

"I see."

Pete bristled. "What the hell do you see, Harvey? That I was a jerk? I know that. Just tell me what the hell to do to get this monkey off my back."

"It doesn't work that way. What do you *want* to do? Everything in life starts at the beginning."

"So what you're telling me is I should go back to California and do whatever I have to do. I did try to locate Lily. For some reason, I couldn't find her in the yearbook."

"Why didn't you hire a private detective to find her? It would appear you didn't want to find her badly enough. It's not like you can't afford the best of the best, Pete."

"I guess I'm afraid." Pete sat back down on the recliner. "You need a bigger place, Harvey. This is too cozy, too comfortable. You need more light in here, too."

"I'll take it under consideration. Why didn't

you follow through on the promise you made to yourself? Did you think it was too far over the top—one of those things you say because the moment seems right at the time—or did you really believe there was something sinister about the facility?"

"Probably a little bit of both. I have to go back to the beginning, don't I?"

"It's a good place to start, Pete. You do realize you cannot invade people's lives, don't you?"

"Hell, yes. That's one of the things that's killing me. God, I was so stupid. Why the hell didn't I just take a semester's leave, work my ass off, then finish up? Why?"

"Is it because you are so goal-oriented? So on target, so anal, you can't get sidetracked in any way? There are people like that, you know," Harvey said quietly.

"You mean that in my haste to become a millionaire at the age of forty, I didn't give two shits about anything except myself?"

"Something like that. Do you want some advice?"

"Yeah. Yeah, I do, Harvey."

"Then find the elusive Miss Lily and take it from there. It's not that misery loves company, but more like you two have so much in common, maybe you can help each other. I'm just a phone call away, Pete."

"I can't unring the bell. This is never going to go away, right? I have to come to terms with what I did and didn't do. I guess I've known that all along, just didn't want to face it."

"No one is perfect; nor is it a perfect world we live in. We all make mistakes, and we have to live with them. Sometimes you get up to bat again, and sometimes you don't. You have to make the best of it."

"And that about ends our session," Pete said, getting up off the chair.

Harvey clapped Pete on the shoulder. "It's not the end of the world, Pete. It might seem like that right now, but eventually there will be light at the end of the tunnel."

"I'll call you."

"From California?" Harvey asked.

"Yeah, from California."

Chapter 2

Lily Madison stared off into space. She was jolted out of her thoughts when the office manager of Sandcastle Ltd. entered her workroom to drop her personal mail on the desk. Penny Lyons knew better than to intrude when her boss was designing. Lily looked down at her sketch pad. Lines. Nothing else. It wasn't happening that day. The truth was, it hadn't been happening for some time. All of her creativity seemed to have vanished into thin air. She wondered, and not for the first time, why she'd left her teaching job years ago to go into designing children's clothing. *Because,* she answered herself, *I didn't want to deal with children. And, yet, here I am, designing and managing one of the largest children's clothing lines in the country.* Nothing made sense anymore.

Children.

It always came back to children.

The story of her life.

Better not to dwell on that at the moment.

Lily slid off her drafting stool and walked over to her desk. She felt a head rush when she saw the large square envelope from her old alma mater. Now what did they want? She'd sent an extremely generous check, and that should have been the end of it, but here they were, writing to her yet again. Her heart jumped up into her throat as she slit open the envelope with her nail. Her sigh of relief was so loud it bounced off the walls of the workroom. A thank-you card. She was so light-headed with relief, she sank down on her chair to pull herself together. Seconds later, she was rummaging in her desk for her scribbled notes. She'd called PAK Industries twice to try and locate Pak, as he'd introduced himself to her years ago, to no avail. Mr. Peter Aaron Kelly was out of town, she'd been told. She'd even tried through the Alumni Association to find Pak's home address, but they wouldn't give it out. She supposed that was a good thing.

Lily sighed again when she struggled with her thoughts in regard to the head of PAK Industries. She'd thought of him often during the past years because they had so much in common, and yet they didn't really know each other. A brief encounter, a five-minute lunch, yet she still remembered him so clearly. He had become one of the richest men in the world. She was no slouch in that department herself. While her revenues couldn't quite match Peter Kelly's, they were up there with so many zeros she often got dizzy when she looked at her financial statements.

How clearly she remembered the day she had

decided to track down Peter Kelly. It was the day the first invitation had arrived. She told herself that if there was a way for her to find out if he was attending the fund-raiser, she would consider going herself. She needed to talk to him. Or someone. Preferably him.

Lily pushed the thank-you card around on her desk with the tip of a pencil. She moved it one way, then another until she finally tipped it into an open drawer. Good. Now she didn't have to look at it. She slammed the drawer shut with way too much force.

The phone on her desk chirped. She pressed the button for the speakerphone to activate.

"Are you ready for your lunch, Lily?" Penny asked.

"Sure, send it in. And bring the paper and two cups of coffee." Like she was really going to eat lunch. These days she nibbled, and that was about it. She wasn't sleeping either. A dangerous combination, Penny had chastised her. Half the time she was walking around like a zombie. Why? She knew why but didn't want to face up to her past. No sense lying to herself. That was why she wanted to talk to Peter Kelly.

Lily looked up when her lunch was set in front of her. It looked good, but, as usual, she wasn't hungry. She reached for the coffee and gulped at it as she opened the paper. She always went to the financial section first. Coffee cup in hand, she looked down at the photo and article that took the entire half of the financial page above the fold. The cup dropped from her hands as she stared at the man she had just been thinking about. She stared at the picture for a long time as she tried to control her trembling body until she realized it wasn't Peter Kelly she was now staring at but Senator Hudson Preston.

Why did this particular picture of those two men put her in such a state of panic? When she couldn't come up with an answer, Lily sat on her hands to stop them from shaking. What was wrong with her? It was Peter Kelly who rendered her witless. She didn't even know Senator Preston.

Almost an hour later, Lily managed to get up off the chair she'd been sitting on. Her hands felt numb. She gathered up the newspaper with averted eyes and scrunched it into a ball. Then she mopped up the spilled coffee that had soaked into the blotter and puddled on the carpet. While she was doing that she was talking to her secretary, instructing her to book a flight to San Francisco so she could attend the fundraiser at Berkeley. "An early flight tomorrow morning."

Lily leaned over her desk, her hands gripping the edges. She'd made a decision. She'd actually made a decision. Not just your run-of-the-mill decision but an important one. So important, she felt like her very life hung in the balance. At least that was how she felt at the moment.

Lily jammed her cell phone into the pocket of her jeans. She looked around to see where she'd tossed her straw bag. She slung it over her shoulder, but not before she jammed a matching straw hat on her head. She almost ran from the office, shouting orders over her shoulder.

Before she ran into her private elevator, she shouted, "I'll call, and you'll see me when you see me."

How blasé that sounded, Lily thought as she climbed behind the wheel of her Range Rover minutes later. Her stomach in knots, her thoughts all over the map, she barreled out of the parking lot and on out to the road that would take her to Interstate 26 and downtown Charleston, where she lived on the Battery. A half-hour drive, depending on traffic. Time to buy an outfit for the black-tie dinner at Berkeley. Maybe another new outfit for the day after. A travel outfit. Lily tried to remember the last time she'd gone clothes shopping. When she couldn't, she gave up. She wondered if she had enough time to get a facial and a haircut. Just the thought of getting a haircut sent shivers up and down her spine. Some inner instinct warned her that she needed to look as successful as she was if she was going to see Peter Kelly. Assuming she would meet Peter Kelly if he even showed up for the fund-raiser. Well, she'd just have to make the time. The worst-case scenario was that she would have to pay extra to have the beauty shop stay open to accommodate her.

As Lily drove toward Charleston, she let her mind wander back to her past and the years leading up to the present. She had so many regrets these days. She'd hoped to be married with children by now, but that wasn't happening. She didn't think it would ever happen. Maybe it wasn't such a bad thing. She was married to her company and would just be cheating a husband. She had no motherly instincts, but there was a reason for that. A reason she didn't want to dwell on. How sad.

Lily tried to remember the last time she'd had a real date. Well over a year ago. Penny said it was because she was too intimidating. Penny also said her standards were way too high, and at her age, she needed to stop being so *picky*. Lily didn't even bother to offer any rebuttal because Penny was right. If things continued the way they were, she was going to end up an old maid, rocking on her verandah and staring out at the ocean.

Lily continued with her soul-searching. She'd always been a methodical kind of person. And analytical. She rarely made a mistake, but when she did, it was usually of the mega kind. To date she regretted only two things she'd done in her life. The first one was going into the teaching field. She simply wasn't teacher material. While she admired all teachers, she herself had no desire to mold young minds. The second mistake was to donate her eggs to that awful clinic. How young and stupid she was back then. How needy, how greedy, how goal-oriented she was during that last year at Berkeley.

With all that on her shoulders, it still boggled her mind that she'd made a go of the little business she'd started in her grandmother's garage. These days she ran a company that netted a billion dollars annually.

All of that, and still she was an emotional wreck, teetering on the edge. For months she'd known she had to do something to turn her life around. Then when the invitation arrived to attend the special fund-raiser, her mind had kicked into high gear. Why she thought Peter Kelly could help her was beyond her comprehension. Some deep part of her gut said that since he was part of her past in a minimal way, the answers had to lie with him. "Maybe I'm in the throes of a nervous breakdown and too stupid to know it," she muttered to herself.

Lily had reached Charleston. She parked by the outdoor market and made her way to a specialty shop on King Street—a shop named Olga's—where she bought a ton of clothes that Olga herself paraded in front of her. She explained that she was going to the hairdresser at Charleston Place and paid extra to have her purchases delivered to her home on the Battery.

At seven o'clock, when she left the beauty shop, her long crop of hair was sheared, sunstreaked, and highlighted. Her mane of curly hair, what was left of it, was now styled into a becoming skullcap hairdo that curled winsomely around her face. She liked the change because she looked totally unlike herself. The beautician said she looked ten years younger. The woman's testimonial pleased Lily so much that she purchased two shopping bags of products she knew she would probably use once. Her face glowed and tingled, but she was zit- and blackhead-free. She hadn't even known she had zits and blackheads, which probably just meant she needed glasses.

From time to time when she parked her car in her driveway, Lily would stop and look at her house. She would marvel at how far she'd come in life, from the ramshackle house she'd lived in with her grandmother to this historical house that she had restored. A house that was far too big for one person. Oh, she had a housekeeper and a gardener, but they went home at five o'clock. It was a house that begged for children and pets, not a young single woman who rarely got home before nine at night and left at six in the morning.

Lily pressed the code to the gate in her walled-off courtyard. The solar lights guided her toward the kitchen, which was awash in light. In fact, every light and every television set was on inside the house, something she insisted on. She hated coming home to darkness and silence.

Lily set her shopping bags on the counter and poured herself a glass of wine that she carried out to the courtyard, where she settled herself in a comfortable cushioned glider. She leaned back and closed her eyes, but she couldn't turn off her mind.

If only . . . if only . . .

Lily woke a little past midnight bathed in sweat. The damn dream again. She dropped her head into her hands and started to cry. It was always the same dream: children, dozens of them, dressed in clothing she'd designed, and who looked just like her at their age, picketing with faceless parents outside Sandcastle headquarters. Everyone was screaming and shouting, but she could never make out what they were saying. Until a week ago—when she had the dream again, and the words were so crystal clear it felt like they were burned into her brain just the way they were minutes ago when she woke.

Lily choked on her own sobs as she struggled to get herself together. The words— *"See, see, it is a big deal"*—wrapped themselves around her very soul.

What a fool she'd been. She knew she was still being a fool to think Peter Kelly could help her. First, she needed to help herself. She needed to talk to someone, to try and unload the guilt she'd been carrying around for so long. At the very least she needed a professional to help her come to terms with what she considered "Lily's folly" so many years ago.

Lily was stiff from the damp air. She picked up her empty wineglass and made her way into the house, where she climbed the stairs to the second floor to take a shower. She knew there would be no more sleep for her that night, so she might as well pack and get things ready for her early-morning trip to the airport.

The image in the bathroom mirror startled her until she remembered her makeover just hours ago. "The new me," she mumbled as she stepped into the shower. *This new me is going to turn her life around or die trying.* With that promise, her spirits lifted. Maybe, just maybe, she would finally be able to get a handle on her life.

Fifteen minutes later, a luxurious towel wrapped around her, Lily padded out to her bedroom to look at what Olga called her "traveling attire." She stared at the pale green linen suit with matching sandals and winced. Linen?

How had she allowed Olga to talk her into linen? She'd be one wrinkled mess before she even got to the airport in Charleston. She hung the suit in the spacious closet as she moved hangers this way and that. She finally chose a pair of off-white capri pants with a matching top. She rummaged through her shoe rack until she found a comfortable pair of straw sandals for the trek through the Hartsfield-Jackson Atlanta International Airport, where she had a layover.

She just needed one more thing. Her old hat, the one she'd been wearing when she had first met Pak/Peter Kelly. He'd even commented on it. Said he liked it. How weird was it that she would remember a detail like that after all these years?

In the dressing room off her bedroom, there were shelves and shelves filled with head busts wearing hats. All from back when she first thought she wanted to be a hat designer. Hats, she'd been told back then, were in the tank, so she'd given up on that idea and designed hats only for herself. There it was, her very first creation. A denim fishing hat with the brim rolled up. A huge silk sunflower was pinned to the middle. She smiled. She'd always loved that particular hat, maybe because it was her first design. The sunflower wasn't the least bit faded or droopy. Nor was there any dust on the denim hat. She plopped it on her head and sashayed out to her bedroom where she got dressed, still wearing the hat. It didn't exactly go with her outfit, so she changed the capri pants to a pair of soft denims with a design around the hem. They weren't jeans, so that was okay.

Lily realized she was feeling better and better as the time moved forward.

It was four thirty when Lily descended the stairs to leave her oversize piece of luggage by the front door. The limo driver could carry it down the front steps when he arrived at five thirty to take her to the airport.

With time to kill, Lily made coffee and toast. While she waited, she scribbled off a note to her housekeeper, saying she would call when she was certain of her return date. She looked around the pleasant kitchen, pleasant because her housekeeper had made and hung the checkered curtains. She had also sewed the place mats, and the padded cushions on the wooden chairs. Nelda had also brought in the green plants and looked after the little herb garden on the windowsill. The ceramic-tile floor was spick-and-span, all the appliances sparkled. She smiled when she remembered the day one winter when Nelda asked if Lily would mind if she bought a rocking chair for the kitchen. Nelda liked to sit and rock in front of the fire she always had blazing because of her arthritis. Lily had sat in the rocker on many occasions herself, watching the flames and daydreaming. It had been a good decision on her part to repair and rebuild the old kitchen fireplace, since it was now the focal point of the big room. She looked upward, startled to see a lush philodendron climbing the bricks.

She wondered when that had happened. Obviously, she needed to spend more time in her kitchen.

Her eye on the clock, Lily tidied up the breakfast things. With minutes to spare, she was on the front verandah waiting for the car service promptly at five thirty.

Please, please, she pleaded silently as she settled herself in the back of the Lincoln Town Car, *let this be the right thing that I'm doing.*

Chapter 3

Garment bag over his left shoulder, battered duffel on the other, Pete Kelly sailed through the security checkpoint, the shoelaces of his battered Nikes flapping in his own breeze. He headed straight for a kiosk, where he bought a bottle of iced tea and a paper. He settled himself on a blue hard-plastic chair and settled down to read the paper. He liked to brag that he read the paper cover to cover, line by line. Those people foolish enough to question a particular article or phrase usually ended up with sheepish smiles on their faces when they walked away after he snapped out the correct answer.

Settling his New York Mets cap more firmly on his head, Pete reached into his pocket for his reading glasses. He didn't look up once for the next ninety minutes as he read the paper from beginning to end. If he had looked up just three short minutes before he closed and folded the paper, he would have seen the woman he was so desperate to find walk right by him.

The paper and iced tea finished, Pete got up to throw them in the trash just as the first boarding call was announced for the flight to San Francisco. He sprinted to the men's room and was back within minutes. He looked around to see why the airport had suddenly gone quiet. Then he looked up at the television screen that everyone seemed to be looking at. As he fumbled for his boarding pass, he blinked, then blinked again as he tried to hear what an excited Anderson Cooper from CNN was saying. The second boarding call for seats at the back of the plane was announced. He knew he could have boarded at any point because he was flying first class, but his feet were rooted to the floor.

The crowd that had assembled at the base of the huge screen was beginning to thin out as passengers ran to board their flights. Pete didn't move, and the woman standing in front of him didn't move either.

A man standing next to Pete let out a string of profanity. "Poor kids. Where in the hell did the guy get that gun? Where the hell are his parents? Well, shit, they just said it was a group home for teenagers! Where are the teachers and counselors? Nowhere, that's where. Someone is to blame for this. Look! Look! They look like the kids next door. Twelve dead! Two escaped. Well, good for them. Book deal! Movie deal!"

"Shut up!" Pete said through clenched teeth, as the man hurried off to board his flight.

Lily, hearing the tirade, looked up just as a picture of two young men appeared on the screen. Stunned at seeing Pak, she swiveled around to see his exact likeness on the screen. "Oh, my God!" Suddenly she felt her hat being removed. She turned again.

"Lily! Jesus, it really is you! I've been trying to find you. You weren't in the yearbook." All this was said with his eyes going to the screen above him. "Look!" he hissed.

"I saw it," Lily hissed back. "I was in the hospital with an appendectomy when they did the yearbook pictures." She reached for her hat and jammed it back on her head. "I called your company to find you, but they wouldn't put me through."

Pete reached for her arm and held it in a vise-like grip. "Are you going to the fund-raiser? Are you on the flight to San Francisco?"

"Yes, and that was the last boarding call. Come on, we can talk on the plane."

Pete followed Lily blindly. His heart was beating too fast. "That kid looked just like me when I was his age," he mumbled as he handed the woman gate agent his boarding pass.

"I know. That's how I remember you, even if you were five years older."

"What do you think are the chances of us meeting like this, then seeing . . . seeing what we just saw?"

Lily felt light-headed as she grappled for an answer. "One in a trillion! Two trillion! This is my seat," she said as she extricated her arm to slide into her place.

Pete looked down at her. "How are we going to talk?" He sounded so anguished, Lily looked over at her seat companion, a corporate type with tortoiseshell-rimmed glasses. "Sir, would you mind changing seats with . . . with my fiancé? We couldn't get seats together. I would so appreciate it."

The corporate type looked up, saw and recognized Pete. "Aren't you . . . ?"

"Yeah. Shhh. We're running away. We're trying to keep it a secret. No one knows," Pete whispered.

"You mean I'm the first to hear?"

"Well, yeah," Pete said as he stepped aside for the man to move to Pete's seat. He settled down next to Lily and buckled up. He immediately turned the bill of his baseball cap backward so he could see Lily better.

"I like your hat."

"I made it myself."

"Yeah, yeah, that's what you said that day we met. Do you know how many times I thought about you over the years? A lot. I don't know about you, but I'm having a hell of a time. I am so damn glad to see you. By the way, my name is Pete. Some of the guys back at Berkeley used to call me 'Pak.' " He was babbling, the way Millie babbled when she did something wrong and he caught her at it.

"Pete, that boy looked like you. *Exactly* like you. Do you think . . . ? Is it possible? They said it was a group home. Why would one of . . . ? Why a group home? They said the one that looked like you got away. So did the other boy. That's a good thing. At least I think it's a good thing. God, I don't know anything about anything these days. What does all this mean? This is so bizarre," Lily said, running out of breath.

"Why were you looking for me?" Lily asked when she finally caught her breath.

Pete leaned in closer to Lily. "Because . . . I see kids that look like me everywhere I look. I can't sleep. At first it wasn't so bad. I was working, then I went off on my own. I was so tired I'd fall asleep standing up. But when things leveled off, it started all over again. Dreams, then nightmares. I wanted to talk to someone. I really did look for you. I thought . . . hoped you would understand, and maybe together we could get a handle on it. Assuming, of course, you were having similar problems. I know you said back then that it was no big deal, but . . ."

"I lied," Lily whispered. "It was a big deal from the git-go. I'd give anything if I could turn the clock backward and go to those counseling sessions. I mean it."

Pete leaned even closer. Lily could smell his aftershave. "I started seeing a shrink a while back. It really didn't help because I didn't open up until the session yesterday, when he threatened to dump me for wasting his time. He used to be my company's softball coach, so he can talk to me like that. He said I had to go back to the beginning. That's why I'm on this flight. I was going to hire a private detective to try to find you. Your turn."

"My story is pretty much the same as yours. It was a big deal. I hated that I sold my eggs. I was so desperate I thought I didn't have any other choice. I didn't want to deal with what I'd done, and I sure as hell didn't want to go to counseling sessions and talk about it. Unlike you, I didn't go to a shrink, but I did think about it. I decided to go to the fund-raiser, hoping you'd be there. I didn't think beyond getting there."

"Do you . . . do you want to see the kids we . . . ? Is that what you want?"

Lily bit down on her lower lip. "I have this business. I design and manufacture children's clothing. It's called Sandcastle Ltd. I went nuts when I would see all the child models in the beginning. I *knew* that each one of them was mine. How stupid was that? I finally had to stop going to the photo shoots because I was getting obnoxious and grilling the parents. I even changed the employment forms so I could check on the parents. How sick is that?"

"I'm no better. I started sending computers to just about every school in the Berkeley area. Then I'd send my people there with video cameras to film the kids. Then I'd torture myself by looking at the videos, thinking, swearing to myself, they were all mine. I was teetering on the edge for a while back then. I tried talking myself out of it. I fought going to a shrink because I didn't want anyone to know. For some reason I thought . . . I didn't mind . . . if you knew. Ah, you know what I mean. And here we are. By the way, does your company have a catalog? I think I saw it on my secretary's desk. Millie has five grandchildren, and she orders from catalogs a lot."

Lily smiled. "We do. It comes out twice a year. Christmas and early summer."

"What happened to teaching school?" Pete asked curiously.

"I gave it a shot. It wasn't for me. Every one of those kids was mine. End of story. What if that boy we saw on television was . . . yours? He's out there all alone, with no one to turn to. I only say that because he was living in a group home, so that must mean he doesn't have a family or else the family put him in a group home because of . . . what, I don't know. I hope he's with the other boy. Together, they might be okay. You know, strength in numbers. Two heads are better than one. They will be okay, don't you think?"

They were airborne by then and about to level off at thirty thousand feet. The flight attendant was serving coffee, pastries, and little bunches of grapes on square white plates. Pete and Lily ignored the food and kept on talking in whispers.

"The shooter got away. He might be looking for the boys. I'm going to call my office and have them get everything they can on the case, and it will be ready for us when we land. How about we blow off the fund-raiser and try to find the kids?"

"I'm okay with missing the fund-raiser, but what makes you think we can find the kids? The police are on it. It's national news now. They won't let us anywhere near that group home. I don't care how much money you have or how famous you are. If anything, your presence nosing around might hurt you."

"You're right, and I know that. My shrink said

I had to go back to the beginning. That's where we'll go."

"And you think they're just going to open up and tell us what we want to know! I don't think so."

Pete slouched down in his seat. "I knew I should have bought that goddamn business and burned it to the ground. I said I was going to do it that day I met you, and I never followed through. When I made my first million, that was my number two priority. I had nightmares about that, too."

"Even if you had, it would have been too late, Pete. Our donations were distributed long before you became successful."

Pete bolted upright. "Are you always right?"

"No. Just sometimes. You already knew it. I just said the words out loud."

Pete nodded. "Do you remember how . . . I don't remember if it was you or me, but one of us said there was something sinister about *that place.*"

"It was you. I agreed, as I recall. I asked you about the building in the back, the one with no doors or windows. I think we were both just spooked. It was an emotional time for both of us. It's probably a giant freezer to . . . you know, store all those donations. I wonder how much they'd want to sell that place. I bet if we could find that out, we'd get a sense of how big an operation it is. There must be blueprints at town hall. I know that when I built my office building and the warehouse, my blueprints were there for anyone who wanted to look at them."

Pete started to crack his knuckles out of frustration. "That boy was the spitting image of me, wasn't he?"

"Yes, Pete, he was. It took my breath away when they showed his picture. That group home—or was it a school?—what little they showed of it, looked pretty upscale to me. Not like a place for wayward youngsters. I didn't hear any names, did you?"

"No. I was so stunned I didn't see half of what you saw. God, I hope my parents or my brothers didn't see it. They'll think for sure I have an illegitimate child out there somewhere. My mom is like a dog with a bone when she gets an idea in her head. She's forever nagging me to get married and have kids. She said it's not natural to be my age and not married. By the way," Pete said, his eyes wide, "you aren't married, are you?"

Lily grimaced. "Only to my business."

"I can relate to that. We need to make a plan, Lily. The minute we get off this plane, we need to have a definite objective, and this time we're both going to follow through to the end. No matter where it takes us. Agreed?"

Lily nodded solemnly. "Agreed."

Chapter 4

By the time Flight 2107 landed in San Francisco, Lily and Pete were fast friends.

As Lily commented, "It's like we've been transported back to the day we met."

Pete agreed as he juggled his garment bag and duffel. Lily had a firm grip on her own carry-on luggage as they made their way out to the concourse.

Pete ushered Lily to the side. "Someone is going to meet us right here to hand over whatever information my guy Marty was able to get. And," he said, turning around, "here comes my shadow. Lily, meet Zolof Kuchinsky. Zolly, meet Lily."

He was bigger than a bear, almost as tall as a giraffe.

Lily looked up in awe at the bald-headed man who appeared larger than life. "Nice to meet you, Zolof." Lily extended her hand, certain it would be crushed. It wasn't.

"Everyone calls me Zolly."

His voice was a surprise, it had a light timbre with a cadence Lily couldn't identify. His bright blue eyes sparkled, and a slight smile tugged at his lips. Lily couldn't help but smile. A "shadow" had to mean he was Pete's bodyguard. It made sense that someone of Pete's stature would have a bodyguard. It was probably mandatory. She knew in her gut that the Pete she'd just gotten to know on the flight had probably put up a fight but in the end saw the good sense of having someone watching his back.

"I can meet you by baggage claim, Zolly. Get Winston, and make sure he gets some water." Winston was Pete's one true love—his German shepherd—and he never traveled without him.

"No way, boss. You know the rules. We stick together. There's your package."

He was so fast on his feet, Lily could only gasp when an arm bigger than a tree trunk reached out to intercept the manila envelope a flight attendant was holding out to Pete.

"You get used to it after a while." Pete grinned. "He's my nanny." Pete waited patiently until Zolly opened the envelope to scan the contents. Satisfied, Zolly handed it over.

Pete slapped the thick envelope against his leg as he waited for Zolly to take a call on his cell phone.

"Winston's up and ready," Zolly said as he clicked off. "An attendant is getting him some water because he's panting. He probably has your scent already, boss."

"Then let's go. Winston hates to be kept waiting."

Five minutes later, all hell broke loose in the airport. Screams seemed to be coming from every direction. Zolly looked at Pete, and Pete looked at Zolly. Both men were grinning from ear to ear.

Pete looked over at Lily and explained. "Winston doesn't have much patience. If we stand still, he'll find us." Pete whistled shrilly, a high, piercing sound. He was rewarded with a bark from somewhere in the airport.

"How the hell did he get loose?" Zolly grumbled.

"Here he comes!" Pete laughed.

Lily watched as people stepped to the side, their eyes on the black streak barreling down the center of the concourse and heading straight for them. One hundred and twenty pounds of pure dog bent on reaching his master, airport security and police hot on his trail. Pete whistled again. The black streak seemed to slow down in midair and finally came to a standstill in front of Pete. He held out one huge paw, and Pete shook it.

"That wasn't nice, Winston."

The shepherd hung his head but only for a moment before he stood on his hind legs to put his paws on Pete's shoulders. He looked over at Zolly and barked a happy greeting.

The authorities were not pleased, but when they saw the shepherd's owner, they adjusted their attitudes. The dog had been crated, but it was airport personnel who let the animal get away from them. They knew it, and Pete knew it. Apologies were all over the place as Zolly reached into a cavernous bag on his shoulder for a leash and collar.

Security followed what became known as the "Kelly party" out of the airport. At least that's how it was reported on the evening news. If Peter Aaron Kelly went to the drugstore, it was news. If he went on a plane trip, the stock market went wild wondering what he was up to. Suddenly, Lily was in awe of the man at her side.

Outside the airport, a caravan of four Hummers was waiting. Three contained PAK Industries security. Zolly had his own Hummer, which was the third car in line. Pete, Lily, and Winston climbed into the second Hummer, and they were off.

Winston barked his pleasure as he tugged at his seat belt.

"I taught him to do that," Pete said proudly. "And he's only two years old. I had his parents, but they . . . they got old and went peacefully in their sleep. I have a whole menagerie back in Georgia."

Lily laughed as Winston kept slapping her hand with his paw. "What other kind of animals do you have?" She wondered why she'd never gotten a pet.

"I have a big old cat named Agatha. She just wandered by one day, decided she liked me, and stayed. She's pretty much the boss. Winston treats her like a lady because she hisses at him. I have two Golden Retrievers named Jam and Jelly. They're sisters from the same litter. They're only a year old and they've already chewed through a couch, a chair, an air conditioner vent, and two door frames. They were working on the floor when I left. My house is definitely lived in, and not very pretty. A month ago someone dumped a basket of newborn pups in my driveway. I have that sort of thing going on all the time. But I have a nine-to-five vet seven days a week who keeps it all under control. I'm just a sucker for animals. I could never turn one away." He looked over at Lily, and said, "I guess they're the kids I never had."

Lily's eyes filled. She dabbed at them. "Understood. At least you had the good sense to go for it. I never even had goldfish."

"I have those, too. I've even got a koi pond. You name it, and I have it. You have to come see for yourself." Pete's eyes bored into hers as he waited for her response.

"If that's an invitation, I accept. South Carolina is right next to Georgia."

Pete felt like pounding his chest. "I'll send my plane for you when you're ready."

Lily adjusted her hat and smiled. "I have my own plane, thank you very much. But with the cost of fuel these days, I'll be glad to fly in yours. Why aren't we looking at the stuff in the envelope?"

"Because I can't read in a moving vehicle. I get sick to my stomach."

"How weird. Me, too."

Pete felt like beating at his chest again. Instead, he leaned back and closed his eyes. "I'm thinking," he said.

"And I need to know this . . . why?"

"When I think I don't talk. I don't want you to think I'm being rude."

"Oh," was all Lily could think of to say. She, too, leaned back and closed her eyes, but unlike Pete, Lily fell asleep.

The caravan of Hummers came to a stop under the portico of a secluded hotel. A doorman in a top hat and tails sprang to attention as bellmen hustled when he snapped his fingers. *The man* had arrived. At the foot of the long circular driveway, reporters and photographers with their zoom lenses snapped pictures and shouted questions, all of which Pete ignored.

Within minutes, the Hummers were driven off and the guests shepherded to private villas at the back of the hotel. Pete looked around at the lush landscaping as he tried to gauge the privacy he always demanded when traveling. He made a mental note to send Millie some flowers to show his appreciation.

Pete looked over at Lily, his eyes apologizing for the clamor below the driveway. "I guess I should have warned you about this, but I didn't think . . . I should have known that somehow those guys would get wind of my travels. Tonight, they'll have me trying to buy Microsoft, or Microsoft trying to buy me, or else I'll be here to fight off some nonexistent legal battle. We might have to start some rumors if we have any hope of going off on our own. I'm sorry to say I didn't think this through. Like you, I didn't expect to see you at the airport, and I sure didn't expect to see what we saw on the airport television screen. That's another way of saying I need to fall back and regroup.

"I hope you don't mind that I took the liberty of getting you a villa. Well, I didn't really get you one, I always book the suites on either side of me for privacy. You might want to have your secretary cancel your other accommodations. You aren't upset, are you?"

"No, not at all. I think we need to be close together. What I mean is . . ."

"I know what you mean." Pete laughed. "Okay, let's settle in and see what kind of information my people sent me. Then we'll make a plan. Does that work for you?"

Lily looked up at the tall man standing in front of her. She smiled. He smiled. *I think I like this guy,* Lily thought. *A lot.* "Definitely."

Pete smacked his hands together. He reached out his hands to squeeze her upper arms. "Good. I think we're going to make a good team. In business it's all about teamwork. I really like that hat."

Neither one moved. It was Zolly who poked his boss in the back. "I don't like it when you stand out in the open so much, boss. Let's move it inside. Sorry, miss."

"No problem." Lily took a moment to wonder why she didn't have security like Zolly. That was right up there with never even having goldfish. She moved off to enter the villa assigned to her.

The high-priced villas—and it was easy to see that they were high-priced because while each was distinctive in its own way, all looked like a cozy cluster of Swiss chalets—were perfectly landscaped to afford the utmost in privacy. Inside, Lily looked around at a plush living room whose main focal point was a fieldstone fireplace that rose from the floor to the ceiling. The kitchen was state of the art, the dining room elegant yet homey. The two bedrooms sported king-size beds. The décor was citrus in nature with vibrant greens, oranges, and yellows. The two interconnecting bathrooms were marble, and mirrored from top to bottom. *Five grand a night,* Lily thought. *Maybe more.*

Lily unpacked, hanging her clothes in a spacious closet before she laid out her cosmetics and toiletries on one of the marble vanities. With her chores completed, she opened the refrigerator and popped a cola. The huge basket of fruit sitting on the dining room table looked tempting, but she wasn't all that fond of fruit, preferring candy, cookies, and anything else made with sugar. Instead, she opened the sliding door, to discover a garden so beautiful she gasped in delight. Colored lounge chairs circled a small table with a rainbow-striped umbrella. In the corner of the small sanctuary was a hot tub for two nestled among a kaleidoscope of colored flowers. Lily couldn't ever remember seeing anything as pretty or as peaceful as this small private garden. She wondered if Pete's patio was as nice. *Probably nicer,* she thought.

Lily settled herself on one of the colored chairs as she sipped at the cola in her hands. How surreal this all was. In a million years she

could never have hoped for this particular outcome, and yet here she was, and Pete Kelly was
right next door. She pinched herself to prove
she was awake and not dreaming. The thought
occurred to her that she could duplicate this little slice of paradise at her residence in South
Carolina. More likely than not, she'd never do
it, and she'd never use it even if she did do it.
Real life in South Carolina was a lot different
from this.

Pete Kelly wasn't married. She wasn't married. Pete Kelly had baggage just the way she
had baggage. God, where was this all going to
end? Would it end?

Lily heard the delightful chime when the
front door to the chalet opened, but she didn't
look up. She turned only when she saw Pete's
long shadow on the patio. "This is so nice, Pete.
Thanks for including me." She noticed that he,
too, was holding a cola in his hand. She motioned for him to sit down on one of the colored chairs. "I love bright colors. The more
vibrant the better." Such brilliant conversation.
What she really wanted to do was ask him if he
was involved with anyone.

"You don't mind if Winston joins us, do you?"

"Not at all. I love dogs. I had a little furball
when I was a kid. Unfortunately, she didn't live
all that long. I was so crushed when she died. I
guess that's why I never got another pet, the
pain of losing her was too much to bear. With
no parents around, my grandmother did her
best to console me but it didn't work. She
bought me a stuffed dog. It wasn't the same."

Pete sat down and stretched out his long legs. Lily smiled at the battered sneakers, lack of socks, and jeans so well worn they were thread-bare at the knees. And this guy was a billionaire at least thirty times over. She was impressed.

"So, what's in the envelope? What's our next move? You look . . . I don't know . . . scared? Are you?" Lily asked in a jittery-sounding voice.

Pete bit down on his lip and grimaced. He watched Winston check out the hot tub and the flowers before lying down, his huge head on his paws. "It's not really a group home per se. It's called the California Academy of Higher Learning. The names of the youngsters who . . . didn't make it hadn't been released when Marty sent off the packet of information because the media weren't sure if there were parents that had to be notified. I just called him again, and their names have still not been released. The media is all over it. The two boys who escaped are almost eighteen years old. There's an APB out on them. The boy, the one who looked like me, is named Josh Baer. The second boy is Jesse Rabe, and the shooter has not been identified. It seems this all happened at a midmorning break when the two teachers and all the students were in the same room.

"And before you ask, no cell phones are al-lowed during school hours. It's not a big school, just ninth through twelfth grades. Grades nine through eleven left early on a field trip that was scheduled months ago. The intercom system was deactivated, so someone had to have planned this and acted accordingly. In other words, the shooter had a plan and is detail-oriented. No motive has surfaced so far."

"Are there parents or aren't there parents?"

"I don't know. Marty—who, by the way, is Marty Bronson, and is my right hand—said he would feed me information as he gets it. In case you haven't noticed, this delightful hotel does not have televisions in the villas. My people know how much I hate television and never watch it, so they took that into consideration when they booked these villas. Right now, I would kill for a TV."

"Then why don't we go someplace that has television? Aren't you a computer guru? Can't you bring it up on your laptop?"

"I didn't bring it with me, Lily. Come on, let's go. I'll find us a place even if it's some sports bar. I could use a drink anyway."

Winston was already inside by the time Lily got to her feet. "I don't have a good feeling about this, Pete."

"I don't either, Lily."

Chapter 5

Her nerve endings twanging all over her body, Lily was about to exit her villa when she heard Pete and Zolly. It sounded like they were right outside. Unashamedly, she pressed her ear to the door and listened to the muted conversation she could barely hear.

Zolly scratched at his bald head, his brow furrowed. "Boss, is something going on here I don't know about? You know the rules, so let's hear it. I also want you to tell me, do you and the lady inside this villa have some kind of history together? It reads like you do."

A history. Well, that was one way of putting it. Lily pressed her ear harder against the door to hear Pete's reply.

"In a manner of speaking. A very *short*-lived history. It's personal, Zolly, so don't go reading something into this that isn't there. Lily and I met by accident at the airport, and since we were going to the same fund-raiser at our old alma mater, it made sense to invite her here so we could catch up on . . . This is none of your business, Zolly."

"Everything you do is my business, boss. Don't fight me on this, or we're going to have sharp words. Like I said, you know the rules. I'll stay out of your way. Just to keep you in the loop, I ran a background check on your friend." The security guard jerked his head in the direction of Lily's villa to indicate she was the one he ran the check on.

On the other side of the door, Lily heard Pete groan.

"Boss, the good news is, I think it's safe to say she isn't after your money, chance meeting or not. She's got quite a pile of her own. A really, really big pile. She's not in your league, but she's damn close. Her kids' clothes, they call them her *'dee-zines,'* win prizes in the garment business. Her creds are five-star."

"I don't care about that, and you had no business doing that check without my authorization. She's a friend. I hate when you pull this shit, Zolly. Dammit, what if she finds out?"

"I was discreet, boss. The rules say I check everyone you come in contact with."

Grinning from ear to ear, Lily jumped away from the door when she heard a rat-a-tat-tat knock. She moved farther into the room and shouted so her voice would carry through the door. "Be right there!"

Lily stepped out into warm, golden sunshine. Winston sidled up next to her, hoping for a pat on the head. She did better than that. She dropped to her haunches so that she was eye level with the huge dog. She rubbed his belly, his rump—the only place he couldn't scratch himself—and tickled his ears. Then she nuzzled him, nose to nose. When she was upright again, she knew she'd made a friend for life. A four-legged friend.

Winston was in love.

Pete smiled and smiled as he ushered her forward to a black Chevy Suburban that was waiting under the portico. "We have to do this, switch up vehicles, from time to time when the press gets obnoxious."

Lily didn't know what to say, so she just nodded as she climbed into the huge vehicle.

"Where are we going?"

Pete threw his hands in the air. "To that place you and I spent hundreds of hours in a lifetime ago. The Berkeley Library. We'll use their computers."

"Great idea. Any updates?"

"No. We're going to have to make our own updates. All I need is a computer, and if there's something out there, I'll find it. You aren't having second thoughts, are you?"

She rather thought she was having second thoughts, but her answer didn't betray that indecision. "No, not at all. Maybe we should get a newspaper. Do you have the power to authorize a stop at some convenience store to get one?" Lily let loose with a giggle to show she was teasing. She tried to remember the last time she'd giggled over anything. In the end she gave up, then laughed outright when the Suburban pulled to the curb.

Zolly hopped out and was back within minutes, his arms full of newspapers. Winston took that moment to unbuckle his seat belt to barrel to the back, where he sat at Lily's feet to gaze up at her adoringly.

Lily stroked the big dog's head as Pete divvied up the papers. "We can read them in the library. I think my dog likes you. He hasn't been around women much except for my housekeeper. Up till now I would have said the only people he likes are me and Zolly."

The GPS on the dashboard came to life as it told Zolly where to turn and where to park. Pete leaned toward the window. "It looks the same," he said quietly.

"Nothing is the same," Lily said flatly. "Nothing," she said adamantly.

There was nothing for Pete to say, so he remained quiet. The moment the Suburban came to a stop, he hopped out to hold the door for Lily. He offered his hand. She took it and jumped to the ground.

Suddenly she was surrounded by a group of men that Pete seemed to know. Security.

"See you, big guy," Pete said, tussling with the shepherd for a minute.

Winston growled to show his displeasure until Lily turned to hug him. He settled down immediately, to Pete's chagrin.

They moved off, one of the security detail staying with Winston, Zolly in the lead. Once inside the library, he would discreetly move away, the other security scattering to keep their eyes on the boss and his companion.

Lily looked around. Pete was right, she'd spent hundreds and hundreds of hours in the library. It looked the same, and yet it looked different. Possibly it was the shrubs and the trees on the outside. Maybe it was the ivy growing up the brick walls. She shivered when she entered the quiet building. How young the students looked, bent over tables, books open in front of them. A long time ago she had looked just like them. Once she had loved this place. So long ago. She sniffed the familiar smell of books, waxed floors, and dust on the windowsills. A lifetime ago, just for fun, she'd traced her name in the dust on one of the windowsills. For one wild moment she felt like doing it again. That, she told herself, would be regressing, and she really needed to move forward.

To Lily's surprise, no one so much as looked at either her or Pete. All this macho security, and none of the students cared about Pete Kelly. Shrugging, she followed Pete to the computer area. He logged them both on, then nodded to the newspapers, indicating Lily should go through them. She moved off to the side of the long table to spread out the papers. Nothing on page one. That was strange. Normally the media ran with anything involving children. She quickly scanned the rest of the papers to find the story relegated to page two in most of them. Beyond strange. Two young boys gone missing, eleven others dead, and it was on *page two!* She stared down at a small picture of the two missing boys. No mention of parents.

Lily leaned over and whispered her findings

to Pete. "Page two?" he hissed. Pete frowned. "I bet the FBI put a lid on it. That's the only thing that makes sense to me."

"Yes, page two. No mention of parents. Two boys missing, and it's four lines. Two very, very small pictures of the missing boys. I don't get it. Have you had any luck?"

"About the same as you. It was a massacre, and they're playing it down for some reason. I suppose it could have something to do with the missing boys, but I don't understand what it could be. No, it's got to be the FBI in charge. They like to be in control and keep things close to the vest. They aren't saying if the shooter was one of the kids or a stranger. Maybe a disgruntled staff member. If it's not the FBI, then there must be some big money involved in the academy to keep it this buttoned-up. Let's see if we can find out who owns the California Academy of Higher Learning. I'm not hopeful we're going to find out anything since we don't have the proper software. I'm going outside to call my office. See what you can find out about the working staff."

Lily nodded as she flexed her fingers. While she wasn't as proficient on the computer as she knew Pete was, she knew her way around the Internet.

An hour later Lily sat back in disgust. So much for her computer expertise. Other than the names of some of the staff, she was unable to come up with telephone numbers or addresses. She didn't discount the fact that maybe the staff lived at the academy since it seemed to be a boarding school of sorts, and from what she'd been able to gather, the students lived there, too. She was about to get up to search for Pete when she saw him striding toward her. She threw her hands up to indicate she'd had no luck.

"Marty's on it. So, if you're up to it, let's hit the town hall and see who owns what. As in the clinic and the academy. We'll probably come up dry, but what the hell, it beats standing around here sucking our thumbs. My notebook is on the way. One of my guys will pick it up when the flight gets in. I want to find a TV, too. You okay with this, Lily?"

"I'm okay with it. Let's do it." But she wasn't okay with it, and she knew it. She wished Winston was with her, so she could hug him, and she didn't know why she suddenly felt the need to have someone close to her even if it was an animal.

Thirty minutes later, Pete and Lily entered the hall of records.

"It smells almost like the library, but I can also smell coffee brewing somewhere," Lily said.

She was struck again at how young everyone looked. It was obvious that those with the gray hair, glasses, and potbellies were the ones in charge. All of the others looked like part-time Berkeley students. Everyone looked harried, and the lines for assistance were out the door. Both Lily and Pete patiently waited their turn.

Two hours later, the couple looked at one another in disgust.

"Corporations within corporations, holding companies within holding companies," Pete said.

"Everything is over the top and out the kazoo. We need a map just to follow all the companies involved in that academy and the clinics. In the end, it will be some group of wealthy investors offshore or someone in Switzerland behind it all. It must be a bigger cash cow than I first thought." He shrugged.

Lily's heart fluttered in her chest. She could tell Pete was starting to get angry. Her voice was a bare squeak when she said, "For someone to go to all that trouble . . . They must be hiding something, and for some reason I don't think it's just money. That's my take on it anyway."

"I'll put Marty on it. He's better than a junk-yard dog. The guy never gives up until he has the answer he's looking for. If anyone can find a bona fide name or legitimate corporation, it's Marty. I say we cruise by the clinic. We might as well get everything that we can done while we're here. I'm all for going in and announcing my-self and rattling some chains. What's your feel-ing, Lily?"

Her feeling was she wanted to run like hell. "Let's do it, 8446!" Good Lord, how brave that sounded.

"Oh, my God, you remembered my donor number?"

"Yep! And mine is 1114. Do you think we might be expunged from their records by now? It was all a long time ago."

"Trust me, we're in their archives some-where," Pete said, his voice sounding ominous.

Yes, the big guy standing next to her was defi-nitely getting angrier by the moment.

Lily leaned in closer to Pete and whispered, "What about Zolly and your other security? What are they going to think?"

Pete shrugged. "They're paid by PAK Industries to protect me, not to think about where I go and what I do. They all signed confidentiality agreements." He shrugged again, then laughed uproariously when he said, "By six o'clock tonight everyone at PAK Industries will know the boss went to a sperm bank with some chick."

In spite of herself, Lily laughed. "When we get there, what are we going to do?"

"Be brazen as hell and go for the gusto. I know that was my kid we saw on television. And if we can find him, DNA will prove it. Just so you know, Lily, I don't plan to hide behind anonymity. At this stage of my life, I don't care if the world finds out I sold my sperm to get an education. That kid is what's important. You're a woman, so it's different for you. You deal with children in a sense. Am I off the mark here?" he asked anxiously, his eyes sparking dangerously.

This was her out *if* she wanted out. Did she? Part of her said yes, and part of her said no. She had to stop this ridiculous waffling. She squeezed Pete's arm and smiled. "No anonymity for me either. Right now the only important thing on our agenda is the two boys." Suddenly, Lily felt like a hundred-pound weight had been taken off her shoulders.

They were back in the Suburban, with Winston doing his best to get between them. He was like a puppy as he vied for attention from both Pete and Lily. When he finally calmed down,

Pete rattled off the address of the sperm bank. Zolly keyed it into the GPS, and they were off.

Lily squirmed under the constraints of her seat belt. She felt so wired, she thought she would explode. They were apparently going to march into the clinic and demand answers, if she understood Pete correctly. She poked Pete on the arm, and whispered, "Do you think we might be tipping our hand by going to the clinic first? Maybe we should have gone to the academy first."

"I think it's one of those either/or things. Don't you think someone at the academy would call the clinic *if* they're involved? At this point, we are just assuming the sperm bank and clinic are tied together. We'll know soon enough once we see their reaction to our demands."

"I guess that makes sense."

Sensing her indecision, Winston whined. Lily stroked his big head, and he calmed down immediately.

"Boss, it says here the address you gave me is a sperm bank. Are you sure it's the right address?"

"I'm sure, Zolly," Pete said cheerily.

Lily turned away so Zolly couldn't see her amused smile in the rearview mirror.

Fifteen minutes later, when Zolly pulled the Suburban to the curb, the others falling directly behind, Zolly looked into the rearview mirror. "Ah . . . boss, is this one of those . . . ?"

"Uh-huh. Stay in the car, Zolly. There's only one way out of this place, and you're looking right at it. Give me Winston's lead. I'm taking him with me."

"Oh, jeez, boss, I thought . . . never mind what I thought. Winston, huh?"

Pete couldn't resist tormenting his protector. "No, it's not for Winston. I'm taking him for protection. I mean it, Zolly, stay in the car."

A moment later, Pete, Winston, and Lily were striding up the walkway to the entrance of the sperm bank.

Lily did her best not to look to the left, where the entrance to the egg donor clinic was. It was déjà vu all over again. She swallowed hard and was right behind Pete and Winston when they walked through the door.

This is a mistake. This is a mistake. This is a mistake.

"Pete," she hissed, as he was about to walk up to the receptionist. "If we do this, our lives are never going to be the same. You know that, right?"

Pete turned around and pierced her with his level gaze. "Yes, Lily, I know that. I have to do this. I really do. You don't. Right now you can turn around and walk out that door. Your call." He waited, hardly daring to breathe, for her answer. He reached for her hand and squeezed it. At the same moment, Winston tried to wiggle his way between them.

Lily looked up to see something change in Pete's eyes. She didn't know how she knew, but she knew right then, at that very second, that he wanted to kiss her. And she wanted to kiss him.

Winston, sensing the mood swing, slapped two big paws on the countertop. The sound was louder than a gunshot. A sharp *woof,* then an ominous growl drew the receptionist's attention.

No more waffling. Lily squeezed Pete's hand so tight, her knuckles turned white as she stepped up to the plate and stood beside Pete when he spoke to the receptionist.

Lily's heart fluttered wildly when she heard what Pete was saying. "I'm Donor Number 8446, and this is Donor Number 1114," he said, pointing to Lily, "and we have some questions for whoever owns this joint."

Chapter 6

At the sight and sound of the massive dog, the office receptionist, a thick-around-the-middle woman trying to look nineteen, screeched, "Dogs are not permitted in this clinic. Remove that animal immediately."

Winston whined, his huge paws still on the countertop.

"See, now you've hurt his feelings. I'd like to speak to the owner of this clinic," Pete said nonchalantly.

"So would hundreds of other people. We deal in confidentiality, sir. Take that dog outside immediately!"

A door opened to the right of where Pete was standing. A young man emerged, a blank look on his face. Pete swung around and eyeballed him. Even though he kept his voice low, Lily and the receptionist could hear every word he said.

"Kid, if I ever see you here again, I'll kick your ass all the way to the Nevada border. Now, get your butt back in that room and retrieve your donation. NOW! Here," he said, pulling three hundred-dollar bills out of his pocket. He jammed the crumpled bills into the pocket of the young man's IZOD T-shirt.

"Now see here. You cannot . . ."

Winston took that moment to back up to the doorway. With a running start, he cleared the counter with ease, at which point he sat back on his haunches and watched the woman whose hands were fluttering wildly.

Pete was back at the counter. "Winston, your manners are appalling. Shake hands with the lady. Now, as I was saying, we would like to speak to your superior. Or if that's plural, we can handle that, too. Today is not a good day to try my patience."

"I can't help you. There's no one here but the staff. All communications are done via computer, fax, or phone. I don't even know who owns this clinic."

The young man in the IZOD shirt, a panicked expression on his face, raced out the door and didn't look back.

"Now, see here, you cannot be interfering with our business. I'm going to call the police. Right now!"

Pete shrugged. Winston growled.

"I'm going to need a contact number. You won't mind if I use your computer, will you? A *yes* would go a long way in keeping Winston happy."

"Obviously, I can't stop you, but this will all go in my report to the police. This is highly irregular. We go through channels here. We do not deviate. That's why we've been in business all these years."

"I totally understand," Pete said as he opened the door to enter the receptionist's lair, Lily right behind him. Within minutes he was in another world, clicking away at the speed of light. He spoke once. "Where are the old files? Where are they archived?"

Winston growled, the hair on the back of his neck standing on end.

"I don't know. I swear to God I don't know. I'm allergic to dogs and dander. I'm also afraid of dogs."

"You should work to overcome those fears," Lily said. "I'd also consider another line of work if I were you."

The receptionist gaped at her. It was Lily's turn to shrug as Winston offered up his paw. The woman ignored it. Winston growled. He offered up his other paw.

Lily said, "I think if I were you, I'd shake his paw."

Tentatively, the woman touched the big dog's paw, then withdrew her hand as though she'd just touched a snake. Winston barked happily.

"What you're doing here is illegal," the woman said. Suspicion ringing in her voice, she addressed her next comment to Pete. "Don't I know you?"

Pete half-turned in his chair. "I doubt it. People say that about me all the time. Now, which one of these e-mail addresses is for the person you have the most contact with?"

The receptionist pursed her lips. "I'm not

telling you anything. Furthermore, I signed a confidentiality agreement when I was hired. I have no desire to be sued. I need this job and the benefits."

His face buried in the computer, Pete said, "Winston, take care of it."

Before the woman could gasp, Winston had her arm in his mouth and was leading her toward Pete. He gently released her arm when Pete said, "Thank you, Winston." The big dog took up his position next to the receptionist.

Pete swiveled around and locked his gaze on the woman, whose nameplate said she was Ina Jones. "Listen to me very carefully, Ms. Jones. I want my old donor records, and so does my friend," he said, pointing at Lily. "I never take no for an answer. Having said that, I now want to give you a heads-up on what's going on. I'm sure you saw the news and the massacre at the boys' school." Pausing for a second, Pete continued by laying out for the frightened woman what he was increasingly becoming sure was correct. "Those youngsters originated in this . . . this place. Now, where are the old files?"

The woman started to wail. "I told you, I don't know. I just collect the specimens, keep the records, and create the files. And I pay the donors. That's the total of my job description. I'm sure you're wrong about what . . . what happened at that school."

"What do you do with the files, say, for the past month?"

"A courier picks them up the first of every month. There weren't many lately. Spring is always a slow time. Actually, both spring and early summer are slow." Ina was babbling now, her face mottled with fear.

"Do you call the courier, or does he just show up?" Pete asked.

"He comes on the first Monday of every month. I always have the package ready for him. He signs a slip and leaves. I have no idea what he does with the files or who he gives them to. I wouldn't . . . I wouldn't work for a firm that wasn't ethical. What you're implying is absurd."

"Where are the donations?"

"That's none of . . ."

Winston growled.

"In the clinic. There are two nurses back there who handle the specimens. Talk to them."

"I will. Where is the emergency number you call if something goes awry?"

"What . . . how . . . ?"

"Winston." The one word was a command the shepherd acted on.

"All right, all right." Jones rattled off a number that Pete committed to memory.

"Call the number now and tell that person there are two people here demanding their donor information because they say that information has something to do with the shooting at the school."

Ina Jones sighed as she picked up the phone.

"Speakerphone, please," Pete said.

The woman pressed a button. A rich baritone invaded the room. Winston's ears perked up as he tried to figure out where the voice was coming from.

"This is Ina Jones at Unit Four." Pete watched as the woman kept her eyes on Winston. "There are some . . . there are two people and a killer dog standing right here in the office who are asking for their donor files. He said . . . he said their . . . donations have something to do with that private school shooting. Here," she said, thrusting the phone at Pete.

"And you would be who?" Pete asked coldly. "Me? I'm Donor 8446. My friend is Donor 1114. The dog doesn't have a donor number. Police? That's probably the best idea I've heard all day. If you don't call them, I will." Pete listened, his expression stoic. He finally interrupted the rich baritone. "Scratch the police, I think the FBI would be a better bet. Yeah, well, that was then, and this is now. You led me to believe I would be helping childless couples back when I made those donations. The media said the kids gunned down at that school were *orphans*. Right off the bat, you people lied to me, and you probably lie to every other donor who walks through these doors. I saw my kid at that massacre, and I sure as hell am going to want a DNA sample."

Pete turned to Lily when the telephone unit emitted a high, keening sound. "The bastard hung up on me!" His eyes accused Ina Jones, who clasped both her hands over her heart, fear showing in her eyes.

Lily reached down to scratch the shepherd's head. She could feel his huge body tremble against her leg. Clearly, the dog was reacting to the stress in his master's voice.

"If there's anything you know, anything at all, this would be the time to tell us."

"What . . . what . . . you said just now . . . Is it true? Was one of those boys your son? How . . . how can you know that for sure?"

"I know," Pete said. "He's one of the ones who got away. At least I think he got away. What if anything do you know about that private school?"

"I don't know anything. That's what I'm trying to tell you. This is just a run-of-the-mill job. There's no stress, the pay is decent, and it provides good benefits. It's an eight-to-six job, with plenty of time for me to catch up on my reading."

"Where does your check come from? Who pays the bills? Who signs those checks?"

Tears were rolling down the woman's mottled cheeks. "I don't know who pays the bills. I assume some management company. My check and those of the staff come by UPS overnight every Friday. I hand them out. The bank is First Sovereign here in town. I can show you my check since I haven't deposited it yet. I was going to do it yesterday, but I didn't get to the bank on time."

"Let's see the check," Pete said.

Ina bent down to open one of the desk drawers to get her purse. She pulled out her check and handed it over. Pete eyed the amount, then the signature, which was illegible. It didn't matter. The bank would have the signature on file. He copied down the account number. "Nice pay for a receptionist—$980 a week clear after deductions."

"I'm also the office manager," the woman said defensively.

"You pay the donors in cash. Where does that money come from?"

"It . . . it's in a separate envelope with the payroll checks. I get cash twice a month. I have to keep meticulous records. We don't have a petty cash drawer. If I need to buy a lightbulb or something, I have to use my own money, get a receipt, and I'm reimbursed with my check."

"How many people work here?"

"Right now, two nurses. In the fall and winter, when we're really busy, it can be as many as three doctors and four or five nurses. Six-hour shifts. None of them are friendly."

Lily decided it was time to weigh in. "What do you know about the fertility clinic?"

"Absolutely nothing. I'm not lying," Jones said at Lily's skeptical expression. "The fertility clinic is totally separate from the sperm bank. There's a full staff over there, and the only reason I know that is I see them coming and going. They never come in here, and I've never been over there. That is the God's honest truth. I don't believe this is happening," Ina wailed dramatically.

"You've been here eight years, you said. During that time do you remember anyone coming here who might be involved in the company? Think carefully. Did you ever hear the doctors or nurses say anything that might help us?"

"No. Never. This is really a boring job. It's the

same thing every single day. The routine never changes. Like I said, fall and winter are busy, with more donors coming through the doors."

"Where are the personnel files?" Lily asked.

"I don't know."

Pete knew there was nothing more to gain from interrogating Ina Jones. He picked up the CD he'd copied and stood up. "Thank you for your help, Ms. Jones. You can call the police now if you want to. I'd call that number I just called before you do that, though."

Ina Jones started to cry. She was dabbing at her eyes when the phone rang. The trio looked at one another. "Answer it and use the speaker button," Pete said.

"Berkeley Sperm Bank," Ina said in a jittery voice.

The rich baritone snarled a greeting. "Are those people gone? What did you tell those people?"

Ina closed her eyes. "They're gone, and I didn't tell them anything because I don't know anything. I told you, they had a killer dog with them. They copied everything that was on the computer. I quit. I'm leaving right now."

"You will do no such thing. Do you hear me?"

Pete's eyebrows shot up to his hairline at the threatening tone he heard coming from the speakerphone. To his and Ina's surprise, Winston licked her hand.

"I guess you didn't hear *me*. I said I quit. I'm going to lock the door, leave my key in the mailbox, and go, depart, vamoose. I will also turn out the lights. Good-bye, whoever you are."

The phone rang almost immediately the moment the connection was broken. Ina ignored it as she set about turning out lights and gathering up her purse and other belongings.

Ina ran her fingers through her hair as she turned off the computer and straightened the calendar blotter to the middle of the desk. She looked Pete in the eye, and said, "I'm going to cash my check before they stop payment on it. Please, follow me out." Pete and Lily had no other choice but to trail behind her. Winston followed, his eyes alert.

Ina was at her car, a maroon Honda Accord, when she turned to Pete. "I really hope you're wrong about all this. I'm going to have a very hard time of it if I find out you're right and I was even an unknowing part of this. I wish I wasn't afraid of dogs. Winston seems like a nice one."

Winston barked happily at the mention of his name.

The engine running, the window rolled down, Ina had one more thing to say. "I know I know you from somewhere. I never forget a face. It will come to me," she muttered to herself as she drove away.

For the first time, Lily realized it was drizzling. "It's raining!" How brilliant was that? "Now what?"

Pete looked down at the woman standing in front of him. Even with all that was going on he wanted to kiss her. Lily, reading his intentions lifted her head slightly. The world tilted, rocked, then tilted again. She knew she'd waited all her life for this moment. She said so when they finally drew apart.

"Damn!" was all Pete could think of to say. "Well, damn!"

Lily laughed. She linked her arm with Pete's as she led him up the walkway to the fertility clinic.

What looked like a hastily printed sign that said CLOSED was taped to the door. Pete tried the door handle. It didn't budge. He gave the stout metal door a hard kick. When nothing happened, he cursed under his breath.

"We could sit out here and wait for people to leave," Lily said. "They can't stay in there forever. There are eighteen cars in the parking lot. Staff, donors? Do we want to waste our time here? This is just a guess on my part, but I think the procedure at this clinic is the same as the one at the sperm bank. In short, Pete, we aren't going to get any information. Maybe we should try the police or the FBI to see what if anything we can find out about the school. What do you think?"

Pete kicked the door again. "Okay, let's try the police first even though the Feds are on it. Sometimes the police get pissy when the Feds stomp on their turf. They might be willing to give up something."

"It's worth a try," Lily said.

"Lily . . . what just happened . . . it wasn't because of . . . this, was it?"

"Way back when, we . . . you and I . . . we let the moment get away from us. I never forgot about you. I dreamed of you more often than I care to admit. Always, I wished we had gotten together somehow. I told myself that particular moment in time wasn't right for us. These moments, right now, feel right to me."

"Damn! Well, damn. That's exactly how I feel. Felt. We're not too bright, now, are we?"

Lily fiddled with the hat on her head. "Oh, I don't know, Pete. I think that was a pretty bright move you executed back there in the parking lot. I was bright enough to respond. So where does that leave us?"

"How does 'together' sound?" Pete asked.

"I think it sounds perfect. Listen, Pete, are you sure you want to go public with all this? You're so high-profile, I'm thinking it could damage your reputation. Stockholders are a funny lot. I'm nowhere near your league. I could use a different name. Zolly could help me. We could report back to you. I'm thinking out loud here."

"It doesn't matter. When this is all over, I'm retiring. I'm going to move out to my ranch in Montana. I made up my mind ages ago. It just took me a long time to get around to it. Right now, that's my game plan. Can you see yourself living in Montana, Lily?"

Lily threw her head back and laughed. Her hat sailed away on a gust of wind. Winston chased it and caught it in midair before it could land in a puddle.

"It's still pouring rain," Pete commented.

"I know. I had a dream about us once. We were walking in a park in our bare feet in the rain. You were holding my hand. I wanted you to kiss me so bad. But there were other people walking in the rain, and you were shy. You actually admitted to being shy. I was so impressed that you were a sensitive guy."

Pete listened intently. "Then what happened?"

Lily tried not to laugh. "I don't know. I woke up. We could pretend we're in the park right now." To move things along, Lily removed her sandals. She reached for Pete's hand and led him to the biggest puddle in the parking lot. She stomped in it. Pete joined her, then Winston joined them.

Zolly and Pete's security team watched from their cars, their jaws dropping. Zolly clamped his hands over his eyes when the boss planted a liplock on his companion that lasted so long he didn't think it was possible. He peeped between his fingers to see if either of them had suffocated.

" 'Bout time, boss," he muttered.

Chapter 7

It was like a Halloween night—wet and cold, the naked, arthritic trees bending under the torrential rains falling like raging rivers from the black hole in the sky.

The windowless concrete building had its own symphony of sounds to match those of the elements: rats skittering across the floor, the howling wind invading the dark space through the many cracks in the deserted old building. Even cement floor offered up its own set of weird, frightening sounds.

It was obvious both occupants of the room were nervous because they jumped when an owl hooted its displeasure at the weather invading its space in the tree outside the concrete building.

The witches and goblins this night were mortal. One wore a power suit and shiny wing tips, and carried a briefcase that cost more than most mortals earned in a month. The other goblin—more boy than man—it was hard to tell—looked like he had just stepped off the soccer field, with the grass stains to prove it. And yet, he smelled like Ivory Soap.

Even in broad daylight, it would be hard to tell either person's age—a teenager perhaps or a thirtysomething with a baby face. A nonthreatening goblin.

The power suit was a plain-looking man. Possibly in his late fifties. Definitely a pampered individual. Plain face, plain, thinning hair, plain stature. It was the suit, the shoes, the briefcase that shrieked *power and money*. Then again maybe it was the man's arrogance, or the man's defiant eyes—eyes black as the night.

The other man/boy hated the plain man. Hated and distrusted him. He waved his wrist in the general direction of the man—a test. A test to see if the power suit had any idea at all that what he thought was a heart monitor on his wrist was really a miniature digital recorder. In this line of business, you never knew what could go down in the blink of an eye. Satisfied, the man/boy held out his hand. The plain man slapped a thick brown envelope into his palm.

"It's all there," the plain man said.

"Yeah, well, I never take things for granted." The man/boy stuck the small penlight between his teeth so that the powerful tiny light beamed down on the thick stack of currency inside the envelope. The man/boy counted slowly and methodically, spitting on his index finger from time to time when the bills stuck together.

Outside, the owl hooted again and again. The rain continued to river downward. Holes in the roof allowed spits of water to hit the dirty concrete floor with delicate little plopping sounds.

"I told you it was all there," the plain man said when the man/boy shoved the thick envelope inside his zippered Windbreaker.

"Nice doing business with you," the man/boy said as he pretended to kick an imaginary soccer ball.

The plain man in the power suit looked at the man/boy, whose job description was "contract killer," and winced. "I hope you remember the rules," he said coldly.

The man/boy laughed. It was a pleasant sound. "'Go to the main library every Tuesday and Friday morning and check out the James Bond book *Never Say Die,* and if you need me, there will be a yellow Post-it on page two hundred telling me the time and the place for our next meeting.'" Like he was really going to do that. He'd be outta there the minute he hit the highway. He'd done a clean job with no loose ends. His first rule of business was, "Never stick around to watch the cleanup."

In the far corner of the concrete building, two rats screeched at one another. The owl hooted again. The minute the door opened, lightning ripped across the dark night like a spaceship gone amuck. Both men ran toward their vehicles, the plain man to a high-powered Mercedes, the man/boy to a junkyard pickup truck.

The last sound to be heard was the eerie hoot of the owl before the night turned totally black.

* * *

The plain man's house was palatial, even by
the standards of the megarich. He shed his
soggy power suit jacket and tie, kicked off the
sodden wing tips, and yanked at his soaking-wet
socks before walking up the circular staircase to
his bedroom. He stripped off the rest of his
clothing as he made his way to the bathroom. As
always, he took a moment to stare at the room.
It was a grotto, featuring a sunken whirlpool,
with vines and plants somehow growing out of
the brick walls. Water trickled down the stone
walls and into a trough that led into the
whirlpool. It was such a soothing sound he felt
his eyelids start to droop. He pinched his stomach hard as he stepped into the shower. First the
icy-cold spray, then steaming spray so hot his
skin felt like it was on fire. When he thought he
couldn't stand the heat one second longer, he
switched back to the icy-cold. At least it woke
him up.

Shivering, he towel-dried himself and dressed
in a pair of flannel pajamas decorated with fat
white bunnies, a gift from one of his grandchildren. He couldn't remember which one.

That night he had the California house to
himself. His family and the two full-time ser-
vants were back East in an almost identical
house. He liked it when he was alone.

Wearing slipper socks, he padded down the
circular staircase to the state-of-the-art kitchen,
where he made himself a grilled cheese sandwich and a cup of hot chocolate. People were always surprised that he knew how to cook.

As the plain man chewed his sandwich, he noticed that his hands were trembling. As he was always in control of his emotions, the tremor bothered him. He realized for the first time that what he was experiencing was fear. He didn't like the feeling at all. Not one little bit.

He stared across the room at the huge bay window in the breakfast nook that took up one entire wall of the kitchen. All he could see was total blackness. A shiver ran up and down his arms as he tried to remember if he'd set the alarm when he entered the house. He slipped and stumbled as he made his way to the foyer, where he quickly punched in a set of numbers.

Alarms were a joke. If someone was intent on entering a house, alarm or not, they'd get in. Like that lowlife he'd just paid off.

The slipper socks slapped at the imported marble floor as the man made his way back to the kitchen.

The black window drew him like a magnet. Was someone out there watching him? *Now, where did that thought come from?* he wondered. Though he could see nothing, he could still hear the pouring rain.

Suddenly, the man felt vulnerable, standing exposed in his bunny pajamas at the window. He moved rapidly to turn off the bright overhead lights. When the kitchen was as dark as the night outside, he slithered to the side of the window. Did he just see movement by the bougainvillea trellis? He felt trapped as he crept back to the entry hall, where he reached up for the panic button that was held in place by a magnet. He clasped it in his hand as he made his way to the second floor.

At the top of the steps, he pressed a switch, and the entire first floor lit up like a football field at a night game. The light made him feel a bit better. But only for a moment. Even if he pressed the little red button on the panic gizmo, he could be dead before the police arrived. He must have been out of his mind to hire that psycho.

He entered his home study. He looked at his computer and wondered if there was some wiseass out there who could find what he'd gone to such great lengths to hide. He cursed his father then, in all four languages in which he was fluent. If it wasn't for him, he wouldn't be there sweating like a Trojan. A fearful Trojan.

Like the old man cared. Crippled with arthritis, Parkinson's, and a weak heart, he was going to die soon and leave his son holding the bag. "And there go all my political aspirations," he mumbled as he turned on the computer. "There goes the goddamn White House!"

Senator Hudson Preston sat down in his ergonomic chair and leaned back to wait for the computer to boot up. He felt proud of himself that he'd personally contacted Peter Kelly and harnessed the man's expertise in setting up foolproof firewalls that, according to Kelly, even the Pentagon couldn't penetrate. And in return for that expertise, the senator had ordered thousands of computers to be sent to the local school system, all compliments of Preston Pharmaceuticals.

Peter Aaron Kelly didn't like him, and Preston knew it. "Tough shit, Mr. Kelly," the senator said aloud.

He started to type, recording everything that had happened in the past three days. When he finished, he raced out of the room to his bedroom, where he'd tossed his keys on the dresser. He grabbed them and removed the memory stick that looked like a child's whistle painted in psychedelic colors. To anyone who asked about the strange doodad hanging from his key ring, he said it was a gift from one of his grandchildren. He removed the memory stick, plugged it into the computer, and copied the file he'd just created. When he was finished, he returned the two-inch cylinder to his key ring and laid it on the top of his dresser.

The senator deleted all the files and turned off the computer. He was ready to go to bed. He crawled between the covers, knowing full well he wouldn't be able to sleep. But he had to try because he needed to forget all the carnage he'd seen on the news. If he tried, he could almost live with that. What he couldn't live with was the picture he'd seen of Peter Aaron Kelly on the evening news, along with Lily Madison.

The senator started to shake under the covers.

PAK Industries *versus* Preston Pharmaceuticals.

One winner. One loser.

Unless . . .

Chapter 8

They were in someone's yard. A family's backyard. Josh Baer could see into the kitchen, where a family was seated around a big table. He'd seen scenes just like this on television. This was different, though. This was a real, flesh-and-blood family. Not actors pretending to be a family.

Even though he was soaking-wet in his khaki trousers and navy blue blazer, he couldn't tear his eyes away from the scene in front of him. He wished more than anything in the world that somehow he could be part of the family inside. Just once. Just to see what it felt like to have a father put his hand on his shoulder. For a mother to hug him. For a sister or a brother to take a poke at him. Families did that. He knew his eyes were filling up with his loss, so he tried to refocus his thoughts. Why was this family eating so late? Dinner at the academy was promptly at six o'clock. Not five minutes past six, not one minute past six, but promptly at six. He could see the big, round kitchen clock over the doorway through the window. It said the time was seven fifteen.

Josh did his best to forget how wet and miserable he was as he watched the family get up and leave the kitchen. A minute later he heard voices in the driveway as they got into a car and drove off. He blinked at the fact that lights were left on and food was still sitting on the table. He knew Jesse was hungry. Maybe he could sneak into the house and take some food. He didn't stop to think but ran toward the house, though not before he cautioned Jesse to stay hidden in the thick shrubbery. He returned with the bucket of chicken, some clothes from the dryer by the back door, and a headful of wonderful scents. He now knew what a family's house smelled like. He felt giddy at the sudden knowledge.

They ate first, devouring the fried chicken and biscuits. They had fried chicken at the academy, but it had never tasted like this chicken.

"That was very good," Jesse said. "We're having a real experience, aren't we, Josh?"

"This is as real as it gets, Jesse. Quick now, change your clothes. You'll feel better when you're dry and comfortable. We have to leave here and find a place to sleep tonight. The police are going to be looking for us. So will the . . . lots of people are going to be looking for us. We have to look different so we . . . so we blend in."

Josh Baer prodded his companion. "Come on, Jesse, we have to keep moving, or they'll find us. We have to find a place to ditch our old clothes. Jesse, are you listening to me?"

Jesse mumbled something as he tried to keep up with Josh. "Why are we running away? Let's go back, Josh. They're going to punish us."

Josh drew a deep breath. He'd taken responsibility for Jesse, who was mentally challenged, when they were five years old and living in that first awful place. "No, they aren't going to punish us because we aren't going back. Promise me you're going to do everything I say. Promise, Jesse."

"I promise. Where are we going? Who was that person with the gun? Are they going to catch us?"

"I don't know where we're going yet. Someplace safe. He was just a guy with a gun, and I don't know who he was. If you do what I say and listen to me, they won't catch us. Do you understand me, Jesse?"

"I always do what you say, Josh. You're my brother."

"Except for yesterday, when you couldn't find your book bag and we were late for class. Being late for class yesterday was a good thing, Jesse. If we had been on time for class, we'd both be dead."

"I'm getting tired. I wish I had some more of that chicken."

Josh was losing his patience. "I'm tired, too, Jesse. We have to get as far away from school as we can. It's better if we move around at night because no one will be watching for us in the dark. Please, Jesse, try to keep up. We'll find a place to sleep pretty soon."

Staying in the shadows, skipping from yard to yard, the two boys trudged along for hours as they sought a safe haven. The rain had stopped, and the cloud cover moved on, leaving the moon riding high in the sky. Josh wasn't sure, but he thought it must be around midnight. He knew Jesse was more tired, but he was gamely putting one foot in front of the other. Jesse was always a good sport.

If only Jesse had been smart enough not to swallow those pills. Well, there was no point in thinking about that now. Maybe someday he'd be able to tell someone who cared enough to listen.

His eyelids drooping, Josh saw the bus in the empty lot out of the corner of his eye. He half-dragged, half-carried Jesse to the bus, praying that the door would be open. It was. They crawled in, and Jesse was asleep the minute he stretched out across the long seat at the back of the bus. Josh sat down, propped his feet up against the seat in front of him, and closed his eyes. Tired as he was, sleep would not come.

He played the scene over and over in his mind. Why? He felt bad about stealing money from Mr. Dickey's wallet. He felt even worse for taking all the money in Miss Carmody's purse. He told himself they were dead and wouldn't need it. Still, he'd stolen it. More for Jesse than for himself. Altogether it was $140. Enough to buy food for a little while until he could figure out what to do.

He was smart. All those doctors who checked him all the time said he was exceptionally smart. The tests proved it. But he wasn't smart in the ways of the world. How could he be? He had lived in group homes, under close supervision, then at the academy. He'd never gone anywhere in the outside world to gain any practical knowledge. He thought about the family he'd seen earlier. They looked so happy. He wondered if he would ever be happy.

Josh did his best to curl into the fetal position on the narrow seat. His last conscious thought before drifting off to sleep was that he knew in his heart, in his mind, in his gut, that somewhere out there in that strange, alien world he was just coming to know, he had a mother and a father. He wasn't a test tube kid. He wasn't. No matter what they said or did to him, he would never, ever believe that.

The memory came almost immediately.

He was back in the white building dressed in a long white shirt and standing in a long line with other children. To get the colored candies. The men in the white coats said they were M&M's. He looked up at the pictures on the wall of the little candies dancing across a poster.

He didn't know how he knew, even at the age of six, that it wasn't candy on the little white dish. Maybe it was because the other children got sick after taking the candies.

* * *

He kept the colored candy under his tongue, then spit it out when no one was looking.

Then again, maybe it was the way the men in the white coats whispered when he was next in line to receive the candies.

They wrote a lot on the paper that had his name on it. Someday, when he learned how to read, he was going to search for those papers to see what they had written about him.

He moved out of the line and waited for Jesse. Jesse was like him when they first came to this place, but he was different now. Sometimes he couldn't remember his name and Josh would have to remind him. "What's your name today?"

The chubby six-year-old laughed as he ran out to the playground. He always laughed when he couldn't remember his name. Josh followed him, trying to understand why Jesse couldn't remember his name. Everyone was supposed to know their names. Jesse used to know his name before they started giving out the colored candies.

Fifteen minutes to play on the swings and monkey bars, then the monitors would line them up to go back indoors. He moved closer to Jesse. "You have to remember your name, or they'll put you in the slow line," he whispered.

Jesse laughed again as he scampered away from the swing he'd been swinging on.

Josh followed him and watched as Jesse struggled

with the monkey bars. He turned when he heard the whistle. Time to line up. The fast line and the slow line. Josh took his place in the fast line with another boy and one girl. Jesse waved as the monitor led him to the slow line, where the majority of the children were waiting. He waved again as he took his place in line. Josh didn't wave back.

Josh moved closer to the boy in front of him. When the monitor wasn't looking, he whispered, "Do you like those candies, Tom?"

"Heck, no. They're bitter. When no one is looking, I spit them out. Don't tell on me, okay?"

"I won't tell," Josh said solemnly. He turned to the girl and asked the same question. "Do you like the candy?"

The girl, whose name was Sheila, giggled, and said she put them in her ear when no one was looking. "Promise not to tell." Again, Josh solemnly promised.

Following the monitor inside, Josh knew if they swallowed the candies that he, Tom, and Sheila would go to the slow line, the line where the kids couldn't remember their names.

Josh stirred, then woke. Groggy, he looked at the darkness surrounding him. It all came back to him in a rush. He crept to the back of the bus to check on Jesse, who was still sleeping peacefully. Josh walked back to his seat and tried to go to sleep again, but sleep was elusive. His weary mind kept going to the family he'd watched from his hiding spot in the bushes. What he'd seen earlier was real—really, totally real.

Josh knew that the outside world he was in

was very different from the cloistered one he had lived all his life. He, Tom, and Sheila whispered about this other world after lights-out. They talked and planned what they'd do when they left the academy at eighteen. It was Tom who came up with the plan. Sheila, the bravest of the three, said it would work if they all did their part.

They did have one fear, and Josh was the one who'd expressed it over and over: "What if the authorities don't believe us?"

Tom's response was, "I have the goods."

Sheila said their remarkable memories would serve them well. All Josh could do was nod and hope they were right.

Now he was on his own, with only Jesse to help him. He blinked away the tears forming in his eyes. He was never going to see Tom and Sheila again. Ever. If he was lucky, maybe he could find out where his two best friends were buried so he could visit them. He had to tell them how sorry he was that he was alive and they weren't.

Josh wondered if that would ever happen. His eyes finally closed, and he was asleep.

A hard shake to his shoulder woke Josh hours later. He blinked as he raised himself on one elbow to look out the bus window. The sun was just creeping over the horizon.

"I have to pee, Josh. I'm hungry. I don't like it here. I want to go home. Let's go home, Josh."

Josh stood up and had to duck. His six-foot-two frame was too tall for the bus. He crouched over as he led Jesse outside.

Ninety minutes later the two young men stopped at a roadside shack, lured in by a sign that said it served the best bacon-sausage-and-egg sandwiches in California. Josh ordered six and two bottles of orange juice, seriously depleting his money supply. They wolfed down the food and asked the man behind the counter for directions to the nearest library.

The day was beginning. People were walking in little groups, some walking dogs, others running, some jogging. Traffic was heavy in all directions. Overhead the birds were awake and singing their morning songs. Josh wished he had the time to enjoy and savor what was going on around him.

Josh did a double take when he saw a sign for the university and realized they must be headed for the Berkeley Campus Library. He didn't know if it was a bad thing or a good thing. He told himself there was probably more information to be gained from a college library than a public library.

"I want to go home, Josh. Why are we going to this place?"

Josh whirled around. "Listen to me, Jesse. We can't go back. They . . . closed the school. The doors are all locked. We have to find somewhere else to go. You have to listen to me, Jesse, and pay attention. That man with the gun back at the school . . . He will come after us."

"Why?"

Josh knew he wasn't going to get through to Jesse, but he tried nonetheless. "He's one of the bad guys. He doesn't like us. He wants to kill us

the way he killed Mr. Dickey and Miss Carmody
and all our friends. When we get inside, you can
open your backpack and draw while I work on
the computer. Maybe . . . maybe the people in
the library will let you hang up your pictures.
You have to be real quiet in the library. You
can't talk to anyone, Jesse. Do you hear me?"

"Will they really hang my pictures, Josh?"

"Yeah. I promise. You're gonna keep quiet,
right?"

Jesse squeezed his lips shut with his fingers
and giggled.

Josh's eyes were everywhere as he walked
through the security line, Jesse right behind
him. It was a nice library. A big library. They
could get lost inside for many hours. Even at
that hour there were hundreds of people,
mostly students, milling about. The only thing
he didn't like about libraries was the deathly silence. When you made a sound, everyone *looked*
at you. Just then he didn't want anyone looking
at him.

Two strolls up and down the aisle later, Josh
picked out a table at the back of the library and
settled Jesse. "Listen to me," he whispered, "I'm
going to be over by the computers. Do not move
from this chair, Jesse. Stay here until I come
back for you. If you get lost, someone will take
your book bag, and they won't give you anything to eat." He hated saying things like that to
Jesse, but sometimes he had to do it so Jesse
wouldn't blow things out of the water. As Josh

had found out over the years, there was no telling what Jesse would do at any given time.

Josh waited until Jesse had his colored pencils and his art tablet in front of him before leaving. He looked back once, and saw that Jesse was in his own little world. For the moment.

Josh headed for the racks of current daily newspapers. He carried them to a small table, opened them, and proceeded to read everything printed about the carnage at the academy. *What a crock,* he seethed under his breath. He had a good mind to send the newspapers a scathing e-mail, telling them they had it all wrong. Maybe he would do that.

As he pondered what he'd just read, his gaze was everywhere. He spotted it then, two backpacks with baseball caps stuck in between the straps. Josh looked around to see if anyone was watching. He snatched the caps, perfectly ordinary khaki-colored billed caps. In the blink of an eye he was back at Jesse's table. He reached down for a bright-blue marker and scribbled the word "Jack" on the bill. On the one he plopped onto Jesse's head he wrote "Bill." Jesse looked up and smiled, but he didn't take off the cap.

Back at his own table, Josh gathered up the newspapers to carry them back to the rack. He positioned them just the way they were when he got them. Behind him, a woman in a hat with a big flower on it was waiting for the papers he'd just read. He mumbled, "Excuse me," and went back to his table.

Feeling slightly invisible with his curly hair

tucked under the cap, Josh bent over the computer and logged on. He took one last look at Jesse, who was contentedly filling page after page with his drawings, before Josh lost himself in the only world he truly knew. The Internet.

It was fast approaching the noon hour when Josh looked up at the clock on the wall. Jesse would be getting hungry. He clicked the mouse one last time and almost passed out when he saw a picture of himself on the screen. He slouched down in his chair as he read the small caption under his picture.

KILLER LOOKS LIKE BOY NEXT DOOR!
DEAN SAYS JOSH BAER WAS A TROUBLED BOY.

He could hardly believe what he was reading. They were blaming him! They were blaming him for killing Tom and Sheila and all the others. Even the teachers. Were they crazy? Why would the media accuse him? He wished Tom and Sheila were there so he could talk to them. What would they do or say? He turned off the computer just as a tall man, almost as tall as he was, walked by his table.

Josh was about to get up when he saw the tall man heading toward the lady in the pretty hat. He watched out of the corner of his eye to see if they would notice or pay attention to Jesse. They talked for a minute, then they left together, but not before the woman pointed to Jesse, who was bent over his drawings. Josh felt his heart flutter in his chest. Why did she point to Jesse? What did it mean? Instinctively, he knew they had to get out of the library immediately.

Josh did his best to hurry his friend, but Jesse refused to leave until his drawing was finished. Josh looked down and got dizzy at what he was looking at. Jesse had perfectly captured what had happened that morning at the shoot-out. Right down to the guy who looked like a soccer player holding the automatic weapon. Jesse's art more than made up for his other inadequacies. Josh had never been able to figure that out. In the earlier years, Sheila had said God gave Jesse his art so he wouldn't miss being normal. Even back then Josh hadn't bought that theory, but he couldn't come up with anything better to explain what a wonderful artist Jesse was.

"I'm done. Will you hang them up now? I'm hungry."

"When we come back I'll hang them up. We have to go now. I'm hungry, too." Josh expected Jesse to give him a hard time, but he was agreeable to leaving. Probably it was the mention of food. You could always tempt Jesse with food.

The sky was overcast as the two boys left the library. Josh looked around anxiously to see if either the lady with the hat or the really tall man was anywhere in sight. He let his breath out in a loud *swoosh* when he didn't see anything out of the ordinary. "Let's run, Jesse. We haven't had any exercise in a few days. We have to stay in shape."

Jesse giggled as he lumbered off at an awkward trot, Josh pounding the pavement behind him.

Fifteen minutes later, burgers, fries, and milk shakes under their belts, Josh asked for directions to the public library.

By two o'clock, Jesse was settled with his art pad, pencils, and markers, while Josh logged on to the computer. His mind raced as he looked down at the sickening pictures Jesse had drawn. As far as he could tell, Jesse hadn't left out one detail of that awful scene. He hated what he knew he had to do next. But, he told himself, there was no other way. He had to do his best to protect and keep Jesse safe. If he kept Jesse with him, it was only a matter of time before they were caught. All the money in his pocket would go to feed Jesse. He didn't mind that, but what would they do when the money ran out?

Josh logged on to the computer and typed up an e-mail to the FBI. He gave his name and his student ID number from the academy. The letter was short and succinct.

Dear Agents,
    I did not kill my friends or the teachers at the academy. I don't have a gun and wouldn't know where to get one. You have to keep Jesse safe. When you see his pictures, you will understand why. Jesse likes to eat and draw. He's like he is because of what the people who own the academy did to him. Only eight of us that I know of are normal. I am not a troubled young man like the dean said in one of the newspaper articles. Tom had all the proof, but that man killed him. He kept the proof hidden at the academy. Only Sheila

and I knew about it. They're dead now, so only I know.

I am going to try to find the truth and the proof, then I will give it to you. I know that man is going to come after me.

Please take care of Jesse.

Josh typed his name at the bottom of the e-mail. He read it through several times until he had it committed to memory. Then he clicked on the SEND button.

As Sheila would have said, "The fat's in the fire now." Tears burned his eyes at how the three of them were always so in sync. No more.

Josh looked around the library, which was almost deserted. It didn't look like anyone was paying attention to either him or Jesse. Did he dare risk going up to the librarian to ask if he could buy an envelope from her? He didn't stop to think but marched right up to the desk, and asked, "Ma'am, can I buy a large mailing envelope?"

"Of course. That will be a dollar. Do you need stamps?"

"No, ma'am, I have some," he lied.

Back at the computer, Josh clicked and clicked until he found the address of the nearest FBI office. He clicked on MapQuest for directions. He printed out the information, studied it thoroughly. He then typed up another letter to the FBI and printed it out. He photocopied Jesse's pictures before he put everything in the brown envelope. His plan was to take Jesse to the office and send him inside with the envelope and make tracks. They would take care of Jesse, he was sure of it.

The clock on the wall said he had a lot of hours to kill until it got dark. Maybe he could find a movie with a double feature. Jesse would like that. Then, when it got dark, he'd send Jesse into the building. He'd buy him some pizza so he wasn't hungry.

Josh knuckled his burning eyes. *I don't have any other choice,* he told himself over and over. *When this is all over, I'll come back for you, Jesse,* he promised silently.

Josh turned off the computer and walked over to Jesse. "Want to go to the movies? We can get some pizza, too."

"Did you hang up my pictures?"

"I sure did. Everyone liked them," Josh lied, his fingers crossed behind his back. "What did you draw this time?"

Josh almost exploded out of his shoes when he looked down at the likeness of himself and the lady with the pretty hat then at the one with the man.

Jesse started to laugh at his reaction. "He looks like you, Josh. Isn't that funny?"

Josh could barely get his tongue to work. "Yeah, Jesse, real funny. Come on, put all your stuff back in your bag and let's go."

Chapter 9

Lily wrapped her arms around her legs, which were drawn up to her chin. She stared across the table at Pete, who looked so glum she wanted to reach out to him, but she held herself in check. Winston, lying under the table, whined softly at the silence around him.

A waiter appeared to take away the breakfast dishes.

"This is nice," Lily said, breaking the silence as she motioned to the little walled garden at the villa. "It's so peaceful, so colorful. It was nice having breakfast out here, wasn't it?"

"We missed something," Pete said flatly as he ignored Lily's question. He did allow himself a nod at her comment, however.

"Pete, we went to the police. They said they're searching for the two missing boys. They admitted the boys are on the run. They're looking. I, for one, do not believe for a minute they think Josh Baer is the killer. I think it was all for publicity or just to keep the press quiet. And it was like you said, the FBI is in charge. The locals always get annoyed when the FBI steps in—at least that's the way it is on television. Then again, this is the real world and not make-believe."

"At least the locals agreed to talk to us. It's more than we got from the FBI. We've been here four days, and we haven't gotten past square one. We made four trips to the local FBI office. I called at least a dozen times. No one is calling us back. All the agents are unavailable. That's as in unavailable *ALL* the time. Or is it just when we call or show up? Us, Lily. Me and you."

Lily let go of her legs and leaned forward. "Pete, you are almost as famous as the president of the United States. When your name is mentioned, people know who and what you are. It's called name recognition. Having said that, you must know *someone,* somewhere, who can pull a few strings for you to get a response from the FBI."

"You'd think so, wouldn't you? I've made so many calls, my cell phone went dead. I've sent twice as many e-mails. It seems like half the people in my world are either out of the country, on vacation, or want nothing to do with me. In addition to all of that, we can't get within a mile of that goddamn academy. The fertility clinic and the sperm bank are closed until further notice. What are we onto here?"

"Whatever it is, it isn't good. Maybe we need to start thinking like those two boys and try to find them. We aren't so old that we can't put ourselves in their place. What would we do if we were in their position? They have to be panicking by now. Do they have money? Where are they? Two boys! Someone must have seen them. If we had bios of the boys, it would help. Can you hack into the academy's computers?" Lily asked breathlessly.

"Well, yeah, ordinarily I could, but by now the FBI has them under lock and key. In the damn movies, there is always a snitch lurking in the background willing to give it all up for money. I don't see that happening, do you? No matter which way we turn, we hit a brick wall. Why all this damn secrecy where that school is concerned? Everything is buried so deep even Marty, with all his digging, can't come up with a thing. You're right, we have to find those boys."

Winston reared up on his hind legs when he spotted a small brown bird alight on top of the wall enclosing the garden. He trotted over and watched with unblinking intensity as the small creature eyed him right back. He let out a soft *"woof"* to announce his presence. The bird chirped, ruffled his feathers, and continued to eye the dog before he flew off. Winston lay down, crossed one big paw over the other, and went to sleep.

"He really is an amazing dog, Pete. And he's devoted to you. Lucky you."

"Yeah, I know. If I was one of those kids, I think I'd try to find a way to hook up to a computer. An Internet café. The library. One or the other of them must know someone, somewhere he can call on to help them. What? You look like you just saw a ghost. What?" Pete asked, alarm ringing in his voice.

Lily stared into Pete's eyes. Her toes started to curl up. "That . . . that day in the library, when I was going through the papers, there was this young boy across from me. He had a baseball cap on that said "Bill" on the beak. I assumed Bill was his name. He was drawing in one of those art books. He had all kinds of colored pencils and markers. You know how it is when someone is sitting fairly close to you, and you're minding your own business, but you can still sense or see movement even when you aren't aware of it. Do you know what I mean?"

Pete nodded, wondering where all this was going.

"There was another boy there. He had a baseball cap on, too. It said "Jack" on the bill. He was really tall, like you. I was behind him when he returned the daily papers to the rack. When I went back to my table, I had to walk behind the boy Bill. I looked down at his drawing. It all happened in the blink of an eye. Me walking by, sneaking a look. The drawing had a lot of red in it, figures. Just my quick impression. When I sat down with the papers, he looked up. I hesitate to say he was retarded, but there was a certain blankness to his eyes and expression. It was like he saw me, but he didn't see me. That kind of thing. I do know this, the boy can draw. The lines, the shapes were clean and sharp. He knew what he was doing. I guess he was either drawing from memory or creating something. Do you think it means anything?"

"What about the other boy?" Pete's voice was so tortured, Lily wanted to cry for him.

"I don't know, Pete. I really didn't pay much attention to him. That wasn't where my mind was at that moment. I don't even know what color his hair was. He was wearing baggy clothes like kids wear. You can pick my brain from now until tomorrow, but I've told you everything I recall."

"Two boys in the campus library?"

"Pete, there were hundreds of students in the library that day. It's a campus library, kids are supposed to be there. Don't you remember how many hours you and I spent there?"

"In one of those newspaper articles the dean said Josh Baer was a troubled youngster. You said the boy doing the drawing looked . . . different."

"He wasn't the boy we saw on television at the airport, Pete. And, like I said, I was behind the other boy, so I didn't see his face. I'm so sorry, Pete. I wish I had seen something that would help us. Maybe we should try to find the dean."

"The guy is probably in protective custody. He's not in the phone book because I looked. I suppose it's a possibility he lived at the academy, but I doubt it." Pete looked down at his watch. "The boys have been on the run for over ninety-six hours. I'm starting to think they're pretty smart to have eluded the authorities for that long. Do they have a destination in mind, or are they holed up somewhere afraid to make a move? I keep asking myself what I would do besides panic, but I can't come up with an answer. I don't know anything about teenagers and what makes them tick."

"I know even less," Lily said mournfully.

Pete moved his chair closer to Lily's. "I probably don't have any right to ask you this, but how . . . how much longer can you stay here with me?"

This was no time to be coy or to pretend she didn't know what Pete was talking about. "As long as you want me to stay, Pete." *If you want me to stay forever, I will.*

"I know you have a thriving business to run, Lily, and I know I'm being selfish in wanting you to stay. I think you and I . . . What I mean is . . . we found . . ."

Damn it, just say it, Lily screamed silently. When it looked like Pete wasn't going to finish what he was trying to say, she blurted, "Each other?"

The relief on Pete's face was so comical, Lily laughed. "Well, yeah."

"Now that we have *that* all straightened out, let's put *us* on the back burner and concentrate on finding the boys. It's obvious no one is going to help us, so let's just go for it ourselves. Between us, I'm sure we can make whatever bail they set if we get arrested. Let's also give some thought to hiring a private detective." *Oh, God, did I just say all that? I sound like a gung-ho criminal out for blood.*

"You are indeed a girl after my own heart." To

prove his point, Pete dramatically placed his hand over his heart and let out a heartfelt sigh. "In solving any problem, you have to go back to the beginning. For us, the beginning is the clinic and the sperm bank. I say we break into the clinic and the sperm bank tonight. I'm sure Zolly knows how to deactivate an alarm system. He knows all kinds of stuff like that, and what he doesn't know personally, he knows someone who does. You up for a little B&E?"

Lily didn't have to stop and think before she replied. "Works for me."

"Let's take one more crack at the local FBI office. Then I say we go to both the campus library and the public library to see if anyone remembers seeing those boys. I'm going to download the picture of Josh Baer off the Net. It might trigger some kind of recognition if we show it around. It's worth a try."

"Then let's do it. When are you going to tell all this to Zolly? You go on ahead, talk to him, while I powder my nose. I'll be ready in ten minutes. Five if need be."

She was so close to him, she could smell his aftershave and the melon that he'd had for breakfast. She knew she was falling in love with Pete Kelly. Maybe she'd been in love with him all along, and that's why she'd never had a serious relationship. Did she dare hope he would return the feelings? All indications were *yes*, but when this was all over, would he feel the same way? She simply didn't know. *If I get my heart broken, then it wasn't meant to be,* she told herself as she headed to the bathroom to do a little primping and maybe add a spritz or two of that sinful perfume she'd bought a month or so ago.

In spite of herself, Lily burst out laughing when she heard Zolly's roar of disapproval through the open bathroom window. Winston's angry bark at the raised voices should be enough of a warning for both Zolly and Pete that he wasn't going to put up with bad human behavior. He barked again to make his point. The voices still sounded angry but decibels lower. She giggled when she heard Pete say, "You're fired," three different times.

Lily decided the time was right to exit her villa so she could embark on a life of crime with this man. *I wonder if they'll give us separate cells when we get arrested.* Just the thought of going to jail made her stomach muscles quiver.

"I'm ready," Lily trilled as she tripped down the path to where Pete and Zolly were standing.

Zolly had a murderous look in his eye when Lily joined them. He mumbled something under his breath that didn't sound complimentary to her. Obviously, Winston thought the same thing because he let loose with a horrendous howl of displeasure.

"See, Zolly, Winston approves. Now, get your ass in gear and let's go. You can map out a strategy while Lily and I see what we can come up with, if anything, at the FBI office."

As Zolly lumbered toward the SUV, he called over his shoulder, "You know I have to report this to the board."

"Before or after I fire you—again?" Pete snapped back.

Zolly's shoulders slumped. Winston growled.

Forty minutes later, Pete and Lily walked into the local FBI office. Both were surprised at the small quarters and lack of agents milling about. Local office meant just that. Four rooms and an entrance foyer with a coatrack, a wastebasket, and a receptionist.

Pete stepped up to the window, and said, "I'm Peter Kelly from PAK Industries, and I'd like to speak to one of the agents in charge of the shooting at the California Academy of Higher Learning."

Lily noticed that the receptionist didn't look impressed, and it also appeared like she didn't recognize Pete's name. "All the agents are out in the field, sir. I can patch a call through for you to Agent Robbins, but I don't know if he'll pick up or not."

"If you tell me where he is, I can go there. This is really important. I think I have some information he might be interested in."

A few minutes later the receptionist said, "Agent Robbins said to give me your cell phone number, and he'll call you in a few minutes." Pete rattled off his cell phone number.

Trying to be helpful, the woman said, "You should go outside to take the call. The reception here inside the building on cell phones is terrible. You can barely hear, and nine times out of ten the connection gets broken."

Pete thanked her for the heads-up and ush- ered Lily through the door. "Let's see if this is for real or she just blew us off." Pete barely had the words out of his mouth when his cell phone rang.

Lily almost jumped out of her sandals. She lis- tened to Pete's end of the conversation, her jaw dropping as Pete fumed and snarled and bab- bled about taxpayers' money, after which he threatened to go to the media with his informa- tion.

"What that means is, I share, you share, and we compare notes."

At least he had the agent's attention because Pete suddenly swung into listening mode.

"Hell, yes, I am Pete Kelly, and, yes, PAK In- dustries is mine along with a bunch of stock- holders. No, I am not some kind of kook. I've had enough of this bullshit. Either you meet me somewhere, anywhere you want, and we talk, or I take what I know to the media. Right now, Agent Robbins. I do not give a good rat's ass about blowing your investigation. Now, what's it going to be?" He listened for another minute, then said, "Damn straight I have a few big guns in my Rolodex. Actually, Agent Robbins, the whole goddamn Rolodex is full of big guns. I don't know anyone who isn't a big gun. Before I pull out the artillery, I want to give you the cour- tesy of a meet and greet so we can both do a show-and-tell. Thirty minutes, in front of the Berkeley Campus Library. Be on time, Agent Robbins." Pete hung up.

"Zolly!" Pete bellowed.

Zolly lumbered forward. Winston stood at attention. Both animal and guard knew *that* tone of voice. Winston was actually quivering with excitement, while Zolly felt the need to keep his hand on the gun butt in the holster strapped to his waist.

"Yeah, boss."

"Saddle up, big guy. We're going to the campus library to meet an FBI agent. I want all of us to be on our good behavior. All of *you*, that is." Pete looked pointedly at Zolly, who met his gaze head-on but was the first to look away.

Winston barked happily as he raced to the SUV.

"What does the lady in the pretty hat have to say?" Pete drawled.

"She says, let's rock and roll."

The breezy statement had the desired effect on the software giant. Pete laughed and reached for her hand.

"Do we have a game plan, Pete?" Lily asked the moment Zolly had parked the SUV and turned off the ignition.

Everyone scrambled out of the vehicle. Winston did his best to wiggle between Pete and Lily. It probably wasn't a bad thing, Lily thought. One formidable presence in the form of Zolly was one thing but two, counting Winston, well, that was something else.

"Which means, of course, that Pete and I are chopped liver in this gig," she mumbled under her breath.

"Not really, but I'm working on it," Pete responded grimly as he strode toward the front doors of the campus library, where a nattily dressed man was lounging against a waste container. Like all Bureau agents, he wore the requisite aviator glasses and talked into his sleeve or shirt collar.

Agent Robbins was tall but not as tall as Pete. Lily thought he must be independently wealthy from the looks of his HUGO BOSS suit. If there was anything Lily knew about it was fabric, clothes, and fashion. For some reason she didn't think government employees like Special Agent Robbins made the kind of money it took to buy a HUGO BOSS suit and Bali shoes. The tie looked kind of pricey, too. The pristine white shirt was linen. Linen?

Lily continued to size up the agent behind her own drugstore sunglasses. He was a good 210 pounds, and she could tell he worked out. The word "buff" came to mind. His wheat-colored hair was styled, and his pearly whites guaranteed he was his dentist's poster boy. In short, Agent Robbins was a hunk. A threatening hunk.

Pete stepped forward, his hand outstretched. Agent Robbins did his best to crush his hand, but it was Pete who exerted enough pressure to make the agent's lips thin out in a grimace.

Lily and Winston found themselves being introduced. Lily merely nodded as she clasped the agent's hand. Winston, although always a gentleman, did not offer up his paw. Clearly the jury was still out on Agent Robbins where the dog was concerned.

Robbins took the lead. "Mr. Kelly, you said you had information you wanted to share with me concerning the shooting at the academy. I'm here to listen."

"What I said, Agent Robbins, was this: I said I had information to share, and if you share yours, we can compare notes and, hopefully, solve this case."

"The FBI does not, I repeat, does not, share information on a crime with outsiders. I don't care if you *do* run the biggest software company in the whole world. If you have information that will aid in this investigation, this would be a good time to share it. Otherwise, I'll run you in and charge you with obstructing justice."

Lily turned around when she heard Zolly mutter, "Oh, jeez, it's turning into a pissing contest."

She looked up to see if Agent Robbins had heard Zolly's assessment of the current situation. If he did, he wasn't letting on.

"Well, how's this for starters? That school is tied to the Berkeley Sperm Bank and the fertility clinic next door. Both of which suddenly closed their doors within minutes of my visiting and asking questions. Your turn."

Agent Robbins smirked, then leaned back against the side of the building as he fired up a cigarette and blew a perfect smoke ring. "Well, that is certainly creative. I can't even come close to matching that information. All I can say is an off-the-wall kid got hold of a gun and decided to kill his teachers and classmates. The kid is on the run, but we'll find him. We always get our man."

Pete let loose with a loud guffaw of disgust.

"See, there you go. I was being honest with you, and you up and tell me a big fat old lie. Shame on you. There were two boys on the run."

"Oh, yeah, the other kid. He gave himself up. Just walked into the office cool as you please the other day with his backpack. He had a note or something from the other kid—the shooter. The kid with the backpack is in la-la land. Doesn't even know his name. He giggles a lot, I'm told. Your turn, *Mister* Kelly." He made Pete's name sound obscene.

Lily decided in that moment that she hated the nattily attired Agent Robbins. Winston came to the same conclusion and growled ominously.

Pete's mind raced. He now had more information than he had had a few minutes ago. "That's it for now. Anytime you care to share more, call me. Just so you know, if there's one thing I excel in, Agent Robbins, it's computers. I have every hacker, every expert in the business working on ownership. As in who owns that academy, the sperm bank, and the fertility clinic. You know that old saying 'you can run, but you can't hide.' I'll find out sooner rather than later. If it's later, you might be a ticket taker at Disney when we meet again."

Agent Robbins bolted upright as he stepped on his cigarette, then picked it up. "Is that a threat? Did I just hear a threat?"

"Hell, no, Agent Robbins, that was a promise."

Robbins's voice dripped ice. "What's your interest in all this, Kelly?"

Pete eyeballed the agent standing a foot away. "That kid you're looking for . . . the one the dean from the academy said was a troubled youngster. He's mine. And he sure as hell isn't troubled. Actually, I think he's pretty much a chip off the old block. What that means to you, Agent Robbins, is this: that kid did not kill anyone, and you and your Bureau are misleading the public. It also means he is incredibly intelligent. Just like me. We'll see if you always get your man. I'm betting in this case, you're the loser." As Pete turned his back on Agent Robbins, he wondered if what he'd said was the truth.

Agent Robbins's jaw dropped. He removed the dark glasses to gape at Pete as he tried to decide if he was lying or not.

"Where's Lily?" Pete asked Zolly.

"She went into the library. Maybe she had to go to the bathroom or something?" The boss had a kid and he was just finding out. Who cared where the chick went. A kid. The boss had a kid that was supposed to have killed . . . Zolly couldn't quite wrap his mind around what he'd just heard. Was he supposed to say something? How was he supposed to react? For the first time in his life, he was confused. A kid. A grown-up kid. A nanosecond later he wondered if Lily was the mother. Oh, sweet Jesus, the board was going to explode when they got downwind of all this.

Winston whined as he brushed against Pete's leg. Pete reached down to scratch his big head.

"We'll talk about this later, Zolly." He looked up to see Lily standing in the doorway, motioning frantically.

Pete raced off on a dead run. "What? Is he in there? What, Lily?"

"No, no, not the boy. The man, the kid, whatever he was, the one the other boy, Bill, was drawing that day in the library. I just saw him. I followed him, but he was too fast for me. That is, I think it was him, Pete, but I'm not sure. It was the soccer outfit that . . . that's what the boy drew."

"Is he still in here?" Pete asked, as he raced up and down aisles, Lily right behind him.

"I don't know, Pete. I didn't see him again. Even though I only caught a glimpse of the drawing that day, it certainly did look like him."

Thirty minutes later they accepted that the man Lily had seen was gone.

Chapter 10

He noticed that his hand trembled slightly when he reached up for the novel listed under the *F*'s in the Fiction aisle. He knew there would be a sticky note inside. His guts churned. He was supposed to be a thousand miles away already. His credo and the reason he'd survived in this business was: do the job, then remove yourself from the scene. Even when the outcome didn't go as planned. One opportunity was all you got. If you blew it, or Fate blew it, you damn well still moved on. It wasn't working out like that this time. That was the reason his hands were shaking. *Shift into neutral, shift into neutral,* he told himself over and over as he stared at the yellow sticky note in his hand. He noticed that his hand was still shaking when he replaced Ian Fleming's book on the shelf. The note went into the Velcro pocket of his soccer shorts.

The soccer player didn't like libraries. The truth was, he didn't like any public place where people milled around. He was phobic about being around lots of people, but he wouldn't admit it. He looked around to see if anyone was watching him. Where the hell was the woman in the funny-looking hat who had stared at him? Really stared. Stared right into his goddamn eyes.

If there was one thing he was good at, besides blowing people away, it was reading people's expressions. A requisite of his job. She looked like she recognized him. But from where? He had a phenomenal memory for faces, and he knew he'd never seen her before. His heart kicked up an extra beat. If he didn't get out of there right now, things would start to close in on him. He couldn't let that happen.

The first thing he always did when entering any building was to take a full minute to check out the EXIT signs and plan his way out. *Move! Move! Move!* his mind shrieked. Another minute, and he knew he would be in full panic mode. He saw her at that precise minute with a tall dude almost running down the Fiction A aisle. He was almost to the door when an equally tall boy, a damn replica of the man with the woman, literally bumped into him. Their gazes locked as the door swished open. He saw the open door, correctly read the instant recognition in the kid's frantic gaze at the same moment. He had to go through the open door. He had to.

The soccer player took huge gulps of air to steady himself. *Mind over matter. Get hold of yourself. This is a weakness you can control.* His pep talk wasn't working. His heart was hammering so hard, he thought he was going to pass out. First the woman, then the kid. What the hell was going on?

He had to get out of there before the woman and man came back outside. He knew in his gut they were searching for him. The kid—the kid was a bonus. He could have whacked him right there with one smack to his nose, driving it right up into his brain. But the soccer player's hands were shaking too badly to do it, not to mention the panic that was welling through him. He turned around, realizing that even though only seconds had gone by, the kid was gone.

Never linger. Fall back and regroup. He didn't stop to think or to ponder his options because at that moment it seemed there were none. He plowed through a group of giddy youngsters walking four abreast. He heard himself being cursed out in the way only the young could do when they believed there was strength in numbers.

The soccer player managed to get to his vehicle, a battered brown Toyota he'd heisted the day before from a Target parking lot. His heart continued to slam against his rib cage as he put the pedal to the metal. Even his leg was shaking. If he hadn't been so consumed with what had just occurred, he would have seen the boy, who was trembling as badly as he was, lurking behind a black minivan.

The minute the brown car was out of the lot, Josh Baer raced away, to the shouts of, "Hey kid, hold on!" The words just fueled his brain. He was thankful that he'd worked out with Tom back at the academy. He was the best hurdler at

the school because of his long legs. Tom had
been the best sprinter. Sheila had been their
cheerleader. They were calling him—the lady
with the hat and the tall man with her. Why?
How had they found him?

He was winded when he finally stopped to
grip his knees to steady his quivering body. He
struggled to take deep breaths. First the guy in
the green-and-white shorts, now the lady in the
hat. Who was the big guy with her? It was *his*
voice that had shouted, "Hey kid, hold on!" Josh
didn't have even one doubt that he was the kid
the man was yelling at. What did that mean? He
damn well knew what it meant. They wanted to
talk to him so they could turn him in to the authorities. That's exactly what it meant.

He had to get to a computer to see if there
was an e-mail from the FBI. He had to find out
about Jesse. The moment his breathing returned
to something close to normal, Josh settled the
cheap nylon backpack more comfortably on his
back. He'd been forced to buy it so he could
keep copies of his e-mails and Jesse's drawings,
which he'd photocopied before dropping him
off at the FBI office that first night.

Josh closed his eyes to conjure up the route
to the public library. He started off at a hard
run and didn't let up until his breathing became tortured. He thought about Jesse then, although actually Jesse was never really out of his
thoughts. Where did they take him? Were they
feeding him? Was he happy and safe? His eyes
burned with regret at what he'd done.

What to do? Where to go? He wished he'd

read more spy novels to see how the good guys outwitted the bad guys. He rather thought the trick was knowing exactly who the bad guys were. Was the lady in the hat a good guy or a bad guy? Did it even matter? Just then he couldn't trust anyone, not even the FBI.

The big guy—the one with the lady in the hat. He'd seen him somewhere. Probably on television or in the newspaper. Maybe he was an important person. Maybe the lady was an important person. Jesse's drawing of the man had been bothering him from the minute Jesse had offered it up for his approval. He was glad now he hadn't given up those drawings to the FBI. Who *was* he? Sheila had always said you needed to pay attention to your gut instincts. How right she was.

As Josh jogged along, he wondered if it would be possible to hitchhike to downtown San Francisco or Sacramento. He had to get away from the area as quickly as possible. He also needed some kind of disguise. The money in his pocket was dwindling faster than he liked. Before he could even think about leaving the area, he had to check for that e-mail. He crossed his fingers that Jesse was okay even if he was in his own world. He couldn't help but wonder what Jesse thought about being dumped at the FBI. Poor kid. One way or another, someone was going to pay for what happened to Jesse and all the others. Especially Tom and Sheila. Every time he thought about them, his eyes started to burn. He made a mental note to check the obituaries when he got to the library. Maybe he could find out about the burial service for all the students who were gunned down. Maybe the name of the funeral home would be in the paper, and he could call them for information.

Josh wanted to cry at the situation he was being forced to deal with. So many things to do and so little time to do them.

Who were those people back at the library?

Looking over his shoulder every few minutes, Josh finally made his way to the public library, where he collapsed on a chair at the very back. He had a good view of anyone coming his way. There was also an EXIT door just a few feet away. He had to think and plan. "I wish you were here, Tom. I don't know what to do. I don't know how long I can keep this up," he murmured to himself.

"I'm right here, buddy. Fire away."

Josh whirled around, his face a mask of fear. "Tom? Is it you? Where are you?"

"Yeah, it's me, good buddy. You didn't think I'd desert you, did you?"

"But . . . but you're dead. Where are you? How can you talk to me like this?"

"I'm right here next to you. Sheila is in the other chair. You said you needed me, so here I am. Get hold of yourself."

"Are you . . . are you a ghost? I don't believe in ghosts. You don't either. Explain that, Tom."

"I'm a spirit. I'm here. We're talking. I rest my case."

"I'm dreaming. Just because you were smarter than me doesn't mean I'm going to fall for this. Show yourself, then I'll believe it."

"No can do, buddy. Because Sheila and I met our

*demise so violently, we can't rest or get to the other side.
I need your help, too, Josh. All Sheila does is whine.
She wants to get to the other side. By the way, those
tests said I was only one point ahead of you. That
means you're just as smart as I am. I guess we both
came out of the same test tube."*

"Do . . . do you know about Jesse? I didn't
want to take him there, Tom, but I didn't know
what else to do. Do you know if he's safe?"

*"He's safe, Josh, and you did the right thing. Sheila
agrees. Now, let's tackle your problem."*

"I saw the guy that killed you, Tom. We were
eyeball-to-eyeball. He could have killed me right
then and there, but he kept going. He was at the
same library. I don't know how he found me.
He scared the bejesus out of me. I have to hide
somewhere, and I don't have much money. I
need to take a shower, too. A change of clothes
would be really good. Help me out here, Tom."

*"Go back to the academy, but go at night. You know
the grounds like the back of your hand. You know
every stick and stone, every blade of grass. There's a
hundred places to hide. You can hide out there and
take a shower and get clean clothes. There's probably a
few guards, but you can outwit them. You have to believe in yourself, Josh."*

"Will you be there, Tom?"

*"Sheila and I will be with you every step of the way.
Trust me, you won't be alone. The academy is the last
place they'll look for you. It's buttoned up good by now.
Remember how we used to sneak in and out? All those
good places. They'll never catch on. Hey, you might
even be able to snag a laptop. Remember how
Mr. Dickey used to hide his and thought we didn't*

know? I bet there's so much pornography on it you'll be blushing if you snag it. You do remember where he used to hide it, right?"

"Yeah, yeah, I remember."

"Then you'll remember that he used to keep a stash of money there with his weed, too, right? Josh, don't trust anyone but yourself. Hey, I bet there's still all kinds of food in the kitchen. You can stuff yourself. Bet there's even ice cream in the freezer. You can eat it all. You could use a little fat on your bones, buddy."

"I know all that, Tom. I'll think about you when I eat all that strawberry ice cream. The last I checked the FBI hadn't responded to my e-mail. I'm going to check for it again. Why is that, Tom?"

" 'Cause you can't trust them, that's why. You're smarter than that jerk in charge. I think he's part of the whole thing. Betcha I'm right, too."

"Not much in the papers. My picture. I don't have access to a TV, so I don't know what if anything they're saying. Do you know, Tom?"

"It's all being downplayed. It's those guys that run the academy. You have to find them, too, Josh. When you get to the academy, get the magic number book. When you find someone you can trust, show them the book. All our lives are in that book. Now, aren't you glad I had a photographic memory?"

"Yeah. I miss you, Tom. Tell Sheila I miss her, too."

"We know."

"I wish I knew who that guy was at the library."

"Which one, Josh?"

"What do you mean, which one? The guy that

looked like the soccer player. The one who eye-balled me. The one that killed you, for crying out loud."

"Well, since the soccer coach didn't show up that day, I think it's safe to say that guy got through security by saying he was his assistant or something. The coach is probably dead somewhere. That's just a guess on my part, okay?"

"Yeah, that's pretty much what I thought. This is scary. I'm just a kid. How can I outsmart the FBI? Hey, guess what? Jesse and I saw a real family having dinner. We watched them through the window. I stole food from them, and clothes. I did it mostly for Jesse. You don't think God will punish me, do you, Tom?"

"Nah. You're trying to do good. Remember how Miss Carmody made a joke one time and said God watches over babies, drunks, and fools?"

Josh smiled. "Yeah, I remember that. All that stuff is buzzing in my head. I need a game plan. I can't think clearly. There was another guy at the library with a lady in a pretty hat. Jesse drew his picture. He looks like me, Tom. Or else, I look like him. What's that mean? How come Sheila isn't talking to me?"

"I don't know, Josh. You didn't call Sheila, you called me."

"Okay, I'll remember that. It's different out here in the real world, Tom. I'm not ashamed to admit I'm scared. You know what, though, it's just the way we thought it would be. I wish you and Sheila were here with me. You know, to share the experience."

"Josh, you're as smart as me and Sheila. You can

figure this out. Think it all through. Make a plan. Stick to it. You have the biggest and the best tool of all going for you, the Internet. It's been our lives. Now, make it work for you. Those jerks in your real world don't know half of what you know. Just use that knowledge. I'll be right here with you every step of the way. Listen, Josh, don't stay here too long, okay? Check the e-mail and get out of here."

"Okay, I will."

"Sounds good to me, Secret Agent Josh Baer, also known as Number 8446. I'll see you when you get back to the academy. This is Secret Agent Tom Bower, also known as Number 8211, signing off for now."

In spite of himself, Josh gurgled with laughter. Tom always knew how to make him laugh, to take the edge off things.

"Ooops, sorry, young man," a woman pushing a toddler in a stroller said as she bumped into Josh's chair.

"Th . . . that's okay." Josh turned away, every nerve in his body twanging. Did he fall asleep and dream about Tom and Sheila? Or, was Tom here talking to him? Tom's spirit? He looked around in full panic to see if anyone was paying attention to him. No one was. The lady with the stroller was gone. He had the whole back end of the library to himself. His heart was pumping so fast, he was light-headed. Did he just have one of those out-of-body experiences? Did he just talk to his dead friend?

Focus, Josh. Focus. Think. Calm down. Deep breaths. Focus.

When he was certain he was okay, Josh made his way to the computer station, where he logged on to check the new Hotmail e-mail account he'd set up. There was no response to the e-mail he'd sent off. He then clicked on Map-Quest to get directions back to the academy. The moment he memorized the route, he left the library and headed to a movie house, where he bought a ticket. He would stay there until it got dark, then make his way back to the academy.

Thirty minutes later Josh slouched down in the last row of seats. His agile brain sifted and collated everything he and Tom had discussed at the library. He then gave his mind free rein to go even farther back in time as he tried to make sense out of what was happening to him.

Those people back at the library were out of breath from chasing Josh Baer, aka, Jack-something. Winston was panting, and Zolly was cursing under his breath.

"Boss," Zolly gasped, "this would be a real good time to tell me why we were chasing that kid who was faster than greased lightning."

I definitely have to start going to a gym, Lily thought as she sat down on the ground next to Winston. She rubbed the big dog's belly until he relaxed. "We were *that* close, and we lost him," she mumbled to no one in particular.

"Boss, did you hear what I said?"

"Yes, I heard you. I think he's my son. *Think,* Zolly. I can't prove it. Yet." Pete sat down on a patch of grass next to Lily. He reached for her hand and squeezed it.

"What would I do without you?" he whispered in Lily's ear. "I was oblivious to what was going on around me at the library. How in the hell is that possible?"

"Because you didn't see the drawing. You didn't see the boys either. Stop being so hard on yourself. Even though I saw what I saw, a lot of good it did us."

"It bears out one thing. I was right about the boy using the library. Which he probably won't do again. He'll start going to Internet cafés where he thinks he'll be safer. There are probably thousands around here. The old proverbial needle in a haystack."

"What about a private detective?" Lily asked.

Pete dropped his head into his hands.

Lily felt so sorry for him, she wanted to cry. "Listen to me, Pete. I'm really concerned about something else right now, and that's the guy who looked like a soccer player. What was he doing at the library at exactly the same time the boy was there? Logic tells me he must be searching for the boy, too. The big question is *why?* The only thing I can think of is he's the one who gunned down those kids and teachers. Somehow he missed the boys the first time, and he has to kill them. I sure hope that kid knows what he's up against. The other boy, I suppose he's Jesse, drew his picture, so that has to mean something. I'm going out on a limb here, a very fragile limb, but give this some thought. What if the guy Jesse/Bill drew in the picture was the shooter? What if Josh/Jack and Jesse/Bill saw him, and he knows they saw him? That puts Josh in danger. Thank God Jesse is in FBI custody. No offense, Pete, but I'm starting to think we might need a little more help than just Zolly and Winston."

"Do you think he's my son, Lily? Tell me the truth."

Lily chose her words very carefully. "I don't know, Pete. He certainly does look like you did when you were a few years older than he is. He's a kid, okay? No matter who his parents are, he doesn't deserve to be going through what he's going through right now. He must be scared out of his wits. Him against the authorities, him against the world. Even a man would crumble at having to go through that all alone. We shouldn't be thinking about who he belongs to right now and concentrate on finding him and bringing him to safety. For all I know, he could be my son, too. But you know what, Pete, I can't think about that right now. Neither can you. Now, let's put our heads together and try to figure out the best way to find and help him."

"Like I said, what would I do without you? You're absolutely right. I just want him to be mine," Pete whispered.

"I know, Pete. I know."

Chapter 11

Twilight. That shady time of day when the purple-gray haze warned that the darkness was coming within minutes. The perfect time of day for clandestine meetings. More so if you factored in the light rain that was falling.

The soccer player paced the confines of the cheap hotel room. He checked the small recorder on his wrist to make sure it was working. He'd checked it ten times in the past ten minutes. No, he wasn't nervous. Plain and simple, he was pissed that it had come to this. He hated sleazy motels almost as much as he hated the people he had to deal with.

It was eight o'clock. Outside, he could hear the steady drip of the rain. The sound didn't muffle the opening of the motel room door. There was no knock, there never was. His gaze was trained on the doorknob. He watched it turn.

The soccer player looked at the wizened man, who could have been thirty, forty, or fifty. Or sixty, it was hard to tell. An underling. Well, that figured.

"You failed." The voice didn't match the shrunken figure, it was deep, thick, and gutturalsounding. The soccer player wondered why he was surprised.

"Yeah, well, your intel was a tad faulty. It wasn't like I had a lot of time to do a head count. If you want your money back, just say so. I'm already breaking one of my rules by meeting you here."

"It won't be necessary to return the money. You honored your contract. We just want you to finish the job. We concede the fact that you had no way of knowing the two boys would be late that morning. We had no way of knowing that either. We're willing to pay an additional sum of money for you to finish the job."

"Well, that's not going to happen, dude. You're just going to have to take care of that yourself. The feebs," the soccer player said, referring to the FBI, "have the one kid. I don't mess with the FBI. You want to put your neck in the noose, be my guest. The other one is probably halfway to Vegas by now."

"I'm authorized to pay you whatever you want. Name a figure."

What the hell. The soccer player rolled his tongue over his square white teeth and grinned. "A million dollars. All cash. All up front."

"Done. Give me a time frame."

The soccer player laughed. "Now, you know I can't do that."

The wizened man adjusted his wire-rimmed glasses, which were sliding down his bony nose.

"The FBI has your picture. I'm told it's a perfect likeness. The boy drew your likeness from memory. Right down to all the carnage you left behind."

"What the hell are you saying?"

"You heard me the first time. One of the boys is a superior artist. He captured you on paper, and, like I said, the carnage you left behind. The FBI hasn't released the picture to the media yet, but they will at some point. That means your window of time is . . . let's just say, very small. Having said that, we have another job for you. Five million wired to an account of your choice."

The soccer player's mind raced. Six million bucks! He could retire to some island and live happily ever after—providing he was still alive to enjoy the six mil. He wondered if the man standing in front of him was lying. The feebs had a picture of him? Well, damn, that did put a different light on things. Alive to live off six million bucks. The thought was so unlikely, he laughed out loud.

Puzzled at the soccer player's reaction, the wizened man took two steps backward.

"I do not see anything funny in this situation. Is it a *yes* or *no*?"

String him along. They're going to throw me to the wolves. But first they want me to finish up their dirty work. "What's the other job?" He was asking out of curiosity, no other reason. Who the hell was worth six mil?

"*Yes* or *no*?" the wizened man asked. He jerked at his glasses again.

The soccer player forced a laugh. "Tell you what, I'll get back to you."

"That's not good enough. My instructions . . ."

"Take a good look at me, you little creep. Do I look like someone who cares about your instructions? I-do-not-care. You know what else, I'm not going through that library crap again either. Give me a number to call, and when I make my decision, you'll be the first to know. That's a take-it-or-leave-it answer."

The wizened man backpedaled. "But the picture . . . the window of opportunity . . ."

"Let me worry about that. How long will it take to get the million together? Since the window of opportunity is so small and the feebs have the picture," the soccer player drawled.

"The money is at my disposal. I can get it to you within an hour if you agree to our terms. If you agree to the second job, the money can be wired to your account within an hour."

The soccer player's stomach started to churn. Six million dollars was a lot of money to turn down. Still, finding the kid was going to be like finding a particular grain of sand at the beach. "Who's the second hit?"

"*Yes* or *no?*"

"It doesn't work *that* way. Either tell me, or I'm outta here. Think of me as a priest and you're confessing. I don't talk. Whatever you say is sacred." The soccer player smiled. His guts were still churning. He knew that the way things were going, he was about five minutes away from a panic attack. He moved toward the door.

The name shot out of the wizened man's mouth like a bullet. "Peter Aaron Kelly."

"Whoa! Whoa! The software giant? Now I know you people are frigging crazy. I-don't-think-so."

"Five million dollars for the hit!" the man said forcefully.

"Hey, dude, you look like you could use six mil. Get yourself some new duds, some contact lenses, some wing tips, and I bet you could have a whole posse of women chasing you around. Give me your cell phone number, and I'll get back to you."

The wizened man sighed as he rattled off the ten digits.

"Feel free to order room service," the soccer player said as he closed the door behind him.

The cool rain felt good on his face. Five minutes later, he was out of sight. Should he wait for the little shit to leave and tail him or not? Nah. The soccer player shrugged as he concentrated on his breathing to ward off the impending panic attack. Satisfied that he was under control, he climbed behind the wheel of a snappy BMW that he'd heisted from Gold's Gym.

He avoided the main arteries and stuck to back streets as he headed for his favorite hangout, an oyster bar where no one would bother him. Taking an hour or two out of his busy schedule certainly couldn't hurt the current situation. With a possible six-million-dollar payoff in the offing, he owed it to himself to consider any and all possibilities. Absolutely, he owed it to himself.

* * *

While the soccer player was contemplating the business offer he'd just been presented with, Lily and Pete were circling the block in the SUV and Zolly was walking the same route with Winston on a leash. Just a normal early evening, rain and all.

The night was quiet except for the muted drizzle. No one was out and about. The crickets and tree frogs didn't count. Traffic was extremely light.

"Looks okay to me. What do you think, Lily?"

"I don't see anyone. Zolly's been around the block three times. He said he wouldn't go in until he was certain no one was watching either place. He's got so many gadgets and gizmos in his backpack, he can deactivate anything. I don't know if it was a joke or not, but he said one of those things could pick up someone breathing a mile away. If there's a security monitor, it will just appear to fritz out. Zolly wasn't sure how much time we'd have before alarms go off. There's likely to be a hypersonic alarm around somewhere. Winston will pick up on it if there is one.

"Let's go over this one more time, Pete," Lily said as her partner parked the SUV. "Zolly will deactivate everything. He's going to take on the sperm bank, and you and I are doing the fertility clinic since the entrance to that mysterious room is at the back of the clinic. I'm not a gambling person, but I'm willing to bet five bucks we aren't going to find anything."

"Don't be negative. Let's cross our fingers

and hope for the best," Pete whispered as they trotted along, staying as close to the shrubbery as they could. They were almost to the door of the fertility clinic when the skies opened up. Rain sluiced down, soaking both Pete and Lily. They barely noticed as Zolly held the door open for them.

"You're lucky there are no windows in this dump, boss. You keep Winston with you. He'll pick up on any high-pitched frequencies. I have this," he said, holding out a square black box with blinking green lights. "Move fast and don't waste time. You're both wearing the latex gloves, right?"

Lily and Pete held up their hands for Zolly's inspection. He nodded sourly as he let himself out of the building. The lock snapped into place.

It took only ten minutes to realize there was nothing to be found in the clinic. Not even a paper clip in the trash basket. Pete shook his head in disgust as Lily tugged at his arm. Holding the flashlight directly in front of her, she ran down the long hallway to the vaultlike door. She wanted to cry when she saw the stout locking mechanism.

"Easy does it, Lily. Zolly unlocked it with that magic box of his. Just press the bar, and the door will open."

Winston squirmed and whined at Pete's feet. Lily pressed her weight down on the bar, and it slid inward on well-oiled hinges. Pete reached in to fumble at the wall. Bright fluorescent light flooded the room.

"Oh, my God!" Lily gasped.

Pete looked around the blinding white room. "It looks like a . . . like a . . ."

"Operating room?" Lily asked, pointing to the bright circular lights above the table in the center of the room. "It's a minisurgery. See those tables with the stirrups? Obstetrics," she called over her shoulder as she left the main room to check out the smaller rooms off the hallway. "Labor rooms. I think women gave birth to babies in here. See if you see anything that looks like it could be a nursery."

"It's right here," Pete said in a hushed voice. He pointed to his left.

Lily felt light-headed as she stared around at the tiny beds. A nurses' station of sorts was in the back of the room. Modern-looking incubators lined one wall. Another wall held a bank of refrigerators and sinks. Sealed canisters, holding God only knew what, lined a third wall. The only thing on the fourth wall was a gigantic row of clocks, all showing different times.

"What the hell?" Pete sputtered.

Lily licked at her dry lips. She could barely get the words out of her mouth, but she tried. "Our donations didn't go to couples wanting children, Pete. This place . . . this is . . . oh, God, I don't know what it is. Baby trafficking? All over the world? Why else would they have all those clocks on the wall? Count the baby bins, Pete. Twenty-two. And there are nine labor rooms. This was big business.

"Think about it, Pete. We made donations thinking, at least I did, that my eggs would help a childless couple have a child of their own. For a fee, of course. As a donor I was paid very well. If this is a black market operation, the price for a child could go through the roof. Some wealthy couples will pay anything to get a healthy child."

"That doesn't make sense, Lily. How does it explain the academy and the boy we think is my son? Does he have a birth defect of some kind? You said that Jesse looked different. That school had ninety-two kids in it. And all of them except for Josh and Jesse's class were on a field trip that day. Never to be seen or heard from since. The dean said Josh was a troubled youngster. I'm going to stick my neck out here and say this is some kind of testing lab. I don't know how I know it, but I know the babies born here did not go to parents hungering for a child."

Lily leaned against the wall under the clocks and stared at Pete. She wanted so badly to cry. It looked like Pete felt the same way.

Pete turned the corner and opened another door. He whistled at what he was seeing. "It's a laboratory. Obviously at one point it was fully equipped. Son of a bitch! My mind is going in all directions. What the hell were those people doing here? How was all this kept quiet?"

Winston yipped as he raced to the open door. He yipped again as Zolly filled the doorway. "Zip, boss. The place was cleaned out. I even checked the air vents. What do you have here?"

Pete told him.

"Jesus, boss, what the hell did you get yourself mixed up in?"

"I wish I knew, Zolly."

Suddenly the fur on the back of Winston's neck stood on end. He growled deep in his throat at the same moment the box in Zolly's hand emitted a high-pitched, keening sound.

"Out! Out! Move, boss! *NOW!*"

Zolly led the charge down the hallway, Winston racing ahead of him. "Move, boss! They're onto us. The hypersonic alarm went off. No one but Winston heard it. Head for the car! Goddamn it, will you two move! My grandmother can run faster than the two of you."

Zolly slammed through the open front door. Off in the distance, the wail of a siren could be heard. Flashing lights could be seen through the heavy rain. Even a dummy would know it was a parade of police cars the way the sky was lighting up.

As one, the foursome tumbled into the SUV. Zolly turned on the ignition but not the headlights. They were moving, and that's all Lily cared about. She hugged Winston, who was busy trying to snuggle with both her and Pete at the same time.

"You okay, boss? Ma'am?"

"Hell, no, Zolly. What went wrong?"

"Look, boss, I'm a security guard. This is my first time at breaking and entering. I think I did okay considering it was my maiden voyage into the underbelly of whatever the hell you got yourself involved in. I don't know what went wrong. If you want me to guess, I'd say there's a thirty-minute delay for whoever enters either the clinic or the sperm bank to call in to the alarm company. That's a guess, okay? Don't look a gift horse in the mouth. We got away, didn't we? Now, where do you want to go? The night's still young. We could take on a bank, maybe a convenience store? Your call, boss."

"You're a wiseass, Zolly. Take us home. We need to fall back and regroup."

"That's the smartest thing you've said in days," Zolly growled.

Pete ignored him. "You know what we need, Zolly? We need a police scanner so you can listen in and figure out what they're doing if anything. Can you get one for the FBI, too?"

"Sure, boss. You name it and I'll put it on my shopping list. You want a couple of Uzis, maybe a rocket launcher?"

"Like I said, you're a wiseass, Zolly."

Pete was so deep in thought on the ride back to the villa, Lily had to poke him in the arm to get him to move when Zolly brought the SUV to a stop.

Outside in the walled garden, Lily ordered a room service dinner for the two of them and two chopped steaks for Winston, along with a plate of vegetables. Winston was partial to carrots and green beans, or so Pete said.

"What are your thoughts, Pete? I know something is twirling around inside that head of yours."

Pete looked around the peaceful garden with its ground lighting. It was all so perfect, so serene, so surreal, unlike his emotions, which were all over the place. "I am worried about that kid. I'm trying to put myself in his place. What would I do? What would be my next move? He's taking on the world, and he can't possibly be equipped for that kind of fight. Knowing someone is out to kill you either has to put an edge on you or take off your edge, assuming he even has an edge. At this point I'm not even sure what I'm talking about. Maybe I can put Marty Bronson on the dean of that school, and if Marty can get us an address, we can go and talk to him."

"Don't you think that either his employers, whoever they might be, have him in a safe place or he's gone to ground? It sounds good, but I think it's going to turn into another dead end."

Pete nodded, knowing she was right. "If you were the boy's age, where would you go, Lily?"

"As far away from the scene as I could get. Kids his age hitchhike all the time. Seventeen-year-old kids are fearless, you know that."

"He's had a couple of days to get out of town, but he's still here. There has to be a damn good reason why he didn't split this scene. He's trying to do something. He goes to the library, and I'm thinking he was trying to do something on the computer. Obviously, that avenue failed. We saw him, that other guy saw him, too, so now he's running. Again. What's left for him? I think he's scared, but he isn't panicking. That's a good thing. It means he's thinking logically. I think he's looking for someone to trust."

"Okay, standing in his shoes, what would you do, Pete?"

Pete's clenched fist slammed down on the glass-topped table. "Me? I'd go back to the place where it all started. Think about it, Lily. The school is closed down. At best a skeleton force for security is in place now that it's no longer under control of the authorities. I bet that kid knows the school, the grounds, everything, like the back of his hand. Kids always sneak away after lights-out. Tell a kid he can't do something, and he'll find a way to make sure he does it. Pranks, whatever. He would know how to get in, out, to hide. There's food there. His bed is there, his clothes. That school represents the only security he's ever known. It's his home. If he's as smart as I think he is, no one will even know he's there.

"The big question is, what is he trying to accomplish? Does he have information? Does he know or suspect that something was going on? If we take the fertility clinic and all we saw there and extend it to the school . . . maybe . . . oh, hell, I don't know. My brain is like a beehive," Pete groused.

Lily leaned across the table to reach for Pete's hand. "No, no, don't stop now. I think you're onto something. Go back to the clinic, the operating room, the lab, all those labor rooms. Where did those kids go after they were born? Maybe there's more than one school like the California Academy for Higher Learning. Remember all those clocks on the wall? Maybe the other schools are in different countries.

"Oh, God, Pete! Maybe . . . maybe the babies born there were guinea pigs for some kind of . . . experiment? Think about Jesse. Maybe he was a result of an experiment gone wrong. Maybe some of the kids weathered it, and some didn't."

Pete stood up. He smacked his clenched right fist into the palm of his left hand as he started to pace. "And the massacre . . . why?"

Lily was on her feet, too. "Run with it, Pete. The experiment is over . . . Someone found out . . . They tracked the experiment for what . . . seventeen-plus years, and they no longer need the kids? So they get rid of them."

"What about all the other kids, the ones who went on the field trip that day? It's not computing."

"Yes, it is, Pete. Remember the clocks. They moved the kids. The other kids weren't the same age as Josh and Jesse. That means their monitoring time isn't up yet.

"Think in time increments. Maybe testing didn't start until the babies were older, say two or three years of age. Maybe it was a fifteen-year study. The oldest boys at the academy were seventeen. If you do the math, it would be a fifteen-year study. Am I crazy, or does this make sense to you?"

Lily was suddenly flying through the air as Pete picked her up and twirled her around. "I think that's it. I think you hit it right on the button. God, I love you!"

"You do!" Lily was back on the ground again, her head whirling.

"You know what, I do. I do, Lily. I fell in love with you all over again when I saw you at the airport in Atlanta. I wanted to tell you a dozen times but this . . . life . . . all of this," he said, waving his arms about, "just got in the way. Oh, my God, I'm in love. Tell me you love me. You aren't going to break my heart, are you, Lily?"

Lily could hardly believe her ears. Pete loved her. "Depends on what you have going for you. It's a joke, Pete. Yes, yes, yes, I love you, and, no, I am not going to break your heart. You better not break mine either. How did this happen, Pete? It was all so many years ago, yet here we are. It's all pretty damn amazing."

"Tell me about it. No, don't waste time telling me about it." He was kissing her then as he again twirled her around and around and around.

Winston barked as he raced to the doorway.

"Excuse me, where would you like me to set out your dinner?" asked the waiter.

"Anywhere," Pete mumbled as he broke for air, then continued kissing Lily.

"I'm not hungry, are you?" Pete asked.

"Only for you."

Winston tilted his head to one side, then the other. He finally figured out he was going to have to serve himself when Pete and Lily danced their way into the villa, leaving him behind. He hopped up onto one of the chairs, nosed the lids off the plates, checked it all out, then ate his dinner. He jumped off the chair, made the rounds of the small garden. He eyed the table again, then got back on the chair to eat his master's dessert, coconut cream pie. He very carefully nudged all the silver domes back onto the plates before making his way to the doorway. He lay down, his huge body filling the entire doorway. He didn't sleep. He was, after all, a guard dog.

Chapter 12

He felt drunk, so he must be drunk. Shuffling along outside the oyster bar where he'd shucked and consumed three dozen oysters along with three pints of ale, the soccer player weaved his way among the parked cars in the lot to the newly stolen BMW he'd arrived in. He looked at himself in the rearview mirror. He didn't look drunk, so his earlier opinion had to be wrong, and he wasn't drunk. Even if he was drunk, which he wasn't, he deserved to tie one on, what with all he'd been through this past week. He felt pleased with his mental assessment.

This was the hard part, making a decision he could live with. Days ago he had convinced himself if he killed a bunch of kids, he could live and deal with anything. Now, he wasn't so sure. Taking on the software giant even for five million dollars was a tad out of his league. In time, with a plan in place, he might be able to pull it off. This catch-as-catch-can project wasn't something he really wanted to think about. Still, the lure of five million dollars was tremendously powerful.

The kids, now that was something else. He'd had a plan. A good plan. He'd made numerous trips, a dozen to be exact, to the academy. Once he went as an electrician with the proper credentials and disguise. The second time he'd gone as a cook with an armful of recipe books, since the school prided itself on good, nourishing food that didn't taste like institutional glop. Like he really knew the difference between ground chuck and ground sirloin. The third time he went to the school, he was a gardener looking for a job. That was an all-day visit so he could tramp the grounds to see what was what. On either his fourth or fifth visit he turned into an exterminator so he could inspect every inch of the fifty-five-thousand-square-foot building as well as all of the outer buildings. A schematic of the building that had been left behind in the basement proved to be invaluable. For the life of him he couldn't remember what he did on the other visits except for the last one, where he was a traveling missionary complete with black suit, a clerical collar he'd put on for effect, and a full-grown beard. In that guise he met the class he was to exterminate.

No way would he get away with a plan like that if he agreed to take on the software giant. He vaguely remembered seeing sound bites on TV about how Kelly traveled with heavy-duty security and a killer dog. Exactly what you'd expect for someone of his wealth and stature.

The soccer player, whose name was Diesel Morgan, turned the key in the ignition. The powerful engine kicked to life. He was on the highway in less than a minute, heading toward the motel he'd been staying at for the past few days.

The special cell phone in his pocket chirped. Morgan had a hard-and-fast rule that he never answered his phone after midnight. No matter who it was. After midnight was when he did his best thinking. After midnight was when his mind, for some strange reason, clicked into high gear. If his routine and habits didn't work for other people, that was their problem.

The best things that could be said for his motel room were that it was clean and there were lots of thick towels in the bathroom, which was just as clean as the bedroom. The staff wasn't interested in minding his business, which was fine with him.

Morgan stripped down and headed for the shower. He stood under the hot water until it turned cool. He toweled off, pulled on a pair of boxers, and climbed in bed. He shoved the three foam pillows behind his back, turned on the TV, and let his mental gears run freely. While his mind raced, his index finger was flipping the channels to the twenty-four-hour news stations. After five minutes of watching the chaos in the world, he decided everything was going to hell. One small sound bite at the end of the local news was that the investigation on the school shooting was ongoing and leads were being followed. To Morgan that meant the authorities had squat, and he was treading on safe ground.

Where in the hell was that damn kid? He had to take care of him before he could even think about Kelly and the five million dollars. Loose ends could be fatal to someone in his position. Not to mention his employer.

Morgan fired up a cigarette even though he was in a nonsmoking room. Cigarettes helped him think, and it was the only time he smoked. As he puffed and blew smoke rings, he gave his mind free rein. What exactly did the kid *know*? How did the feebs capture the boy who had drawn his picture? How did the other one get away? Were the feebs looking for the boy to pin the shooting on him, or were they looking for him to keep him safe? Any other times the media had coverage of something like this non-stop, wall-to-wall, hashing and rehashing twenty-four/seven. Was the kid hitchhiking somewhere? If so, where was he headed? Washington, D.C.? Los Angeles? New York? Or was he staying local because it was familiar to him?

The kid had used the library, or tried to. What was he looking for at a library? Maybe that was where he hid out during the day. He'd simply blend in with all the other kids, and no one would give him a second thought or look. Where did he spend his nights?

Morgan lit a second cigarette. What would he do if he was that kid? Where would he go? *If I was him, what would I be looking for? Proof? Proof of what?* "Crap!" he snarled to the empty room. He was going about this all wrong. *Maybe this isn't about me at all, maybe the kid is looking for proof about what went on at the school because something sure as hell was going on to warrant a total wipeout of the class.*

"Shit!" *That's where I'm going wrong! I never asked the why of the shooting. What would make someone order a killing like that? Maybe that's what the kid is looking for, the why of it. Smart kid.*

A third cigarette found its way to Morgan's lips. He fired it up. He knew he was onto something. *Keep puffing, keep thinking,* he told himself. He patted the minirecorder on his wrist, which he was never without. Insurance.

A little while later the room was so cloudy with smoke, Morgan got up and opened the door to the balcony. The smoke poured outward. He lounged in the doorway, a fourth cigarette between his lips. Why? Why?

If I were that kid, where the hell would I go? Get in his head, Diesel. Think like the kid, Diesel. Where are the answers he's looking for?

Morgan put out his cigarette and tossed it over the balcony. He was grinning from ear to ear. "Hell's bells, I'd go back to where I think I might find the answers. Oh, yeah," he drawled as he backed into his room and shut the door. He quickly packed his travel gear, dressed, and left the motel. He was paid up for another day, but he could afford to lose eighty-nine bucks.

Morgan drove for an hour until he turned into a middle-income housing development. He knew his neighbors slightly, saying hello from time to time. He paid someone to maintain his yard and the garden in the back. His MO there in the development was that he was a traveling salesman and was gone three weeks out of every month, oftentimes going to Europe for months at a time. It was a mind-your-own-business kind of neighborhood of fifty- to sixty-year-olds who still worked during the day. The only times he'd ever seen kids around there were when someone had their grandchildren for a few hours on a weekend. He didn't even have to worry about mail because when he did get mail it was slipped through the slot on the front door. He paid a year ahead on his utilities. The outside light and a lamp in the living room were on timers. At a local bank he maintained a three-thousand-dollar checking account and had seven thousand in a passbook savings account. A respectable absent member of the community. The name he used at that address was Daniel Marley. He had the same kind of house and arrangement in six other parts of the country. It all worked for him.

Morgan let himself into his house. He hated the musty, closed-up smell, but there was nothing he could do about it. He turned on all the lights as he walked from room to room to see if anything had changed from his last visit. He always set little traps, a thread here, a speck of paper, a dropped paper clip. Satisfied that everything was exactly the way it was three months ago, he made his way to the basement.

Morgan moved a battered dresser to the side and leaned down to open the floor safe, from which he removed his semiautomatic weapon, two clips, and a battered canvas bag full of various disguises. He fished around in the dark for an oilskin pouch that held dozens of different driver's licenses and passports. He pondered each of them before he came up with the one that he wanted: FBI Special Agent Lionel Lewis, D.C. Bureau. Underneath the name it read, "Group Leader of Special Task Force." Complete with *Major Attitude.* Morgan flipped open the authentic gold shield and polished it. It certainly did pay to have friends in high places.

The last item to be carried out his front door was a garment bag with everything he needed to make him look like a real agent. Almost like Halloween, his favorite time of year.

All he needed to do was lock up the house, ditch the BMW, and heist a new set of wheels more appropriate to his self-created status. A Range Rover, maybe, or one of those Porsche Cayennes, although there was every possibility he might have to settle for a Jeep if the pickings were bad.

Morgan was on the road ninety minutes later, driving a Toyota Land Cruiser. His destination: the California Academy of Higher Learning. The time was 3:20 AM.

Lily woke with a start as she tried to figure out what had woken her. Bleary-eyed with sleep, she squinted at the digital clock on the nightstand. The red numerals read 4:30 AM. A soft whine at the side of her bed made her sit upright. Winston nudged her arm.

"What?" she whispered. "Do you have to go

out?" Where was Pete? Winston whined again. It was obvious the dog wanted her to get up.

In the dim light of the bedroom, she could see that Pete was gone. She peeked into the bathroom, but he wasn't there. Winston nudged her again. This time she knew the shepherd wanted her to follow him, which she did. She stopped short when she saw Pete hunched over the patio table, his head in his hands.

Every emotion in the book flowed through Lily's body as she remembered the lovemaking that had gone on for hours. Each and every endearment was carved into her heart. She knew she'd been waiting forever for this special time in her life.

Was Pete having second thoughts? Was he regretting what had happened last night? Or was it something else? Did she dare to intrude? Winston nudged her leg to move her forward.

Lily reached out to touch Pete's shoulder. "What's wrong, Pete?" She found her way to Pete's lap and laid her head on his chest. He felt warm and strong. And tormented. He stroked her hair.

"I have to find him, Lily. If I never do another thing in my life, I have to do this."

"Then let's do it. As soon as it gets light out, let's start calling everyone under the sun who might be able to help us. Between the two of us, we can become a pimple on someone's ass. The newspapers are an option. I know we've shied away from that, but I say we go for it as soon as possible. I also say we call Agent Robbins and ream his ass out, too."

"Wow! When did you get so feisty?" Pete asked in awe.

"When you made love to me and rocked my world right out from under me. You're my man, Peter Aaron Kelly, and I am going to be the woman behind the man. Well, in this instance anyway."

Pete burst out laughing. Winston barked his approval.

"Lily . . . about . . . I never thought . . . I love you."

"You gonna make an honest woman of me?" Lily teased.

"The minute you say the word, I'm all yours. I'm walking into the sunset, Lily, and I want you with me. I'm turning things over to my people. Can you walk away?"

"In a heartbeat. Now that we have that all straightened out, let's make a plan here that we can activate as soon as it gets light out. We're going to find that boy, Pete. I promise. Now, I have an idea. Want to hear it?"

"You bet." Pete continued to stroke Lily's hair, marveling at how silky it felt and how good it smelled. He nestled his chin against her as she outlined her plan.

"For starters, I think we need to hit the ground running and go to the press. You're what they call a 'media darling,' so every reporter who dreams of a Pulitzer will be dying for this scoop. I like that reporter Tessie Dancer. I say you get in touch with her. At the same time, you call that guy in Washington, the one you can't stand, Hudson Preston, who, by the way, has presidential aspirations. I saw it in the paper yesterday. Actually, I just read the headline. Above the fold, Pete. He'll turn himself inside out to be aligned with you. All that free press is any candidate's dream."

"You're kidding. He's going to take a shot at the presidency? How did that get by me? I can't stand that pompous SOB."

"So, are you up for it or not? It means going public, Pete. The whole world is going to know what . . . what we did. And, before you can ask, I'm okay with going public for myself. First, though, I have to call my office and give them a heads-up so when the stuff hits the fan, they can deal with it. I suggest you do the same thing."

"You have been thinking, haven't you?"

Lily decided in that split second that she'd never been happier in her life, even with all the misery that would descend on both their heads very soon. She squirmed closer as she burrowed her head into Pete's neck. His grip on her was so tight it was almost painful, but she didn't make a sound because this was what she'd been waiting for all her life.

"Yeah, Pete, I have," Lily murmured.

Chapter 13

Josh shivered in his wet clothes as he circled the perimeter of the school property. The good thing was he knew exactly where he was. To his left was the stable and to the right was the gymnasium. The school sat smack between the two buildings, with wide expanses of lawn separating them. To the far left of the gym were the pool and the pool house. Behind the pool house was a gardener's shed. He could make his way to any of the outer buildings and be temporarily safe. But, if he fell asleep, he would wake up to daylight and wouldn't be able to make his way to the main building, where his room was.

If he decided to stay in one of the outer buildings, the stable would be his best bet. He'd always liked the stable, and so did Tom. Sheila said she could take it or leave it alone. The seven horses were gone. Mr. Dickey had explained that the school was downsizing because of the enormous amount of money it took to feed and care for the horses and the salaries for the groomsmen. Tom said there was something fishy about that explanation. Sheila had agreed.

The gym was another case of downsizing. They had cut back from two gym teachers to one, who wasn't worth a dime. All he did was talk on his cell phone while he made the students do laps around the gym. Tom said that was fishy, too.

"So what are you waiting for, Josh?"

"Tom! I was just thinking about you." Josh felt light-headed with relief. He wasn't alone.

"I know, that's why I'm here. You need to make your move NOW. Didn't you see those rent-a-cops patrolling the grounds?"

"I saw them. I've been watching them to see how often they patrol the back end of the building. I counted four. How many did you count?"

"Four. Sheila said there's one who's way back by the electric gates in the service area. He's asleep."

"Yeah, he's the first one I checked out. He's pretty fat, so I don't think he can run very fast. He's got a gun, though. They all have guns. What is it they're protecting, Tom? Are they afraid of vandalism or what Miss Carmody called 'lookie looks'?"

"Probably both. C'mon, let's go. You have to get inside. Sheila and I are right behind you. Hit the service door on the side. Once you're inside, let your eyes get accustomed to the dark, then head for the dormitory and the showers. You need to get out of those wet clothes, and you stink, Josh. Okay, buddy, double down and run like the dean is on your ass for stealing the ice cream."

Josh choked on his laughter as he raced across the lawn. He thanked God for the rain and darkness.

"That was pretty good. You're almost as good as I was. Sheila said congratulations."

"Tom, do you think they'll know if the water is running that someone is inside?"

"No, I don't think so. Maybe if they were looking at a water meter they would, but the school uses well water. Remember when Mr. Dickey showed us the old cistern and how they'd drilled a new well?"

"Yeah, yeah, I remember. You gonna wait for me, Tom?"

"I'm right here, buddy. Anytime you need me, I'll be by your side."

"I need to talk to you seriously. I'm getting scared, Tom. Right now, though, I just want to shower and get into some warm clothes and find some food. Please don't go away."

"I'll be right here waiting for you, buddy."

Josh made his way to the huge open shower area where he stripped down to stand under the steaming spray. He shampooed his hair three times and washed himself four times before he felt clean enough to towel off. A sweat suit from his hurdling days felt warm as toast. Dry socks and clean running shoes were the last to go on as he kept up a running dialogue with Tom.

"I kind of feel like the old me right now, but I need food. Talk to me, Tom. Tell me what to do. Help me out here. And let's get some input from Sheila."

"Sheila said no lights. You have to do everything in the dark, Josh. There's all kinds of stuff in the storage

*room. Canned stuff, too, crackers, peanut butter. I
don't think you should use the stove or microwave.
Some smart-ass might check the utility bill when it
comes in and see that kilowatt hours were used after
the shooting. I think they can tell stuff like that, so
don't give them the edge. You have to pretend you're in
lockdown mode and still function. You can do it, Josh.
You need a plan, and you need to focus.*"

"I know, I know," Josh said as he wolfed down
a can of mixed vegetables. When he'd finished,
he rinsed out the can, flattened it with his foot,
and hid it in one of the cabinets. He cut off a
thick wedge of cheese that was wrapped in
Saran Wrap and proceeded to gnaw at it as he
rummaged for crackers in the storage room. He
washed it all down with a quart bottle of apple
juice. He hid the plastic bottle. He made sure
there were no crumbs and that he'd left no
other telltale evidence that he'd been in the
kitchen and storage room.

"I'm going to see if I can find Mr. Dickey's
sleeping bag. I think I'll sleep in that makeshift
wine cellar the teachers created that no one
knew about. The one John Blane found last
year. He also said he thought the dean knew all
about it because he kept his wine there, too. I
think I'll be safe there, don't you, Tom?"

"*Yeah. That's perfect, Josh. Don't be afraid to fall
asleep. I'll stand guard while Sheila checks around to
make sure Mr. Dickey's computer is still where he kept
it hidden. When you wake up, you're going to have a
lot to do. Maybe you'll dream and think of something.*"

Josh's eyes were half-closed as he made his

way to his old teacher's quarters. He found the L.L.Bean sleeping bag without any trouble. Holding it in front of him like a buffer, he made his way back to the kitchen and the door that would take him to the basement.

The moment he was snuggled and zipped into the sleeping bag, Tom spoke again.

"The sun will be up in about thirty minutes, Josh. Try to sleep all day, and tonight Sheila and I will help you figure out what's going on. Remember, I'm right outside this crappy wine cellar. With all the money those people poured into this place, you'd think there would be a decent wine cellar, one that's climate-controlled."

Josh was half-asleep when he replied, "This is a school, Tom, alcohol is forbidden. Everything in this damn place was forbidden. After I leave I hope it burns to the grounnnnd."

Nine forty-five seemed like the perfect time to appear at the academy, Morgan thought as he drove his stolen Toyota Land Cruiser up to the yellow tape the FBI had stretched across the long driveway leading to the California Academy of Higher Learning.

Morgan looked different today, in his Brooks Brothers suit and shoes. A subdued tie and white shirt with monogrammed cuffs completed his outfit. Not showy, not understated. His face was a little puffier, thanks to silicone patties he plastered to the inside of his cheeks. The mustache was neat and trimmed with just a hint of gray. His sideburns were the same speckled shade. An expert application of latex created a little more than a hint of jowls. Wire-rimmed glasses and dark brown contact lenses changed the whole structure of his face. He felt one hundred percent comfortable in his disguise.

An agent who said his name was Drew Warner asked for his ID. Morgan handed it over, watching the agent carefully for any sign that his creds were suspect. "Special task force, huh? Work fast, okay? I'm sick of standing here. Anything in particular you're looking for?"

"Anything and everything. Anything you want to share? How's that guy Robbins who's in charge? What can you tell me about him?"

"He's the show horse and the rest of us are the plow horses. He's full of himself. That help you at all?"

Morgan raised his eyebrows. "That tells me he isn't popular with the rank and file. Have you come up with anything, anything at all? I just got in on the red-eye, so I'm not a hundred percent up on all that's been going on. Appreciate any help you can give me."

"Nah. The guy made a clean getaway. I just want to know what kind of sick, sorry son of a bitch like that can blow kids away."

"Just like you said, he's a sick, sorry son of a bitch. No clues on the kid that got away?"

"No. The one who turned himself in is in protective custody. Robbins said Josh Baer took him to the station and waited till he got inside. The other kid's name is Jesse, and he's mentally challenged. Says Josh is his brother. Other than that he doesn't appear to have a clue. Lives in his own little world. They've had the best of the best looking and testing him, but so far, nothing. I'm thinking Josh is pretty smart. He's got to be smart to outwit the FBI. Doncha think?"

"We always get our man, or in this case, kid. You know that, don't you, Agent Warner?"

"Nine times out of ten. Right now we can't come up with one good reason for the shooting. At first they thought it was this Josh kid, but it's someone else. We assume the kid saw the shooter, saw it all go down. Jesse was probably with him. Going on the run, Jesse would have slowed him down so Josh does the next best thing, takes Jesse to headquarters, where he knows he'll be safe. I'm telling you, the kid is smart. How long you going to be here, Agent Lewis?"

"Till I get the job done. Thanks for the input. So, tell me, where can I find Agent Robbins?"

"Probably in one of the bathrooms admiring himself. He was royally pissed when they put a clamp on this gig. He was all set for photo ops. Even got a haircut, and it looked to me like he took a few shots at a tanning bed to make himself look good."

Morgan laughed because he knew he was supposed to laugh. "The next guy you see going down this driveway will be Agent Robbins. Call ahead to let him know I'm on his radar screen. We'll talk again, Agent Warner. By the way, how do I reach you down here if I need to ask you something?"

"There's a squawk box on the wall by the

front door. Just press it and talk." Agent Warner offered up a snappy salute, grinning from ear to ear.

A four-man welcoming committee walked toward the Land Cruiser. Morgan took his time reaching over to the passenger seat to retrieve his well-worn but expensive briefcase.

Introductions were made at the speed of light. Morgan thought Robbins held his credentials a little too long. "Is there a problem, Agent Robbins?"

"Why didn't someone notify me you were coming? This is the first I'm hearing about a task force."

"Maybe you weren't supposed to know, Agent Robbins. I suppose, if you want to put your ass in a sling, you could call your superiors or my superiors, or, hell, maybe the director of the Bureau to find out why you weren't told. You want to turn this into a pissing contest, you're going to be the one doing the pissing. I'm outta here." Morgan turned toward the Land Cruiser and pressed the LOCK button.

"Hold on, hold on. All I said was that procedure is that I'm to be notified about all changes."

"I just did. Notified you, that is. You're relieved as of now. All of you except Agent Warner. The rent-a-cops can stay. You all are immediately to go directly to the airport and book flights to New York City. An agent will meet you at the gate on your arrival, and he will take you to the White Plains office. If you have any questions, now is the time to ask them."

"Where's the rest of your task force?"

"En route. I was in San Francisco, so I got here first. The others will be here in the next few hours. Is there anything I should know?" Morgan asked.

"My file is on the desk in the main office. I'd like to make a copy."

"I'll take care of all that, Agent Robbins. I'll forward it on to you. Nice meeting you."

A round of handshakes followed as the stunned agents headed toward their cars.

In the foyer that led down a long hallway, Morgan spotted the squawk box. He pressed the button and listened as Drew Warner identified himself.

"Lionel Lewis, Warner. Agent Robbins and his four agents are leaving the premises. They are not to return under any circumstances. Are we clear on that?"

"Affirmative, Agent Lewis."

"Good."

Morgan immediately headed for the office, where he scanned Robbins's file. It took him all of three minutes to realize there wasn't one thing in the entire file that could in any way incriminate him. He'd done a clean job. The feebs had squat. He tossed the file back on the desk as he tried to figure out how long it would take him to search the fifty-five-thousand-square-foot building as well as all the outer buildings. The kid was here, he could feel it in his gut.

His gut also told him Robbins was no dumb rookie. Sooner or later he'd get a bug up his ass and call someone to find out why he was being transferred to New York. Morgan would have only a few hours' leeway while everyone scrambled to figure out what was going on. At best he had six, maybe seven hours to do what he'd come to do: find the kid and kill him. By then it would be dark, and he'd be able to get away unscathed. Hopefully.

"Josh! Josh! Wake up but be real quiet. Someone is in the basement. Listen!"

Josh opened his eyes to total darkness, but he could hear someone moving around.

He bit down on his lower lip as he dug his nails into the palms of his hands. He wanted to talk to Tom, to reach out to him, but he knew he couldn't do that. Not yet.

He'd been scared the day of the shooting but it had all happened so fast, he'd known the only thing to do was to run. This was different. He knew he couldn't run if his life depended on it.

"Listen to the sound of his walking. Is it familiar? Is it one of the guards from upstairs or is it the guy with the gun? Are you listening to me, Josh? Pay attention. It might be the guy with the gun, and he killed all the agents up there. He'll kill you, too. He wants my book. But more than that, he wants you, Josh. Are you listening?"

Of course he was listening. Did Tom think he was nuts? Whoever was out there was moving stuff around. Would he get to the pile of junk in front of Josh? How much time would he spend in the cellar? Wasn't he taking a chance with agents upstairs? Or was Tom right, and he'd killed them all?

In his cocoon of darkness, Josh strained to hear every little sound. The man was cursing. He sounded angry. It sounded like he was kicking stuff out of the way. Josh could hear things toppling over, perhaps blocking the man's path. The noise was as loud as thunder to Josh's ears. Someone from upstairs should have heard what was going on. They should have come down to investigate. For sure they were dead. He wondered if, when he went upstairs, whether he would see the same bloodbath he'd seen the day of the shooting.

A door slammed shut. Josh remained quiet. "Tom, are you there?"

"Right here, buddy. He's gone. Who was it? Could you tell by the way he walked? From the sounds he made? He was swearing up a storm. Did his words ring any bells?"

"I can't be sure. What should I do, Tom? I thought I'd be safe here."

"I thought you would, too. I really think this is the safest place to be right now. I don't think he's going to come back down here. The thing is, Josh, I don't know how long he's been here."

"Do you know what time it is, Tom?"

"Probably midafternoon. If he stays through the night, he'll need lights or at least a flashlight. You can get around in the dark, so that gives you an edge."

"Some edge. If it's the guy with the gun, he'll shoot me dead. You won't be able to help me, Tom."

"*That's why you have to be careful. Now, here's the game plan. You stalk him instead of the other way around. First chance you get, bop him over the head and run like hell. You can do that, Josh. Remember, this is your turf, not his.*"

"You were the sprinter. I was the hurdler. Remember?"

"*So, after you bop him, you jump over him and bop him again. What's so hard about that?*"

Josh sighed. "Bullets from automatic weapons fly all over the place. It would be just my luck that one would find me in midhurdle. Come up with a better idea. Otherwise, I am staying right here until someone finds me, or I die from lack of food and water."

"*I don't like the way that sounds.*"

Josh pressed his face into the soft down of Mr. Dickey's sleeping bag. "I don't much like it either."

Chapter 14

Pete Kelly paced the confines of the walled garden like a caged animal, the huge shepherd dogging his every step. Lily watched man and dog while sitting at the table under the colorful umbrella. From time to time she sipped at a frosty cola.

"You sure about this reporter, Lily?"

"No, Pete, I'm not sure. All I can tell you is she's always in the alumni news. Since you said you never read the newsletters, and I just started reading them a year ago, it's all I can tell you. She graduated a year ahead of us. She works for the *San Francisco Chronicle*, and she's won all kinds of awards for her reporting, including two Pulitzers. The newsletters played her up big. She got more press than either of us, and look who you turned out to be. That's it! Now you know as much as I know. She sounded eager when I spoke with her, and she said she'd be here at four o'clock. It's only ten minutes to four. Fortunately for both of us, she also recognized our names since we're also alumni and made the newsletter from time to time. She did like the sound of the word 'Pulitzer.' Maybe three is her magic number. How it will play out is anyone's guess.

"Another thing, Pete, reporters have sources they'll go to jail to protect. She didn't get where she is without knowing a few people she can trust. Reporters can go where others fear to tread. We're both batting zero right now, so we have nothing to lose by telling her our story. If you want to change your mind, tell me now, and I'll call her back."

"No, no. Maybe we should have called someone like that guy in Washington who writes all those books."

Lily looked properly appalled. "Are you turning this into a guy/girl thing? A guy can do the story better, is that what you're saying?"

Pete stared at the love of his life, who was huffing and puffing with indignation at his words. He backpedaled immediately. "I just meant he's an investigative reporter with years of experience under his belt. And he knows how it all works. Look how long he kept the Deep Throat secret. See, what I'm saying is we need someone like him. We really don't know much about what's-her-name."

"What's-her-name, by the way, is Tessie Dancer, and she has excellent credentials. And I'm positive that she can keep a secret, too. You aren't a closet chauvinist, are you?"

She sure as hell was making him sound like

one. "Good God, no! I've always been a champion of women's rights."

"*Harrumph,*" was Lily's response.

A heartbeat later, the *harrumph* changed to a strangled sounding, "Oh, my God!" when the sliding door leading to the garden blew open and a two-hundred-pound hurricane blasted through the open doorway followed by Zolly with a gun in his hand.

The hurricane whirled around, and said, "For heaven's sake, put that silly thing away before I squash you like a bug. And as for you," the hurricane said, pointing a long, red-tipped finger at Winston, "one more peep out of you, and you're going to the pound. You can lick my hand now."

Winston whined but obeyed the order.

"Now that we have that all straightened out, I'm Tessie Dancer, and you must be Pete Kelly. I had a crush on you my senior year, but you couldn't see me for dirt."

Taken aback, Pete struggled for words. "I . . . I didn't know."

"Of course you didn't know. Not to worry, it wouldn't have gone anywhere. And, you, lovely lady, must be Lily Madison. I buy your kid clothes for my friends' kids. Great quality. My friends say they wash and wear beautifully. You two," she said, jerking her head in Pete's direction, "are you an item? Is that what this scoop is all about?"

Lily found her tongue. "Not exactly. It's a long story. However, we want your word that you won't print anything until we give you the word to do it. Or, if you think that is beyond something you're comfortable with, you'll keep your source confidential."

Tessie jerked at the leopard-skin leggings she was wearing—complete with matching top—as she eyed Zolly. She nodded to Lily that she agreed to the terms. As she advanced on Zolly, both Lily and Pete sucked in their breath. Winston whined again.

"I told you to put that silly thing away. I meant it. This is also a private meeting, and I do not recall hearing that you were invited. Now, if you want to get together later, I might be able to accommodate you. I am an expert in everything I do, and that"—she lowered her voice to a whisper—"includes sex. I even have a pole for dancing in my bedroom. Now, scoot. That means leave, skedaddle, take off, or, in plain English, get the hell out of here."

Zolly backed toward the door, his face nine shades of red. To Tessie's delight, he jammed the gun into his pants.

"I hope you have the safety on. Okay, kiddies, let's sit down right here at the table and talk. I'd like a double scotch on the rocks and maybe some munchies. I tape everything so there is no misunderstanding later. You okay with that?" Both Pete and Lily nodded.

Lily called room service and placed the order before she took her seat at the table. A devil perched itself on her shoulder. "Miss Dancer, my friend Pete isn't sure you're the one for this job. I, on the other hand, insisted you are. He wanted someone like that guy in Washington who writes all those books and stirs stuff up. He can't understand why, if you're as good as I said you were, you aren't in New York or Washington or maybe Chicago."

Tessie crossed one very plump knee over the other and eyeballed Pete. "When I told that *wuss* with the gun that I was an expert in everything I do, I meant it. You take Mr. W, your pick there in Washington, he writes books. I don't write books. Not because I can't but because I don't want to. I have had offers to go to his paper, the Gray Lady, and just about every other paper in this country. I choose to stay here because of my elderly parents, whom I support. I already have two Pulitzers to my name. I have sources Mr. W can only dream about. He likes to see himself on TV. I do not, for obvious reasons. My bottom line is I am only as good as the story that's given to me.

"I've read all the stuff written about you, Mr. Kelly, and you're boring as hell. Ditto for you, Miss Madison. Just so you know, I do not do human interest, so you better have something with some grit to tell me, or I'm out of here. So, start sucking up right now."

Pete eyed the reporter's flaming red hair, sparkling green eyes, and contagious smile. He thought she was pretty, and for some strange reason he believed everything she was saying. He risked a glance at Lily, who was obviously enjoying the reporter's performance.

He was about to sit down when Zolly tapped at the door with a tray in his hands. Pete set it in the middle of the table and watched the reporter go at it as he and Lily started to talk.

An hour later, the peanut and chip bowls were both empty, and Tessie Dancer was on her second double scotch when Pete finally wound down.

"And I thought you two were boring. Okay, what do you want me to do?"

"Find out from those sources of yours what the hell is going on. Why is there a lid on this shooting? Where did those orders come from? Where's the kid they have in custody and where the hell is my son? I want to know who owns that goddamn sperm bank and fertility clinic and the academy as well. They buried it so deep no one can find true ownership. We can't do anything until we have that information."

"Hold on there. You don't know for sure that the other boy is your son."

"The hell I don't. I *know* it. I know it, okay? If you don't believe me, this is not going to work. He's in danger, and we have to find him. I don't have time for bullshit, so are you in or out?"

Tessie toyed with the glass in her hand. "I'm in. Is everything you two have told me the gospel as far as you know it?" Both Pete and Lily nodded. "You didn't leave anything out?" Both Pete and Lily shook their heads. "Okay, I'm going to need at least twelve hours to try to get some answers. When I'm on a story I never sleep. So that means I might show up here at three in the morning, and I don't want that clown out there with the gun getting in my way. We straight on that?"

"We're straight on that. We're going to take a drive up to the academy. There was something about Agent Robbins that didn't sit well with me. I want to nose around on my own, so we're going to wait till it's dark. You're welcome to come if you want to."

"No. I have too much to do. Give me your cell phone number and make sure you answer when I call. Do not, I repeat, do not, ever, as in ever, put me on hold."

"I will never put you on hold, Miss Dancer," Pete said solemnly.

"Okay. Call me Tessie, and you're Pete and Lily. What's that gorilla's name out front?"

"Zolly."

"And the dog?"

"Winston."

"I think I can remember all that," Tessie said as she turned off the recorder. "By the way, are either of you artistically inclined? What that means is, can either one of you draw a rough sketch of that guy at the library, the one you think is after your son?"

"I only design clothes, but I can take a stab at it. Let me get some paper," Lily said.

Tessie zeroed in on Pete. "Go ahead, ask me. I can tell you're dying to ask me something, so go for it."

"Are you always so blunt? Do you read minds or something?" Pete asked.

"Yes and no. You gonna make me beg you to ask the question?"

"No. Are you as good as you say you are?"

"Better. I was being modest."

Pete let loose with a laugh. He decided he liked this brash woman with the fiery red hair. He decided to play with her a bit. "How is it you're not married, Tessie?"

"I'm too much woman for any man. Men don't know what to do with me. I'm not hiding my light under a basket so some guy can feel he's superior to me. You certainly waited long enough to latch on to Lily there. If this mess hadn't surfaced, would you be a confirmed bachelor?"

Pete wished he'd never asked the question. "I think I would have found her one way or the other. One of these days the right guy will come along. You really got a pole for dancing in your bedroom?"

"Yep. And, I know how to use it."

Pete decided there was no comeback to that, so he clamped his lips shut.

Lily handed over a sheet of paper. Pete looked at it. He nodded. "I think his eyes were set farther apart. His chin was a little more square, but it's close enough."

"Doesn't look like anyone I know," Tessie said, pocketing the picture. "I'll be in touch."

Lily and Pete looked at one another. Tessie looked at them both. "Trust me."

Lily sighed. Pete sighed. Tessie laughed.

Outside, Tessie winked at Zolly, who kept his distance as she sashayed her way to a sleek, candy-apple red Ford Taurus. "See ya, big guy." In the blink of an eye, she went from zero to ninety.

Chapter 15

Lily looked at her watch. It was five thirty. "I thought that went rather well. Do you agree?" She hated that her voice sounded so anxious.

"If she can deliver what she promised, yeah. Either she's full of herself and believes her own press, or she's as good as she says she is. I can tell by your expression it's the latter with you." Pete grinned.

Lily laughed. "Once in a while you meet someone who falls into the category of 'I-can-do-this-better-than-anyone-else,' and can actually deliver the goods. The only part I'm not real happy with is the fact that she doesn't sleep and conducts meetings in the middle of the night."

"That's pretty much the story of my life. You'll get used to it. It's like a thread on a sweater that's unraveling. You have to keep at it until there's a resolution. All things considered, I think it's a good thing. I'm going to call Agent Robbins and bust his chops." At Lily's startled look, Pete said, "It's something to do. I'm not good at this waiting around stuff. All he can do is blow me off."

"Why waste your time? He pretty much ran us off when we were at the academy. He's not going to give up anything. Now, there's someone who is full of himself."

"We won't know if we don't try. People like Robbins hate people like me. He thinks of me as a pain in the ass. He gets off on pulling rank. I'm just going to jerk his chain a little. Sometimes when people get angry or annoyed, they let something slip."

"The guy's a skunk, Pete. I don't see him giving up a thing. If anything, he's the one who will be jerking your chain," Lily said as she played tug-of-war with Winston over a plush toy.

Pete shrugged as he scrolled through the numbers on his cell phone until he found the one he wanted. He pressed SEND, then waited. "Just listen," he whispered.

"Agent Robbins, Pete Kelly. I was wondering if you wanted to go on the record as to our meeting at the library yesterday. I'm about to give an interview to a reporter at the *Chronicle* named Tessie Dancer. I, of course, can repeat our exchange, but I think it will have more credibility if you speak with her yourself. I don't want the article to appear biased in any way." Then Pete listened, his jaw dropping.

"What do you mean you're in St. Louis and you and your men were reassigned to White Plains, New York? Of course I understand English. What task force? Jesus, I thought you were an FBI agent. Are you telling me some guy waltzed into that academy and sent you packing? Yeah, yeah, I guess you are telling me that. Did you even check his credentials other than to eyeball them? Yeah, yeah, I do think you're stupid. I'm talking about a phone call. Guess you didn't do that, huh, Robbins? So, can I quote you for the *Chronicle*? I'll just sit here and wait for your return phone call. If you don't call me back in ten minutes, I'm going to tell Dancer to put her own spin on the article, then I'm going up to that academy with a whole boat-load of police, and I don't give two shits if the FBI is in charge or not. You were snookered, Mr. FBI Agent," Pete snarled.

Pete looked at the phone and snapped it shut. "He hung up on me. We need to call Tessie and head back up to that academy right now. A few hours ago some guy, probably the shooter in disguise, just waltzed in there and booted Robbins and his guys out. What does that tell you?"

"The shooter is in charge and he's looking for the boy and he thinks he's at the school and that Agent Robbins is stupid. Okay, let's go. We can call Tessie on the way. You have to admire the guy's boldness. Like you said, he snookered a seasoned agent. What are we going to do when we get there?"

"Bluff our way in the way that guy did. Hell, I don't know, Lily.

"Zolly!" Pete bellowed.

"Yeah, boss, what's up?"

"Get your boys together, we're going up to

the academy again. Don't argue with me. We're going *now*. Like this instant."

"I need ten minutes, boss. You want fire-power, I need ten minutes."

"You have nine minutes left. Move, Zolly." The big man was out the door before Pete finished speaking. A second later Pete's cell phone was back in his hand.

A second after that, Tessie identified herself, then listened to Pete's monologue. "Can you hold on until I make a few calls to see if Agent Robbins was relieved of duty? I'll get back to you in a few minutes. Sit tight, Pete."

Tessie was as good as her word, she was back on the phone in seven minutes. "No task force is in place. Agent Robbins is still the agent in charge. The only problem is that Agent Robbins is in St. Louis on a layover to White Plains that was not authorized. He's waiting for the first available flight back to San Francisco. The guards patrolling the grounds are rent-a-cops hired by the Bureau. You have maybe, maybe, Pete, a four- to five-hour window. Call me if you need bail."

Pete digested the information. "How'd you get all that so fast?"

"You know better than to ask a reporter to divulge her sources. I told you I was good. Be careful, Mr. Peter Aaron Kelly."

"I will, Miss Tessie Dancer."

Pete snapped the cell phone shut and turned to look at Lily, who was still tugging at a toy with Winston. He repeated his conversation with Tessie.

"What if there's a guard posted at the bottom of the driveway? How would we get past him? Do you have a plan to deal with those rent-a-cops, assuming your intent is to go into the building?"

"Actually, Lily, I don't have a plan. I've always been pretty good at winging it in a crisis. I think this pretty much qualifies as a crisis."

Pete's tone was so upbeat, Lily cringed. The man was beyond fearless. She crossed her fingers that some of Pete's fearlessness would rub off on her. By then she was one raw nerve ending.

Lily's entire body started to twitch when she walked with Pete and Winston out to the parking lot. Zolly's *firepower* consisted of six men who could have qualified as linebackers for the Raiders. She knew they were all wearing shoulder holsters under their custom-made jackets just the way Zolly did. She had no doubt the heavy artillery was in the back of one of the SUVs. AK-47s, rocket launchers, etc. Like she would recognize any of them even if she tripped over them. Her knowledge of weaponry was strictly from TV.

Winston growled, but with pleasure, his body trembling at what he was seeing, which translated to one word: "action."

"I hope to hell you know what you're doing, boss," Zolly mumbled under his breath as he shifted gears in the specially equipped SUV.

"Well, we'll know soon enough, won't we?" Pete asked, his voice ringing with cheer as he settled back to watch the scenery.

Fearless and stupid, Lily thought.

* * *

Morgan stomped the hallways as he cursed up a storm. Where was the damn kid? He whirled around when he thought he heard a sound. "Come on, kid, show yourself. I'm going to find you, so make it easy on yourself." His cell phone took that moment to ring. Just what he needed. He flipped it open.

"What? Where the hell do you think I am? I'm here, and so is the damn kid, but he's holed up somewhere. I don't have much time, as you know. I have another hour at the most, then I have to get out of here. Stop thinking the FBI is stupid, okay? I pulled it off, but it's temporary, and I'm not going to prison for you or your boss. You got that?"

From his position in the air duct to the left of where the killer was standing, Josh listened to the cell phone conversation. Did that jerk really think he was going to show himself so he could pump him full of bullets? All he had to do was stay safe for another hour. The guy didn't want to go to prison. Well, who did?

"Okay, Josh, back up and find another vent. Screw with his head. You've got the edge. He said he doesn't have much time. Let me do the talking. You just listen."

Josh slid backward until he was satisfied with his location. He looked through the vent to see the dean's office below. The plant on his desk looked dead. Like that really mattered.

"Okay, bellow like you used to do when I was crossing the finish line, then get the hell out of here and move to the next location."

Josh took a deep breath and yelled as loud as he could. "Come and get me, you son of a bitch!"

"That was good, Josh. Cursing is ten demerits and two laps around the track. Now, move forward to where you were before. Make the bastard chase his tail. Can you make it to the infirmary? Be careful, don't make any noise."

Josh slid backward again, his eyes straining to see in the darkness as he passed one vent after another. He looked down and saw the sterile whiteness of the infirmary. What should he taunt the jerk with this time? "Hey, jerk-off, I called the FBI office, and they're sending a new team of agents. The local cops are on the way. And I have a gun, too. Say something, you piece of crap," he bellowed at the top of his lungs.

"Damn, that was good, Josh. Sheila is impressed. Quick, get to the main hall and don't move or say anything until I tell you. Shhh, his phone is ringing. Can you hear what he's saying?"

"Yeah, yeah, I can hear."

"Yeah, Agent Warner, what's the problem?" Morgan listened, the color draining from his face as his eyes sought the nearest EXIT sign. "My team is approaching the entrance to the academy? That's impossible. I just spoke to them, and they're thirty-five minutes away. What you have there, Agent Warner, is a situation. Take care of it. I'll join you as soon as I finish what I'm doing here. You have a gun, so use it if you have to."

Morgan's mind raced. What the hell was going on? "Five SUVs, you said?"

"Yes, and those boys look meaner than snakes."

"One more thing, if Agent Robbins tries to contact you, do yourself a favor and don't answer your cell unless you want to be assigned a shit detail like he has. Are you following me here, Agent Warner? Your only priority right now is those SUVs."

"Yes, sir. Agent Robbins is actually calling me right now. His name just popped up on the ID."

"And . . . ?"

"I'm not answering, sir."

"C'mon, Josh, give him one more blast."

Josh was directly overhead now and about to slide backward to where the vent in the industrial kitchen was located. He sucked in his breath, and shouted as loud as he could, "Hey, dickweed, I thought you were going to find me! You couldn't find an elephant if it was standing on your dick. I told you I called the FBI and the local cops. You better run, dickweed, or you're going to get caught. Run, run, run, you piece of shit."

Morgan looked upward as he realized where Josh was. So that was how the damn little snot had outwitted him.

Josh couldn't resist one last parting shot. "Give it up, you turd. It would take you hours to find me up here, and before you can sneeze, I'll be safe and sound." He saw the weapon being raised at the same moment he started to slide backward. In his life he had never moved so fast, not even when he was in top form and hurdling. His heart was pounding louder than the hail of bullets that were ripping into the ceiling.

"Holy shit! Get out of here, Josh. You had to do that, didn't you? You okay, you didn't get shot, did you?"

"I'm okay, I'm okay. Yeah, I did have to do that. He killed you and Sheila. I liked Mr. Dickey and Miss Carmody. The other kids, too. He's on the run now. Oh, shit, no, he isn't. That's his team down by the guardhouse. Or is it? Just for a minute I thought it was the cavalry. What should I do, Tom?"

"No, it isn't his team. He acts alone, but he does have a boss who gives him orders. Get to the hidey-hole and stay put. No matter what you hear, don't come out until I tell you it's safe. Swear to me, Josh."

"I swear. That's all I've been doing today. Good thing Mr. Dickey can't hear me."

"Oh, he can hear you, all right, and he's appalled. I'm joking, okay? Listen, Josh, are you sure that guy spraying the bullets is the same guy who killed us all?"

"I am damn sure. He tried to disguise himself, but I just closed my eyes and tried to remember Jesse's picture and stripped away the stuff he added to his face. It's him, all right. And, he had that same watch or whatever it was on his wrist."

"I'll see you later, Josh. I'll be back when I figure out what's going on. Remember, now, don't make a sound. Take some cheese and crackers in case you get hungry. And a flashlight. I think there's one in the kitchen drawer. You also need a weapon. Take that mallet the cook uses to pound meat. It's better than nothing."

"Okay. You're going to watch over me, right?"

"You bet. I told you, I'll always be right by your side. First, though, I want to check things out down

the driveway. We have to figure out a way for you to get my book and who it's safe to give it to. I'll be working on that while you hide. It's gonna be okay. I promise, Secret Agent 8446."

"I'll be waiting for you, Agent 8211," Josh responded, but this time he wasn't laughing the way he usually laughed when Tom called him Agent 8446.

Exhausted with all he'd been through, Josh scurried to the kitchen, where he grabbed a small wheel of cheese and the box of crackers he'd opened the evening before. At the last second he remembered the flashlight and stuck it in the pocket of his sweatpants. He longed to take a shower because he was filthy from crawling through the ductwork, but he knew that was out of the question.

Safe in the makeshift wine cellar, Josh curled himself into a tight ball inside Mr. Dickey's sleeping bag. He was so tired he ached all over, but he was afraid to go to sleep, and he needed to think. Was he losing his mind? Had he really been talking to Tom? Or was he in overdrive? It sure sounded like Tom, but how was that possible? Was he so desperate, so scared, he'd conjured up Tom out of thin air?

Josh's eyelids started to droop. He jerked upright. He wished he'd been smart enough to go to the electrical panel and pull the lever that put the school in lockdown mode. Why didn't he do that? He remembered the time Tony Polaro pulled the lever and the panic that ensued. For days his ears rang with the high-pitched sounds. It took hours for the instructors to figure out how to unlock everything. Poor old Tony had to walk the grounds for a full month. Tony was dead now. Maybe he'd pull the lever in his memory before he left this place.

Josh had to leave, he knew that now. He had to get Tom's book and go to a newspaper. The hard reality he was forced to recognize was that he couldn't trust the police or the FBI. He'd known all along the only person he could trust was himself. And now Tom.

Josh's last conscious thought before drifting into a sound sleep was to wonder if Jesse was safe and if he would ever see him again.

Chapter 16

Tessie Dancer glared at the small recorder she was listening to as she drummed her fingers on the desktop. When the tape ended, she pressed the OFF button. She rewound the tape and listened to it for the tenth time, knowing she could almost recite the words verbatim at this point. She had a tiger by the tail, and it wasn't a baby tiger. Oh, no, this tiger was the granddaddy of all tigers. *The* scoop of a lifetime. Possibly a third Pulitzer. Front-page stuff, big byline, above the fold. It didn't get any better than that, and she knew it.

The problem was, and it *was* a problem, how should she tackle the story? Should she go with bits and pieces? A tease, so to speak. Or should she wait, the way Kelly wanted her to, and do it all in one shot? Or . . . go to the source? Once she found the source.

Tessie turned off the recorder and turned on her computer to check her e-mail. She'd sent out over fifty e-mails to her sources, friends and

families of those sources, and anyone else she
had thought of who might have information for
her.

As Tessie stared at her blank e-mail screen,
her fingers continued to drum on the desktop.
A nervous habit just like biting her nails was.
She thought about Pete and Lily's story. How
sad that was. Two high-powered people who
were wealthy beyond anyone's dreams, and they
were miserable because of something they had
done in their youth, something they had no way
of knowing would bring them to this place in
time. They made their donations for the right
reasons, not only because they needed the
money but because they hoped they would be
helping childless couples. And now, those ac-
tions had come back to haunt them.

Who are the principals in the sperm bank
and fertility clinic? Her cursory trace was so
complicated, she'd given it up and turned it
over to a computer wizard who owed her big-
time for a favor she'd done him a few years
back. Why bury ownership so deep if the principals weren't trying to hide something? Why?

Tessie thought about Lily's description of the
lab and minihospital. Why would a fertility
clinic need something like that? Where did the
money come from to outfit something like that?
First rule: Follow the money.

Then there was the California Academy of
Higher Learning. Ownership of the academy
was buried just as deep. Same owners? Probably.
Who put the lid on the media? Someone high
up in the food chain. What were they hiding at

the school? Where did everyone disappear to? Who was the boy Josh Baer? Was he Pete Kelly's son? Pete seemed to think he was, and Lily had agreed.

Years of experience had taught her one thing. When people went to so much trouble to bury something, it meant it was either drug-related or the principals were politicians with deep, dark secrets. Tessie's eyes narrowed. Her gut told her it was fifty-fifty.

What kind of person would hire a contract killer to snuff out an entire class of seventeen-year-old kids, one of whom was mentally challenged? The same kind of person who was hiding ownership of the school, the fertility clinic, and the sperm bank. That had to mean all three were connected. Tessie scribbled notes to herself.

Where were the other kids and their teachers? Where was the dean? Did all the records disappear before the shooting or did the FBI confiscate them? Tessie made more notes. How could a large group of students disappear with no one seeing them? Private charter flights to ... somewhere. Maybe there were other schools like the California Academy of Higher Learning. Why? For what purpose?

Who was the shooter? Where was the boy? Were the kids at the school geniuses?

Every private school she'd researched had a Web site; not so for the academy. Well, she had one of her sources working on that, too.

Tessie's guts started to churn when she thought about the missing boy, who might possibly be Pete Kelly's son. How long could he stay safe? Her blood started to churn at what could happen to him. She'd been a child advocate for the past fifteen years. In fact, her first Pulitzer was a heart- and gut-wrenching article on child advocacy. Her thoughts shifted to Pete Kelly and the academy. She didn't know how she knew, but she knew that before the end of the day, he was going to be in jail. She was so deep into her thoughts she almost missed the e-mail that popped up on her screen. The moment she saw it, she jerked upright to read the terse message.

Are you nuts, Tessie? What the hell did you get yourself mixed up in? I'm not putting stuff like this in an e-mail. Meet me where you always meet me, and we'll talk, but first you better hire yourself a top-notch attorney.

Tessie's eyes almost popped out of her head. She sent back an e-mail asking for a time to meet. The response to her e-mail was: One hour.

Little Slick, the e-mailer, was the best computer hacker known to man. He must have found something really important. Little Slick had his own computer lab and sixteen employees. Not many people knew Little Slick was on retainer to the FBI, the CIA, and the rest of Alphabet City, also known as the nation's capital. Little Slick had appeared on her radar screen when one of his kids needed a neurosurgeon and someone gave him her name. She'd called in favors and promised far more than she should have in the hope the five-year-old could be saved. It had all turned out well, and Little Slick worked overtime to pay off what he considered his debt to her. She, in turn, sent small gifts from time to time to the little boy who called her Aunt Tessie.

With Little Slick requesting a meeting, whatever he'd found had to be red-hot and top secret. Tessie felt giddy at the thought.

Tessie looked around, suddenly aware of how quiet it was. A sigh escaped her lips as she looked out the window. Eight o'clock. She should be home fixing her parents' dinner. The home health aide she'd hired to fill in for her was worth every hard-earned penny she paid her. Still, she felt bad that she wasn't the one making the meat loaf that both her mother and father loved. She'd long ago given up the idea that she could be all things to all people. All she could do was her best, and if that wasn't good enough, so be it.

Tessie reached into her desk drawer for not one but three power bars. She scarfed them down, then swilled the rest of her cold coffee.

Tessie reached for her cell phone, which had been strangely silent these past few hours. Most days it rang nonstop. Was the silence an omen of some kind? She wasn't the least bit surprised when Pete Kelly didn't answer his cell phone. She wondered how he would like a few hours in jail. She sent off another e-mail to Little Slick advising him of the current situation with Pete:

Lose the paperwork in the computer and don't let him get booked if he's brought in.

Morgan cursed long and loud. How the hell was he going to get out of there? Five SUVs? Obviously they weren't FBI reinforcements. Then who? No one in his right mind messed with the FBI except maybe someone like him. Outsiders. The guy from the library? What the hell difference did it make who they were? All that mattered was for him to get out of there in one goddamn piece.

Morgan looked up at the ceiling. Did he get the little bastard? Too late now; saving his own skin was paramount. He'd just have to figure out another way to get the kid, or else he'd pack it in, give back the money, and move on. He didn't like the flip side of that coin very much. People as powerful as the ones he was dealing with would find a way to get to him and kill him. Well, that wasn't going to happen.

Morgan ran from the building to the stolen Toyota, climbed in, and raced to the bottom of the hill, where Agent Warner was standing guard over the five SUVs. He thrust open the door the moment he brought the Land Cruiser to a stop, his automatic weapon drawn. He hit the ground running, the safety off. He motioned for Agent Warner to step out of the way. Within seconds all five SUVs had flat tires. Morgan was surprised that his gun wasn't smoking. "Take care of this, Warner. My team hit a roadblock ten miles down the road. I have to take care of it. Run these people in and I don't give a good rat's ass if they claim to be friends of the president of the United States. I'm glad you had the good sense to keep them in their vehicles. Did Agent Robbins call back?"

"Don't know, sir, I've been kind of busy with this," Warner said, waving his arm toward the line of SUVs. "They have a dog inside."

Morgan pulled out his cell phone, pretended to dial a number, then spoke to himself, his back half-turned to Agent Warner but still within ear-shot.

"Special Agent Lionel Lewis. I'm up at the California Academy of Higher Learning. My task force is stuck at a roadblock ten miles away, and I'm on my way to straighten that out. We have an incident here, and this is a request for additional agents ASAP. I'm leaving Agent Warner in charge. No IDs but obvious fire-power. Civilians or media would be my guess. They aren't going anywhere, I shot out all the tires. There is a K-9. Send four of ours. I thought it best not to bring the rent-a-cops into it, ma'am. It was my call. I'm in charge here. Fine, fine."

Morgan clicked the cell phone shut. He'd never make an FBI agent. He'd totally forgotten the rent-a-cops. He turned to Warner, and said, "Get those rent-a-cops down here and keep these people in their vehicles. Now, Agent Warner."

Agent Warner ran over to the guard shelter and used his squawk box to call in the rent-a-cops, who responded on the run.

Morgan could feel a panic attack coming on. He had to get out of there before it all blew up on him. The moment the rent-a-cops skidded to a stop, he was in the Toyota, speeding out to the highway.

"Josh, wake up! Wake up! I hear gunfire! C'mon, c'mon, wake up! You have to see what's going on."

Josh struggled to a sitting position. Tom was right. He clamped his hands over his ears, his eyes burning. It sounded just like that day when all his friends were killed. Where were the gunshots coming from? Inside or outside? Outside, he decided. Who was that skunk shooting this time? The guards? The police? *Maybe someone was shooting at the shooter.*

"C'mon, Josh, you have to check it out. You need to stay on top of what's going on. If you don't, they're going to catch you, and you can't let that happen. Can't you move any faster?"

Josh picked up his feet and ran, staying close to the wall as he hit the first floor and the long hallway that led to the main entrance. He looked down once to see hundreds of shell casings littering the floor. He'd seen the same casings that day when all his friends had been gunned down.

"Don't look at them, Josh, they're just pieces of metal. You need to keep your wits about you and you also need a weapon. Think . . . Agent 8446."

"The baseball bat in the dean's office. The one Adam hit the grand slam with last year. I can break the case it's in. Adam . . . Adam doesn't . . . won't . . . He won't ever need it again. Maybe I can kill someone with it to avenge him."

"Just get the damn thing and worry about killing

someone later. It's to protect yourself. You're no killer, Josh. C'mon, c'mon, hurry up. You got lead in those legs today. Move it!"

Josh raced back down the hall to the dean's office. He took a second to stare at the dead plant on the desk, wondering if he should water it. *I must be crazy to think about watering plants at a time like this.*

A heavy glass paperweight in his hand, Josh smashed the glass case that housed the winning bat and baseball. He pocketed the ball and gave the bat a few wild swings. Now he felt like he had a little control.

"You just going to stand there, or are you going to do something?"

"What? What? You want me to go out there and show myself with that crazy guy shooting people? I don't think so. I have to get out of here. I just want to see what's going on down by the gate. What if he shot everyone? If he did, then I have to call the police."

"Well, if that did happen, there's nothing you can do. When you're dead, you're dead, and calling the police can't help them."

"They might not be dead, just hurt. I have to help."

"At the risk of getting caught?"

Josh debated the question. "Yes."

"Go out through the kitchen, walk behind the shrubs. They're so thick against the building, no one will see you. Just don't make any noise. I'm here, Josh, right beside you. Be careful, now."

"If he's gone, he'll be back. I have to get out of here, Tom."

"Yeah, yeah, yeah. First things first. Check out the situation first. If that guy even thinks about coming back, he'll know you're gone. No more talking, now. Be as quiet as you can."

Josh looked around to study the terrain. Even though he knew it intimately, he studied each bush, shrub, and tree to see what would afford him the best cover. He eyed the sycamore tree with the low branches that were thick with fresh green leaves. Before he shinnied up the tree, he slid the baseball bat under a bush. With the dark gray of his sweat suit, he'd blend in with the foliage.

Josh climbed steadily. He didn't like the idea that he had to go as high as he was going. Talk about being a sitting duck. But, if he wanted to see all the way to the guardhouse, he had to go midway up the tree. The limb was sturdy, so there was no problem about its holding his weight. Still, as he stretched out his body, he hung on for dear life.

The view was startling and definitely not what he expected. People, lots of people. No shooter. The guards with guns, the FBI agent. He knew it was an agent because it said "FBI" in bold yellow letters on the back of his Windbreaker. Eight men. Five big utility vehicles, all with flat tires. Shell casings all over the place. The lady and the man from the library.

The FBI guy was holding a gun on the people. The lady in the hat looked like she was going to cry. The guy with her, the one from the library, looked pissed to the teeth. The dog looked like he wanted to take a chunk out of someone. Josh closed his eyes, and whispered, "What's this all mean, Tom?"

A strong gust of wind whipped through the trees just as Tom was about to respond. *"Uh-oh, get out of here right now, Josh. That dog just picked up your scent. Quick. He's straining at the leash and looking right here where you are. Try not to disturb the branches. Move, Josh, hurry. Everyone is looking at this tree."*

"Oh, shit!"

"Yeah, oh, shit!" Tom said.

"Okay, okay."

Chapter 17

Pete and Winston saw the movement in the sycamore tree at the same moment. *The boy!* So he'd been right after all. He was going to lose him again if these dumb clucks didn't get out of his way. Still, did he want to take on the FBI and the rent-a-cops, who were all holding guns pointed at the SUVs? He looked down at the driveway to see all their own firepower as well as all their cell phones in a tidy little pile.

"This is bullshit!" Pete said, opening the door and stepping out onto the concrete apron. He and the others would have been fools not to hear the click of seven guns. Even Winston knew enough to freeze in his tracks. Pete raised his hands high over his head. Winston, at his side, growled menacingly, the fur on the back of his neck standing straight up. Inside the SUV Pete could hear Zolly's and Lily's protests.

Even though his hands were high in the air, Pete's eyes were on the sycamore tree and the branch that was weaving and bobbing. Without the interference he was facing, with his long legs he could have snagged the boy before he slid to the ground. Goddamn it!

"That's far enough, mister," Agent Warner said.

To Pete, his voice sounded shaky. His firing hand didn't look exactly stable to him either. The rent-a-cops looked nervous.

"Look, we didn't do anything. We stopped at the taped line when you told us to. We came here to see if we could find the boy. I think I know him. Now, either let us go or charge us with something. We have all the paperwork to carry those guns lying on the ground. What's it going to be?"

"You're staying right where you are until I get orders telling me otherwise. Now, get back in that vehicle and stay there."

"See, now that's where you're wrong. We're leaving, and we're taking our property with us. You want to shoot me, then damn well shoot me. Before you can get that gun into firing position, this dog will have your throat ripped to shreds. I also want to remind you that I'm the CEO and founder of PAK Industries and have friends in some very high places, like 1600 Pennsylvania Avenue, for example. I bet with one phone call I could have your ass booted out of the Bureau with no trouble. And those rent-a-cops—well, I understand Walmart is looking for help. And the bill for all these tires is going to be sent to the Bureau since you allowed a bogus agent to use an Uzi to flatten all our tires. Bogus agent, Mr. FBI Agent. How's that going to look in your file? So back off, hotshot."

·Agent Warner longed for a deep, dark hole to swallow him up. During his nine years at the Bureau, this was his first confrontation. Damn that stupid Robbins. Everything this guy said made sense. Still, to back down in front of all these people was going to be one hell of a humiliating experience. Sometimes you just had to bite the bullet.

Warner holstered his weapon, the rent-a-cops did the same.

"This is a crime scene, so get your gear and your posse and get the hell out of here. Don't let me see you within a mile of this school again. You hear me?"

"Screw you and the horse you rode in on," Pete responded. "Zolly, get the guys, and let's go!"

On the short walk to the road, while Pete called for transportation, Zolly was stewing and fretting. "We could have taken them, boss."

"Yeah, I know," Pete replied, snapping his cell phone shut. "We don't have time to spend in custody waiting for bail and the paperwork that goes with it. That asshole got away, and I saw the boy up in the tree. I told you he'd come back here. Now he's going to run again. I need to get back up there. Me and you, Zolly, and, of course, Winston. We need to find a way in through the back, and this time I'll let you take on the rent-a-cops. We can do it, Zolly, but we have to do it right now. That bumpkin back there won't think we have the chutzpah to do something so quick. You game?"

"Yeah, boss." Zolly's honor was at stake here, and he knew it. "It's almost dark, so let's go for it. What about Miss Lily and the others?"

"They'll wait for our transportation."

"Do not ever make the mistake of speaking for me again," Lily warned. "I'm going with you. I have as much invested in this as you do, Peter Aaron Kelly. Don't give me any guff either. Let's go."

Zolly rolled his eyes as he cut through a mass of brambles at the foot of the long driveway, with Pete, Lily, and Winston bringing up the rear.

Josh raced into the kitchen, where he fell against the counter as he struggled to bring his breathing under control.

"That was certainly an experience to write about in your journal. They saw you, you know. What's your game plan now?" Tom asked.

"No shit! Why do you think I'm standing here breathing like a racehorse? I need to get the book, Tom. Then I have to split, but I don't know where to go. Do you have any ideas? That's my game plan unless you have a better one," Josh gasped.

"Actually, I do have an idea, Josh. Mr. Dickey kept an apartment in town. He went there on weekends. If you can find his address, you could go there and hide out. It's a complex. He told us about it, don't you re-member? He told us about all the weird people who

lived there and how hard he had to work to get along with them."

"Yeah, yeah. Just what I need, more weird people. Like this isn't weird enough," Josh said, waving his arms about. "That means I have to go back to the library."

"That's exactly what it means, Josh. You should be safe at his place because the FBI went through everything there already. I bet his rent is paid to the end of the month. But maybe the people who own the apartment already rented it out. It's a chance you have to take. Sheila agrees."

That was all Josh had to hear—his two best friends agreeing on a course of action.

"So do I take the book with me or not?"

"Yeah, yeah, take the book, but I don't think you should leave it there. Sooner or later the apartment will be up for rent. Maybe you can find a place in the library that will be safe. You know, some book no one will ever look at. I think you should make copies first, though."

"I can do that. Yeah, yeah, I can do that. It's almost dark out. Should I leave now?"

"First go get the book and, yeah, go out the way you got in here, through the back. Stick the book in your pants and, for crying out loud, don't lose it. It's all you got going for you, buddy, to prove what's been going on around here."

"Wait for me, Tom."

"You know it, buddy. Sheila's here, too. She said to tell you that you're going to need an ice pick to open Mr. Dickey's lock. You better take some food, too."

Josh's mind raced as fast as his feet as he ran through the building. Fifteen minutes later he was back in the kitchen, Tom's spiral-bound notebook tucked securely in his sweatpants. He jerked at the string holding up his sweatpants to make sure the book was secure.

Within seconds he had an ice pick in his pocket and a paper sack filled with food. "Wait a minute, I forgot something. I have to go back."

"Josh, there's no time. I hear a commotion outside. What's so important you have to go back for it?"

"My photo album with all our pictures. I can't leave without it. I don't ever want to forget what you and Sheila look like. Our other friends, too."

"All right, all right, but hurry up."

"Fan out, people," Pete hissed. He placed a cautionary hand on Winston's head to warn the big dog to stay close. Winston whined.

Thirty minutes later, Zolly had taken out three of the rent-a-cops. "They're sleeping like babies, boss, and, no, I didn't really hurt them. They might have a headache when they wake up a few hours from now, but that's it. Do you want to go inside, or are we just checking the grounds?"

"I'll take the inside, you do the grounds. Keep Winston with you. Lily, come with me. You take the first floor, I'll take the second."

"Pete, it's pitch-dark inside, we aren't going to be able to see a thing. The boy could be standing in the same room with us, and we'd never know it. This isn't going to work unless we feel our way around and call his name. We both know he isn't going to answer us. We need a better plan."

Pete knew she was right. How did he get to be this stupid? "You're right. You stay here, and I'm going to wander around and call his name. I can't leave here without giving it a shot." There was such anguish in his voice when he said, "I have to try, Lily."

"I know, Pete. I'll do the same. There's a little light coming in some of the windows. Don't call out too loud," Lily warned, as Pete moved off.

Lily ventured forth, wishing she had Winston at her side. From time to time she called out to the boy, hoping he wouldn't pick up on the fear in her voice and know she was in a state of panic. Thirty minutes into her search she also knew she was hopelessly lost. Her heartbeat kicked up several notches as she broke out into a cold sweat. "Pete!" she croaked. "Can you hear me? I'm lost."

Josh Baer stopped dead in his tracks. Was his mind playing tricks on him or did he just hear a female voice no more than a foot away? He thought his heart was going to explode right out of his chest. He moved quickly to the opposite side of the hallway that led to the biology lab.

"Oh, shit! Be careful, Josh. This isn't good, buddy. Don't even breathe. Let her pass you. She sounds scared. We both know scared people do crazy things."

Josh flattened himself against the wall, hardly daring to breathe. He clutched at the spiral-bound notebook and the thin photo album he'd stuck in his sweatpants. He just knew they were going to fall out, so he pulled them out and stuck them under his sweatshirt, which he tucked into the sweatpants. Too bad he didn't have a Windbreaker with a zipper.

"C'mon, c'mon, you ditzball, get the hell out of here. She's calling someone who must be upstairs. How'd they get by us?"

Did Tom really think he was going to answer him? The woman was whimpering, or it sounded like she was whimpering, although he'd never heard anyone doing that. Who was she? What was she doing here? Who was the guy upstairs? Tom was right, he had to get out of here. He moved then, the toe of his sneaker sticking on the slick tile underfoot. He'd made a noise. Damn.

"Pete, is that you? Thank God. I thought I heard something. I have to get out of here before I pass out. You know the way out, don't you?"

"I know what you're thinking, Josh. Don't do it. Do you hear me, don't do it!"

Josh wished he could tell Tom to shut up. Instead he whispered, "Follow me." He felt movement then, the air stirring around him as he started down the hall. *Please,* he prayed, *don't let this be a mistake. Please, please, please.*

Lily was babbling as she followed him, but he was so intent on getting safely away that he had no clue what she was saying. At the doorway that led into the kitchen, Josh reached out and pushed her forward. He whispered, "Kitchen. Wait." He raced past her and out the door.

"That was probably the dumbest thing you've ever done in your whole life. Now, how the hell are you going to get out of here? There are people out there, and they have that big dog. What are you going to do, Josh?"

"I'm going to pretend I'm you and run like hell; then I'm going to go back to being me and hurdle any obstacle that crosses my path. You know, like Superman. Unless you have a better idea."

"Go for it, buddy."

And he did.

Lily listened to the sound of the door closing and frowned. Why was Pete leaving her alone? She called his name, knowing he couldn't hear her.

"What's wrong, Lily? You sound scared out of your wits," Pete said as he came up behind her. He put his arms around her shaking shoulders.

"P . . . Pete? Didn't you just go out the kitchen door? How did you get back in here so quick?"

"What are you talking about? I didn't go out the kitchen door, I just got here. I was looking for you. It's too damn dark, so all I could do was call his name. But Josh didn't answer. Did you have any luck?"

"No. I got lost, then I panicked. I thought you led me out here to the kitchen. Someone whispered, 'follow me,' and I did, then he went out the kitchen door. I thought it was you. Oh, God, it was Josh, wasn't it? He was right here with me, and I didn't even know it. Oh, Pete, I am so sorry."

Pete kept his arm around Lily's shoulders as he led her out of the school into the dark night. Within seconds, Winston bounded to his side, followed by Zolly.

"He got away, boss! Winston tried, but he tripped on some roots, and the kid was like a streak of lightning. At least I think it was the kid. Man, can he move! He's gone!"

"Yeah, I know. C'mon, we might as well join the others. I hope they're waiting for us. He's not going to come back here, that's for sure. Jesus, what does he know? Why did he help Lily, then run?"

"He doesn't know who to trust, Pete. Hey, he could have left me back there blithering like an idiot or bopped me on the head, and he didn't. And, he's afraid."

"Not as afraid as I am," Pete muttered as he followed Zolly and Winston to the area where they'd invaded the school grounds. "Are the guards okay, Zolly?"

"Yeah, they'll be waking up soon with bad headaches. This has been a hell of a night, boss. Someday you have to write a book and send it to your stockholders at Christmastime."

"Smart-ass," Pete mumbled.

"Takes one to know one, boss."

"That's the truth," Lily said, weighing in.

Chapter 18

Tessie Dancer parked her red Taurus in the dimly lit parking lot of the Belly-Up Bar in a less-than-desirable location in town. She looked around at the rows of pickup trucks and battered cars the Belly-Up's customers arrived in. It was a strip bar with pole dancers who were shy about removing their clothing, saying they danced for the art of dancing. Tessie considered the dump educational because she had visions of wrapping herself around one of the poles and going for it. Not that she ever would, but every girl deserves to have a fantasy. Little Slick hated the place, but he was the one who found it and said it was the only safe place in town for people like him and Tessie to discuss business.

The Belly-Up Bar had a private room for such discussions, and for forty bucks, it was theirs for a solid hour. One free drink each and a bowl of peanuts came with the deal.

Little Slick, who really wasn't so little at six two, climbed out of a Jeep Wrangler and walked toward Tessie, who was just getting out of her car. "Evening, Tessie," he drawled.

"We have to stop meeting at dumps like this. It's not good for my image," Tessie drawled in return. She looked pointedly at Little Slick's hands, knowing full well the hacker never carried anything with him. Among other things, Little Slick had a photographic memory.

The Belly-Up was smoky. The patrons, as they were called, didn't give a shit about ordinances and the people who issued them. Anyone brave enough to enter the Belly-Up with the intention of enforcing any of the ordinances was never seen or heard of again. Or, so said the owner, a barrel-chested ex-wrestler who kept not one but six guns under the bar.

Tessie and Little Slick waved to the owner behind the bar as they headed for the private room that was so in demand a reservation had to be made in advance. Usually ten minutes prior to arriving qualified as a reservation.

Knowing the rules, Tessie and Little Slick went in and sat down at an old Formica-and-chrome table with bright red chairs, complete with brass nail heads, and waited. There was a certain ritual that had to be adhered to. Little Slick said it was the owner's version of a class act. A knock sounded and the door opened. A bowl, as big as a watermelon, filled with peanuts was placed in the middle of the table. Five minutes later two bottles of BUD LIGHT were on the table, along with two skimpy cocktail napkins.

The moment the door closed, Little Slick

leaned across the table, his eyes boring into the reporter's. "Tessie, what the hell are you involved in? Girl, this is not good. Are you listening to me?"

Tessie bristled. "Well, I would if you'd tell me what you're talking about. What?"

"Give me some background. I'm not divulging anything that's going to get you wiped off the map until I know how you . . . how you got involved in whatever this is."

Tessie could feel her stomach start to churn. "It fell in my lap. I got a phone call and I responded. Credible people. What, Slick?"

Instead of answering the question, Slick asked one of his own. "How credible?"

"As credible as they come," Tessie snapped.

"Who? I need names, Tessie."

"Well, you aren't going to get any names. You know better than to ask me something like that. Either you trust me or you don't. For God's sake, what?"

Little Slick moved his beer bottle on the table, making round wet circles, his eyes cloudy with worry. "Call your friend or whoever it is and ask him or her if you can give me their names. I'm not giving up a thing until I know what this is all about. It's for your own good, Tessie. Mine, too. This is all too far up the food chain for either one of us to go off half-cocked. The retaliation could be deadly. Either you do it, or I'm outta here."

Tessie couldn't believe her ears. In all the years she'd known Little Slick, this was the first time she'd ever seen him so concerned, looking this worried. She bit down on her lower lip. "I guess I can do that. Why don't you go out to the bar and buy us another beer while I make the call."

Little Slick stood up. "Don't even think of snowing me, Tessie. I'll know if you try to put one over on me."

Tessie waited for the door to close behind Little Slick before she pulled out her cell phone. She pressed in Pete Kelly's cell number. When there was no answer, she tried Lily Madison's cell. She picked up on the third ring.

"Lily, it's Tessie Dancer. Listen, I've run into a bit of a problem. If you know anything about reporters, then you know we don't reveal our sources and don't mention names unless we have permission. I have a long-standing source right here with me who has information Pete needs, but he's telling me he won't give it up until he knows who it is that wants it besides me. Are you following me here? Good, now, can I talk to Pete?"

As Lily handed the phone to Pete she told him who was on the line.

"Tessie! I was just going to call you." Before Tessie could tell him why she was calling, Pete launched into the happenings at the California Academy of Higher Learning. "Lily was *that* close to him, Tessie. He actually led her out to the kitchen. He's gone now. So for now he's lost to us again. I was right, though, he did go back to the school, where he felt safe. That bastard shot up the ceiling, so I'm assuming the boy was crawling through the ductwork. There were hundreds of shell casings in the hallway floor. Somehow or other the kid got away, thank God. I hope you're calling with better news."

Tessie digested the information, sifted and collated it with her reporter's brain. She cleared her throat. "Listen, Pete, I'm meeting with one of my best sources. At the moment he's not with me, so he can't hear what I'm saying. I want you to believe me when I tell you this guy is the best of the best. He has something, but he won't divulge it unless I tell him who you are and how I came by the story. My thinking, and he pretty much verified it, is that this is so far up the food chain he's afraid. And, trust me, I did not think there was anything in this world that could scare this guy. I've gone to jail twice to protect my sources, and I'll go again. It would just make it easier if you give me the okay to mention your name. He's not going to do anything with the info. It's strictly for his ears only. What say you, Pete Kelly?"

The sudden silence on the other end of the phone caused Tessie's stomach muscles to crunch into a tight knot. When Pete finally started to speak, she felt light-headed with relief.

"You're the reporter, Tessie. Whatever you decide is okay with Lily and me."

"Okay, I'll get back to you in a bit. Tell Lily to think about the shooter and the changes to his appearance. I'll bring the drawing she made, and she can sketch in the changes. You're telling me there isn't going to be any fallout with the FBI over your visit?"

"So far so good. Other than a mess of flat tires and a bunch of tow trucks, we got away clean without being hauled in."

"Okay, good. We'll talk in a bit."

Tessie clicked her cell phone shut and stared at the only picture on the wall. It had a black velvet background with a glow-in-the-dark image of Elvis Presley decked out in a white rhinestone-studded, one-piece suit. A true work of art. She really loved tacky crap.

Her eyes glued to the artwork, Tessie heard rather than saw Little Slick enter the room, two bottles of beer in hand. His eyes questioned her.

"His name is Peter Aaron Kelly, CEO and founder of PAK Industries, and his lady friend, Lily Madison, doyenne of children's clothing."

Little Slick's expression gave away nothing. "The rest, please."

"Being as smart and astute as you are, I'm surprised you haven't figured it out. Pete donated his sperm, Lily donated her eggs. A lifetime ago, nineteen years, to be exact. The kid that got away . . . Pete thinks it's his kid. Which then begs the question of why would some crackpot blow away a whole classroom of kids? Somehow the shooter missed the boy and his friend. The friend, by the way, is mentally challenged and in the protection of the FBI." Tessie leaned back and stared across the table at Little Slick.

"Tell me the rest."

Tessie sighed. "With the help of Pete's security, they broke into the clinic and sperm bank. Both places were deserted, wiped clean. The sperm bank was pretty much what you would expect. The clinic was different. In the back was a complete minihospital. Delivery rooms. Labs. Just like a regular hospital, only scaled down. Not so much as a paper clip was left behind. Both buildings were abandoned within hours of their visit, during which they asked some real serious questions. That's it, Slick, it's all I have. Now it's your turn, and don't leave anything out."

Slick pointed to the picture on the wall. "True art."

Tessie knew he was stalling for time. Well, she had all the time in the world.

"What happened first, Tessie, the shooting or Kelly getting in touch with you?"

"The shooting. Pete and Lily were in the airport in Atlanta, both taking a flight here for a fund-raiser at their alma mater. They met by accident, although they had met nineteen years ago. A brief encounter. Both of them have some severe problems where all this is concerned. It seems neither one of them took advantage of the counseling that was suggested back when they were . . . uh . . . making their . . . donations. Yes, they made those donations for money, but they also made them believing the donations would go to childless couples. That doesn't seem to be the case, in my opinion.

"Another thing, Slick, where are the other youngsters who attended that school? All I can find out is that they left several days before the shooting. As far as I know, no one knows where they are. How do you secret away so many kids, and why? The shooting was a contract kill. Who in the hell orders something like that? What kind of sick bastard would do something like that? Well?" Tessie asked through clenched teeth. "Do you know, Slick?"

"Let's just say I know where all the threads lead. Can I prove it? In time, yes, if I stay alive long enough. That goes for you, too, Tessie. You know that dream you have of getting a house on the water so you can putz and putter around and maybe write a book? That might not happen if you stick with this. Anyone capable of killing a bunch of kids isn't going to think twice about killing a reporter and her friend. *Me* being said friend.

"I'm willing to give up all I know, but then I have to back off. From here on in, you're going to have to forget you know me. I have to think about my wife and kids. Your call, Tessie."

Tessie eyed her friend across the table. She'd never seen him this *frightened*. The Slick she knew didn't have a bone of fear in his body except maybe when it came to one of his kids. For one wild moment she wanted to heed his warning, grab her bag, and run, but the reporter in her wouldn't allow it. She offered up a salute to Elvis as she nodded to Slick. "Lay it on me, big guy!"

Morgan blitzed his way down the highway, knowing he had to ditch the Land Cruiser and heist another set of wheels. An all-night supermarket was the most likely place, he told himself. He was rattled, and he admitted it to himself. He still couldn't believe he'd gotten away with that show he'd put on back at the academy. But he was on borrowed time and he knew it.

He had to get back to the Daniel Marley house so he could fall back and regroup. No way was he ever going to get another chance at the school and the kid. If the snot was half as smart as he seemed to be, he was already long gone. This whole thing was getting way too dicey for Morgan. He needed to distance himself from the whole scene as soon as possible. He knew how to disappear. The others involved could stay and pick up the pieces. He'd worry about the damn money later. For now he had to think about saving his own skin and getting rid of this vehicle.

Morgan was careful to stay within the speed limit so as not to attract any attention to himself. Twenty minutes into the ride, he spotted a twenty-four-hour supermarket. He pulled in, cruising up and down the aisles as he looked for the darkest section of the parking lot. Near the Dumpster was a battered rust-colored Chevy just begging to be stolen. Hell, he'd be doing the owner a favor if he hot-wired it and drove it away. He parked the Land Cruiser at the opposite end of the parking lot and, with all his gear, walked back to the Chevy, which was just waiting for him, without drawing any attention to himself.

Morgan was back on the highway in less than ten minutes. Fifteen minutes from the Marley house, he stopped at a farm store where he bought two six-packs, six burritos, and a copy of the *Chronicle*. He asked for a shopping bag, paid for his purchases, and was quickly back on the road. Two blocks from his house, he ditched the Chevy and carried his belongings with him as he jogged all the way to his house.

Morgan fell into his well-trained soldier mode as he carried his weapons to the basement to secure them. He hung his suit in the closet, careful to pull the zipper of the storage bag all the way to the top so no dust could invade the quality suit. His shoes went on shoe trees, his underwear and shirt in the hamper. He showered, dressed in a baggy T-shirt and flannel pants. He walked barefoot back to the kitchen, where he wolfed down all six of the burritos and washed them all away with three beers.

He felt calmer, more alert, and not nearly as hyper. He flipped open the newspaper to see what was going on in the world. On page three he found what he was looking for. His jaw dropped, his eyes popped, and his fist shot upward.

The pot of gold at the end of the rainbow.

Well, damn.

No, double damn!

This time both clenched fists shot into the air.

Chapter 19

The television was on, the sound low, and the remains of a late-night room service dinner sat on the table. Winston was curled up on the couch next to Lily and Pete, who were cuddling in the corner. Pete was stroking Lily's hair. She smelled like summer and warm sunshine rolled up together. After all these years he'd found her. The gods were truly smiling down on him. He gave her a little squeeze. Lily snuggled even closer.

"I'm sorry, Lily. For so many things. Right now this all seems to be about me and the boy. We haven't even touched on your . . . you. I just want you to know when we find Josh, we're moving into high gear and will find all of them, and we'll start with you and any children you might have out there. I just want you to know I never make a promise I can't keep. The fact that you haven't said one word about your needs is mind-blowing to me."

"Pete, it's okay. Right now, Josh is the most important thing to both of us. My turn will come soon enough. But, I think we need to be realistic and recognize the fact that all the others . . . We might never be able to find them. We'll do the best we can and hope it's good enough. We have good people watching over us and helping, so we should be grateful for that. Tessie won't let us down. I just feel that in my gut. As a woman, with a woman's intuition, I feel the boy is going to be okay. Josh is smart, Pete. Look at what he's accomplished so far. If he stays focused, he's going to come out of this okay. Now, let's talk about something else for a little while. Tell me about your ranch in Montana."

Pete chuckled. "It's great, Lily. Big Sky Country. The cleanest, clearest air in the whole world. The house is pretty big. Six thousand square feet. Perfect for a bunch of kids and animals. Speaking of animals. I have a herd of cows and nine horses there. Plus two barns and one milk barn—everything is electric and climate-controlled. In a separate building I have an indoor tennis court and a heated pool, a Jacuzzi, and a steam room. The main house has a state-of-the-art kitchen. Open beams with green plants growing all over them and up the fireplace. It has one of those racks that hangs over the island with dozens of copper pots and pans. Latest appliances. You can actually cook in the fireplace. Out-of-this-world bathrooms, stone with waterfalls and recessed lighting that makes you look really good. The floors are heated throughout the house. The master bedroom is actually a suite that's bigger than this whole villa. The views from all the windows are totally breathtaking. They tell me that's what women look for in a house. A glorious deck that surrounds the house for summer pleasure. The house has six fireplaces, all fieldstone. You could roast an ox in any one of them.

"The only thing it lacks is a woman's touch. At the moment there's lots of leather in the place. I guess the decorator believes that myth that men like deep dark leather furnishings. I think it's kind of cold in the winter. You might want to change all that."

Lily snuggled even closer. "It sounds wonderful. I can't wait to see it. How often do you get to go out there?"

Pete laughed so loud Winston woke up, then looked around and went back to sleep. "I went once for the grand opening. Stayed a day and a half. The decorator and builder were a little miffed at me, but I had to get back to work. Oh, did I tell you it has its own helicopter pad? I have one of those, do you?" He made it sound like he was bragging about a new vacuum cleaner.

Lily giggled. "You're just showing off. Don't want one of those, the rotors mess up your hair when they're twirling around. Nope, I just have a company plane."

"Winston loves going up in the twirly bird. He can even buckle his seat belt. He's going to love living out there in God's country. Do you know how to bake pies, Lily?"

"Doesn't everyone? The short answer is *yes*. What's your favorite?"

"Banana cream, followed by strawberry rhubarb and after that blackberry, and I really love blueberry."

"So, most any kind of pie will do, is that it?"

Pete chuckled. "That pretty much sums it up. What's your favorite food?"

"Anything Italian. I make a pretty mean lasagna. Well, I used to. I haven't cooked much lately."

"No kidding. Anytime I have a choice, I pick Italian food, and second, Japanese."

Lily sat upright. "No kidding! I love Japanese food."

"God Almighty, do you have any idea how lucky we are that we found each other?" Awe rang in Pete's voice.

"I know. I think about it every second. We should go to bed, Pete. It's late. What's on our agenda for tomorrow?"

"I don't have a clue. I guess it pretty much depends on what Tessie comes up with. Now that the boy is gone, I don't have a clue where he might go. He's probably hitchhiking to Outer Mongolia. Kids today are fearless. He could be lost to me, Lily."

"Don't even *think* that, Pete. That kid isn't going anywhere far. He's going to stick around to see how this all plays out. He's gone to ground. That means he has survival skills of some kind. I think in the end, he's going to find us, not the other way around. It's a gut feeling, but it feels right to me."

"Let's go for a walk, Lily. I always like to walk around my yard at home before I go to bed. Looking at the stars relaxes me."

"Do you make a wish?" Lily teased.

"Always. For as long as I can remember, I've wished that I would find the right person to spend my life with. I always wish that I can be as happy as my parents. I think you'll like my mom and dad. I know they'll love you. They're simple people, Lily. Stuff, big bank accounts, fancy cars—none of that means a thing to them. My mom lives for the county fair where she can enter her quilts and jam. She always wins. My dad's passion in life is fixing tractors and tinkering with his pickup truck. Growing up, I remember how his dream was to someday own a John Deere tractor. You know what, Lily, he cried the day I showed up with one. My dad cried. This great big guy who looks like a bear, hugged me and cried. Jesus, in that one minute, I would have tried to climb to the heavens to get him the moon and the stars if I could have.

"When I had a car dealer deliver a brand-new truck, he sent it back and called me up to tell me I shouldn't waste my money like that. It was the fact that he called long-distance that made me sit up and take notice. My parents do not, ever, ever, make long-distance calls, so I had to bite the bullet and accept his decision. Mom, now, that's a different story. She didn't have one bit of trouble accepting the Ford Thunderbird so she wouldn't have to depend on my dad to drive her around. She wears her apron when she drives it. Don't ask!" Pete laughed.

"I love them already. You said something about a walk . . ."

Josh backtracked his way to town as he kept up a running conversation with Tom.

"I have to find a telephone book. I know that Mr. Dickey lived in the Castle Gate Apartments, but that's all I remember. Maybe I should take a taxi if I can find the address."

"Maybe you shouldn't. Never leave a trail if you can help it, Josh. Taxi drivers log their trips. You're going to have to hoof it. Look for an all-night fast-food joint. There's bound to be a phone booth with a phone book. Someone inside will probably be able to give you directions. You have to do this in the dark, buddy. Once it gets light out, you're a sitting duck."

"Yeah, yeah, you're right. I'm really tired, Tom. I don't know how much longer I can keep this up."

"Sounds to me like you're whining, Josh. Knock it off. Look, there's a hot dog stand. C'mon, look smart now, pick up your feet, and move. Stop shuffling. Get some hot food, coffee. That'll wake you up. You need to be alert from here on in."

Josh did as ordered. He tripped up to the Hot-dog Haven and headed straight for the phone booth at the end of the building. He cussed under his breath when he realized the lightbulb was burned out in the booth.

"Look alive here, buddy, it's not the end of the world. You have the penlight in your pocket. Did you forget that?"

"Yeah, I did forget." Within minutes, Josh had

the tattered book up on the skimpy shelf and was leafing through the pages. He sucked in his breath as he rolled the little light down the pages. He almost blacked out when he saw the name he was looking for: Dickey, A, 9 Castle Gate Apartments.

"Got it, Tom. Boy, what a relief. What time is it?"

"I don't know, Josh. I told you, time here is irrelevant. Go get some food and coffee. Looks like an older man behind the counter. He can probably give you directions. You have to keep moving. Hey, get the works on the hot dog. Relish, onions, mustard, sauerkraut, and chili."

In spite of himself, Josh laughed. "I'll keel over if I eat that."

"Humor me, buddy. Sheila wants one, too."

The hot dog stand was almost deserted except for two men who Josh thought might be hobos or street people. He stepped up to the counter and ordered two dogs with the works and a large black coffee.

Josh watched the older man with the crippled hands as he fixed the hot dogs and handed them over. Why was such an old man working in the middle of the night? He made a mental note to ask Tom, who knew everything. Josh paid for his food and waited for his change.

The man's hands shook as he counted out Josh's change. He looked like a grandfather. "Sir, do you know where Castle Gate Apartments are?"

The man's voice shook almost as much as his hands. "Sure do, young fella. I live there. In the cheap seats. Two sections, one for people with more money, then the other one for people like me on a limited income. What number are you looking for?"

"Apartment 9."

"That's where I live. I'm in 16. I can make you a map while you eat your food. It's not far. Did your car break down or something?"

"No, I don't have a car. I'm looking for a friend to spend a few days with. How far is 'not far'?"

"Maybe three miles. A young fella like you can get there in no time. Eat your food before it gets cold. I just cooked those wieners a few minutes ago, so they're fresh."

Josh savored every bite of food in front of him while Tom kept up a running commentary about everything and nothing. The coffee was so strong and bitter, he felt as if his eyeballs were about to stand at attention.

The two homeless people shuffled toward the counter, where Josh could hear them thanking the man behind the counter. They called him Charlie. Somehow or other, Josh thought the man named Charlie gave the two men free food. He hoped he was right.

Josh finished his coffee and carried his trash to the container by the front door. He walked back to the counter and waited patiently until Charlie handed over the map that would take him to Adam Dickey's apartment.

"Thank you very much, sir."

"You're welcome, young fella. We had some excitement at the Gate a while back. One of the tenants was shot and killed at the school where he worked. The FBI came out and talked to all of us. The manager was pretty upset. She said she wouldn't be able to rent out the apartment if people found that out. Those fancy boys told her she couldn't rent it out anyway because, while it wasn't a crime scene exactly, it had to do with a crime scene. At least that's what I think he said," Charlie said fretfully.

"So, it's not rented?"

"No, one of my neighbors told me the man who lived there was paid up for six months, and the FBI knows that. They told Clarissa, she's the manager, if she tried renting the apartment before the rent ran out, they'd throw her in jail. They had that yellow tape all over the place. It's not there anymore, though. Don't know if kids took it down or if the FBI took it down."

Six months. He could hide out for six months. Not likely. Josh thanked the man for the information and the map. At the last second, he handed over a dollar for a tip.

Outside in the dark, Josh looked down at the map and started off.

"*Sometimes you just step in a bucket of luck, right, buddy?*"

"Yeah. But three miles is a hike in the middle of the night. Cops are patrolling like crazy," Josh said.

"*Just look like you know where you're going. If anyone stops you, you have a destination in mind, 9 Castle Gate Apartments, or you could say 16 Castle Gate. You aren't doing anything wrong, just walking to a destination. How were the hot dogs?*"

"Terrible. You wouldn't have liked them. That coffee was so strong and bitter it curled the hair on my chest."

"Liar, liar, pants on fire—you don't have any hair on your chest," Tom said. *"I'm up for a jog, how about you? Sheila is going to get there before us. Boy, can she run! You gonna let a girl beat us?"*

"Not likely!" Josh called on all his energy and sprinted off. Thirty minutes later he skidded to a stop, his breathing shallow, at the entrance to the Castle Gate Apartments.

Even in the dark there was nothing appealing about the apartment complex. Dead brown grass could be seen under the halogen lighting. Rusted wagons, bicycles without wheels, and assorted broken-down toys littered the small patches of lawn in front of most of the apartments. Junkyard cars were everywhere, some minus doors. Most with flat tires. Josh just knew wild animals lived in these rat traps.

"Okay, get the ice pick ready so you don't have to hang out too long by the front door. Go in and don't turn on any lights. I betcha if you just give the pick a few twists the door will fly open."

Tom was wrong. It took four twists of the pick and lots of jiggling before the door swung open. Josh was inside in a heartbeat. He thought he could smell Old Spice aftershave or cologne, something Mr. Dickey wore all the time.

"Let your eyes get accustomed to the dark before you walk around. The walls in this place are probably paper-thin. You don't want to make any noise. Get out your penlight and shine it downward. All the blinds are pulled, and I didn't see anyone outside, so

I think you're probably safe. You can take a shower before you go to sleep. I like the fact that there's a dead bolt on the inside of the door. Once you lock the door, no one can get in. Okay, okay, you can move now. Leave your shoes by the door so you don't track in any dirt. Cops look for stuff like that."

Josh walked through the small apartment, surprised at how neat and tidy it was. The furniture in the living room, while there wasn't much of it, was nice and looked comfortable. A big-screen television covered one wall and there was a DVD player. The bedroom surprised him. Bigger than the living room, it had a king-size bed, a large double dresser with a double mirror, a comfortable chair, and a second TV.

Josh moved the penlight and was startled to see the framed picture on the double dresser. "Look at this, Tom. It's Mr. Dickey and Miss Carmody. He has his arm around her. Do you think . . . ?"

"Yeah, he was sweet on her. Most everyone knew it. We talked about it, Josh. Didn't you notice they were always making moon eyes at each other? You can look at all this later and think about it. Take a shower so the people sleeping next door don't hear the water running. You don't know who goes to work during the day and who stays home. I'm sure Mr. Dickey has some clothes that will fit you."

"Damn, Tom, I don't think I can wear a dead guy's clothes. Especially his underwear."

"Get over it. You're in the outside world now. You have to adapt and do what you have to do. We're talking about your survival, Josh."

"Okay, okay, but I don't like it. I don't know if

I can sleep in his bed either. Jeez, what if they . . .
you know . . ."

*"Had sex in the bed? It's a given they did. Get over
it. You need sleep, so move. Before you know it, the
sun will be up."*

"I really liked Mr. Dickey. I don't feel right
about any of this," Josh muttered as he stepped
into the shower. He lathered up, washed his hair
and rinsed, then did it all over again. A towel
wrapped around his middle, he padded out to
the bedroom and started to go through Adam
Dickey's drawers. He found a pair of pajamas
that smelled just like their former owner. He
winced when he put them on, but when nothing
happened, he shrugged. "I'm sorry," he mumbled.

Suddenly he wasn't as sleepy as he'd been
when he had first entered the apartment. He
used the time to munch on the cheese in his
bag as he rifled through the teacher's drawers.

"Hey, look at this, Tom. Mr. Dickey had a
passport. He'd never used it. Do you think
maybe he was going to go on a honeymoon?"

"Maybe."

"There's $260 in an envelope. I guess I have
to steal it. For sure I'm going to go to hell for all
this stuff I'm doing." Josh moved on to the
closet, where he checked the contents. A ring of
heat spread around his neck when he recognized some of Miss Carmody's clothes hanging
next to Mr. Dickey's.

His head whirling and twirling, Josh headed
over to the huge king-size bed and pulled down
the covers. It looked like the sheets were clean

and fresh. He sniffed them. They smelled like detergent. He sighed with relief as he settled himself between the covers. "Keep watch, Tom, okay?"

"You know it, buddy. Sweet dreams."

Chapter 20

Walking hand in hand, Pete and Lily, Winston at their side, walked past Zolly's villa. Winston stopped when the big man loped down the path to confront the late-night strollers.

"This is a no-no, boss."

Pete sighed. "Don't you ever sleep, Zolly? We're just strolling before turning in. Winston's with us. It's three thirty in the morning. You should be in bed."

The big man reached down to stroke Winston's head. "The short answer is no, I don't sleep. How can I when you keep breaking the rules? Will you be returning to your own villa or the one next door?"

Lily grinned in the darkness as she waited for Pete's reply.

"I'm going to pretend you didn't ask me that. Good night, Zolly."

As they walked along, Lily sniffed at the fragrant evening. How lush all the flowers were, how deeply scented, how perfect everything seemed to be in the quiet of the night. The sky was star-spangled, some of the stars winking at her as she gazed upward. She searched for and found the Big Dipper and the Little Dipper and smiled to herself. A childhood thing. Almost perfect. She took a moment to wonder if things were ever actually perfect. Probably not, she decided.

Pete waited till they were out of sight of the villa and Zolly before he said, "I don't know how to tell Zolly he won't be going to Montana with us. I put a retirement package in place for him, but he's going to fight me. So will the board. Winston will miss him, that's for sure. I just want to be John Q. Citizen again. God, if you only knew how anxious I am to get out there and start a new life."

"I think I know, Pete. Zolly will adapt. What's that noise?"

Winston backed up and raced off, leaving little clumps of grass in his wake. "Must be a rabbit or something," Pete muttered. Seconds later when the noise grew louder, he added, "Or an elephant."

"I hear voices," Lily whispered.

Pete reached for Lily's hand as they ran off, trampling through the flower beds. The grass was covered with dew, soaking through their sandals. Pete stopped short when he was within eyesight of the villa. He jerked Lily backward and hissed, "It's Tessie. Listen."

Both Pete and Lily stepped deeper into the shrubbery as they unabashedly listened to the conversation.

"So, big guy, what—are you some kind of vampire, or do you always walk around with a gun at three thirty in the morning?"

"What are you doing here at this hour, Miz Dancer?"

"If I told you that, I'd have to kill you. Where's your boss?"

"That's NTK, in other words, need to know, Miz Dancer. The boss didn't tell me he was expecting visitors. He always tells me when visitors are expected. That means you were not expected, so you need to leave. Like now."

This last was said so defensively, Pete found himself grinning. His money at the moment was on Tessie.

"What are you? A nanny, a babysitter, a squatter, or just a royal pain in the ass? Get your boss and stop jerking my chain."

"Ladies shouldn't talk like that. Ladies are supposed to be refined. And, for your information, I am a security guard. The board of directors of PAK Industries has entrusted the care of Mr. Kelly to me. I take my responsibilities very seriously. Now, get on your broom and fly off and come back after breakfast but be sure to call for an appointment." Zolly waved his gun for emphasis.

Lily clamped her hand over her mouth to keep from laughing. Pete stomped his feet in the wet grass. Zolly had met his match.

"Is that big old bad gun supposed to scare me? I could take you out right now and not even break a sweat. Wanna see me do it?"

"You and what army?" Zolly sputtered.

"No army. Just me. Well?"

Tessie reached into her bag and brought out a cigarette. She stuck it between her lips, then talked around it. "See this cigarette? It isn't really a cigarette, it's a dart. If I blow it right at your privates, woo-hoo, you're out for . . . like . . . a long time. And then you'll never be the same again. In . . . uh . . . that area. What we have here is a stalemate. Now, where in the hell is your boss? My patience just ran out."

Winston whined and nudged Zolly's leg, which meant, give in already.

Before Zolly knew what was happening, the reporter was pressed up against him, then she was kissing him so hard he thought he was going to black out.

Winston yelped and pawed the ground at these strange goings-on.

"That's to remember me by and do not, I repeat, do not, ever try to tell me you've been kissed like that in your whole life. Now, again, where in the hell is your boss? I have business with him. You . . . I'll get back to you later, and we can pick up where we left off."

Winston pushed hard against Zolly's leg to get him to turn around. When that didn't work, he ran back to where Pete and Lily were desperately trying not to laugh. He tugged at Pete's pants leg to get him to move.

"Whatever you do, Lily, do not let either one of them know we heard what just went on," Pete hissed. "Let's go now and pretend we just got here."

Pete stepped out of the shadows, pulling Lily

behind him. "I thought I heard voices," he said. "Tessie, what a nice surprise. Lily and I just took a stroll since it's such a nice night. Come in, come in. Good night, Zolly."

"Don't mind him. He just had a life-altering experience. He'll be okay by morning. Nice doggie, take Mr. Zolly back to his lair while your master and I have a conversation." Tessie giggled.

The shepherd eyed the big woman, listened to her tone of voice, and decided it was in his best interest to obey the order. He pushed and growled until Zolly finally moved in the direction of his villa. Winston then marched forward to Lily's villa and waited for her to open the door.

Pete led the parade straight to the sitting area. "What's up?"

His voice sounded so anxious, Tessie patted his arm to reassure him. "Which do you want first, the bad news or the terribly bad news?"

"Does it matter, Tessie?"

"No, I guess it doesn't matter. My source is extremely upset at what he says we are mixed up in. This particular source is pretty unflappable, but he was flapping big-time this evening when I met with him. He wouldn't part with any of his information until I told him who you were. Once I told him it was you and Lily, he was okay with telling me what he found out because he said you two could take care of yourselves because you're so high-profile."

"What . . . what did he find out?" Lily asked.

"That minihospital attached to the fertility

clinic. It seems nineteen years ago, which is our time frame, there was a surrogate program. He managed to track down one of the surrogates. They were artificially inseminated, monitored for nine months, then gave birth at the fertility clinic. This particular surrogate was paid fifty thousand dollars. It was all legal. Lawyers and all. My source traced one of the lawyers, but found he died three years ago. The lawyer's widow was less than forthcoming, and she's old now and in frail health. Still, the proper authorities can have a go at her when the time is right."

"Well, where the hell did the children go?" Pete demanded.

"My source doesn't know. He hit a blank wall. He has suspicions. He thinks the lawyer's widow knows. The surrogate might know, but she clammed up because she has a family now and doesn't want them to know what she did back then. My source thinks it was a ring back then for . . . nefarious purposes."

Pete sucked in his breath. "What . . . what kind of nefarious purposes?" He could feel Lily start to tremble next to him. He put his arm around her as they both waited for Tessie's response.

"Human testing of some kind, which was probably illegal. Guinea pigs, for want of a better term. I don't know, Pete. What I do know is if they were paying fifty thousand dollars to a surrogate to deliver a baby, the return on that money would have to be substantial. Do the math. The one thing I can tell you for certain is your, uh . . . donations did not go to childless couples, directly or indirectly, as you were led to believe. There is absolutely no record of that anywhere, and if there was, my source would have found it."

"Are . . . is the school involved in some way? Did your source find out who owns the sperm bank, the fertility clinic, and the school?"

"Yes and no. It's a consortium. Four organizations. Well, that's not quite true, it's four individuals from very wealthy organizations. Three foreign and one American. The American is the one who calls the shots because the sperm bank and fertility clinic are here in California. There are other schools besides the California Academy of Higher Learning."

Pete leaned across the table, his eyes blazing in the lamplight. "Do you have a name for the American?"

"My source has it. He wouldn't give it to me for what he said was my own good. He said even you, Pete, as high-profile as you are, are not immune to this guy's power."

"That's bullshit! Are you afraid, Tessie?"

Tessie thought about the question. " 'Afraid' isn't the right word. 'Cautious' might be a word I'd choose. The man I'm thinking of is ruthless. Having said that, even ruthless people have an Achilles' heel. I've found over the years in my line of work that there are more ways than one to skin a cat."

"Do you *think* you know who it is, Tessie?" Lily asked.

"I think I have a pretty good idea, and my source is right—he's as powerful as they come."

"Is there anything we can do to get to him?" Pete asked.

"Do you mean like having a Plan A, B, or maybe C? I have to think about it. I rushed over here to tell you as soon as I got myself together. This is one of those rare times when you have to take a step backward and think about the repercussions of continuing. I can handle my end of it, I am a reporter. My paper, now, that's a different story. I want to say *yes,* but I do have some reservations. Like I said, Pete, I want to think about this a little more."

"Who is it, Tessie? C'mon, this involves my kid, and, yeah, he's mine, and I'll never believe otherwise. Even if he wasn't my kid, I'd still be standing here talking to you and pleading my case," Pete said.

"Why don't we just say for the moment if it is the guy I'm thinking it is, he has many friends in high places and can waltz in and out of 1600 Pennsylvania Avenue any time of the day or night."

Diesel Morgan stepped off the red-eye and headed for the restroom, where he washed his face and ran the razor over the stubble on his cheeks and his now-bald head that he'd shaved before leaving the Daniel Marley house.

Traveling as David Mason, he wore a conservative Armani suit that hung exquisitely on his lean frame. He pulled a fresh white shirt and tie out of a carry-on that he would ditch the minute no one was looking. He stared into the huge mirror until he was satisfied with his image before he departed the men's room in search of breakfast.

Two cups of coffee, six pancakes, three eggs, and assorted bacon and sausage later, Morgan felt prepared enough to hail a taxi to take him to his employer's prestigious home in Georgetown. He felt giddy as he anticipated the look on the man's face when he stepped into what Morgan knew would be an elegant home. Yessireee, the pot of gold at the end of the rainbow.

He'd been able to learn his employer's schedule by finding an article by a *Washington Post* political reporter who had been given access to the man's daily routine, so Morgan knew what he needed to know. Morgan looked at his watch. He had a good thirty-three minutes until his quarry would step out of his house, all pressed and smelling good, and into the waiting limo that picked him up every morning to take him to his office, where he toiled to make the world a better place to live.

Before he headed for parts unknown, Morgan made a promise to himself that he would kill the guy to save the world from his bullshit. Yeah, yeah, that's what he'd do, then he'd send a letter to every newspaper in the country telling them about his act of generosity.

The moment the taxi cruised to a stop outside a redbrick Colonial house on P Street, Morgan handed the driver a fifty-dollar bill and told him to keep the change. He walked up the brick path leading to the front door and rang the bell. A Hispanic-looking maid complete with gray uniform, white apron, and some kind of fancy white lace thing on her head opened the door.

"Yes?"

"I have an appointment," Morgan said, shouldering his way inside past the startled maid and made his way to the dining room, where he knew his quarry would be having coffee.

"Good morning, sir. I thought I'd join you for a cup of coffee. You might want to call your driver to tell him you're running late this morning. Do it!" Morgan said, steel ringing in his voice.

"*Señor, señor,* you cannot . . . sir, he . . ."

"It's all right, Consuelo. Fetch some coffee for my guest and call my driver and tell him I'm running late."

The man was livid and trying to control his emotions. But, he appeared unafraid. Morgan thought that very strange. He wondered if something was going on that he didn't know about. Like all things, he'd just have to play it by ear.

"I told you we were never to meet. What part of that didn't you understand?"

Morgan propped his elbows on the linen-covered table, with its array of silver-domed plates and crystal. The rich really did know how to live. "The part where I do what you say when you say it. Our contract didn't specify details like that, as you well know. I came here to tell you that I cannot fulfill the second half of our contract. I thought I owed you that much. I did try, but the FBI got in the way, not to mention that computer guy. Your ass is in a sling, mister, and they're closing in on you. I also wanted to tell you I am not returning your money. So, if you have anything to say, say it now before I leave. Oh, there is one other thing I want to show you in case you get any funny ideas."

The maid entered the dining room through a swinging door that Morgan assumed led into the kitchen. She placed an exquisite china cup in front of him. He waited until the door swung shut behind her before he spoke again.

"Listen to this," Morgan said as he shoved his arm next to the man's ear.

The man's face drained. "Shut that thing off. What do you want?"

"Ten million dollars wired to the Caymans will buy my silence. Wired within the next ten minutes. And the contract canceled. Your word will do. Consider it collateral damage. No questions asked. For whatever it's worth, the kid is gone. Will he resurface at some point? I don't know, and I don't care. Your people did not have good intel, and that's why things didn't go according to plan. You're on your own now. Sir," Morgan added as an afterthought, "do we agree on all of this? A simple *yes* or *no* will satisfy me."

"Very well."

"I'm going to take that as a *yes*," Morgan said as he pressed a button on his wrist. "I can see myself out. I think I'd be remiss, sir, if I didn't tell you that if I were you, I'd get the hell out of Dodge."

The man's zany laughter floated around the dining room as the single diner pounded his fist on the table in frustration. "Bastard!" he seethed.

Chapter 21

Josh woke to a sound he couldn't immediately identify. He lay still and listened intently. Rain! Hard-driving rain beating at the windows. His tense muscles relaxed until he remembered he was sleeping in Adam Dickey's bed. He hopped out at the speed of light.

"Where are you, Tom?"

"Right here, buddy. It's just rain, don't go getting spooked. You can't go anywhere anyway. You're socked in until this evening. What's your game plan?"

"I don't have a game plan. I'd need a computer and a telephone to have a game plan. Do you have any ideas?"

"Maybe. Sort of. More or less. Didn't that guy from Hotdog Haven tell those homeless people he was working the day shift today?"

"Yeah, I did hear him say that."

"Well?"

Josh's mind raced. "You want me to break into his apartment at Number 16 and use his phone, is that it?"

"*He might have a computer. You could leave some money for the use of those things. It's not like you're breaking and entering to steal or destroy his apartment. I think you could do it and get away with it. It's really raining hard. No one will be paying attention to anyone out in the rain. It's worth a shot, Josh. You have to get dressed and check this place out. Who knows, maybe Mr. Dickey left some clues here that will help us.*"

Josh was already in the kitchen checking out the refrigerator. He found some yogurt that was past the due date, two oranges that were still edible, and a package of English muffins. Josh ate it all and washed it down with two bottles of water.

The kitchen was neat and tidy, just like Mr. Dickey. It was obvious by just looking around that Adam Dickey was not a collector of anything. He had a set of dishes for four, one fry pan, two pots, and silverware for four. There were four glasses in one of the cabinets, some boxed crackers and canned soup. The rest of the cupboards were empty.

Josh sat down on one of the kitchen chairs as a feeling of grief came over him. He had really liked Mr. Dickey, who'd told Josh so many things about the outside world, things he said Josh would need to know when he went off on his own. "Always be courteous," Mr. Dickey had said. "Never do anything to anyone you wouldn't want done to you." "Always treat women like the ladies they are and respect them." "Be kind to your elders and all animals." "Work hard and save for a rainy day." "Never judge people, only God can do that."

"What's wrong, Josh?"

"I was just thinking about how nice Mr. Dickey was and how good he was to all of us. I'm sorry he's dead, and I'm sorry I'm here using his things. Do you think he had any family?"

"He said he was an orphan. Miss Carmody was an orphan, too, I do remember that. I guess that's why they got along so well. Why, is it important?"

"Maybe. It doesn't seem right that no one is claiming his things. I know it isn't much, but someone out there should want them. I would if I could. It bothers me that he died the way he did, and now people will just throw his things away. If that happens, no one will remember him but me. It's not right. He didn't say anything about this kind of stuff going on in the real world."

"Yeah, I know. Remember how he used to tell us that every day would be a new experience, and we'd have to adapt a little bit at a time? Okay, enough of this, let's get to it and make a plan. Get dressed and make it snappy, Number 8446."

Josh ran to the closet, pulled out pants and shirts, and didn't stop to think about dressing in his teacher's clothes, which were a little too small, and his sneakers, which were a little too big. But it all worked. At the last second, he reached for a hooded zip-up sweat jacket and carried it to the kitchen with him. "Where are you, Number 8211?"

"Right here. So, what's the game plan?"

"Like I said, I need a phone and a computer. What do you think about me calling a newspaper and telling my story to a reporter? They won't know where I'm calling from. I can ask questions, get a sense of what's going on. Reporters on television never tell about the people who give them scoops."

"Their sources," Tom volunteered. *"Reporters go to jail to protect their sources. Good thinking, Number 8446. I bet that guy Charlie gets a newspaper. You can pick a reporter out of it and call. Remember, though, there's that thing called 'caller ID.' The person you're calling can see where the call is coming from. Keep that in mind."*

"Okay, Tom. Boy, I don't know what I'd do without you."

"You'd manage. It's time to go. You want to get in and out before Charlie gets back from work. Do you have the ice pick? Where's the book?"

"I have both on my person. I'm ready. Should I go out the kitchen door or the front door?"

"The back door, you goose. Why call attention to yourself?"

Ten minutes later, soaked to the skin, Josh was twisting the ice pick into Charlie's lock. The tumblers clicked, and the door slid open. Josh rushed inside. A small lamp was burning on a table in the living room. The blinds and curtains were closed. Josh sniffed as he tried to identify the smell that seemed to be all over the apartment. He finally identified it as BENGAY, the same junk he used to rub on the calves of his legs after a hard hurdling session. He realized he hated the smell.

It was a cluttered apartment, with stacks of newspapers and magazines on all the tables. Empty coffee cups and candy wrappers littered the kitchen table, along with a lot of crumbs. Charlie needed a wife, Josh decided. He sighed with relief when he saw a yellow phone hanging on the wall in the kitchen. Now, if he could just be lucky enough to find a computer, he'd be all set.

Josh spied a stackable washer and dryer in the kitchen. He peeled off his wet clothes and stuck them in the dryer. He padded around in Mr. Dickey's underwear to check out the bathroom, which was neat and clean, then went to the bedroom, whose bed was unmade. In the corner were a card table and a wooden chair. He closed his eyes in relief when he saw the computer. He checked it out and was glad it was a newer model. He turned it on and sat down.

Ever mindful of the time element, Josh quickly scanned the headlines in all the newspapers, then logged on to the identity he'd created at the library to see if he had any e-mails. There were none. So the FBI didn't want to be bothered with him. Obviously, the police thought he was a weirdo because they hadn't answered either. He was angry as he typed out an e-mail to each of them informing them that he had records that were going to be turned over to the *Chronicle*. He then did a Google search and fired off another e-mail to CNN.

"That'll work," Tom said.

"No, it won't. Don't you get it, Tom, they don't care? They probably get tips like this all the time and don't have the manpower to follow up. I think our best bet is going to the newspapers. I can send an e-mail instead of calling. What do you think?"

"What I think is if you e-mail, you might not be able to get back in here to check the e-mail for a response, whereas if you call, you have a real person on the other end of the phone. I vote for the phone call. If they trace the call, Charlie won't know a thing about it when they show up to question him. If you need to make a second call, you'll have to use a phone booth or buy one of those throwaway phones. Find a paper and pick a reporter."

Josh turned off the computer and pushed the chair back to its original position. Charlie would never know that his territory had been intruded upon.

Yesterday's edition of the *Chronicle* was on top of the pile. Josh scrutinized it carefully and finally whittled down his list of possible reporters to call. He looked around for a piece of paper and a pencil. He found a pencil next to a crossword puzzle that seemed to have stymied Charlie, since it wasn't finished. Josh couldn't help himself, he finished it and made a star at the top of the puzzle. He then ripped a corner off one of the older newspapers and wrote down his short list: Desmond Quigley, Amanda Summers, Phil Coster, and Tessie Dancer. "Which one would be your choice, Tom?"

"Think Captain Queeg. Amanda sounds like a flirt. Phil sounds like a fuddy-duddy. Tessie Dancer

sounds like she's got it going on. I think I'd go with her. What do you think?"

"Tessie Dancer it is." Five minutes later Josh had the main number for the *Chronicle*. He dialed the number and asked for Tessie Dancer. He almost fainted when he heard a female voice announce her name—"Tess Dancer. What can I do for you today?"

"Miss Dancer, this is Josh Baer. I'd like to talk to you about . . . some . . . some things. Will whatever I tell you be held in confidence?"

"Josh Baer! The kid from the academy?" Tessie bolted upright in her chair, the power bar in her hand all but forgotten. She quickly snapped on her recorder, and said, "A reporter is just like a priest. We never give up our sources, and once we give our word, it's golden. I'm giving you mine. Kid, where the hell are you? Everyone and their brother is out there looking for you."

"I can't tell you where I am. I'm okay. I tried to go to the FBI and the police, but they wouldn't help me. Doesn't anyone care about all those kids and teachers that were killed? I don't see anything in the papers or online."

Tessie's heart raced as she tried to come up with something compelling that would keep the boy on the line. "That's because some very powerful people put a lid on it."

"I sent them a picture of the man who did the killings. I didn't see it on the news or in the papers. Where's Jesse?"

"I didn't know that. Can you send it to me? I don't know this for sure, but I think the FBI has

Jesse safe in a secure location. I can try to find out more. How can I reach you?"

"Are you crazy? I can't tell you where I am. I can call you from time to time, but that's it. That crazy guy almost killed me yesterday. He wants me dead because Jesse and I saw him kill all those kids and the teachers. He keeps following me. I don't know how he knows where I am, but he does. He changes the way he looks. And some big guy keeps showing up with a dog and a lady."

"Listen, kid . . . Josh . . . the big guy, the dog, and the lady are the good guys. Trust me on that."

"I'm sorry, Miss Dancer, but I can't trust anyone. I don't even know you. I have a book with all the numbers in it. Me and my friend Tom wrote it all down. Tom and Sheila are dead, and now I have the book. When you catch that guy, I'll turn it over, but only if I'm sure it goes to the right person. You work for a newspaper. Why aren't you writing about the shooting? All those kids are dead, and no one cares. I care, dammit, they were my friends, and now they're dead. They were my brothers and sisters."

"All of them were your brothers and sisters?" *What the hell?*

"Jesse was. I think. They said we were all related. Mr. Dickey . . . Mr. Dickey said that was impossible. Miss Carmody said it could be true. They were going to get married, but no one knew but me and Tom. Now they're dead. Mr. Dickey knew a lot. He was going to quit. I don't know about Miss Carmody. Maybe she was going to quit, too. They killed them. They don't care."

Tessie was beside herself as she struggled to give this tormented boy some kind of hope. "I care, Josh. I really do. I'm working with that tall man with the dog and the lady. He wants to find you desperately."

"Why?" Josh snapped.

Truth or lie? Somewhere in between. Find the right words without scaring the daylights out of the kid. Try to get him to trust you. "He wants to help you. He doesn't live here in California, but he's visiting right now. He's a good man, so is the lady. They were at the school yesterday. The guy doing the shooting shot out their tires. You helped the lady get to the kitchen. She was scared out of her wits."

Josh threw Tessie for a loop when he asked, "Are you a mother?"

"I wish I was, but, no, I am not a mother. I have a mother, though. And a father. I take care of them. Is it important to you for me to be a mother?"

"Mothers are protectors. They don't let bad things happen. Miss Carmody taught us that. She cared about all of us. She used to tell us what it was like to have a family and how families did things."

"Sometimes, Josh, when mothers and fathers get old, the roles reverse, and the children have to take care of them. Do you have a mother or a father?"

"No."

Tessie bit down hard on her tongue. She wanted desperately to tell him he did have a father, but this wasn't the time. Then again, maybe this was the right time.

"Josh, what would you say if I told you I think you do have a father, and I might know who it is?"

"Josh, don't fall for that. We both know we don't have parents. We're artificial kids. She's lying to you to gain your trust. Don't trust her. Hang up right now."

"I don't believe you. If what you said is true, it would have been in the newspapers because that's news. Your newspaper doesn't care about me or the others. No one is looking for that guy who wants to kill me. Tell me I'm wrong, Miss Dancer."

"If it was up to me, Josh, I'd have it plastered all over the front page of the paper and it would be on the news twenty-four/seven. Unfortunately, I just work here. You can trust me. Maybe between the two of us, we can figure out the best way to handle all of this."

Josh broke the connection, his hand shaking when he replaced the phone in its base. *Shit, shit, shit. Now what am I supposed to do?*

"Get out of here right now. Hustle, buddy, and don't forget to leave some money for Charlie."

Josh was almost to the door when he realized he was still in his underwear. He grabbed his clothes from the dryer and dressed. He was back in Mr. Dickey's kitchen within minutes. He was huffing and puffing as he stood in the center of the floor, shaking all over.

"Okay, okay, calm down. Let's talk about this calmly and rationally. That's what Mr. Dickey used to tell us when things got out of hand."

Josh snorted in disgust. "None of that stuff we learned is worth anything. This world is nothing like the make-believe one we were taught. I'm getting scared, Tom. There's no one out here I can trust. What's going to happen now?"

Josh felt like crying when there was no response from Tom.

Chapter 22

When the boy broke the connection, Tessie sat in stupefied amazement as she listened to the tape over and over until she had it virtually committed to memory.

She felt like worms were crawling all over her. She racked her brain for what she could have said, as opposed to what she did say, to Josh Baer to make her feel like this. Why had he called her, of all people, in the first place? She should have asked that. Yes, she'd taped the call, but what good was that going to do her? She would have traced the call, but the paper didn't have those capabilities. The boy had sounded so nervous, so frightened. He mentioned a book. A book he and Tom wrote. What the hell was in the book? Copied files or records? Poor kid. And then that business about her being a mother . . . What did that mean? Whatever it was, it must be important to the boy.

The bottom line was she'd failed the kid. Maybe he'd call back when he replayed the call over in his mind the way she was doing. In her own defense, she thought she'd sounded motherly on the phone. But did her tone ring that way in Josh's ears?

Tessie heaved herself up out of the chair and was halfway to the door when she walked back and sat down. She yanked at her cell phone to call Little Slick. When he picked up, she started to babble. "Look, Slick, I know you said you were walking away from this and I was on my own, but can you do one more thing for me? The boy called me here at the paper. I taped the call but I need to know where the call came from. I know it's a piece of cake for you to find that out. The kid's in mortal danger, Slick. If the situation were reversed, you know I'd move heaven and earth to do it for you." Tessie clinched her little speech with, "He's got no one, Slick, and he reached out to me. Please."

"You're breaking my heart, Tessie. Okay, okay, I'll do it. Give me fifteen minutes, thirty tops, if you want a profile, which I know you do."

Tessie's sigh of relief was so loud she startled herself. She reached into her drawer for a power bar and made a vow to stop eating such crap. Tomorrow she'd bring some raw veggies and crackers. She knew she'd do no such thing, but vowing that she would made her feel better. It was like promising herself she'd go to a gym on Monday morning. On Sunday afternoon it always seemed plausible to make a promise like that to yourself.

With nothing else to occupy her until Slick

called back, Tessie reached for a ragged, tattered picture of a beach house she'd clipped from a travel folder twenty years ago. She referred to it as an incentive to make things work for her and her aging parents, and someday, maybe, she'd be able to retire to something close to what she hungered for in the picture. Just a one- or two-bedroom bungalow on or near the water, pre-ferably on the water. A small garden so she could plant a few vegetables and maybe some flowers. A front porch. Not a deck. A deck was for yuppies. She wanted a front porch with a few rocking chairs. Maybe some potted flowers for color, a few hanging ferns from the beams. A bachelorette home. A big old fireplace, a sunken bathtub. Maybe a pretty kitchen where she could pretend to cook once she learned how. Not that she literally couldn't cook. Anyone could make meat loaf. She had over two hundred recipes for chopped meat. She wanted to branch out, maybe pork chops that were stuffed, rack of lamb, even though she hated lamb. "Come on, you dumb shit, call me. What's taking you so long?" she seethed.

Almost on cue, Tessie's cell phone rang. "Didja get it?"

Slick sighed. "Didja think even for a minute that I wouldn't?"

"No, no, not even for a minute. I owe you my life, Slick. Shoot it to me."

"The call was made from 16 Castle Gate Apart-ments. The phone is listed to a Charles Garri-son, age 73, a widower. He has two sons, one lives in Boston and one lives in Delaware. He has six grandchildren. He's a retired master chief in the navy. He currently works at a place called Hotdog Haven and makes ten bucks an hour. You happy now? Swear to me you won't call me again."

Well, that was certainly more than she needed to know. "I'll try not to. Thanks, Slick."

"Tessie, when are you going to get it through your head you can't save the whole world?"

"The same time you do. We're the good guys, remember?" When Tessie realized she was talking to a dial tone, she hung up.

Tessie turned her computer back on and went to the MapQuest Web site and typed in "16 Castle Gate Apartments." Then she typed in the address of the hotel where Pete Kelly was staying. She printed out the directions, turned off her computer. She took a moment to call home to tell the health aide she wouldn't be home for dinner, then gathered up all her gear for the trip to pick up Pete Kelly. It was almost five o'clock, rush hour. She shuddered at the thought, but it didn't stop her. She had a lot of thinking to do, and what better place to do all that thinking than in her car while stuck in traffic.

Winston heard Tessie's footsteps even before she turned the corner of the path leading to Pete's villa. Zolly appeared out of nowhere and groaned when he saw who the early-evening visitor was.

Tessie marched up to the security guard and stuck her face in his. "Can you tango, big guy?"

"Huh . . . What?" Zolly sputtered.

"Guess that's a *no*. Not a problem, I can teach you. You really need to loosen up. This dog has more finesse than you do, don't you, little fella?"

Winston whimpered as he licked Tessie's hand. "Bet you can't even do the two-step."

"I can fox-trot," Zolly blustered.

Tessie just laughed as she made her way to Pete's villa. She didn't bother to knock but just opened the door and announced herself. "Saddle up, guys. I found the boy. Move, move, move!"

Pete and Lily both stood rooted to the floor. Zolly stood in the open doorway, listening.

"And I have directions," Tessie said, waving the printout for everyone to see.

Awe rang in Pete's voice. "You actually found him! How? When? Are you sure this isn't some false lead? Hey, I'm ready. Let's go."

Lily was as dumbfounded as Pete. She gripped his arm for support. "You didn't call the police or the FBI, did you, Tessie?"

"No way. I really think Zolly should stay here, and we go in one car. No sense spooking the boy. He's going to be watching us. On the drive up here, I knew there was something I was missing. I figured it out when I hit the parking lot. The teacher, Adam Dickey, lived at the Castle Gate Apartments, but my source told me the call came from a phone listed in the name of Charles Garrison. He might be the boy's friend or someone the teacher knew. I just don't recall the number of the apartment for Adam Dickey.

Anyway, that's where the boy is. I should have figured it out sooner but I didn't. I'm sorry. Sometimes my brain goes on overload. I'm driving," Tessie said firmly.

Zolly lumbered into the room. "You can drive, but I'm going. I better not hear another peep out of you, either."

Tessie whipped around. "Why are you being so nice to me all of a sudden?"

Zolly was so befuddled he threw his hands in the air. He thought he was being nasty. "Just make sure you drive the speed limit."

"If you think you're going to tell me what to do, think again, big guy. Is the dog going, too?"

"That's a really stupid question even for you, Miz Smart-ass. The dog goes everywhere we go. We should take the SUV, because there's more room in it. I'll let you drive it," Zolly said.

"I suppose you think I don't know how to handle an SUV. Well, I do, Mister Smart-ass. Can we just leave already?"

Pete and Lily barreled through the door to follow Tessie to the parking lot, where the SUV waited. Zolly tossed Tessie the keys, and she caught them in midair. She unlocked the door.

"Mr. Authority here sits up front, you two and the dog in the back. We all agreed?"

Zolly started to mumble as he strapped himself into the passenger seat in front.

"I hope you aren't one of those people who feels the need to talk when she drives."

"Actually, I do talk when I'm driving. I even taught myself Spanish and Italian from tapes.

I'm studying Greek right now. Being multilingual is a definite asset in my line of work."

Not to be outdone, Zolly said, "I speak Polish, Russian, and Japanese."

In the backseat, Pete and Lily rolled their eyes. "It's the mating dance. They're flirting with each other, and neither one knows it. Well, maybe Tessie knows it. Zolly is a little slow on the uptake," Pete whispered in Lily's ear.

While the give-and-take banter went on in the front seat, Lily leaned closer to Pete, and said in a low voice, "I'm so excited for you, Pete. I know I feel relieved, and know you must feel the same way. We'll get him to safe ground, then the powers that be will have to listen to him and keep him safe. It will happen that way, won't it?"

"If it were a perfect world, yes, it would happen that way. But this is far from a perfect world, Lily. What can go wrong will go wrong. I'm hopeful, though."

"Tessie said he had a book that he and his friend Tom made up. What do you suppose . . . Do you think they know about whatever it is that was going on?"

"Obviously the two of them knew something they thought was important enough to commit to paper. Having said that, the short answer is *yes,* and that's why he's so afraid to trust anyone. I would be, too, if I were in his shoes.

"He's out there all alone fending for himself with no friends. The friends he did have are all dead and only by the grace of God is he still alive. Living in a group home all his life hasn't prepared him for the world as we know it. So far he's doing okay, though. We both know that can change in a heartbeat. I think right now he's getting desperate. Otherwise, he wouldn't have called Tessie. He sees the authorities as the enemy and not to be trusted; and then there's that maniac who's after him. The kid has guts, I can tell you that. I hope to God he is my son. Do you think he is, Lily? Tell me the truth."

"I do, Pete. I really do."

"Well, if he is my son, he's never going to understand any of this. Seventeen-year-olds have minds of their own. When this is all over, and he has to move on, how does he go from what he's known to me? I tried putting myself in his place, and I stunned myself with my reaction."

"What?"

"I'd say to me, 'Go pound salt and get out of my life.' I would be bitter and hateful. He thinks he's artificial. So he knows, or thinks he knows, about the donations, the artificial insemination, the surrogate mothers. He probably knows more than we're giving him credit for."

"Don't go there yet, Pete. And don't sell that kid short either. I see a whole other scenario. Oh, look, Tessie is slowing down. We must be almost there. You ready?"

"As ready as I'll ever be." It was a lie, and Pete knew it. In a million years he could never ready himself for the moment when he would be eyeball-to-eyeball with his son.

* * *

"*What's your problem, Josh? Why are you pacing around like this? You're safe. You have that big-screen TV over there to watch. You're not hungry, and you're not tired. So, why all the pacing? What's the problem?*"

"For one thing, even though it's dark in here and no lamps are on, televisions give off a glow. Someone outside might see it. I should go outside to check it out. I don't think I should have called that lady reporter. I think it was a mistake. I'm scared, Tom, and I don't feel safe here. I think I should leave now, while I can."

"*Where will you go? Besides, it's pouring rain outside. This is as safe as it's gonna get, Number 8446.*"

"I'm going outside to check to see if any light can be seen. You coming with me, or are you staying in here?"

"*Scaredy-cat.*"

"Easy for you to say, you're dead. I don't want to be dead. I want a family, and I can't find one if I'm dead. Don't give me any more of your bullshit either." Josh flicked on the television and watched as a rerun of *Law & Order* came onto the big screen. He ran to the kitchen and out the door, a towel over his head. He sloshed his way around to the front in time to see a big black car turn into the street. He stopped next to a scraggly bush and watched the red lights of the huge vehicle. His blood ran cold when he thought he heard a dog inside the vehicle start to bark.

In this particular section of the apartment complex, there weren't that many operable cars. Most people walked to the bus stop. He'd watched through the curtains earlier in the day. This vehicle was definitely out of place in this area. He strained to see through the rain. He literally stopped breathing when he saw the red taillights stop in front of Charlie's apartment.

Josh waited a moment longer until the car doors opened. He watched four people and a dog get out, the tall man from the library holding on to the dog with a leash. Faster than lightning, Josh ran back inside. The moment the door closed behind him, he started yelling at Tom. "I told you! I told you! They're here. I have to get out of here right now.

"You're pretty damn quiet, Tom. See, you aren't always right! My gut instincts warned me. I saw a slicker in Mr. Dickey's closet. Oh, shit, I forgot to turn off the TV." Josh rushed back to the living room, turned off the TV, then checked the front door to make sure the dead bolt was in place. He ran back to the bedroom, jammed things into a duffel from the floor, pulled on the slicker, and was out the back door in minutes.

Josh knew he had to run, and he had to run fast because the dog had his scent. He knew it as sure as he knew he needed to take another breath to live.

How did they find him? "How'd they find me, Tom?"

"I guess it was the reporter. She probably traced the call, and the trace led them to Charlie's apartment. You're safe, Number 8446. You didn't see them com-

ing here, did you? No, they went to Charlie's. He doesn't know you broke into his apartment."

"Bullshit, Tom. Those people are determined to find me. All they have to do is turn that dog loose, and I'm toast. Where should I go?"

"You know what, Josh, you're just panicking. Even if they turn the dog loose, he's looking for Mr. Dickey's scent, not you. You're wearing his clothes."

"That didn't make one bit of sense, so I'm going to pretend you didn't say it," Josh gasped as he ran at the speed of light. Before he knew it, he was out of the complex and on a main road. He dodged to the side and tried to stay in the underbrush as he looked for an escape route.

"I got it! Find a church. Any one will do. Churches offer sanctuary. No one can make you leave a church."

"That's bullshit, too, Tom. If I didn't know better, I'd think you were smoking some of Mr. Dickey's weed. They lock churches at night, and sanctuary is a thing of the past. You need to shut up now and let me think. Look, I'm not mad at you, but right now your advice stinks, and I have to concentrate on staying alive. Don't make me remind you again that you're dead."

His heart pounding, his ears buzzing, Josh raced on as he tried to figure out what the next move should be in his quest to stay alive.

Charles Garrison opened the door and peered at the gaggle of people on his doorstep. "What can I do for you?" he asked pleasantly. "That's a beautiful dog you have there. I've always loved animals, but we aren't allowed to have them here. Would you like to come in out of the rain?"

"Yes, we would, Mr. Garrison. My name is Tessie Dancer, I'm a reporter for the *Chronicle*, and this is Miss Madison, Mr. Kelly, and the big man is Zolly. The dog's name is Winston."

Everyone shook hands as Charlie tried to figure out what was going on.

"Look, Mr. Garrison, I know this is probably going to sound very strange, but this afternoon a call came in to me from your telephone number. I'm trying desperately to find the young man who made the call. Were you here today, or did you have any guests who would have called me from your phone?"

A lightbulb went off in Charlie's head when he heard the words "young man." He needed to keep his wits about him. "I rarely have guests, and I was working today. I usually work the night shift, but today I had to take over for Dorothy because she had to go for a CAT scan. As far as I know, no one was here. Check my locks. The place wasn't broken into. Did this young man do something wrong besides making a phone call? Are you sure the call came from here?"

Charlie knew he was old, but he still liked to think he was sharp as a tack. He thought about the young man who'd come into Hotdog Haven looking so lost and hungry. He'd given Charlie a dollar tip, something he never got. Nice kid, polite and respectful. He recalled in perfect detail their conversation of the night before and how he'd told the boy where he lived.

"He's in danger," Tessie said.

Charlie looked from one to the other and decided he didn't give two hoots what they said. The boy was scared, that was for sure. But when reporters and people like this group that were standing in front of him wanted to gang up on a youngster, well, he didn't see any need to help them.

"Zat so?" He thought he was being clever when he asked, "Is it drugs? Did something go wrong? These kids today, you just never know what they'll do next. So, do you want to look around or what? I live alone, as you can see. The place is a little untidy. My cleaning lady only comes once a month. Sometimes she forgets, and I have to call her."

So now he knew who it was that had left the twenty dollars on his kitchen table and who it was that had finished his crossword puzzle and gave him a star at the top. No sirree, he wasn't telling these people a darn thing.

Tessie took Charlie up on his offer and walked around the apartment, opening closets and looking under the bed. When she returned to the living room, she said, "You don't seem concerned that someone broke in here and used your phone. Now, why is that?"

"Because I think you made a mistake. No one broke in here today. I have the only key to this place, and it's still on my key ring. Sounds to me like that young man who you say is in danger is smarter than you think he is. If there's nothing else . . ." Charlie said pointedly, looking toward the door.

Pete stepped forward. His voice was tortured. "Mr. Garrison, are you absolutely sure you don't know this boy?" he asked, pointing to the picture Tessie held in her hand.

"I think I'd remember meeting such a nice-looking youngster. Kind of looks a little like you, mister."

"Yes, he does. Just a little," Pete said in a choked voice.

Charlie walked toward the door. He knew people like these people. They reacted after the damage was done, preferring not to see what was going on before something bad happened. He opened the door and stared at the big, fancy vehicle sitting out there in the rain. *Your secret, whatever it is, youngster, is safe with me.*

Back in the car, Tessie said, "I think he was lying, but I can't tell you why."

"That old man? Winston would have picked up on something. He didn't. Sorry, Tessie, it's just another dead end," Pete said.

"Then how do you explain the fact that the boy called me from Garrison's home phone?"

"I can't explain it. What reason did that man have to lie to us? I watched him. He looked me right in the eye when he was saying no one broke into his home. Maybe the telephone wires got crossed, or they were wet or something."

"That's a bunch of crap, Pete. I just remembered where Adam Dickey lived. Right there,"

Tessie said, pointing a finger at the huge "#9" on the front door of the Dickey apartment. "Call me stupid or whatever, but this is just too much of a coincidence for me to swallow. You up for a little B&E?"

"No!" Zolly bellowed.

"Yes!" Lily and Pete said in unison.

Winston growled. In approval.

Chapter 23

"Boss, this is not a good idea. We got away with it once, so why push your luck? It's not going to look good in the newspapers if we get caught," Zolly pleaded.

"Zolly's right, Pete. You and Lily stay in the car with Winston. He and I will go in through the back, assuming there's a back door. I'll park farther down the road just in case Mr. Garrison is watching us from his front window. It's entirely possible the kid picked his lock and just relocked the door when he left so he'd be none the wiser. I'm telling you, the call originated from his apartment. The fact that Garrison is so steadfast in his denial worries me. Okay, we're here. Come on, Zolly. Stay in the car, Pete. I mean it. I can talk my way out of this if we get caught, but you won't be able to."

"I heard you the first time. Go on. We'll wait for you," Pete said.

"I wonder why that teacher kept an apartment here when he lived at the school?" Tessie muttered to herself as she led the way around to the back of Adam Dickey's apartment building.

"Privacy," Zolly volunteered. "He must have had time off occasionally. Living and working in the same place could get to you, I'm thinking."

"You're probably right," Tessie agreed as she pointed to the back door of Apartment 9. "I think I can pick the lock with my nail file. I've done it a time or two in the past."

"You're not very ethical, are you?" Zolly asked virtuously.

"It depends on the situation, Zolly. Like right now, the end justifies the means, if you get my drift. If you're not up to it, stand out here in the rain and watch my back. Another way of looking at this is that your boss certainly has enough money to bail us out of jail if we get caught. In addition to that, this isn't exactly the kind of neighborhood where the neighbors call the police for anything.

"Okay, it's open. Do you want to go first, or should I? You know, just in case there's a big, bad bogeyman in there."

"Put a cork in it, Miz Smart-ass. I'm not afraid of anything."

"That's a big fat old lie, Mister Smart-ass. You're afraid of me. Admit it," Tessie said, as though she were discussing the weather. She stepped into the kitchen and looked around.

"Where'd you get the idea I'm afraid of you? Don't go flattering yourself. You should think about going on a diet."

"More of me to love this way," Tessie snapped as she opened cabinets and the refrigerator. She checked the garbage can under the sink. "Aha! Someone was here. See the orange peels! You could stand to lose about forty pounds yourself. You look like the Pillsbury Doughboy. Now, shut up, I need to pay attention to details here."

Zolly clamped his lips shut as he followed the reporter from room to room.

"This is a decent enough place, and the rent is probably doable for someone on a teacher's salary who wants a bit of privacy from time to time. Bed's been slept in. Towel's still a bit damp. Yeah, the kid was here."

Zolly opened the clothes hamper and pulled out Josh's sweatpants and shirt. "I bet there's DNA on these clothes. The boss is gonna want these."

"Right. See if you can find a plastic bag. I think I saw some under the sink."

When Zolly returned with a trash bag, Tessie said, "It would be a straight run from this door to Mr. Garrison's back door. He picks the lock the way I picked this one. The big question is, why did he choose Charlie Garrison's apartment?"

"Maybe the kid has been watching to see who lives where and who's home during the day. Maybe Garrison was the only one not home. But, that was by chance. He said he usually works nights, and he would be home sleeping during the day."

"My point exactly. That has to mean the kid met him somewhere and knows him even if it is just slightly. Maybe he's trying to protect the kid. Who knows what he told the old guy."

"So, what's our next move?"

Tessie whirled around, stunned at the question. "Did I hear you right? Did you actually *ask* my opinion?"

Instead of answering her, Zolly stepped forward, grabbed Tessie, and kissed her so hard she thought she was going to black out. "What'ya think of that?" Zolly asked in a shaky voice.

In a voice just as shaky-sounding, Tessie gasped, "What do you do for an encore?"

"Guess you're gonna have to wait and see. You were right, you're a lot of woman."

"Uh-huh."

"Time to get out of here. I think we need to fall back and regroup. How are you going to lock the back door?" Zolly asked.

"It's self-locking," Tessie said as she tried to come to grips with the kiss she'd just experienced. She tried to remember when she was last kissed like that but had to give up when no occasion came to mind.

"You drive!" she said magnanimously.

"Guess I rocked your world, huh?"

"Don't flatter yourself. I need to think and, no, not about you. Kissing is one thing. Performing . . . now, that's a whole different ball game," she said ominously.

Zolly started to sputter and squawk as he climbed into the driver's seat.

Tessie was grinning from ear to ear as she fastened her seat belt. She turned to face Lily and Pete. "He was there. He ate some oranges, and he took a shower. The towel was still a little damp, and it looks like he slept in the bed. We took what we think were his clothes out of the hamper. You can have them checked for DNA, Pete. If it matches yours, you'll know for sure he's your son. Talk about luck."

"Damn. That's great, Tessie. I know just the guy to run the DNA, too. The kid is thinking, that's for sure. Each time I think he's run out of steam, he surprises me. He's a thinker. He plans. Now we have to put our heads together and try to figure out what his next move is."

Lily squeezed Pete's arm. "This is so wonderful, Pete. How long will the DNA take?"

"I'm not sure. Maybe a week. That's just a guess. He's my kid, Lily, I feel it in every bone of my body."

Lily crossed her fingers. "I feel it, too, Pete." *Please, God, let it be true.*

Josh didn't think he could possibly be more miserable. The rain had turned colder, and he was chilled to the bone, not to mention soaking-wet. If only he could get warm. And he was tired. He closed his eyes and thought about his bed back at the academy and how good it always felt when he went to sleep at night. "I can't do this anymore, Tom."

"Yeah, I know. Are you going to go to the police and turn yourself in?"

"What other choice do I have? Nothing's working out. I can't keep running like this. I've been thinking, Tom. If they kill me, I'll be with you and Sheila."

"Boy, is that some dumb thinking. I can't believe

you said that. You need to refocus and think of something else. The last thing you want to be is dead. You have to carry on for all of us. We're depending on you to do all the things we promised we'd do when we came of age."

"Staying alive is a lot of work. I just know I'm going to get sick. You can die from pneumonia. I don't feel good, Tom."

"What are your options? You can't go to a hospital because you don't have any health insurance. If you go to the police, they'll turn you over to the bad guys. That reporter isn't going to help you. Think . . . who can you count on?"

"You, but you're dead. I'm alone, Tom. Look around, do you see anyone here to help me?"

"There is one person. Think, Josh. Think!"

Josh heaved himself upright. "Charlie!"

"Exactly. Return to the scene of the crime. Those people are probably gone by now. Just go up to his door, knock, and beg him to help you. He looked like a nice man."

"I guess because you're dead, your memory isn't so swift, buddy, but when I returned to the scene of the crime at the academy, at your suggestion, it didn't exactly work out."

"Well, if you have a better idea, go for it. The temperature is falling. You need some hot tea and soup. Maybe some aspirin. Turn around and head back. It's not that far. It seems far because you were walking against the wind and rain. Pick up your feet and run. Forty minutes, Josh, and Charlie will have you eating soup and drinking hot tea. I guarantee it."

"Do ya think?"

"Yeah, I do. Get going, Josh. The wind is whipping

up harder, but it will be at your back. You know, like a tailwind. I'll be with you all the way."

Tom was wrong about the time, Josh thought an hour later, when he trudged up to Charlie Garrison's door and rang the bell. When the door opened, Josh asked, "Will you help me?"

Charlie looked up and down the courtyard before he pulled the boy indoors. It took only one good look to tell him the young man standing in front of him did indeed need his help. "First things first, get out of those wet clothes and into a hot shower. We can talk later. Don't worry, I'm not going to call anyone. People were here looking for you, but I didn't tell them a thing. You're safe here with me. I'll leave some warm clothes on the sink for you. While you're showering I'll make you some hot tea and soup. Can you take aspirin?"

"Yes, I can take aspirin. I don't have pneumonia, do I?"

"I doubt it. I'll get you fixed up. I'm glad you came back, and thanks for finishing my crossword puzzle. That one really had me stymied. Appreciated the star, too, young fella. Name's Charlie Garrison. What's yours?"

"Josh Baer. I don't know if that's my real name or not. It's the name they gave me. Thanks for helping me, Mr. Garrison."

Charlie blinked as he tried to figure out what the youngster meant.

In the kitchen, Charlie opened a can of soup and put a kettle on for tea. He added a package of crackers to the soup plate, along with a banana and a slice of pound cake. The youngster looked hungry. He took a moment to wonder if he should add some brandy to the tea. What could it hurt? The boy was going to go to bed, and it might help him sweat out any germs.

Charlie was pouring the soup into a bowl when the boy walked into the kitchen. "Thanks for the clothes, sir. I have to apologize to you. That's another reason I came back. I broke into your house, but I left money for the phone call. I used your computer, too. I swear I didn't touch anything, and I didn't even look in your refrigerator even though I was hungry. I'm really sorry, but I didn't know what else to do, and you were nice to me that night at the hot dog place."

"It's okay, Josh. Sit down and eat the soup while it's hot. We can talk later or when you wake up. You look pretty tired to me."

"I am very tired. I just can't run anymore. I thought you might be able to help me. You're a grandfather, right?" Charlie nodded. "That means you've lived a long time and are wise. This soup is good. We always had soup for lunch at the academy."

"I have more if you want it. Is there anything else you want to eat?"

"No, sir, this is fine. Those hot dogs the other night were very tasty," he said, knowing enough to tell a white lie to make Charlie feel good. "We never had those at the academy because of the contents. That means they're not good for you. I don't understand that. How can something that tastes so good be not good for you?"

This is one strange young man, Charlie thought. For reasons he couldn't explain to himself, he felt an overpowering need to take care of this youngster and protect him. With his life if he had to. *Now where did that thought come from?* he wondered.

By the time Josh finished his soup, his tea, the cake, and banana, Charlie had the couch made up with two warm blankets and two fluffy pillows.

His eyes drooping, Josh got up from the chair and stumbled toward Charlie, who put his arms around his shoulders. "Come on, young fella, I have your bed all ready. I'll sit up and watch over you. Believe me when I tell you, I will keep you safe. We have all day tomorrow to talk because I don't have to go to work until eleven o'clock tomorrow night."

"Thank you, Charlie. Maybe someday I can do something nice for you. Do you think I'm too big to be tucked in? Nobody ever tucked me in. Tom or Sheila either. We used to talk and wonder what it was like."

Who was this strange kid? "You can never be too old to be tucked in," Charlie said gruffly as he made a pretense of straightening the blankets and brushing the hair back from the boy's forehead. "Sleep tight, Josh."

"That's niiiiccce," Josh murmured as he drifted into a sound, peaceful sleep.

Charlie Garrison sat down in his favorite chair and stared at the sleeping boy for a long time. When he was satisfied that he was indeed sleeping soundly, he walked out to the kitchen to clear away the dishes.

His routine off-kilter, Charlie spent the next

hour cleaning up the apartment and toting his trash out to the Dumpster at the corner of the building. Back inside, he fixed himself a cup of tea, fired up his pipe, and sat down to think.

Eventually, Charlie dozed off, and it was Josh who woke him a little after eight the following morning. "Thanks for letting me stay here, Charlie."

"I appreciate the company, Josh. Now, would you like some breakfast?"

"I'd like that a lot. Can I do anything to help you?"

"No, just sit at the table. The kitchen isn't big enough for two people to be moving around at the same time. Do you like bacon and eggs?"

"I love bacon and eggs. I don't think there's anything I don't like. We had to eat whatever was put in front of us at school, or we were sent away from the table."

"Why don't you tell me what's wrong and how I can help you."

"Will you promise not to call the FBI, Charlie?"

Charlie turned around. He raised his hand, and said, "I give you my word whatever you tell me stays with me. Now, shoot!"

"Shoot what? I don't have a gun. That guy who killed all my friends is the one who had a gun. It was a big one, it just kept spitting out bullets. Jesse and I were late that morning because Jesse couldn't find his book bag. We saw him, and we ran. Jesse . . . I think Jesse is my brother, but I'm not sure. He's . . . Jesse is slow. He draws like an angel, though. I had to take him to the

FBI because those people that were here tonight saw us at the library, and Jesse drew these pictures. I couldn't keep running with Jesse. He takes a lot of care and patience. I don't even know if he's okay."

Charlie flipped the bacon in the pan as he listened intently. "Go on, Josh."

"I kept running and hiding, then I went back to the school. I thought I would be safe there until I could figure out what to do. But that guy with the gun showed up, pretending to be an FBI agent. I crawled up into the ductwork when those people that were here last night showed up. Again. That guy started shooting at me through the ceiling. Then he shot out their tires and got away. I was leaving and it was dark and the lady was lost inside the building. I helped her to the kitchen, then I ran. That's how I ended up here.

"Mr. Dickey was always nice to me and to all the other guys. He was as much a friend as he was a teacher. He tried to tell us what it was like in the outside world. My bad luck was he didn't tell me enough. I don't know what to do. Tom has been helping me, but he's dead and he only knows what I know."

Charlie whirled around. "I thought you said Tom was dead. How can he help you if he's dead?"

"He talks to me. I know how strange that sounds, and you probably don't believe me, but he's my lookout. He warns me of danger, and so far he's been pretty good. Each time I manage to get away, he watches my back. You don't believe me, do you? That's okay. When he first started to talk to me, I thought I was going nuts. We made this book. We don't know what it means, but we have it, and I'll turn it over to the right people. The only thing is, I don't know who the right people are. What should I do, Charlie?"

"I need to think about all this, Josh. Eat your breakfast," Charlie said, setting a plateful of golden-yellow scrambled eggs and toast, along with a mound of bacon and hot coffee in front of the boy.

Between bites and sips, Josh said, "I don't understand why there hasn't been more in the papers and on television about all my friends getting killed. Weren't we important enough? Or is it because we're artificial?"

Charlie was tempted to hit the brandy bottle sitting on the counter. *The kid talks to dead people who help him. He's artificial, and he doesn't trust anyone. He's sitting here in my kitchen asking me for help.* Charlie thought about his ditzy sister, Anna, who claimed she talked to her dead husband every night. A dead husband who talked back to her. Maybe it was possible. Or maybe it was a fantasy that enabled both Anna and this boy to block out the horrible losses they couldn't cope with. Okay, he wasn't going to touch that one just yet. "What makes you artificial, Josh?"

"Tom, Sheila, and I think we were test tube babies. No parents. We had numbers, then someone gave us names. Look," Josh said, kicking off one of his slippers. "See that number on my big toe? I'm 8446. Tom was 8211. I forget what Sheila's number was. Everybody had a number on their big toe." He kicked off his other slipper and wiggled his left toe. The number 2003 was clearly visible. "I don't know what they mean, but they must be important. They're tattoos. That's what's in the book—all the numbers. Tom and I used to go around after lights-out with a flashlight and copy all the numbers off everyone's toes. We even wrote down the names the different schools gave everyone. We got them all," he said proudly, "but it took us forever to do it because we had to be so sneaky."

A lump the size of a golf ball settled in Charlie's throat as he stared at Josh's wiggling toes.

Josh finished the last of the eggs on his plate. "Do you have a family, Charlie? What's it like having a family?"

Charlie's head was reeling. Maybe it was better to talk about himself and think about everything the boy had said later. "Yes. But not in the true sense of the word. Not the kind of family you see on television shows. I was in the navy, and that made me an absentee father. I have two sons who live on the East Coast and six grandchildren. I haven't seen them in over ten years. You see, I was always away, out to sea or at a distant port. My wife raised our sons pretty much by herself, and my sons never quite forgave me for not being around for their ball games, birthday parties, and graduations. We're polite to each other, and they call once a month or so. They send pictures. What that means, Josh, is we're not a close-knit family."

"That's very sad. I want a family someday. So

did Tom and Sheila. Nobody ever kissed us or tucked us in. We never got hugs. We used to practice with each other so we'd know what it would feel like. When I'm eighteen, I can do whatever I want. Mr. Dickey said so. I think that's why they killed all my friends. We were all almost eighteen. Everyone was going to leave.

"You should go to see your family, Charlie. Maybe you can say you're sorry and take some flowers. Miss Carmody said when you give someone flowers, it always makes them smile, and then they're happy. You should try that, Charlie."

Charlie's mind continued to buzz. "I did try that, but it was such a strain I knew they wanted me to leave, so I did. The grandkids didn't like me. In all fairness to them, I was a stranger, so I understand their feelings."

"Why? You're nice. Do you still have a wife?"

"No. She died a long time ago. My sons told me she didn't want me at her funeral, so I didn't go. I did go to the cemetery after everyone left. I sat there and cried for hours."

"Do you still go there to visit her?"

"Yes, Josh, I do."

"I want to be able to go and visit Tom, Sheila, and all my friends. Mr. Dickey and Miss Carmody, too. But they aren't buried yet. Do you know why that is, Charlie? I think it's important to go to the morgue to get the numbers off their toes. You know, to match them up to the ones in the book. We put their initials next to their numbers but someone could turn around and say we made it up."

"I don't know why they haven't been buried, son. I can go on the Internet to try and find out. Would you like me to do that?"

"Sure. I tried, but there isn't anything there. You know what else, Charlie? No one is talking about all the other kids and what happened to *them*. Where did over ninety kids go? And why did they leave right before the shooting? Tom said they sent them away to one of the other schools. There are three or four more, you know. We just don't know where they are. Plus, plus, Charlie, all the files, records, and computers disappeared from school a few days before the shooting. We were working strictly with paper and pencils for those days. Mr. Dickey was very upset and worried. I could tell. So was Miss Carmody.

"Did you think about anything to help me, Charlie?"

"No, not yet. I'm going to go out to get one of those TracFones where they can't trace where the calls come from. The Target store isn't that far from here. You'll be safe here if you keep the doors locked. Promise me you aren't going to cut and run."

"I'll promise if you promise not to turn me in," Josh said smartly.

"It's a deal," Charlie said, holding out his hand for Josh to shake.

Chapter 24

It was six thirty when Tessie settled her bulk into her chair at the *Chronicle*. She looked up to see her boss approaching her office.

"Nice to see you, Tess. I was starting to think you wandered off the reservation. The last time I looked you were on salary, but no one has been sitting in your office. And, need I remind you that you're the only one who actually has an office at this paper besides me? An office with a window."

Harry Newton was a big guy with a mess of snow-white hair that was too long to be fashionable. Topping the scales at 240, he was never creased or pressed, and there were always ink stains on his shirt and hands. He had the shrewdest eyes in the business and the best nose for news of anyone Tessie had ever come across. She liked him, but more important, she respected him.

"Harry, Harry, Harry! I'm working on my third Pulitzer. I am also in love . . . Well, that might not be quite accurate but I am smitten with one of the opposite sex. Now, what do you want?"

"We need to talk, Tess. In my office."

"Now?"

"Yeah, now."

Tessie followed her boss back to his stinky, cluttered office. She saw the remains of a bagel and a banana skin sitting on his desk. Both were probably two or three days old. She flopped down and glared at Harry Newton. "What?"

"What the hell are you mixed up in this time, Tess?"

Tessie leaned forward, her hands clutching the edges of the cluttered desk. "Okay, you asked me, and I'm going to tell you," she said, holding his gaze. "But before I spill my guts I want you to know that if you even think about putting a lid on me, I'm outta here, and I'm heading to New York to take the old Gray Lady up on her latest offer. You still want to hear what I'm working on?"

"Spit it out, Tess."

She did. When she finally wound down she watched as every emotion in the book rippled across her boss's face.

"You shitting me about Pete Kelly, Tess?"

"No. And, the little lady ain't no small potatoes either. I have a tiger by the tail, Harry."

Harry Newton's guts rumbled. He knew Tess Dancer, and he knew she never said anything unless she could back it up with two or three sources. He also knew she'd do just what she said she'd do—head off for New York in the blink of an eye. He continued to stare at her until she leaned back in the chair.

"Who got to you, Harry? Why didn't we run with that shooting at the academy?"

"Nobody got to me, and I damn well resent your question and the implication. The owner of this fine paper invited me to his home and told me in the interests of national security I wouldn't be printing anything other than what I was told to print. I quit on the spot, then some other very important people came to see me when I was cleaning out my desk and told me to just sit tight for a little while. If this will make you feel any better, I made the rounds and talked to the *Register, Tribune,* and *Gazette* and they all had the same visitors. We agreed among ourselves to give them two weeks. Time's almost up. Before you can ask, the television channels got the same treatment."

Tessie closed her mouth, which had been hanging open. "You frigging buckled! You!"

There was such disgust in Tessie's voice, Harry Newton cringed. If there had been a rock handy, he would have tried to slither under it. "Yeah, me! I never said I liked it. I figured, like all the others, I could live with the two weeks. How much more time do you need?"

"A few more days. Maybe four, possibly five. This goes all the way to 1600 Pennsylvania Avenue. Just so you know, Harry."

Harry reached into his desk drawer and pulled out a bottle of Rolaids. He dumped a handful in his hand and popped the pile in his mouth. He washed them all down with cold, scummy coffee that was probably as old as the bagel and banana skin. "Feed it to me as you get it. We clear on that, Tess?"

Tess chewed on her lower lip. When she didn't respond, Harry swiped his arm across his messy desk to make his point. Everything flew in different directions. "What? You're saying you don't trust me?" His bellow of outrage could be heard a block away.

"You said it, I didn't. I was thinking it, though. Okay. But . . . and this is a big *but*, Harry, just in case those *very important people* come at you again, I'm making a backup file that will go where it's supposed to go. Are *we* clear on that, Harry?"

"Crystal, Tess. Now, get the hell out of here so I can have my nervous breakdown in peace and quiet."

The cell phone in Tessie's jacket pocket chirped. She pulled it out to check to see if she had to take the call at that moment or wait. Her heart jumped into her throat when she recognized the symbols that indicated Little Slick was on the phone. The same Little Slick who told her never to call him again and who was going to pretend he didn't know her. "Yeah. what's up?"

"No small talk, just listen. The eight-hundred-pound gorilla just flew in on a private jet and is supposedly going straight to the local office. If you leave now, you might be able to catch him off guard. Your call. You know what they say, Tess, keep your friends close, your enemies closer. Be careful."

"Always," Tessie replied before she snapped her cell phone shut. Five minutes later she was out of the building and headed toward the office of Senator Hudson Preston.

Zolly rapped smartly on the door to Lily's villa. "Boss, the guy from Channel 5 News is waiting in the main lobby of the hotel. He said Tessie arranged a three-minute sound bite. You want me to bring him down here, or do you want to go to the lobby?"

"Bring him here, Zolly."

"I want you to stay inside, Lily. Let's not give the press any more fodder than they need. Three minutes can be a lifetime in a situation like this. You're against this interview, aren't you?"

"Yes and no. The media have a way of twisting things, but you'll be live, so maybe it will work. What are you going to say?"

"I'm not good at rehearsing, Lily. I'll just wing it. Trust me, okay?"

Lily looked Pete up and down and laughed. He looked like a beach bum in long pants and high-top Converse sneakers that had seen better days. Pete correctly interpreted Lily's look and laughter.

"'Always keep 'em off center' is my motto. Listen, if Tessie calls, interrupt me."

"No problem. It's kind of early for a call, though."

"Tessie Dancer marches to a different drummer. If you don't believe me, just ask Zolly."

While Pete waited for Zolly and the reporter, he watched a young woman exit one of the villas with her poodle on a leash. Winston growled, and the woman scooped up the little dog and scurried down the flower-bordered path.

Pete's mind raced. He'd lied to Lily. He knew exactly what he was going to say the minute he opened his mouth. He hoped more than anything in the world that Josh Baer was someplace where he had access to a television so he could see the short interview. He also hoped the news channel would air the sound bite throughout the day. If only he could be so lucky.

If there was one thing Pete Kelly hated, it was men with hard-hat hair. The reporter, who said his name was Carlson Cook, had so much hairspray on his hair that gale-force winds wouldn't have caused a strand to move out of place. They did the manly handshake, even Winston.

"So, Mr. Kelly, to what does the fine state of California owe this visit? Are you buying up something to send Wall Street into a feeding frenzy?"

Pete forced a laugh he didn't feel. "No. I came out here to a fund-raiser at my alma mater and decided to stay on for a few days. I'm doing a search on something personal."

"Do you care to share what that might be?" the reporter simpered.

"Well, sure. I'm looking for 8446."

Whatever the reporter was expecting by way of a response, this wasn't it. "What's 8446?"

Pete smiled. "That's why it's personal."

"If you find or locate the mysterious 8446, will it drive Wall Street over the edge?"

"It might," Pete said with a straight face. "By the way, I'm going to step down and retire to my ranch in Montana."

"That *is* news! Now I know the market will go off the charts. When will that happen, Mr. Kelly?"

"As soon as I find 8446. I'd like to talk more, but I have a meeting scheduled. Nice meeting and talking with you, Mr. Cook." Pete offered up his hand, the two men shook hands, then it was Winston's turn.

Back inside, Pete pressed his ear to the door in time to hear Carlson Cook say, "And there you have it, folks. You heard it here first in this exclusive interview with the founder of PAK Industries, Peter Aaron Kelly, and his companion, Winston."

"Oh, Pete, that was fantastic. Of all the things I imagined you might say, that never entered my mind. Is Wall Street going to go crazy? I so hope Josh sees the interview. You did good. I knew I liked you for a reason."

Pete picked up Lily and swung her around until she squealed for mercy. "I love you, Lily Madison."

"And I love you, Pete Kelly," Lily whispered. "What do we do now?"

"We wait to hear from Tessie. And Josh, if we're lucky."

"It's coming down to the wire, isn't it, Pete?"

"Yeah, Lily, I think it is."

* * *

Josh Baer paced Charlie Garrison's small living room as he waited for Charlie to return. The television was on but he wasn't paying attention. Instead he called on Tom. "I'm really nervous, Tom. Do you think Charlie can help me?"

"Yeah, I do. You don't have anything else going for you right now. He's a grandfather, Josh. He won't let you down."

"I hope you're right. Hey, Tom, look at all the pictures Charlie has of his family. I bet his sons don't even know he keeps their pictures all over the place. I feel bad for him. I'm going to ask him if he wants to be my grandfather even if I'm a stranger. I'll tell him more about you and Sheila, and I bet he'll say he'll be yours, too. If I can get somebody to put up a tombstone for all you guys, I'm going to ask him if it will be all right to put his name on it as your grandfather. I bet he says *yes*."

"That would be so great, Josh. Then we wouldn't be nameless. I never liked being a number. Sheila didn't like it either."

"That's because it's not right."

"Josh! Josh! Look at the television. There's that guy Jesse drew. Listen."

Josh stood transfixed as he stared at the man speaking intently on the screen. For one wild, crazy minute it looked like the man was talking directly to him.

"Oh, man, did you hear what he just said? He's looking for you. For 8446. The guy is on television and he's saying your number. Oh, shit, buddy, is that good or is it bad?" Tom asked.

"I know who he is, he's the guy from the library and the academy. He's looking for me. Why? Is it possible he's a good guy?" Josh asked in a shaky voice.

"Mr. Dickey told us about him, how he started from nothing and built his company up to the billion-dollar company it is today. He's famous, and he's Midas-rich. He looks like you, Josh, just older. What do you think that means? How can he look like you? Do you think he's got a number, too? Maybe he's your brother or something since he looks like you. Yeah, yeah, I bet he's your brother."

"Dammit, I don't know. He doesn't look . . . evil. Maybe I should call him up."

Tom laughed. *"Yeah, half the world would love to call up Peter Aaron Kelly. That's like trying to call the president of the United States."*

"Then why did he say what he did? He's looking for 8446. That's me. He looks like me. That has to mean something. Or, was it a warning to let me know he's coming after me? What do you think, Tom?"

"For a rich guy, he sure did look strange. He looked like Mr. Dickey on Field Day. I agree with you that he seemed to be looking right at you. Maybe he said something in code we're supposed to figure out."

Josh snorted. "Code? Get real. Where do you think he is?"

"Someplace only rich people can afford to stay. It looked like there was a Spanish villa behind him. We saw them in a travelogue when we were studying about Spain. Remember? You could call a travel agency and ask them what's the biggest and most expensive hotel in this area. Or you could go online and not make a phone call."

Josh was about to head into the bedroom to use Charlie's computer when Charlie let himself into the apartment carrying a bag that said TARGET on the front. Josh started to jabber all at once while he pointed to the television.

"Whoa! Whoa! Slow down, big fella, and start all over."

Josh took a great, gulping breath and managed to get his story out in one long, breathless sentence.

"Are you telling me the guy who founded PAK Industries is the man you saw on TV and the same man your friend Jesse captured in his drawing? The same guy from the library and the academy?"

"Yeah, Charlie, that's what I'm telling you. So, is he a good guy or a bad guy? How'd he find out about the number 8446? No one but us kids and the people at the school knew ... know about the numbers. I guess that means he's *one of them.*"

"Slow down, Josh. Let's think this through. It doesn't have to mean he's one of them. He could have come by the number legitimately. Maybe it means something to him, and this was his way of telling you so you would reach out to him."

Josh started to pace again. "Telling me what? He should have told me how to reach him if he's a good guy. He said he's going to retire to Montana. That doesn't mean anything to me. What do you really think, Charlie?"

"I think we should call his office once we find out where it is. We can call on this TracFone I just bought. First, though, we have to set it all up and charge it. That's going to take a while. While I do that, go online and find out where Mr. Kelly's headquarters are. And check out five-star hotels in the vicinity. It's going to be okay, Josh. I have a good feeling about this."

"I don't have a good feeling, Charlie. Neither does Tom. Do you think maybe he's my older brother, and that's how he knows about the number?"

"I know you want me to say *yes,* but I can't. I just don't know, son."

Chapter 25

Tessie Dancer eyed the storefront local office of Senator Hudson Preston. She'd heard someone say once, someone who didn't want to be quoted, that politicians' storefront offices were for the little people to come and plead their cases and to walk away with an autographed picture. She wondered if the senator would move this particular location to something a little bigger and grander once his hat was officially in the ring for a presidential run.

Hudson Preston, son of Douglas Preston, founder of Preston Pharmaceuticals, bigger than everyone except Merck and Pfizer. A multibillion-dollar industry. Billion with a *b*. Hudson Preston, with the trophy wife, the first wife languishing in Carmel-by-the-Sea with a dizzying payout to free him up for the trophy wife. There were grandchildren, too, brought out for photo ops from time to time.

Tessie wondered if it was worth going to Carmel to talk to the first wife and to look up the grown children. Maybe a conference call or a videotaped call. She recalled that the first Mrs. Preston did not like the limelight, ditto for the son and daughter, who had forcefully said they wanted nothing to do with politics. Or with the senator, though that part was mumbled under their breath, or so her colleague who had interviewed them told it. But they were perfectly content to take his money. In any event, it was something to think about.

Once she found a parking space, Tessie sauntered down the tree-shaded sidewalk and entered the building. Three nerdy-looking individuals looked up at the same time, curious expressions on their faces. Clearly there weren't all that many visitors to the senator's local office. It also looked like the small staff wasn't expecting the senator. Did Little Slick get his information wrong? Did the senator go to his home first, maybe to freshen up? Well, she was here, so she might as well make the best of it. First, though, she had to call Pete Kelly to find out how the early-morning interview went. She held up her hand to indicate the three nerds should wait a moment while she made a phone call. Pete picked up on the first ring.

"How'd it go, Pete?"

Looking through the plate glass window, her eyes on the foot traffic as well as on the vehicular traffic, Tessie spoke quickly. "Give it to me word for word." Pete did. "That's good. Do you think the boy will call your headquarters?"

"I can only hope. I called the office, and everyone is on alert. There will be a rash of other calls, I can guarantee it, so they'll have to sift through them. My people know what to do, so there's no worry on that end. They'll give him my and Lily's cell phone numbers. By the way, I packaged up the boy's suit and had one of the guards take it to the airport. That, too, is in good hands at the moment. We'll know soon if his DNA is a match for mine."

"Good going, Pete. I'll get back to you," Tessie said. Then she noticed a black Town Car about to pull to the curb in front of the storefront. She quickly snapped the phone shut and pocketed it as she turned around to face the three nerdy-looking staff members.

"Tess Dancer from the *Chronicle*," Tessie said as she flipped open her wallet to show her press card. "I heard Senator Preston was in town. I thought I'd get an early start and see if he wants to do an interview. Well, will you look at that!" she said, pointing to the curb outside. "Talk about a reporter's dumb luck." Tessie stepped aside as the door opened, and a gaggle of men walked into the long, narrow room.

Preston's megawatt smile lit up the room when he saw and recognized Tessie. "Can't hide out from you guys nohow," he said jokingly. "It boggles my mind that I didn't know I was coming here until last night, yet here you are! What can I do for you, Miss Dancer?"

"How about a few words for your constituents? In private."

"Anything for the press. I've always been cooperative, you know that."

Tessie forced a smile as she followed the senator to the back of the room, where there was a table with four chairs. One of the aides hustled to get the senator a bottled water. "Can I get you anything, Miss Dancer?" the young woman asked politely.

"No thanks, I'm good."

Tessie turned her attention to the senator. "So, you're going to make a run for it."

The senator turned coy. It was not a becoming expression. "If the people want me, what else can I do? I live to serve my government, you know that, Miss Dancer. It's how I got to office. I'm on a pretty tight schedule today, so if there's nothing else . . ."

"Well, actually, Senator, there is something else. My readers have written some very strong letters to us at the paper wanting to know why there was a lid put on the shooting at the California Academy of Higher Learning. They want to know why, as their elected official, you aren't demanding answers. I find it rather odd myself, Senator, so if you'd care to comment, I'd appreciate it."

Tessie wondered if it was her imagination or if the senator had stiffened slightly at her question. The man waved his arms expansively.

"Believe it or not, no one asked for my help, and when I did volunteer, I was told in no uncertain terms that my help wasn't needed. I know when to retreat. The FBI is a very fine organization, and they know what they're doing."

"By chance, Senator Preston, would it have anything to do with the fact that along with a bunch of other wealthy investors, you had/have, a stake in that school? And while I have you face-to-face, do you care to comment on your ownership of a sperm bank and a fertility clinic here in town?"

The senator feigned astonishment. "Is it a slow day at the *Chronicle,* Miss Dancer? Where *do* you people come up with this stuff?"

"Hackers!" Tessie said smartly. "The kind that make a living trolling for stuff like this and getting bonuses for a job well done." She felt pleased to see tiny beads of perspiration blossom on the man's forehead.

Senator Preston stood up and held out his hand to signal that the interview was over. "I make it a practice never to comment on gossip."

Tessie stood up, towering over the senator, who was a short man. She took a moment to wonder if he had a Napoleon complex. "But that's the point, Senator, it isn't gossip. I'm talking about actual records. By the way, by any chance did you see the founder of PAK Industries on television this morning? Maybe you were still en route and missed it. The only reason I mention it is that I remembered a photo op you had with Mr. Kelly a week or so ago. Today he said he was looking for 8446. Any idea what that means?"

"Now you *are* talking in riddles. Maybe it's his lottery number or something. I'll call you the next time I'm in town, and perhaps we can have breakfast. I don't like cutting you so short, but I really have to keep to my schedule. Thanks for stopping by."

"I expect to be hanging around here a lot

from here on in, Senator. I can see myself out."
When she reached the door, Tessie called over
her shoulder, "I'll be sure to quote you verbatim, Senator." *Made you sweat, didn't I, you little
prick.*

The moment the door closed behind the reporter, Hudson Preston shifted into high gear.
He issued orders like the general he was, pretended to be interested in what his aides were
saying before he waved airily. He stomped from
the office and headed straight for the Town Car
that would take him to his eighty-plus-year-old
father and his palatial mansion.

By the time the Town Car ground to a stop
under the portico, Hudson Preston thought he
was going to black out. He could hardly wait to
blurt out the news to the old man, who virtually
lived on the second floor of the ugly mansion.

At eighty-six, Douglas Preston was still an im-
posing figure, and he was ordinarily still capable
of making his son cower in his presence, but not
today.

Hudson slammed and locked the door to the
lavish sitting room where his father was watching an old Wimbledon tennis match. He reached
out a stubby hand to turn off the television.
"There's a reporter at the *Chronicle* who's figured out what's been going on. She came to see
me this morning. She knows, Father."

"That's impossible," the old man said, press-
ing the ON button on the remote.

Hudson turned off the set again. "Not only
does she know, there's this guy Peter Aaron
Kelly, the founder of PAK Industries, who gave

an interview on television this morning and announced to the world that he's looking for 8446. Do you want to know what 8446 is, Father, or do you prefer being kept in the dark?"

The old man, who still had all his hair, glared at his son. "I'm assuming he was one of the donors. He'll never find anything. Why do you always get so upset over trivial things? When people like Kelly go on television, it only means he has nothing and is looking for something. I saw the short interview. The man is a disgrace to the garment industry. He looked like a street person. He has a number, and that's all he has."

"Well, guess what, Father! That kid is still on the loose. If those two find a way to meet, your wrinkled old ass is going to be sitting in the slammer. The world won't give a damn if you gave away free drugs to starving nations or not. All they're going to see and remember is the slaughter of all those kids and teachers at the academy."

"Something else you managed to botch up, Hudson. You were told to oversee that project and, as usual, you fouled it up. God help us all if you ever make it to the White House."

The tennis match appeared on the screen again. Hudson turned it off for the third time.

"I want you to listen to me very carefully, Father. This might surprise you, but that man, Peter Kelly, is quite a bit richer than you are. He has more clout than you *ever* had. Or I will ever have. People love the man because he does good, wonderful things for mankind and he does them with very little fanfare. Unlike you, and, yes, unlike me. He's on a mission, and he is not—are you listening to me, Father?—he is not going to give up. On the ride here I accessed the data on my memory stick, and the boy is a match for 8446. That means the kid is Pete Kelly's son. Now you can say something, Father."

The old man seemed to shrivel in front of his son's eyes. "How did this happen, Hudson? It was foolproof. We covered all the bases."

Hudson sat down on a hassock. He wrapped his arms around his pudgy knees. "It happened when you ordered a wholesale slaughter of all those children. That's what happened. I told you to just let them go off on their own once they turned eighteen, but you wouldn't listen. None of this would have happened if you *had* listened to me. Now you are going to be hounded unmercifully, and you'll go to jail, where you will die, but only after you, after we, become a media circus. Your whole life will be aired and dissected, and you will get to the point where you want to kill yourself, which you might well do. Even in death, they'll pick at your bones."

"Then do something about it, Hudson. Make it all go away."

"You must be senile, Father. Tell me how I could do that. Under the guise of conducting research at the fertility lab, they created human guinea pigs, children with no families and no parents . . . who could be secreted away to become the ongoing clinical-testing subjects for the drugs our firm manufactured. You said no regulations to worry about. No government interference, no concerned parents. You said other drug companies would have to spend decades developing and testing on animals before they could even think about giving them to a human subject, but that our company could test them immediately. When they start their probe, they'll see how Preston Pharmaceuticals recovered from the crapper we were in, and the sudden megagrowth will attest to the diabolical genius of your plan. There you have it, Father Dearest. Chew on it, and I hope to hell you choke on it."

"How dare you speak to me in such a manner?" the old man sputtered.

"How dare I? How dare I not speak to you like this? You can do whatever the hell you want, but I'm getting out of here as soon as I can. I have no desire to participate in the free fall that is just around the corner. I simply came here to warn you. Do what you want. Tell me you understand what I've just told you."

"What I understand is that you're a traitor to this family. Get out of my sight. I never want to see you again. Do you hear me, Hudson?"

"Oh, I hear you, all right. But that's my line, Pater. I wish to God I had turned you in to the authorities myself before I ever agreed to help you try to hide this by killing those children." Without another word, Hudson struggled to his feet and left the room. Even before he closed the door he could hear the tennis match come to life on the big-screen TV set.

Hudson Preston suffered through the short ride to his California home. He wasn't the least surprised to find the house empty. He wasn't sure, but he rather thought his wife was in Europe. He vaguely remembered hearing something about fashion shows. Thank God. He headed straight for the bar, where he poured himself a tumbler of hundred-year-old cognac. He downed it in three swallows, his throat burning from the searing liquor. He looked at the empty glass and poured another.

When he felt loose as a goose, he made his way back to his office, where he sat down to contemplate what could very well be a very dim future. He'd always known deep in his gut that this day would come. Well, he'd set up things for this eventuality, so he might as well get cracking on it.

Hudson opened the wall safe and stared at the contents. There was no money inside, nothing valuable, not even his wife's jewelry. He reached for the only thing in it: a plain brown envelope given to him and all the others that made up the consortium. His father had one, too, but Hudson doubted he'd ever use it. Well, he wasn't his father.

Hudson spilled the contents onto his desk as he did his best to remember all the instructions that had been drilled into his head. First, he needed to insert the special battery, kept charged at all times, into the phone. He did so. The instructions for using the high-tech encrypted phone were seared into his brain. All he had to do was make one phone call, then wait six hours, at which point he was to leave and pretend he was going for a walk. He was to dress down, which meant casually. He wasn't to take his wallet, his ID, or anything personal, just his keys. At some point during his walking route he would be whisked away to a safe haven, where others would take charge. He looked down at his watch. In six hours it would be five thirty. A short stroll before dinner wouldn't be out of the ordinary for someone like him. Or, would it?

He'd certainly find out at five thirty. He wondered which banana republic he'd end up in. Or would they simply kill him? He had no way of knowing.

With nothing else to occupy his time, Hudson took a shower and dressed in a running outfit. The last time he'd run or jogged was when he was seven years old. He slicked back his hair, shaved, and went to the kitchen in search of food.

As Hudson bit into his ham-and-cheese sandwich, he wondered if it would literally be his last meal.

Chapter 26

It was a little after four when Charlie Garrison pronounced the TracFone sufficiently charged to start making calls. He felt excited for the boy and hoped something good would come of everything. He was going to miss the youngster when he left, but there was no need to fool himself—the boy *would* leave.

For some reason Charlie felt close to him, almost paternal where the young man was concerned. *He could be my grandson,* he told himself. *He asked me to be his grandfather. It would be nice to be able to spend time with him, to watch him through his college years, maybe visit him on campus, go to dinner with him, send e-mails back and forth. Maybe play a game of chess once in a while, confer about the Times' crossword puzzles. Maybe just to love him because no one else did.* The bottom line was, Charlie realized just how lonely he really was. In less than twenty-four hours he realized something else: he loved this kid with the curly hair and dark eyes and quaintly old-fashioned way of looking at things.

He wanted to take Josh to ball games, to get a pizza, to buy him a dog that would love him to death. All the things he never got to do with his own kids or grandkids.

Josh stunned the old man when he asked, "Charlie, why can't I work at your hot dog place and stay here with you? I can sleep on the couch. I won't bother you. I need to get a job so I can go to college. I was going to ask you if I could go online to apply for aid. Maybe you could help me. I'd really like to continue my education here at Berkeley."

"Youngster, I don't know if that's a good idea until all this mess is sorted out. You can work at Hotdog Haven if you want, and, yes, you can stay with me, but you deserve more than this. Don't worry, we're going to work it all out." Charlie's voice turned ferocious and yet proud-sounding when he said, "If I have anything to say about it, your running days are over. I might be old, but I learned a thing or two in the navy I can use to protect you."

The boy was nervous, Charlie could tell. "Have you . . . uh, talked to Tom lately?"

"As a matter of fact I haven't. The last time I talked to Tom, he said I have you now to help me, and he'd go into a wait-and-see mode. He's like that. If I need him, I just call his name, and he's right there. I miss him a lot. Sheila, too. I bet Tom or I would have married Sheila some-day. She said she wanted us to fight over her. Tom and I said we wouldn't fight each other over her, and she didn't speak to us for a whole week, so we said okay, we'd fight over her, but she had to marry someone else." This was all said in one breathless burst of words.

Charlie laughed. "Women are at the root of all evil. You have a whole life ahead of you before you can think about marrying. Eventually you'll meet some nice girl in college who will blow your socks off, and that will be it. Love comes around when you least expect it. First things first, you have to get a fine education so you can take care of a wife and kids and probably her mother. Girls always come with a mother, for some strange reason."

"No, the first thing I have to do is save enough money to buy a tombstone for all my friends. I'm thinking just one with all their names on it. What do you think, Charlie? How long will it take me to earn enough money at your hot dog place to do that?"

Charlie's eyes started to burn. "Not that long," he said gruffly.

"Then that's what we'll do. You'll help me with that, won't you, Charlie?"

"I will, youngster, I will. Are you ready to make the call?"

Josh disconnected the charger and turned on the TracFone. He turned around to look at the kitchen clock. It was four thirty. "Let's go over it one more time so I don't foul things up. Jeez, this is like debating class. I was never good at that. Sheila was a whiz. She always won."

"You're going to call and ask for Mr. Kelly. Tell them who you are and say you saw Mr. Kelly on television. Tell them your number. If you want, tell them about your book. Ask why Mr. Kelly is looking for you. Then you hang up. If you want them to return your call, you'll have to give them the TracFone number. Or tell them you'll call back in a half hour to get a number where he can be reached. You don't have to do this if you don't want to, Josh. We can just throw the phone away."

"No, I have to do this, Charlie. I have to do it for Tom, Sheila, Jesse, all the others, too, as well as Mr. Dickey and Miss Carmody. Okay, here goes."

Charlie sat back in his chair and watched the boy as he punched in the numbers to PAK Industries. He wished he was clairvoyant.

Josh listened to the operator say, "PAK Industries, how may I direct your call?"

"Hello. My name is Josh Baer, and I'd like to speak to Mr. Kelly, please."

"Mr. Kelly isn't in the office. Can I put you through to his assistant, Marty Bronson, sir?"

Josh smiled and mouthed the words, *"She called me 'sir.'"*

"No. . . . Wait a minute. Okay, I can talk to him."

"Just a minute, sir."

"Marty Bronson."

"Hi, Mr. Bronson. Can you tell me how I can get in touch with Mr. Kelly? My name is Josh Baer. I also have a number that is 8446. I saw him on television, and he said he was looking for 8446."

The voice on the other end of the phone was

smooth as silk and didn't miss a beat. "Mr. Kelly is in California but I can have him call you, Josh. Is it okay to call you Josh?"

"Sure. I know Mr. Kelly is in California. Do you know why he's trying to find me?"

"I'm sorry, Josh, I don't know the answer to your question. I'm assuming it's personal. If you give me your phone number, I will try and reach Mr. Kelly. I'm sure he'll return your call as soon as I reach him. He's a prompt kind of guy, if you know what I mean." When Josh didn't respond, Marty Bronson said, "Josh, are you there? Did you hear what I just said?"

"I heard what you said, and I'm still here. I'm thinking. Why don't you give me his cell phone number? In the interest of expediency. Are you still there, Mr. Bronson? Did you hear me?"

Josh was rewarded with a chuckle on the other end of the phone. *"Touché, Josh."*

"Hang up now, Josh."

Josh whirled around. "Tom! Why?" he mouthed the question.

"Towers. He's trying to track your location."

"Oh, shit!" Josh broke the connection as he struggled to take a deep breath.

"What happened?" Charlie demanded.

"Tom told me to hang up. Something about the towers the cell phone signals go through. They can find me that way."

"He's right, son. I'm sorry, I didn't think about that. Maybe I'm not the right person to be helping you. Guess that means I have to relocate you. That's not going to be a problem. I'll just call Dorothy and tell her she's going to have a few guests for a while. Get your stuff together. We should leave now. I have a key to her house."

"I don't have any stuff, Charlie. Just the book, and it's stuck in my pants. Why do you have a key to Dorothy's house? Won't she mind if we go there?"

Charlie put his hands on his hips. "Now why do you *think* I have a key to her house?"

"I thought . . . maybe she had a cat or a dog or something."

"Sometimes you are so slow you make me crazy. Try the birds and the bees, buddy. Remember that sex education class when Mr. Dickey said there could be snow on the roof and fire in the chimney. It took us five days to figure out what he was talking about, and even then it was Sheila who got the answer," Tom said.

Josh turned pink. "I get it. Dorothy is your sweetheart."

"Among other things," Charlie muttered, as he started throwing things into a bag.

"Will we be safe at Dorothy's house?"

"Youngster, when you meet Dorothy, you'll know nothing is going to happen to you. She can be a one-man, er, one-woman army. Matter of fact, she was in the army once. She's a crack shot, too. Wears combat boots all the time. If she decides to kick ass and take names later, that person is never seen or heard of again. She cooks like an angel. She has two dogs and two cats, and her place still smells like Ivory Soap. You ready?"

"Yeah, I'm ready."

"Then let's hit the road."

The time was five ten.

* * *

Hudson Preston checked to make sure he had his keys deep in his pockets. He took a last look around the house he knew he would never see again. His gaze raked the photos on the mantel and then the huge painting of his father over the mantel. "Rot in hell, you bastard!"

He was almost to the door when he turned around and headed back to the bar, where he poured one last drink of the vintage cognac. As he gulped the fiery liquid, he realized he was too nervous to enjoy it. *Another time, another place*, he told himself as he walked back through the rooms and out the kitchen door. If he didn't make a sound and walked through his neighbor's yard and exited on the cross street, his security detail would never know he'd left the house. He'd eluded this particular bunch in the past, so he saw no cause for worry this time.

His heart thundering in his chest, Hudson played the instructions over and over in his mind as he trotted along. *Don't make eye contact with anyone, don't look to the right or the left. Don't speak to anyone. A car will stop, the door will open, and you get in.* Even an idiot could follow those simple instructions.

Five minutes later, Hudson heard the sound of a car behind him. His feet picked up speed, but he didn't look up. Out of the corner of his eye he saw the black nose of the car slow and pull to the curb. When he heard the sound of the door sliding open, he stepped to the curb and climbed in. The automatic lock slammed home.

Safe.

Twenty minutes later, the privacy partition slid open. The driver turned slightly. "Are you comfortable, Senator?"

There was something familiar about the voice asking the polite question, but Hudson couldn't place it. "Yes," he said curtly.

Another twenty minutes went by before the driver made a sudden stop and pulled to the curb in front of an identical-looking car. "I'll just be a moment, sir. I have to speak to a colleague."

Hudson watched as the driver climbed out of the car and walked around to the back so that he could approach the parked vehicle behind him. He opened the door, looked in, and turned to face Hudson Preston at the same time the automatic doors slid open.

"How's it going, old chum?" Diesel Morgan asked.

"You!"

"Well, not exactly. I'm the new you from here on in. See that car? That was supposed to be your getaway car, but now it's my getaway car. Like I said, I'm the new you. And don't you worry that fat little head of yours, I'm going to pop your old man as soon as I get done with you. Any last words, Senator?"

"It was all my father's idea. He's to blame for all this. Go on, shoot me, get it over with."

Morgan obliged.

* * *

Pete Kelly pounced on his cell phone like it was a lost contact lens. "What the hell do you mean he hung up on you? Marty . . ."

"Pete, I told him I'd have you call, and then the kid asked for your cell number when all of a sudden I could feel this intake of breath, and he froze on me. I think he was with someone. Just like that he cut me off. I did hear him say, 'Oh, shit!' before he hung up. I'm sorry, boss."

"No caller ID?" Pete asked.

"No, a TracFone, I assume. You know how those things work. The kid is smart, but I can guarantee you he's got some help. He knows you're in California. And he saw you on television. He also said he's Number 8446. That's it, boss."

Pete broke the connection. He felt like crying. "We lost him again. He called. Marty thinks he has help now. That's probably a good thing if it's the right kind of help. We need to think about that. Up until last night the boy was flying blind. Now, where in this short span of time did he come up with help? You wanna know what I think, Lily? I think that old guy at the Castle Gate Apartments is helping him. He snookered us. And we damn well fell for it. Son of a bitch!" Pete seethed as he banged his fist into the wall.

"The best part is this. He said he was 8446. That's all I needed to hear. He's my kid! He's mine, Lily! No more guessing. He's mine!"

Lily ran to him and put her arms around him. "Tell me, Pete, what's it feel like?" she whispered.

Pete looked down into Lily's questioning eyes. "Like a thousand Christmas mornings all rolled into one. It's a high and a low all at the same time. I want to tell the world I have a son. Although he probably hates my guts or will if he doesn't already. I don't even care about that. It's the same overwhelming feeling as the one I had when I realized I loved you. Your turn is coming. I promise. I never break a promise, just so you know, Lily."

"I know that, Pete. I'm a patient person. Now, let's put our heads together and see what we come up with."

Pete nodded. "First I have to call Marty and tell him to run an extensive check on that old guy. While he's doing that, I think we should go back to the Castle Gate Apartments as soon as it gets dark. My gut tells me the boy is with him."

"Why wait for darkness, Pete? Let's be brazen and walk right up to the door and knock. I see no reason to let more hours go by when we're so close to finding him."

The phone call made, Zolly at the wheel, the trio, along with Winston, set off for the Castle Gate Apartments. By the time Zolly parked the car, Marty Bronson was on the phone.

"You want to write this down or will you remember it, boss?"

"Just give it to me now, Marty, then text message it, okay?"

"You got it. Charlie Garrison has a few navy buddies. I have two addresses. He owns the Hotdog Haven and works for ten bucks an hour. That's all he takes out of the business. There's a

rift between him and his family. Yeah, I know I
gave you some of this before. He has four employees, and here are their addresses. My gut
tells me to go with Miss Dorothy since she seems
to be of an age with Charlie. Maybe they're an
item. Women are sympathetic to kids and old
men. Start with her. I did a MapQuest check
and she lives about six blocks from the Castle
Gate Apartments. She's a widow and works the
day shift at the Hotdog Haven three days a week
and one day every other weekend. She's ex-
army, so watch it, or she might wipe up the floor
with you. She lives at 982 Sawmill Road. If
there's anything else you need me for, just call."

"Here's the plan, Zolly, go around back and
pick the lock. Lily, Winston, and I will go right
to the front door that you will open when we
ring the bell. Make it quick, Zolly."

Eight minutes later they were in Charlie Garrison's kitchen.

Zolly was the one who found the packaging
from the TracFone in the trash basket by the
back door. "Hey, boss, here's the phone number
of Josh's phone!"

Excitement rendered Lily momentarily speechless. "Are you going to call the number, Pete?"

"Yeah, but not until we get to 982 Sawmill
Road. Zolly will be at the back door, you, me,
and Winston will be at the front. He's not going
to get away from us this time."

Chapter 27

Tessie's cell phone chirped as she was walking to the lot where she'd parked her car. She flipped it open, mumbled a greeting as she fished around inside her carryall for her keys. She stopped what she was doing when she heard Little Slick's voice.

"I'm buying dinner. Fifteen minutes. Be on time."

Tessie blinked. Two calls in one day. Her stomach started to churn at what she tried to imagine this invitation was all about. Something not good, that was for sure. When Little Slick offered to buy dinner, it meant trouble. Big trouble. Secretly, she thought he probably had the first dime he ever earned socked away under his mattress. But she loved the lanky hacker even though he was tighter than a duck's ass.

Tessie hit the highway, then took a turnoff and made the rest of the journey using side streets and alleys until she entered the smelly parking lot of the Desperado Lounge, a place that featured gyrating pole dancers and other assorted live entertainment. Not that she or Little Slick ever paid attention to the performers. They loved the food. At least Slick did. She did her best to take notes on the sly on how to conquer the pole. One of these days . . .

Slick was waiting for her in the back of the lounge, a bottle of Heineken in front of him. One, with the cap still on, was waiting for her. She slid into the booth but remained quiet as she twisted off the cap and took a healthy swig of the beer.

"Hudson Preston is dead! They just found his body. You were the last person to see him other than his security detail. The feebies want to talk to you."

Tessie heard the words as though they were coming from some far-off place. She set down the green bottle very carefully in the exact same wet circle that she had picked it up from. She licked at her lips. "Did he just die, or did someone help him out?"

"Dead is dead. Yeah, someone pumped a few into him. Probably used a silencer because there have been no reports that anyone saw or heard anything on the street. He was left in a Honda Odyssey on the side of the road. A cop on patrol had gone over to check it out because it was in a no-parking zone. Lots of blood. I bet it was the same guy who shot up the schoolkids. I tell you this only because if it is going to get swept under the rug again, you need to present yourself front and center and run with it. It's your call, Tessie. If it doesn't sit right with you, have that dude from PAK Industries stick his neck out. Ah, here's our food."

"How can you even think about food at a time like this?" Tessie grumbled as she tried to imagine the ramifications of Senator Preston's death. She looked around at the biker clientele. Lots of black leather and way too many silver spikes. There wasn't much in the way of décor aside from the posters of every Harley-Davidson ever manufactured that wallpapered the long, narrow room. The Desperado was a beer joint, pure and simple. It was whispered, but not too loudly, that there were other things that went down there from time to time, but no one seemed to care. The owner, according to Little Slick, turned a nice six-figure profit quarterly. "Quarterly" being the key word.

"I can think about food because I haven't eaten since nine thirty this morning. What's your next move?" Slick asked as he tried to bite into the eight-inch hamburger that drizzled the table with all kinds of stuff that was stuck between the meat patties.

"I need to think. You can't just spring something like this on me and expect me to come up with . . . whatever the hell it is you expect me to come up with. I rattled him this morning, I do know that. Help me out here. The feebs can't brush this under the rug; the guy was a goddamn United States senator. That's news. And if he was really going to throw his hat into the ring, that's even bigger news."

Little Slick swiped at his chin with a wad of paper napkins. "Wrong place at the wrong time,

random shooting. Where does it say they're
going to tie him into the school shooting? No
one is going to advertise that little tidbit. Except
maybe you," he said slyly. "Like I said, this might
be a good time to powwow with your friend
Kelly. Always remember you have freedom of
the press on your side. Use it. You can beat the
feebs. Or is that boss of yours a pansy and afraid
to take on . . . you know who?"

Tessie propped her elbows on the scarred
table. "Damn, I've never heard you talk so much
in my whole life. This sucks, Slick."

"Yeah, it does." Slick held up his beer bottle
to signal for a refill. In the blink of an eye two
bottles appeared on the table. "If you aren't
going to eat that burger, push it over here. You
on a diet or something, Tessie?"

"Or something," Tessie responded, her eyes
on the bikini-clad woman slithering up and
down the pole in the middle of the polished
bar. Someday she was going to be able to do
that.

Tessie hated to ask for advice, but she did it
anyway. "Slick, what do you think I should do? I
have the FBI chief's home phone number. My
boss told me some very important people came
to see him and all the other paper owners and
told them to sit on the shootings. They agreed
temporarily. He said I could run with it, but had
to check in with him. You want to listen to our
conversation, or should I take it outside?"

"The less I know, the less I can testify to. Go
for it, Tessie. I'll watch your back."

Tessie slid out of the booth. She was almost to

the bar area when she turned around and walked back to Little Slick. She bent down and kissed his cheek. "Thanks," she whispered.

Tessie made one last stop at the bar and looked up at the slithering pole dancer. "Honey, how long did it take you to learn to do that?"

"Two days."

As she exited the bar, cell phone in hand, Tessie mumbled, "My ass, two days." She punched in her boss's number.

"Harry, Tessie. Hudson Preston was found shot to death about an hour ago. So far it's been kept quiet. I got the scoop. If you give me the go-ahead, I'm going to call the Bureau chief since I have his home phone number. Harry, you still there?"

"You got two sources?" Harry asked in a strangled voice.

"I have *one* source, and I'll die before I give him up. He's so golden he could light the universe. Well?"

"You got it. Feed it to me as you get it, and it will be the headline for the morning paper. Don't make me regret this, Tessie."

"I want a raise," Tessie said because she couldn't think of anything else to say.

"That, too," Harry said.

Tessie's next call was to the FBI's chief, Ansel Montgomery, who, from the way he sounded, was having dinner.

"Mr. Montgomery, this is Tess Dancer from the *Chronicle*. I'm sorry to be calling you during the dinner hour, but I was just told Senator Hudson Preston was found shot and killed a little while ago. I was wondering if you'd care to have your office comment on the shooting. We're going to go with it in the morning. I have a source that tells me the ballistics will match those of the shooting at the California Academy of Higher Learning." Tessie licked at her lips, which were so dry she thought the skin would peel off as she waited for the chief's response. When there was none she asked in awe, "You didn't know, did you? Okay, I can run with that. Nice talking to you, Mr. Montgomery."

Tessie clicked the phone shut and let her breath out in a long *swoosh* of air.

Her next call was to Pete Kelly. "C'mon, c'mon, pick up, Pete."

"Tessie, what's up?"

"Where are you, Pete?"

"Well . . ."

Tessie gritted her teeth. "Pete, where the hell are you? Senator Hudson Preston was found shot and killed over an hour ago and left on the side of the road. According to my source, I was the last one to see him other than his security detail. I'd told him I knew he was one of the principal owners of the sperm bank, the fertility clinic, and the academy. Now he's dead. It's going to hit the papers in the morning. What that means to you is I got the scoop, and the shit is going to hit the fan. I have to run with this. Now, where the hell are you?"

Pete told her. "We're almost there."

"Wait for me, Pete. Promise."

"Yeah, okay. We don't have a tail if that's what

you're worried about. Zolly has eyes in the back of his head."

"Yeah, well, I think it's safe to assume that Senator Preston thought he didn't have a tail, too. I'm not worried about you, Pete. I'm worried about the boy. I should be there in twenty minutes or so."

The second Tessie heard the siren, she knew what was going to go down. The cell phone still in her hand, she dialed Pete's number again. The moment she heard his voice, she said, "The cops are about to pull me over. I'll keep the line open so you can hear what's going on. Have Lily or Zolly call my boss and tell him what's happening. Then I want you to call another number and tell the person who answers the same thing. Just identify yourself and tell him I told you to call him. I don't know where they're going to take me. Local or Feds? Who knows? I called the Bureau chief, and he didn't even know about Preston so I'm thinking the locals are picking me up for a handover. Okay, I'm at a full stop now." Tessie slipped the open-line cell phone into the pocket of her jacket and waited for the tap on her window.

When it came, she rolled down the window halfway. She held out her press card, her insurance card, and her driver's license. "I wasn't speeding."

"Yes, you were speeding, ten miles over the limit."

"Yeah, and my mother's name is Madonna. I was not speeding, Officer. As a matter of fact I was under the limit because I am more or less lost at the moment."

"Tell it to the judge. Get out and lock up your car."

Tessie's heart kicked up a beat. "Why? Just give me the ticket, and I'll work it out in court. What's your name? And I want to see your badge number before I get out of this car."

Tessie could see the indecision on the officer's face. "Well? Let's see it. How do I know you're not one of those guys who dress like a cop and prey on women at night? That's not even an official police car. You just have the light on the top. I'm rolling up my window now, and I'm not getting out of this car. In fact, I'm going to drive off right now, Officer, and I'm going to drive to the nearest police station, so stay behind me. I'm going to call 911 and report this." Tessie reached into her pocket for her cell phone and pretended to dial 911. She talked to Pete at breakneck speed, giving her approximate location, a description of the officer, and the type of car he was driving.

The moment there was a break in the evening traffic, Tessie pealed out, tires squealing. She looked into the rearview mirror to see the cop standing with his gun drawn. He wasn't following her. Why should he? All he had to do was call ahead to one of his buddies, and she'd get stopped again down the road. Her brain racing, she turned off the road, drove over a few lawns, and parked the car at a curb, right in front of a fire hydrant. She got out of the car and ran as fast as she could as she babbled into the phone to Pete on the other end. "I don't know where the hell I am. Can you send Zolly to pick me up?"

"Well, yeah, Tessie, as soon as you give me a clue as to where you are. Damn, you are one hell of a ballsy lady. Zolly is going to be impressed. Scratch that, he *is* impressed. We have a GPS tracker in the car. Give me a street, and he'll find you. I guess I don't have to tell you to stay out of sight. I made your calls, by the way. Your boss was pissed to the teeth, said he was on it. Your source, or your snitch, whoever he is, just grunted and broke the connection. So where are you?"

"I'm in a residential neighborhood. I left my car a couple of streets back. I bet that cop stuck something on my bumper to track me. I can hear sirens. This street is"—Tessie craned her neck to see the sign at the end of the street— "Oliver Terrace. It looks like Martina Place is the cross street. I can barely see the sign. I'll be waiting for you. Tell Zolly to hurry, Pete. I can see flashing blue lights already," Tessie said as she wiggled and squirmed her way into a dense privet hedge. She dropped to her knees and hoped to God she'd be able to get back up.

"We're on our way, Tessie."

The flashing lights were coming down the street at a bare crawl. Tessie crossed her fingers as she leaned as far back behind the privet as she could. She was so busy thanking God for the hedge, for Pete and Zolly, for the dark night, and the fact that no stray dogs were about when she saw a second car with flashing lights crawling down the street. Suddenly front lights came on up and down the street, doors started to open, and somewhere a dog was barking. Tessie's heart started to flutter. "Come on, Pete, hurry up. I'm a sitting duck here," she muttered under her breath.

The minutes crawled by so slowly Tessie thought she was going to lose her mind. The moment she saw a pair of headlights turn onto Oliver Terrace, Tessie punched in Pete's number and waited. "Are you on the street yet?"

"We just turned the corner. Where are you?"

"Three car lengths from your car. I can see your headlights. Slow down, I have to dig myself out of this privet hedge. Pull into the driveway, and by the time you do that, I can bolt for the car. Have the door open." Tessie scrambled from the privet just as a dog raced down the road. Winston leaped from the car to hold him at bay as Tessie made a mad scramble for the backseat. Pete yanked and pulled her into the car, which was backing out of the driveway before he could close the door. Lily opened the other side, and Winston jumped in.

Tessie was shaking from head to toe. Lily wrapped her arms around the stout woman's shoulders. "You're safe, Tessie. Damn, that was close."

Tessie was still shaking when she asked about her boss. "What'd he say?"

"Just that he was on it," Pete said. "Your snitch just grunted. What now, Tessie?"

Tessie already had her cell phone open and was calling her boss. "I'm okay, Harry. Tell me you haven't had a change of heart. Tell me you're going to run with the senator's death by gunshot."

"I'm going with it. Anything else you want to tell me?"

"Wake up Douglas Preston, the senator's father, Harry. He lives in that mausoleum on Wild Orchid Drive. He's a recluse these days, and there doesn't seem to be a great deal of closeness between father and son. Tell him you know everything. See what he gives up. That should keep you busy until my next call. Don't worry, I'll feed it in to the desk as I go along. I think we might have found the boy. If we're successful where he's concerned, we're going to bring him to the paper. He's the key to everything, Harry. Alert everyone, okay? Oh, one other thing, call Montgomery, the Bureau chief, and tell him you're running the story and this might be a good time for him to wash the stink off his hands. This is Secret Agent Tess Dancer signing off for now," Tessie said in a jittery voice.

In the front seat, Zolly guffawed.

"Okay, big man," Tessie said to Zolly in the same jittery voice, "let's go find this man's kid so we can all go home and go to sleep."

Chapter 28

Diesel Morgan eyed the man in the backseat, who was shackled to the door handle. One more stop to make, then he would step into Hudson Preston's shoes. Just one more stop. He met the man's gaze in the rearview mirror and smiled. He laughed when he saw the way the man shivered. "I certainly hope you haven't lied to me about anything."

The man in the backseat said nothing. What was the point?

"Okay, we're here," Morgan said, pulling up under the portico of the Preston family mansion on Wild Orchid Drive. "I won't be long," Morgan said as he opened the car door.

Morgan marched to the side door and rang the bell. A maid, who looked to be an old family retainer, opened the door and peered up at the clean-cut-looking man standing in front of her. "Hudson asked me to drop something off for his father. I don't have much time, so if you show me the way, I can be in and out in a few minutes."

"Eh?" the old woman asked as she cupped her ear to hear better. "Mr. Preston," Morgan shouted. "Hudson sent me," he said, waving a brown envelope under her nose. "Take me to him." When the woman still didn't seem to understand, Morgan brushed past her, taking a moment to pat her on the back in a friendly way.

The woman backed up, then closed the door. Morgan waited to see if she would lead the way. She did, stopping at the bottom of the stairway and pointing upward. She then pointed to her knees, a sign that Morgan took to mean she didn't do stairs, which was fine with him.

The staircase was beautiful, polished mahogany and circular. At the top, a woman in a white uniform waited for him. "Can I help you?"

"You sure can. Hudson asked me to deliver this package to his father. He said I was to place it directly in his hands. I'm in a bit of a hurry as I have a flight to catch. Can you show me the way to Mr. Preston's room?"

"No one called me," the middle-aged woman grumbled. "I don't like my patient's routine altered. Right now, Mr. Preston is watching the US Open. An old one, but he does love to play commentator. I guess it's all right. Hudson was here earlier in the day. Hudson never comes here anymore."

Morgan shrugged and waved the envelope. "No offense, ma'am, but I will need some privacy for this meeting."

The nurse huffed and puffed a little, but in

the end she opened the door to her patient's room and closed it as Morgan was walking toward the elder Preston.

"Who are you?" the old man asked petulantly.

"Why do you want to know?" Morgan asked as he opened the brown padded mailing envelope. He withdrew a gun with a long snout. The old man recognized the silencer and cringed in his chair. "Don't make a sound," the hired killer warned.

The old man started to wheeze as his clawlike hands gripped the arms of the chair. "What do you want? Did my son send you?"

"I want you to write a letter saying what you and your rich friends did where all those kids were concerned. For starters, I know you're the one who gave the order to slaughter those kids at the school. I want you to explain, in detail, how you tested your drugs on all those children from the day they were born. By the way, your son Hudson is dead. I killed him a few hours ago. Now, write," Morgan said as he handed a pen and paper to the old man. "Be quick about it, or I'll start by shooting out your kneecaps."

"I'll do no such thing," the old man wheezed. The words were no sooner out of his mouth than Morgan pointed and fired at the man's right knee. The only thing to be heard was a spitting, popping sound. The elder Preston doubled over, a scream of pain spewing from his mouth. The door opened, and the nurse rushed in to check on her patient, her eyes wide with fear. Morgan shot her right between the eyes. She crumpled soundlessly to the floor.

"Now, write, old man."

Morgan kept one eye on his watch and the other on the old man. "I think you need to write a little faster." He raised the gun and waved it around the room, finally settling on the old man's left leg.

"Why are you doing this?" Preston asked, his voice full of pain.

"Because I can."

"Who the hell are you to judge? You killed those children for money. What makes you any different from me? All we did was speed up the testing process so our drugs could help millions of people. It's called 'collateral damage.'"

There was no reasonable response to the old man's questions or his last statement, so Morgan didn't try to offer any. "Now, write down names and phone numbers."

"I don't have that information. Hudson has all the records. Other people . . . I don't know. I tried to keep my distance in case . . . I just didn't want to be involved. That's the truth, so if you're going to shoot me, just shoot me."

"Okay." The hit man raised his arm, eyeballed the man in front of him. He fired. The old man died instantly, slumping over in his chair.

Morgan reached for the paper, which he stuffed in the brown envelope along with the gun. He then dragged the nurse to the far corner of the room. He checked the air-conditioning unit and turned it to maximum cooling. He gave off a jaunty salute when he left the room.

Downstairs, he headed in the direction of the kitchen, where the old housekeeper was chopping vegetables. She looked up with frightened eyes before the bullet ended her life. Morgan dragged her body to the pantry and closed the door. He looked around for another air-conditioning panel and once again turned the temperature as low as it would go. He locked the kitchen door before making his way to the door that led to the portico.

After exiting the house, Morgan walked from the portico to the car and climbed behind the wheel, humming the lyrics to Rod Stewart's newest song. In the backseat, his passenger cowered in fear. Morgan took a second to look over at the brown envelope on the passenger seat. He had the old man's paper and Hudson's keys. The memory stick with all the records. A hell of a bargaining chip should he ever need to use it. Not to mention a wonderful blackmail tool. Ah, the life of luxury was just his for the asking.

Now, all he had to do was head for the airport and climb aboard the chartered Gulfstream that would whisk him away to a safe land, where he would assume his new identity and commence living a life in the manner to which Hudson Preston was accustomed.

When Zolly parked the SUV six doors away from #982, no one made a move to get out of the vehicle.

"Maybe I should call first," Pete said. "If we go right to the door, the old man or even the boy might opt to call the police. We need to ask ourselves if we really want to tangle with the locals, who will then call the FBI. If we blow it now, we aren't going to get another chance."

Tessie digested the information. "You do have a point. The last thing we want is for the boy to take off again. How about this? Zolly goes to the back door. I station myself at the garage. You and Lily go to the front door. Call the Trac-Fone before you ring the doorbell. Ask for the old man. He might listen and not panic, as opposed to the boy, who is scared out of his wits. If you get the feeling they're going to call the police, Zolly can break down the door."

"Okay, let's do it," Pete said, getting out of the car. "Lily, call Zolly's cell phone so he can keep an open line. Everyone ready?"

Josh was about to bite into his grilled-cheese sandwich when the TracFone on the kitchen counter rang. He dropped his sandwich on the plate in front of him as he got off the chair, but Charlie beat him to the counter.

"I think we should answer it, youngster."

"How did they get the number?" Josh whispered.

"Stupid, stupid, stupid! They broke into Charlie's apartment and went through the trash and found the number on the papers in the trash. Sloppy work, buddy."

Josh closed his eyes. "I can't run anymore, Tom," he whispered. "Whatever is going to happen is going to happen. Maybe I'll be seeing you sooner than you know."

"I don't want to hear that kind of talk. You have things to do, places to go, promises to keep. Just see who it is, and maybe you can cut a deal. Go for it, 8446."

Josh turned to Charlie and nodded.

Charlie clicked on the phone, and said, "Make it quick and state your business."

Outside the front door, Pete blinked. In the voice he used from time to time to rally his staff, Pete went into his spiel. He ended up by saying, "We're the good guys, Mr. Garrison. Do you think I got to be where I am in the business world by bullshitting my way? Everything I told you is the truth. All we want is to take the boy to safety, and the *Chronicle* seems to be the best place at the moment. If that doesn't work for you and the boy, we can go anywhere you might suggest. I give you my word that we will keep the boy safe, and no harm will come to him. You can tell him for me that I am the other half of his number. I'll give you a few minutes, then I'll call you back. Will that be okay, Mr. Garrison?"

Charlie's brain whirled and twirled. "I'll talk to the boy. Give me a little time. Give me a number where I can call you back." Pete rattled off his cell phone number, then ended the call.

Charlie looked at the young man standing across from him. He put both his hands on Josh's shoulders and looked into the young man's eyes. "I believe the man, Josh. He wants to help you. He said he'll take us to the newspaper or wherever else we want—to keep us safe. I think the paper is the way to go. You can tell your story, and the paper will print it. Once it's public, there isn't anything the authorities can do to you except take your statement. I'm thinking Mr. Kelly has some top-notch lawyers who will beat them off with their law books. He also said to tell you he's the other half of your 8446. I don't know what that means. It must be important because no one else knows about those numbers. What do you say, youngster?"

Josh turned around. "Tom?" he hissed. "Tell me what to do."

"I think you got it going on, buddy. Give the guy a chance. If you don't like what he's saying to you, tell him to buzz off. Make him give you his word that if you don't like what he says. you can leave, and he never bothers you again. Remember, you have Charlie in your corner."

"You sure, Tom?"

"I'm as sure as I can be. The rest is up to you, Josh. You have to make a decision now, no more waffling. I think going to the newspaper is the right choice. I have a feeling they're going to make this all right for you, buddy."

Josh turned around and reached for the phone. "Tom said it's okay. You say it's okay. I'll call Mr. Kelly. Read me off the number, Charlie."

Josh punched in the numbers of Pete's cell phone. When Pete came on the line, he said, "This is Josh Baer. I'll agree to talk to you if you promise me something."

Pete grew so light-headed at the sound of the boy's voice, he had to reach for Lily's arm to steady himself. "I never make a blind promise. Tell me what it is, and if I can agree to it in good conscience, then I will give you my promise."

"Take him at his word," Tom whispered. *"What he's saying is fair, Josh."*

Josh waited for several long minutes before

he finally said, "Okay, that will work. When do you want to talk?"

"How about right now? I'm at your front door. Open it, and we can sit down and talk."

Josh turned white. His expression showed panic as he handed the phone to Charlie.

"What?" the old man barked into the phone, his eyes on the young man, who was shaking from head to toe.

"Open the door, Mr. Garrison. I'm on the front porch."

Charlie Garrison wrapped his arms around the boy. "Take a deep breath and sit down. We're ready to listen. You don't have to say a word if you don't want to. It's not going to hurt to listen; you might learn something that will help you. I won't open the door if you don't want me to. What's it gonna be, Josh?"

"Go ahead, open the door, Charlie. I'm ready." And, Josh realized, he *was* finally ready. He took another deep breath and waited.

He's tall, not scary-looking at all, Josh thought. He stood, and said, "You look like me." He didn't offer to shake hands. They were equally tall, he noticed. Strange.

Pete struggled with every emotion in the book. He tried for a light tone, but the words came out gruff and hoarse. "I was just going to say you look like me. Why don't we just say we look like each other and let it go at that? Okay?"

"Yeah, sure," Josh said as he sat down.

Pete turned to Lily and introduced her. Josh simply nodded. "If you don't mind, we have two friends outside. I'd like them to come in if that's okay," he said, addressing Charlie, who nodded his agreement.

Again, introductions were made. Winston prowled the kitchen before he settled down by the boy's feet. *He knows,* Pete thought. Dogs' instincts were so uncanny.

"What do you want? Why have you been chasing me everywhere I go?" Josh asked.

"I want . . . I want to keep you out of harm's way. This lady," Pete said, motioning to Lily, "and I met a long time ago when we were both around your age and going to college at Berkeley. We lost touch over the years and met up in the Atlanta airport the day the shooting occurred. We saw your picture on the screen at the same time. We were both coming here to a fund-raiser at our alma mater.

"But I need to go back to the beginning to when we met, but more importantly, where and how we met. I was . . . poor, as was Lily. It was our last year, and neither one of us had enough money to pay for our room and board and tuition. We both, unbeknownst to each other, made an unwise decision. I donated my sperm to a sperm bank, and Lily donated her eggs to a fertility clinic that was next door to the sperm bank. We met on our way out.

"We had both been told that counseling was available, but neither of us followed through on that. Consequently, neither one of us had an easy time of it wondering how many children were out there that belonged to us.

"On the five-hour flight here, we both agreed to see if there was a way for us to find the children of our donations. In doing so, things pretty much exploded. My donor number was 8446. Lily's number was 1114. We went to the sperm bank and the fertility clinic but couldn't find out anything. The next day when we went back, we broke in, only to find everything cleaned out. There wasn't so much as a paper clip or rubber band left behind. We tried everything to find out who owned those two operations but were not successful. That's why we went to Tessie Dancer of the *Chronicle*.

"She was able to find out that a consortium owns both those operations and the California Academy of Higher Learning. One of the principals is Senator Hudson Preston of Preston Pharmaceuticals. We believe they were testing their drugs on babies born of our donations. When we made our donations, Lily and I both believed that the resulting children born from our donations would go to childless couples to complete their families. That, we know now, was not the case. Those people also had a surrogacy program in place, where women were paid large sums of money to deliver babies who were whisked away to be tested and monitored. You were one of those babies."

"Holy shit!" Tom said.

Charlie touched Josh's shoulder. "Show him."

Josh kicked off his sneakers and held up his toes to show the two tattoos on his big toes. Pete blinked and swayed. He stared at the number 2003 on Josh's left toe. Mother and father. He looked over at Lily. Tears were rolling down her cheeks. Tessie was pretending she had something in her eye. Zolly smacked one hamlike fist into the other, his eyes murderous.

Winston got up, sniffed Josh's feet, then did his best to leap onto his lap. Josh struggled to help the big dog. "Why's he doing this?" he asked curiously.

"I think he likes you," Pete said, his voice so husky he could hardly believe it was his own.

"Where is Jesse?" Josh asked abruptly.

"We're going to have the answer to that real soon. Right now, if you are agreeable, we're going to go to the paper, and Tessie will write your story so it makes the morning edition. You have to talk to her boss and tell him the same thing you've been telling us."

Josh's head bobbed up and down. "What about the guy that did the shooting and killed all my friends? Did anyone catch him? Is he still looking for me?"

"*No* to your first question, and the answer to the second one is probably *yes*."

Tessie spoke for the first time. "Senator Preston, one of those who owned all three facilities, is dead. We just found out a little while ago. With the picture of the shooter, an all-out manhunt will go into effect the moment my story hits the paper. That man, whoever he is, won't be safe anywhere on this planet. I want you to believe me on that."

"You didn't see that guy. I did. He's not going to give up. Charlie said you're rich," Josh said, looking up at Pete. "Is that true?"

"More or less. Is that important to you?"

"No, not to me. I want to make a deal with

you," Josh said. "I'll turn over my book to you if you make arrangements to get a stone with the names of all my friends on it. I want a funeral and a place where I can go to see the classmates that guy killed. I want something really special."

Pete wanted to grab the kid and run as far and as fast as he could. "Okay, it's a deal. First, though, we have to follow the rules."

"How long will that take?" Josh asked.

"I'm thinking not long at all once Tessie's story hits the paper. The FBI will be falling all over itself to do the right thing. At least I hope so. Tessie, do you agree?"

"Absolutely. Listen, guys, we have to leave now if you want this story to hit the morning paper."

Josh stood up and moved over to stand by Charlie. "He comes, too. He's my new grandfather. So, does all this mean you're my father, Mr. Kelly?"

Mr. Kelly. "I think so. The clothes you left behind at Mr. Dickey's house were sent off to be examined for DNA. Do you know what that is?"

Josh nodded.

"When the report comes back in a week or so we'll know for certain."

"Oh, man, are you one lucky dude. Not only do you find your real father, but he's a rich father. One real family coming up."

Josh ignored his friend's comment as he joined the small parade to the front door and out to the SUV.

* * *

It was midnight when things wound down at the *Chronicle.* Two FBI agents escorted the little group out of the building, explaining they needed to get Josh to what they referred to as a "safe house." Josh balked until the agents promised that Jesse would also be brought to the safe house.

"Someone needs to go to the morgue to get the numbers off . . . everyone's toes," Josh said.

"It's being done as we speak, Josh," Tessie said gently. "You look tired. A good night's sleep is called for. Tomorrow is going to be a busy day for you."

"Charlie's coming, right?"

Pete nodded.

"Youngster, I am not leaving you. I'll be with you as long as you need me."

Winston, Pete noticed, was glued to the boy's side. It was right, boy and dog. His heart was so heavy he could barely make his feet work on the way to the car.

"Pete, relax," Lily said. "You just handed that boy a double whammy. Did you really think he was going to fall into your arms and call you 'daddy'?" she asked gently.

"No, but it was what I wanted to happen. I watched him looking at me. He's viewing me as something bad on the bottom of his shoe. How do I change that?"

"You don't, Pete. It's up to Josh now. You've done all you could. He seems like a great kid. I thought I was going to lose it there for a minute when he asked you if you'd buy a stone for his friends."

"That's the last thing I expected to come out of his mouth. You're right, he's a great kid. How many kids that age, going through what he's been through, would be thinking about Jesse and buying a tombstone? None, that's how many. He doesn't like me, Lily, that's the bottom line. He's judging me, I could see it in his eyes, and I came up real short. Hell, if I was him I think I would have punched me out."

Lily squeezed Pete's arm. "It's not about us anymore, Pete. It's about Josh and Jesse and all their fallen friends, and the others who were removed from the academy and sent to the other schools. We have to accept that. Our day in the sun will come."

"You're right, Lily, as usual. What do you make of the fact that Winston wanted to stay with the boy?"

"I think Winston is one very smart dog, and the boy needs someone like Winston right now. And beyond that, maybe Josh smells a little like you. It's a good thing, Pete."

"Yeah, a good thing," Pete murmured as he held open the door of the SUV for Lily.

"Back to the hotel, boss?" Zolly asked, his voice cracking with emotion.

"Yeah. The FBI said no way were we allowed to be with the boy. Just Tessie, since she and her boss called the shots. Tomorrow is another day."

The weariness and sadness in Pete's voice made Lily want to cry. She reached for his hand and squeezed it. "Yes, tomorrow is another day, Pete."

Chapter 29

Instead of going straight to Pete and Lily's villa, Tessie stopped at Zolly's, the morning paper under her arm. Zolly was waiting for her, which surprised her for some reason.

"I knew you'd come here first," Zolly whispered, knowing voices carried in the still air.

"It's all there, everything the boy knows and remembers. We copied everything in his little notebook, then handed it over to the FBI. There's no way anything associated with this story is going to get sat on from here on in. By the end of the day, Ansel Montgomery will be relegated to some outpost far, far away for letting the power boys in Washington dictate to him. Pete gave a half-assed promise not to bring the wrath of PAK Industries down on the feebies. It worked. God only knows what his and Lily's stockholders are going to think when they read the paper this morning."

"I don't think the boss cares a whole hell of a lot what anyone thinks, and that includes his stockholders. For the moment anyway," Zolly said softly.

"The headlines have gone around the world at least twice already," Tessie said wearily. "I got text messages on my BlackBerry congratulating me even before the paper hit the street. Don't even ask me how that can happen because I don't have an answer."

"Well, damn. Will this get you your third Pulitzer?"

"My boss said it will. You know what, Zolly, this time it wasn't about the Pulitzer. It was about . . . a kid, a bunch of kids, and a gaggle of scum who were the Devil's disciples. I called them that in my story, too. You know what else? On my way over here I got a call from my boss who told me he had calls from MI6, Interpol, Scotland Yard, and a few more of the world's police forces. All of them offered their help in tracking down the rest of the members of the consortium and the killer."

"What about the boy?"

"He's a great kid, Zolly. You should have seen him with Jesse when the feebs brought him over to the safe house. Jesse is all he has left from that other life. Challenged as he is, Jesse knew him, hugged him like he'd never let him go. They need each other. Both of those kids need to talk to a shrink. That will be ongoing. Eventually, Josh will be okay, and Jesse, as long as he's with Josh, will be okay, too. Josh *talks* to his dead friend Tom. Tom talks back to him. Josh did admit to me he thought he was nuts—those are *his* words, not mine—the first time Tom talked to him. Then he said he thought maybe it was his own conscience talking to him, or he was in a dreamlike state. Charlie seems to think Josh really does talk to a spirit because he saw and heard Josh having a conversation with Tom. Someone a whole lot smarter than I is going to have to deal with that. Personally, if that's what the kid wants to think and believe, it's okay with me. He got this far with his buddy urging him on from the spirit world. That damn well has to count for something in my book."

"I believe in stuff like that. My parents used to talk about those things in the old country all the time. They were believers, too," Zolly said.

Tessie nodded, her eyelids drooping.

"Zolly, I wish you could have seen the pictures that boy Jesse drew. Every single one of the kids at the school who . . . who . . . aren't with us anymore. Then someone asked him to draw a group picture, and he did it. He drew one of the other classes—one of the groups that supposedly went on field trips before the shooting. The detail was mind-bending.

"We didn't include any of them in the article, but my boss, Harry, is sending them off to the other law agencies abroad. This is global now. I have to go, Zolly. Pete's waiting for me."

"Tessie . . . listen, I'm sorry if I . . . we got off on the wrong foot there in the beginning. I never . . . What I mean is I was jealous of you. I've been the boss's right hand for so long, and I saw you as stomping on my turf. I just want you to know I'm sorry."

Tessie patted the big man's shoulder. "It's

okay, Zolly, I knew where you were coming from. I was just busting your chops. Hey, you never did tell me, can you tango or not?"

"Just like Fred Astaire." Zolly laughed.

Tessie would have laughed, too, but she was too tired.

"Seems weird without the dog here," Tessie called over her shoulder. "He was sleeping next to the boy when I left the safe house." Tessie turned around and walked back to where Zolly was standing. "I hate to say this, but the kid wants no part of your boss. I tried to explain, as did Charlie, but he wasn't buying into it. He even said that Tom, that's the dead friend, said he needed to give the guy a chance. He said he wasn't turning over that book of his till he had everything in writing. I was pretty impressed, and, yeah, even a little proud of the kid when he started cutting his own deals. One other thing, he wants to file lawsuits against Preston Pharmaceuticals. That kid is going to own the damn company when he's through. Mark my word."

Zolly just nodded, then he burst out laughing. "He's the boss's kid, what did you expect? The boss giving up the dog, now, that's something else, but the way I see it is every kid needs a dog for a best friend, and Winston certainly fits that bill."

Tessie waved airily as she shuffled her way to Pete's villa. She was bone-tired. It had been a while since she'd pulled an all-nighter. She must be getting old. Maybe it was time to retire. Like that was ever going to happen. Just yesterday afternoon her parents had said they wanted to go to an assisted-living complex where there were people their own age. They were tired of seeing so little of their only daughter and having to live with the cross-eyed curmudgeon she'd hired to take care of them. Tears welled in her eyes. Didn't they know how hard she worked, didn't they know how every penny she earned went to their care? She couldn't remember the last time she'd bought a new outfit or had her old Ford Taurus serviced.

Tessie sat down on the decorative bench outside Lily's villa to blink away the tears. It was just a bad day in a long line of many bad days. When she looked up, Lily was standing next to her.

"What's wrong, Tessie? Did something happen?"

Tessie sniffed and shook her head. "It's . . . personal. I'm just tired. Here's the paper, first one off the press. I'm going to go home."

"You wait right here, Tessie Dancer, and do not move." Lily took the paper and ran into the villa to hand it to Pete. "I think I might have a small crisis out front so don't come out till I tell you. Promise, Pete."

Pete nodded as he unfolded the paper Lily had handed him. Big, bold black headlines. The whole goddamn front page, complete with pictures. Almost all of page two as well.

Lily went back out to sit with Tessie.

"Tell me," Lily said gently.

And Tessie did because it'd been so long since she'd heard a voice as gentle and caring as

Lily's. She let it all out and didn't hold back a thing. It was a woman-to-woman thing, something she'd needed to do for a very long time.

"Okay, that's enough of that," Tessie said, getting up. "I have to go home and get some sleep. You know what, Lily, that's another thing. I don't have a bedroom anymore. I sleep on a pullout couch. My mother took my room over for her sewing and quilting room. All she does is complain about the pole in the middle of the room. I told her I was going to plant ivy around it but never got around to it. Someday I'm going to write a book. Look, honey, this was all just between us, okay? I just needed to unload. It gets to me when I'm winding down a story.

"Come by the paper this afternoon. The feebs are going to be bringing Josh to us to finish up some things. I know Pete's going to want to see him again. And Jesse, too."

Lily sat back down on the bench, her thoughts far away. She dropped her head into her hands and swayed back and forth, a keening sound escaping her lips.

All those children still missing. She knew in her heart, in her gut, some of them were hers. Pete was the lucky one, and she didn't for one minute begrudge his happiness at finding his son. If only she'd found one of her children. If only. She knew she had to come to terms with the fact that they might all be lost to her forever. How was she going to live with that? To have come so far, to have learned so much, and now it all seemed lost. Tessie didn't think so, but maybe that was wishful thinking on her part.

Lily knew now that if her donations had gone to childless couples, she never would have interfered in their lives. But that wasn't the case. All those parentless children out there never knowing someone was trying to find them. How in the name of God could anyone ever make that right?

Maybe by dedicating one's life to the pursuit of finding them. She and Pete certainly had enough money to do that. Maybe that was what she was supposed to do with the rest of her life. Maybe, maybe, maybe.

Lily rubbed at her eyes with the sleeve of her shirt when she saw Zolly approaching her. "You're just the person I want to talk to, Zolly. I wonder if you would do me a favor."

"Just name it, Miss Lily."

She did, and Zolly's head bobbed up and down. "I'll get right on it. What's the time frame, Miss Lily?"

"Sooner rather than later. Thanks, Zolly."

The sun was up as Lily made her way back to her villa, where Pete was waiting for her. The birds were chirping their morning song. How normal everything seemed, yet there was nothing normal about the beginning of this new day.

Lily opened the door to see Pete bent over the little table, the paper spread out in front of him. His eyes were moist, as wet as her own. She didn't know what to say, so she just sat down next to him and reached for his hand.

Pete pointed to the front page of the paper, where a life-size picture of him and Josh stared back at him. "It's a sterling article, Lily. Heartbreaking, to be sure. I'm certain Tessie will get a Pulitzer for it. She'll be following up for weeks."

"It's not about the Pulitzer for Tessie, Pete. It's about Josh and the kids and what was done to them in the name of profits for a pharmaceutical company. What do you say we get cleaned up, have some breakfast, and head into town until it's time to meet up at the *Chronicle*?" In a lighter note she said, "I'll wash your back if you wash mine."

Pete scooped up Lily in his arms and ran to the bathroom. "Best offer I've had today."

"It's only going to get better," Lily promised.

Josh woke slowly, aware that there was something different going on. He tried to roll over but couldn't move. He opened his eyes, then burst out laughing. Winston was sitting on his chest. He growled softly and licked the boy's face. "You want to play, is that it? No? What, you want to go out?" Winston leaped off the bed and raced to the sliding door that led to a fenced backyard. Still laughing, Josh opened the door, and Winston raced outside.

Charlie and the two FBI agents in charge of Josh's and Jesse's safety looked at one another. The boy knew how to laugh. Charlie grinned from ear to ear.

"Hi, Josh," Jesse said. "Breakfast was real good. The pancakes are better than the ones at school. Did you miss me, Josh?"

"I sure did," Josh said, tousling Jesse's hair. "Did those people treat you okay?"

"Yeah, sure. They liked my drawings. Look at this one."

Josh picked up the drawing and smiled. Winston sleeping alongside him in bed. He laughed again. "Very good."

"Where are we going to go, Josh?"

"With me, young fella," Charlie said, sitting down next to Jesse. "Unless Josh changes his mind."

Winston barked and barked. "I think he wants to eat. What do you feed a dog?" Josh asked anxiously.

"How about what you eat?" the female agent said. "Pancakes and bacon. By the time you shower and dress, I'll have it all ready."

Josh nodded. "Did the paper come, Charlie?"

"It did, youngster. You're famous, and so is your . . . Mr. Kelly. It took a lot of guts for him to go public like that. You realize that, don't you, Josh?"

"Yeah, I guess so. Do you think Mr. Kelly is going to want his dog back? I always wanted a dog. He seems to like me. I think he'd be good with Jesse, don't you, Charlie?"

"Yeah, youngster. We can talk to Mr. Kelly about the dog. Go on now, take your shower and get dressed. Wear those new clothes I put in your room. I got them yesterday when I was out buying the TracFone. You want to look nice today for all the interviews you have to do. If we're lucky, we might have time to get you a haircut."

"That's a hoot, Josh. You going to a real barbershop. Or do you think they'll take you to one of those

fancy places where they style your hair? And you got a dog, too. Not to mention you're now famous. I don't think it gets any better than that."

"You know what, Tom, just shut up. I don't want to talk about any of this. I have a lot of thinking to do, and these people . . . all they want to do is pick my brain."

"Well, helloooo, Mr. 8446. Isn't this what you wanted? You're safe, people are going to take care of you, you got a dog, Jesse is back with you, and you have a rich father. And a pretend grandfather. And if I heard things correctly, you are going to end up owning the drug company. What's your problem? I don't like the way you're acting, and, just for the record, Sheila doesn't like it either. So there."

Josh slammed open the shower door and stepped inside. Tom was right. What was his problem? His father was the problem. All his life he'd wanted a father, and now that it looked like he actually had one, he didn't know what to do about it. He soaped up and rinsed off. "Get out of this shower, Tom. I'm not in the mood for you today."

"Tough shit, buddy. You need to listen to me. Sheila is hounding me to tell you that you need to be nice to your father. We think he's sincere. So what if he sold his sperm? So what? You wouldn't be here today if he hadn't done that. He's a good guy. You could at least be nice to him. Give him half a chance. Meet him halfway, buddy. You might piss him off, then you won't get another chance. He got you to this safe house, didn't he? You'd still be on the run if it wasn't for him."

Josh clamped his lips shut as he dressed in

brand-new khakis, a dark green T-shirt with a polo player on the pocket, and a pair of Docksiders. He slicked back his overly long hair. He did need a haircut. He felt a little like his old self as he made his way to the kitchen, with Tom nagging him every step of the way. He continued to ignore his dead friend.

Winston gobbled his food. Josh ate in silence, Charlie and the two agents watching him to gauge his mood. At least that's what he thought they were doing. Why, he didn't know. He liked it better when no one paid any attention to him.

The minute Josh finished eating, the female agent scooped up his dishes, put them in the dishwasher, and turned it on. "We're ready to go as soon as Jesse's handler gets here."

"Oh, no, oh, no! Jesse goes with me. We aren't leaving him behind again. Just because I'm doing what you want doesn't mean I trust you. Jesse goes with me," he repeated. "Right, Jesse?"

"Yeah, right, Josh. I want to go, too. Can we get some pizza?"

"Sure. Pack up your stuff, Jesse. Go to the bathroom and then we'll go for a ride."

"That's not the way it works," the male agent said coldly.

Josh straightened his shoulders. "Yeah, mister, that's the way it works. You people screwed up my life, and I'm not doing anything you say. You're going to do what I say. I say Jesse goes with me. Go ahead, talk into your sleeve, call the president of the United States, I don't care."

"That's certainly telling them, 8446."

"I'm ready, Josh. Where are we going?" Jesse asked.

"To a newspaper. You can sit and draw there, and we'll get you some pizza."

The two agents looked at one another and shrugged. The woman said, "Okay, Jesse can go with us."

Josh was tempted to say something nasty, but he changed his mind. The end result was all that was important. "Then let's go and get it over with."

The little group walked into the attached garage and climbed into a white van with blackened windows, the agents in front, Charlie, Jesse, and Josh and Winston in the back.

"When will they let me and Jesse go with you, Charlie? Do you know?"

"I don't know, Josh. Maybe not for a while. I can't change any of that. You have to do what they say for your own good. Jesse's own good, too."

"Is that your way of saying I should go with Mr. Kelly? Jesse and I go together."

"I think Mr. Kelly knows that. Josh, he's going through the same thing you're going through. He doesn't know what to do, and I think he's looking to you to make some decisions. I don't know this for a fact, but I think he wants whatever is best for you, whatever will make you happy. When you turn eighteen, you can do whatever you want to do. We talked about that, remember? Jesse needs a guardian. We talked about that, too."

Josh leaned back into the leather seat and

closed his eyes. He had so much to think about. What should he do?

"You know damn well what you should do. So, why don't you just do it and let people help you? What's so terrible about getting help from people who have your best interests at heart? Give some thought to what Jesse is going to need in the future."

Josh ignored the whispered words at first. "Shut up, I'm thinking."

Thirty minutes later, the van pulled into an underground garage. Agents milled around, talking into their sleeves, as the party exited the van.

Eight minutes later, the little group was in a conference room at the *Chronicle,* where Tessie was talking to a group of men and women. Who they were, Josh had no idea. He looked up when Pete Kelly and Lily entered the room. He tried to smile, but his facial muscles wouldn't cooperate. He was so nervous he thought he was going to get sick.

They were talking about him, around him, as though he weren't physically present. His tattered book was sitting in the middle of the long, polished table. It seemed to beckon him for some reason. He got up slowly and reached for it. Conversation came to a crashing halt.

"Ah, so you are getting it, 8446. Good going. Wait for just the right moment to spring it on them."

Josh shrugged but didn't say anything. Conversation picked up again.

Tessie looked over at Josh. "Josh, these two

men are lawyers from one of the biggest law firms in the state. They're very interested in taking on your case as a class-action suit on behalf of all the children at the academy. Since you aren't eighteen, Mr. Kelly, or the *Chronicle*, or Mr. Garrison can oversee things."

"No thank you. I know what a class-action suit is. Mr. Dickey explained it to us. He said no one gets any money but the lawyers. So," Josh said, looking from one hungry lawyer to the next, "I won't be needing your services. I'll file my own suit with a lawyer I have in mind. Mr. Dickey said he was the best of the best. You're wrong about my age. I turned eighteen two days ago according to this book. That means I am a free agent and can do whatever I want. What I want is Preston Pharmaceuticals, and I intend to get it."

"Damn, that was good, Josh. Real good."

Josh took that moment to look at Pete Kelly, who was grinning from ear to ear. He gave Josh a thumbs-up. In spite of himself, Josh smiled.

Tessie did her best to suppress her own laughter as she escorted the two chagrined attorneys out of the conference room.

"Next up is the FBI," she said on her return. "There have been breaking developments since last evening. For one, the elder Preston, founder of Preston Pharmaceuticals, was shot and killed along with his nurse and housekeeper. Early ballistic testing confirms the bullets were the same as those used to kill Senator Preston and the children at the academy. They tell me that agents are on it now like white on rice. There won't be any more cover-ups from here on in.

Help is being offered from the four corners of the globe. It might take a while, but we'll find the man who did the shooting. Know this, though, the orders to kill came from the Prestons, Senior and Junior.

"There are some new agents waiting outside this room to talk to Josh and Jesse, so the rest of us will leave you. Since you told us you are now officially eighteen years of age, Josh, you don't need anyone to monitor the interviews unless, of course, you want someone with you."

"Okay, buddy, this is where the rubber meets the road, when it's time to step up to the plate and hit that home run. This moment will never come again, you need to know that. You can do it, Josh."

Josh nodded. In a voice that ricocheted around the room he said, "I think I'd like to have my dad sit in with me."

"Way to go, 8446."

Pete Kelly felt himself start to sag against the wall. Lily shoved her shoulder into his side to prop him up. "Dammit, say something, Pete."

"Nothing would give me more pleasure, son."

Chapter 30

Pete Kelly packed his bags and carried them to the door. Zolly would take them to the car as soon as Lily snapped the last of her suitcases closed. Pete was so nervous he was twitching from head to toe.

"I'm going to miss you, and you haven't even left yet," Pete said, taking Lily in his arms. "I know, I know, you have things to take care of just like I do before you can move to Montana. Call me on the hour, I mean it, Lily."

"And run my battery down! I promise to call, Pete. You're going to be pretty busy with Josh and Jesse and getting them settled. It is safe to take them with you, isn't it?"

Her tone was so worried, so anxious, Pete hastened to tell her one more time about the protective team of agents assigned to the two boys. She nodded, but he suspected she wasn't really assured.

"I guess I'm just a natural-born worrier."

"Tessie wants us to stop by the paper before

we leave. She said she has something to tell us. I hope to hell it's good news."

"Okay, I'm ready."

Pete opened the door to see Zolly standing to the left of the driveway. "You ready, boss?"

"As ready as I can be. Zolly . . . I . . ."

"Boss, there's no need to go all mushy on me. We had a great run, and now you're going on with your life as Mr. John Q. Citizen. It's the right thing for you and the boys. Just make sure you invite me to the wedding. There was no need for the . . ."

"Now who's getting all mushy? I want you to retire and do what you want to do from here on in. I don't know what I would have done without you all these years, especially these last few weeks, Zolly. Remember now, you're the boys' uncle just the way Tessie is their aunt, and with that goes a certain amount of responsibility. You have to send cards, you have to call once a week, and you have to send surprise presents from time to time. You have to compliment them, pat them on the back, tell them you're proud of them, which means you'll have to come to Montana at least once a month. Then you'll have to get on a horse and go riding with them." At the expression on Zolly's face, Pete burst out laughing.

"Gotcha, boss," Zolly said in a choked voice.

There weren't any handshakes, Pete would have none of that. Instead, he clasped the big man in a bear hug and squeezed as hard as he could.

It was Lily's turn to be hugged. "You know

what you have to do, right, Zolly?" Lily whispered.

"Yes, ma'am, I do, and it's under control," he whispered back.

The bags stowed in the cargo hold, Zolly hit the gas pedal.

"I'm nervous, Lily. I've never been a father before. What if I screw up? What if the kids decide they want to go back with Charlie if they don't like it in Montana? Hell, I don't even know if you're going to like it there."

"I'm going to love it in Montana, and so will the boys. It goes without saying you will screw up from time to time. The boys will screw up, too. It's going to be a learning experience for all of us. Relax. Are you going to show Josh the DNA report that came in last night?"

"Yeah. It's the final confirmation. I think he's going to *need* to see it. In case you haven't noticed, the boy is big on going by the book and having everything official. I've got my lawyers looking into the legalities of everything and that includes adopting Jesse. It will all happen in time, I guess. I just wish there wasn't such a strain between us. It's like we're treading on eggshells."

"That will change. Your job is to be there for them. The foundation they need and never had. They'll do the rest. Patience, Pete."

"When did you get so smart?"

"The day I met you all over again. Where's your present for the boys?"

Pete reached into his travel bag and pulled out two bright-red baseball caps with the initials

PAK written on the bills. He stuck his own threadbare cap on his head.

"Perfect." Lily giggled. "Like father, like sons."

"That sounds so . . . so . . ."

"Perfect?"

"Yeah." Pete laughed.

In the driver's seat, Zolly listened to the conversation behind him. Miss Lily was right, it was all perfect. He hoped his own life would turn out just as well. Well, life was all about hope, wasn't it?

Fifteen minutes later they were all gathered in one of the conference rooms at the *Chronicle*. Tessie pointed to the pile of newspapers in the middle of the table. Even though Pete and Lily had seen the papers before, they listened with rapt attention to Tessie's dissertation.

"What we have here are the issues we published on days two, three, and four after my initial story, and among them are reproductions of all of Jesse's drawings. They've been circulated worldwide and already sightings of some of the children have come in. Interpol is on it as well as others. In addition to that, Harry here got a call from Inspector Zven of Interpol, who said a man with the same build and coloring as the man described by Agent Warner and the housekeeper in Senator Preston's Georgetown place is known to have landed in Zurich three days ago. Interpol has been looking at all privately chartered flights originating on the West Coast.

They've identified the private chartered flight that got him to Zurich. Every available agent is on the man's trail. That was the good news. The bad news is the man has gone to ground. They'll find him eventually. We're telling you this so you can go off to Montana with a feeling of safety.

"The FBI, as well as some very powerful people in Washington, has assured both Harry and me that this matter will be resolved. Everyone was so busy trying to cover their asses that they would have promised anything within reason and even beyond. What that means to you, Pete, is you're golden. That goes for Josh and Jesse, too. Excuse me," Tessie said when her cell phone chirped. She listened, and said, "Send them in."

"Your boys are here, Pete. We just have time for a quick good-bye, or you're going to miss your flight. Those feebies are punctual if nothing else. Ride their asses, Pete, and don't let them blink unless you okay it."

"Yes, ma'am," Pete said smartly. "I don't know how to thank you, Tessie."

"No thanks necessary. I just did my job. Go on, get out of here. I need to go home and get some sleep. Bon voyage, go with the angels, all that stuff. Send me a postcard," she said gruffly.

When the door closed behind the little group, Tessie sat back in her chair and wiped at her eyes. Then she put her head down on the table and cried, great heartbreaking sobs. She didn't look up until she felt a gentle hand on her shoulder. "Zolly! I guess you're wondering why I'm crying. I always cry when a story winds down."

"Liar. Talk to me, Tessie."

"No matter what I did my whole life, I could never make my parents happy or even proud of me. I spread myself so thin there were days when I didn't know who I was. Do you know my parents made their own arrangements last week to move into an assisted-living facility? A high-end assisted-living facility. The cost is three-quarters of my yearly salary. All they needed was for me to sign the papers. I did it. They didn't look back, and they didn't say thank you or good-bye. I just walked away. I don't know what to do, Zolly."

"I'm going to teach you how to say *no*. That's for starters. I'll help you find a place you can afford. Pete can take care of the contract you signed. That's down the road. Right now I'm going to take you to lunch, and I won't take no for an answer. So get your gear and let's go."

"Why are you being so nice to me?" Tessie asked suspiciously.

"Because I like you. You're everything I admire in a person, and you aren't hard on the eyes either. By the way, I officially retired about an hour ago. I'm going to stick around here for a while. I like California."

"Now, that is good news. I hope this is going to be an expensive lunch."

"Oh, yeah. Nothing but the best for you, Tessie."

On the way out, Zolly looked over at Lily and winked. She laughed as she turned back to Pete and the boys. She watched as Josh read the DNA report and pocketed it. He was wearing his new baseball cap, as was Jesse, who was asking Josh if the donuts had jelly inside them. She looked over at Pete, who was in earnest conversation with Charlie Garrison.

"I don't know how to thank you for taking care of Josh, Charlie. If there's anything I can do for you, just ask. I'll make sure the boys call you every day, and I'm going to hold you to your promise to come and visit. There will always be a plane ticket waiting for you."

"That's nice to know, young fella. Listen, Josh likes . . . well, he likes to be tucked in at night. And he's partial to hugs. He likes to be hugged. So if you can see your way to doing that, I think it will go a long way with the boy. I'm going to miss them."

Pete cleared his throat. "I'll certainly do what you suggest. I've never been a father before. Lily says it's a learning experience and ongoing. If you change your mind, Charlie, you have a home with us in Montana. You don't need an invitation."

Charlie nodded. "I guess I'll be saying good-bye, then."

Pete watched, his eyes wet as both boys were hugged and hugged some more. For one wild, crazy moment he wondered if the boys would run after the old man. When they remained at his side, he let out a loud sigh of relief.

"I guess it's just us now. Your protective detail is waiting outside, so I guess we better get this show on the road. You ready, boys?"

"Yeah," Josh said.

"Do you have the donuts?" Jesse asked.

"Bye, Josh. See ya in the funny papers."

Josh turned around. "You think you're getting rid of me, Tom? I-don't-think-so. My dad made arrangements with the FBI to move . . . you know, your bodies out to Montana. There's going to be a private cemetery on his property. Mr. Dickey never said you could do that, but Dad's going to do it. He already ordered this real big, special monument. You're going with us. I'm never going to forget you guys."

"Yeah, well, what about me? I'm not a guy." Sheila piped up.

"Sheila!" Josh shouted loud enough to be heard a mile away. "Hey, thanks for all the help."

"No problem. Make sure you visit often and tell us what a family is really like."

"I promise."

Pete whirled around, his eyes as big as saucers. Lily just shook her head.

"It's just Sheila and Tom," Jesse said as he played with his baseball cap.

"Do . . . you . . . uh . . . do you talk to Tom and Sheila, too?" Pete asked.

"Heck, yeah. All the time. All you have to do is call their names, and they talk to you. They explained why Josh left me that time."

"Okaaaay."

"Come on, kids, time to go home," Lily said,

her mind whizzing this way and that way. *How is that possible?* she wondered. *How?*

Pete held out both arms as the two boys took up their positions at his side, exactly where they belonged.

Outside, Pete took a moment to wave to Zolly and Tessie as they walked toward the SUV. This part of his life was over. He could only hope the second part would be just as wonderful as the first. He looked over at Lily, then at the boys, and knew he was on a roll.

"See ya, boss," Zolly shouted.

"We're here," Zolly said, getting out of the car to walk around to open the door for Tessie.

"I thought you said you were taking me to an expensive lunch. Oh, I get it, some friend of yours is cooking lunch. You know what, Zolly, it's not the same thing. I like to be waited on, and I don't like to have to help clean up, and that's what you have to do when you eat at someone's house," Tessie grumbled.

"Nice house, don't you think? It has a garden, lots of flowers. A plot for planting vegetables. A big deck that overlooks the water. A six-seater Jacuzzi. I like the front porch and all the plants. You should see the inside. Vaulted ceilings, skylights, state-of-the-art kitchen, big plasma TV. Crystal chandeliers, ceramic tile, three fireplaces, six bedrooms, the bathrooms will take your breath away. You won't believe this, but there's a pole in the middle of one of the bedrooms."

Tessie rolled her eyes. "You sound like a real-estate salesman. What's for lunch?"

Zolly tossed a set of keys to Tessie. "Lunch is whatever you make us. This is your house now, Tessie. Compliments of Pete and Lily. There are two Golden Retriever pups in the kitchen just waiting for you to cuddle them."

"What? Did you just say what I think you said?"

"Well, yeah," Zolly drawled.

Tessie had never been speechless in her entire life. This was a first. When she finally got her tongue to work, she said, "Are you moving in with me?"

"Well, yeah," Zolly drawled a second time. "I can't wait to see you work that pole."

"Uh-huh" was all Tessie could think of to say.

"Tessie, you never have to worry about a thing from here on in. Not even your parents. Pete gave me a million shares of PAK Industries as my retirement package. I guess what I'm asking is if you want to share it with me?"

Tessie linked her arm with Zolly's. "Such a foolish question. With or without those shares, you're stuck with me."

Stuck on you, too, thought Zolly.

Epilogue

Six months later

The five hundred guests clapped their hands the moment the minister said, "I now pronounce you man and wife."

The huge white tents were filled to overflowing with PAK staff, Lily's employees, and the couple's friends and relatives. There was no shortage of food or wine. The music was dance music, old nostalgic songs of Lily's and Pete's youth. The guests loved it.

A small group consisting of Charlie Garrison, his friend Dorothy, Tessie, Harry, Zolly, Josh, and Jesse—what Tessie called the insiders—sat together at a huge round table making small talk.

"Do you have any news, Aunt Tessie?" Josh asked.

"Yes and no. The world is still looking for the man who killed your friends. They will find him, Josh. It's just going to take time. I'm on it, and you know me, I'm like a dog with a bone. I have something for you, Josh. Come on up to the house so I can show you."

On the walk up the sloping hill, Tessie asked, "How's it all going, Josh? Is it working out?"

"It is. I'm taking this semester off to get back in the swing of things. Dad bought me an old clunker of a car, in case I wreck it, and taught me how to drive. I go back and forth to the community college every day. I take the SATs next week, then I think I'll go to college here in Montana. I don't want to go back to California. The monument to my friends was finished last month. If you aren't too tired, would you like to see it?"

"I would like to see it very much."

They were at the house. Tessie found her way to her room and searched through her bag for the letter she'd received just a week ago. She looked at it and smiled.

"Did I tell you that you look as handsome as your father?"

Josh laughed. Tessie was startled at the sound. She'd never heard Josh laugh before. She handed over the envelope. "It's just the notification letter. I plan to give the prize to you. I just wrote about it all, you lived it."

"But it's a Pulitzer. You can't give it away."

"Wanna bet? What am I going to do with three of those things? Two's enough for me. Come on, show me the monument."

Back in one of the white tents, Pete looked at Lily. "Where did Josh and Tessie go?"

"I don't know, Pete. I don't see either one of them. The security detail is wherever Josh is, so don't panic. Did I tell you how handsome you look? All the women here are so jealous." Lily giggled.

"Ha! Every man here is shooting daggers at me. You look more beautiful today than you did the first time we met."

Lily laughed. "Go find your son! Tell him they want to take pictures soon."

Pete made his way through the throngs of friends and colleagues. He wasn't sure, but he thought he knew where Josh and Tessie were.

Outside in the brisk early-autumn air, Pete looked toward the hill behind the main house. In the distance he could see two lone figures approaching the black-granite monument he'd worked night and day to have erected. To date, Josh had never invited him to go to the hill. He himself, Pete knew, went up every day and stayed for at least an hour. Pete wondered sadly if he would ever be invited to make that trek with his son. Lily said it would happen, she just didn't say when.

Pete stood at the bottom of the hill willing his son to turn around. He did and motioned for Pete to join them. Another small step in acceptance by Josh.

"What do you think, Tessie?" Pete asked as he approached.

"It's magnificent. A very fitting tribute. Whoever the artisan was who did this is very talented."

"It was all Josh's idea. Notice that Charlie Garrison is the honorary grandfather to all of them. Every symbol on the monument meant something to each of the kids. Sheila liked butterflies. Tom liked baseballs and so on. It's peaceful here under our big sky. It's shady here in the summer, the grass mossy green and perfect as a final resting place. It will be a little stark here in the winter, but it will be all right because spring will be just around the corner."

Tessie looked from father to son, and said, "I should be getting back. Zolly promised to tango with me." She waved airily and started down the gentle incline.

"If you want to be alone, Josh, I can leave, too."

"No. I'm glad you came up here. What took you so long?"

"I was waiting to be invited, Josh. I didn't want to intrude. This . . ." he said, waving his arms about, "is all about you. I am so proud of you for wanting to do this."

"Hey, 8446, this might be a good time to open up a little. I like this place. If it wasn't for your dad, we'd all still be in that morgue," Tom grumbled.

"Yeah, Josh. How about introducing us to your father? By the way, thanks for the butterflies," Sheila said.

Josh threw his head back and laughed until he doubled over. He rolled over and over in the dry grass, not caring about his custom-made tuxedo. Pete watched as his son rolled down the hill laughing his head off. He blinked, then blinked again when he saw a vaporous figure take shape.

"Sometimes they act like six-year-olds," Sheila said.

"Will you promise to take really good care of Josh, Mr. Kelly?"

Pete blinked again. He must have had too much champagne. He whirled around and saw a second vaporous figure. He thought he saw a pretty girl with long, curly brown hair. She was wearing a pink dress with flowers around the sleeves. "I don't understand," he said inanely.

"Josh is afraid none of this is real. He's afraid to let go. That's why he keeps calling on us. He hasn't realized he doesn't need us anymore. He has you and Jesse and Lily. He has a family now, with a new aunt, uncle, and grandfather, and your own family. It's up to you to show him the way. Uh-oh, they're going to punch each other out if I don't put a stop to it. I love it when they fight over me," Sheila said, scampering to the bottom of the hill.

Pete thought he was going to black out for a second when he looked down at the bottom of the little hill. It was the champagne, he was sure of it. He really wasn't seeing two spirits and his son tussling on the ground.

Pete started down the hill. The hard leather of his wedding shoes hit the grass the wrong way and suddenly he was rolling down the hill. He felt more than one pair of arms pick him up. Shaky but determined, Pete looked at his son. "I heard them. I saw them."

"I know. It was time for you to meet them on their own turf. That's the way Tom put it. I went up the hill with Tessie to say good-bye."

Pete wrapped his arm around his son's shoulder. "I don't think you can ever really say good-bye. This place will always be here, thanks to you. If you don't mind, I'd like to go up there from time to time. You know, just so your friends know they haven't been forgotten."

"Sheila will like that. Hey, Dad, wanna know a secret?"

"Sure." Pete felt his chest puff out at the words.

"Sheila thinks we were fighting over her. We weren't. Tom was just paying me back for some of the stupid things I did along the way."

Father and son laughed all the way back to the big white tent.

Lily gasped when she saw the grass stains and dry debris sticking to the fancy tuxedos.

"I'll tell you later," Pete whispered.

"See you two later." Josh laughed. "Tessie said she's going to teach me to tango."

"C'mon, Mrs. Kelly, let's watch our son learn how to dance."

"Then what are we going to do with the rest of our lives, Mr. Kelly?"

"Well, Mrs. Kelly, our lives from here on in will be dedicated to finding each and every one of those children who came out of the fertility clinic. We are going to spend every last cent we have to give them a real life. You okay with that, Mrs. Kelly?"

"I'm okay with it, Mr. Kelly. Oh, look, Josh has the same two left feet his father has!"

"This is one of those times when there is no response, Mr. Kelly. Trust me," Tom said.

"I hear you, son."

If you enjoy Fern Michaels's unique brand of wonderfully entertaining storytelling, you won't want to miss her exciting new series, The Godmothers. Turn the page for a special preview of both

THE SCOOP,

a Kensington mass-market paperback
on sale in April 2012,

and

DEADLINE,

a Kensington trade paperback
on sale in May 2012.

The Scoop

Chapter 1

Charleston, South Carolina

It was an event, there was no doubt about it. Not that funerals were, as a rule, events, but when someone of Leland St. John's stature bit the dust, it became one. The seven-piece string band playing in the downpour, per one of Leland's last wishes, had turned it into an event regardless of what else was going on in the world.

Then there was the tail end of Hurricane Blanche, which was unleashing torrents of rain upon the mourners huddled under the dark blue tent and only added to the circuslike atmosphere.

"Will you just get on with it," Toots Loudenberry mumbled under her breath. She continued to mutter and mumble as the minister droned on and on. "No one is as good as you're making Leland sound. All you know is what I told you, and I sure as hell didn't tell you all that crap you're spouting. He was a selfish, rich, old man. End of story."

Toots's daughter leaned closer to her mother and tried to whisper through the thick veil covering her mother's head and ears. "Can't you hurry it along? It's not like this is the first time you've done this. Isn't this the seventh or eighth husband you've buried? I'm damn glad that preacher said his name, or I wouldn't even know who it is that's being planted. I gotta say, Mom, you outdid yourself with all these flowers."

Toots rose to the occasion and stepped forward, cutting the minister off in midsentence. "Thank you, Reverend." She wanted to say his check was in the mail, but she bit her tongue as she took a step forward and laid her wilted rose on top of the bronze coffin. She stepped aside so the other mourners could follow her out from under the temporary tent, which was open on all four sides. She stepped in water up to her ankles, cursed ripely, and sloshed her way to the waiting limousine, which would take her back home. "That's just like you, Leland. Why couldn't you have waited one more week, and the rainy season would have been over? Now my shoes are ruined. So is my hat, as well as my suit. Too bad you don't know how much this outfit cost. If you did, you would have waited another week to die. You always were selfish. See what all that selfishness got you. You're dead."

"What are you mumbling about, Mom?"

Toots slid into the limousine and kicked off her sodden shoes. Her black mourning hat followed. She looked over at her daughter, Abby, who looked like a drowned rat, and said, "Of all my husbands, I liked Leland the least. I resent having to attend his funeral under these conditions. He was my only mistake. But one out of eight, I suppose, isn't too bad."

Abby reached for a wad of paper napkins next to the champagne bottle that seemed to come with all limousines. "Why didn't you just crisp him up?"

Toots sighed. "I wanted to, but Leland said in his will that he wanted to be buried with that damn string band playing music. One has to honor a person's last wishes. What kind of person would I be if I didn't honor his, even if he was a jerk?"

"Don't you mean if you didn't honor those last wishes, what's-his-name's money would have gone to the polar bears in the Arctic?"

"That, too." Toots sighed.

The woman born Teresa Amelia Loudenberry, Toots to her friends, stared at her daughter. "How long are you staying, dear?"

"I have a four o'clock flight. I left Chester with a sitter, and Chester does not like sitters. There's just enough time for me to grab something to eat at your post feast, change into dry clothes, and get outta here. Can't you hear California calling my name? Don't look at me like that, Mom. I didn't even know that guy you married. I met him at your wedding, and that's the sum total of our relationship. If I remember correctly, you said he was a charmer. I expected a charmer. I did not get a charmer. I'm just saying."

"Maybe I should have said snake charmer," Toots said vaguely. "Leland was like this gorgeously wrapped present that when opened was quite . . . tacky. I was stunned, but I did marry the man, so I had to make the best of it. He's gone now, so perhaps we shouldn't speak ill of him. I'll mourn for ten days for the sake of appearance, then get on with my life. I'm going to find a hobby to keep myself busy. I'm sick and tired of doing good deeds. Anyone can do good deeds. Anyone can garden and grow one-of-a-kind roses. I need to do something that will make a difference, something challenging. Something I can really sink my teeth into. That's another thing. Leland wore dentures. He kept them in a cup in the bathroom at night. I could never get used to that. He wasn't very good in bed, either."

"That's probably more than I need to know, Mom."

"I'm just saying, Abby. I don't want you to think your old mom is callous. You have to admit I did have seven happy marriages. I should have hung up my garter belt when Dolph died. Did I do that? No, I did not. I let Leland sweep me off my feet, dentures and all. Sometimes life is so unfair.

"That's enough of a pity party for me. Tell me how it's going out there in sunny California. How's the job going? What's the latest hot gossip, and who is doing what to whom in Hollywood?"

Abby Simpson, Toots's daughter by her first

husband, John Simpson, the absolute love of Toots's life, was a reporter for a second-rate tabloid, *The Informer,* based in Los Angeles. She was a second-string runner, which meant she had to hit the pavement and find her own stories, then elaborate on them for the public's insatiable appetite for Hollywood gossip.

"Rodwell Archibald Godfrey, otherwise known as Rag to us underlings, called me into his office and told me he wants more product. I can't make it happen if it isn't out there. All the A-list papers seem to get the stories first. I think this is just another way of saying he is not happy with my work. I applied to the other tabloids, but they're full up and not taking on anyone new. I'm doing my best. I just manage to make my mortgage payment every month and have enough left over to buy dog food. No, you cannot help me, Mom. I'm going to make it on my own, so let's not go down that road. My break is coming, I can feel it. By the way, I brought a stack of future issues for you to read. I have stuff in all of them."

"I can't get used to the idea that you people make all that stuff up, then it happens. And you print weeks in advance of what's happening," Toots said.

Abby laughed. "It's not quite that way, but you're close. Well, we're home, and you have guests. You really know how to throw a funeral, Mom."

"Event, dear. *Funeral* is such a dreary word. It conjures up all kinds of dismal thinking."

Abby laughed as she climbed out of the limo and marched up the steps to the wide veranda of her mother's house.

Both women raced upstairs to change into dry clothing before they had to meet with the guests who would be coming by to pay their last respects.

Toots looked at herself in the long mirror in her room. Yes, she did look bedraggled, but wasn't a widow supposed to look a little bedraggled? "Black is not my best color," she muttered to herself as she tossed her mourning outfit into a heap on the floor in the bathroom. She donned another black dress, added a string of pearls, brushed out her hair, sprayed on some perfume, and felt refreshed enough to go downstairs and socialize for an hour or so.

Burying the dead was so time-consuming. Even the aftermath took an eternity. All she wanted to do was retire to her sitting room to read the pile of tabloids Abby had brought with her. Not for the world would Toots ever admit that she was addicted to tabloid gossip. But for now, she had a duty to perform, and perform it she would. She had all evening to read her treasured tabloids and guzzle a little wine while doing so. She'd drink to Leland, and that would be the end of this chapter in her life.

Time to move on. Something she was very good at.

Chapter 2

The minute the last guest walked out the door with a go-bag of food, the bereaved Toots galloped up the stairs and headed for her three-hundred-square-foot bathroom, where she ran a bath. She made two trips to the huge Jacuzzi with the pile of tabloids, four scented candles, a fresh bottle of wine, and her favorite Baccarat wineglass. She paused a minute to decide which bath salts she wanted to use, finally settling on Confederate jasmine since the scent was more or less true to the flower. She was, when you got right down to it, a transplanted Southern belle.

Toots stripped down, and the clothes she was wearing went on top of the sodden outfit she'd discarded earlier. She'd never wear them again. Then again, since she was a stickler for protocol, maybe she'd tell her housekeeper, Bernice, to leave them until her ten days of mourning were up. That way she wouldn't be cheating. And to think she had to wear black, which really made her look washed out, for another ten days. Nine more if you counted today. Well, she was definitely counting today.

Toots sniffed at the delicious aroma emanating from the Jacuzzi. Wonderful! She lowered herself into the silky water and sighed happily. Toots leaned back and savored the first few moments of the exquisite bath before leaning forward to pour herself a glass of the bubbly that Leland had bought by the truckload for his wine cellar.

"To you, Leland," Toots said as she held her wineglass aloft. She turned up the glass and swallowed the contents in one long gulp. Now she could move on. She'd done her duty.

Toots refilled her glass, leaned back, and fired up a cigarette. Smoking was a truly horrible habit, but she didn't care. She was way too old to worry about what was good or bad for her. She was all about living and didn't give a thought to the fact that cigarettes would interfere with that. Besides, she had every vice there was. She loved vices because they made for such good conversations. She liked to drink, smoke, was a sugar addict and a closet tabloid reader. She'd long ago convinced herself that being a vegan made up for all her bad habits. That shit, Leland, was forever giving her grief for her, as he put it, unsavory habits. "Screw you, Leland!"

Toots was on her third glass of wine and on page four of the issue she was reading before she realized she couldn't remember what she'd just read. What was wrong with her? Nothing ever interfered with reading her beloved tabloids. Until now. She closed her eyes and tried to figure out what it was that was interfering with her universe.

Something was lurking somewhere inside her. She'd already scratched Leland. Abby was okay, at least for the moment. Did she feel rudderless? Did she need a man in residence? Hell no, she didn't. Then what was bothering her? The nine days of mourning she allowed herself? She snorted. Any woman worth her salt could get through nine days of mourning by going out to breakfast, lunch, and dinner every day. Fit in a little shopping, and she'd be good to go.

By the fourth glass of wine, Toots decided she needed . . . no, she didn't need, she *wanted* to stir up some trouble. She needed some excitement in her life. Her thoughts carried her back in time to when she was young and full of piss and vinegar with her friends. Friends she hadn't seen near enough throughout the past twenty years. They e-mailed, called, and sent Christmas cards, but life got in the way sometimes. Maybe it was time to call all of them and invite them for a visit. They were, after all, Abby's godmothers. Everyone thought it strange that her daughter had three godmothers. Especially that shithead, Leland. She didn't find it strange at all. Neither did her friends.

Toots peered into the wine bottle. Empty! She climbed out of the tub, dried off with a towel the size of a tent, powdered herself, slipped into a black nightgown—because she was in mourning—and tottered out to the mini-office in her bedroom. It wasn't really an office,

just a little table where she sat to write notes to
people she didn't give two shits about, pay a few
bills that she didn't want her business manager
to know about, and use her laptop to check out
TMZ and Page Six several times a day.

Toots fired up her laptop and proceeded to
type an e-mail to her friend Mavis, who lived in
Maine in a little clapboard house near the
ocean.

*"I want you to come for a visit, Mavis. You were al-
ways the one with the ideas. How soon can you get
here? By the way, I just buried Leland today, and I'm
in a funk."*

Five minutes later, the laptop pinged receipt
of a return e-mail.

*"Sorry, Toots, I can't afford a trip like that. I can't
leave Coco, my dog. She's really my only friend these
days. I'm sorry your dog Leland died. I didn't even
know you had a dog. It's terrible when your beloved
pet dies. Sorry, Toots, I'd love to see you, but my pen-
sion just won't cover a trip at this time."*

Toots blinked. How weird that Mavis thought
Leland was a dog. She wondered why she
thought that, then it dawned on her what her
old friend meant.

She hit the REPLY button.

*"I'll send a first-class ticket for you and Coco. Le-
land was my husband."*

The next response from Mavis was: *"LOL, I
forgot you married again. Too bad, too sad. You'll get
over it, Toots, you always do. I'll be happy to accept
your tickets and look forward to seeing you. It's been
way too long. Are the others coming, too?"*

Toots fired back, *"I'm working on it now. More tomorrow."*

Toots's next e-mail was to Sophie, who'd married a philanderer, now with one foot in the grave and the other on a banana peel, according to Sophie's latest e-mail. It was a known fact among the foursome that Sophie hated her husband and was only sort of / more or less taking care of him because of the five-million-dollar insurance policy she'd taken out on him some years ago. "I'm sticking around long enough to collect, then I'm outta here," she'd said.

"Sophie, I'm e-mailing you to invite you for a visit. I'm willing to send you a ticket if you can clear your calendar. It's been way too long since we've seen each other. I have something in mind that I think you and the others will find interesting. It will be like old times."

Sophie's response came through so quickly that Toots was surprised. *"I can't leave him here alone. This old bird is taking way too long to die. I didn't pay that mountain of premiums all these years to get aced out of the payoff. Besides, I want him to sweat every day and wonder if I'm going to give him his meds and feed him. Which, of course, I do. What kind of person would I be not to do that?"*

Well, Toots decided, she could certainly relate to that. *"Not to worry, Sophie. I'll get you a nurse 24/7 for your husband. So you'll come, then? By the way, I buried Leland today."*

Sophie shot back. *"Okay, I'll clear my schedule that's not really a schedule. Just let me know when my departure date is. Who is Leland?"*

Toots responded to her e-mail. *"I'll get back to you on the date. Leland was my husband. I have to do that ten-day mourning thing. Nine days if you count today. I am definitely counting today. You can watch me and know what it's like, so you'll know how to be-have when that dud you married bites the dust. Mourning is tricky. You have to do it just right, or people will talk about you."*

"What number is Leland?" Sophie queried. *"I think you've been married more times than Elizabeth Taylor."*

Toots quickly replied, *"Leland was number 8, and I am never getting married again. More tomor-row. I have to e-mail Ida now. She's going to be tough. Remember how we hated each other and pretended we didn't? I think she's still ticked off that I married the guy she wanted. She'd be a widow now if I hadn't. I tried to tell her he was a big nothing, but he did have all that money."*

Toots didn't bother waiting for a response before she e-mailed Ida. She got right to the point. *"Ida, it's Toots. I'm e-mailing you to invite you for a visit. Mavis and Sophie have agreed to come, and it will be like old times. I have this plan, Ida, and I want to involve all of us in it. I hope you aren't still holding a grudge against me. It's time for us to forget about all that old silly stuff. Believe it or not, I did you a favor by stealing whatever his name was. Even his money didn't make up for how boring he was. But he was gentle and considerate. So, what do you think? By the way, I buried Leland today. I'm in mourning, have nine days to go."*

Ida's response was short and curt. *"Count me*

in. Tell me when you want me to arrive. Oh, boo hoo about Leland. "

Toots rubbed her hands together and closed her laptop. She was on a roll, she could feel it. Though what this big plan was, she hadn't a clue just yet. She'd think of something. She always did.

Deadline

Prologue

"How can we go to the governor's mansion if it no longer exists?" Mavis asked Sophie, as the Citation X gently lifted off the runway at LAX. "I read about it on the Internet this morning, when I was checking my Web site." Mavis's line of funeral attire, GOOD MOURNING, had blossomed almost overnight since its inception, but she continued to monitor each individual order received from her Web site. Now more than ever, she lived on the Internet.

Sophie rolled her chestnut eyes upward, showing only the milky-colored whites. "It still exists; it's just that it's more of a tourist attraction these days. Ronald Reagan was the last governor who lived there. The *gov-er-na-tor* stays at the Sterling Hotel, which is where we will be staying for the next few days or however long it takes to assist the first lady of California with her nightmares." A slight smile lifting the edge of her full lips, Sophie mimicked the instantly recognizable accent for which the famous former actor turned governor was so well-known.

"Stop being so damn dramatic. You may be a drama queen, but you're not an actress," Toots called out from the seat in front of Sophie and Mavis.

"I didn't say I was," Sophie tossed back.

"Stop!" Ida intervened. "I don't want to hear any smart comments today. I've about had it listening to the two of you squabble."

Laughter bubbled throughout the private jet.

When the four women had boarded the luxury jet, all of them agreed that California's governor flew in style. The cabin was decked out in creamy leather reclining seats, solid cherry cabinetry, and all the latest gadgets, including an Apple iPad2 equipped with high-speed Internet, and built-in telephones, just in case the governor had to make a telephone call and was unable to move about the plane. All four of them: Teresa "Toots" Amelia Loudenberry, Sophie Manchester, Ida McGullicutty, and Mavis Hanover, the last three being Toots's daughter Abby's godmothers, were en route to Sacramento, the state capital. Sophie, in her newfound celebrity, was slated to perform her magic, said *magic* consisting of holding a séance for the Peabody- and Emmy-award-winning first lady, who had begun to be plagued with nightmares about her famous uncle, John F. Kennedy, the thirty-fifth president of the United States, who was assassinated when she was eight years old. When she'd heard of Sophie's success in abolishing ghosts and other *un*worldly beings, she'd personally called to ask for her assistance.

"Oh hush, Ida! If I wanted your opinion, I'd ask." Sophie smirked. "And I really, really do not."

There was a long-standing war of sorts between Sophie and Ida. Though neither would ever voluntarily admit it, if pressured, both would confess to loving the other. It was just that they didn't *like* each other.

"Now now, girls, let's not fuss. We've got a long flight ahead of us, and I, for one, want to relax before we're introduced to California's first couple. I don't want to appear haggard," Toots explained.

Mavis, the most upbeat and positive of the group, said softly, "Oh, Toots dear, you could never look haggard! I believe you're the most gorgeous woman I know."

Toots smiled at Mavis. "You are too kind, but thank you anyway." Ida muttered something decidedly unkind.

As usual, Sophie and Toots ignored her when she mouthed off.

"Hey, this flight might not be as long as you think. Listen to this," Sophie said, holding up the brochure she had removed from her seat pocket. "The Citation X can fly through a half dozen time zones before refueling, and it has a Rolls-Royce engine. Whew! This is some aircraft."

Ida spoke up. "That *is* good news. The less time I'll have to listen to you three run your filthy mouths, the happier I'll be."

Sophie raised her hand above her head so Ida could see her middle finger standing proud and tall. "And it says that the bathroom is marble."

Coco, Mavis's spoiled female Chihuahua, growled from her royal seat, aka Mavis's lap. "Ida, I believe you've upset Coco. She knows full well that I don't say nasty things the way the rest of you do." Mavis grinned, before adding, "Or at least not nearly as often."

It was hard to imagine the woman Mavis had been just two short years ago. A retired English teacher and widow for seventeen years, she'd lived in a little clapboard house near the ocean in Maine before Toots had e-mailed her and invited her to Charleston, South Carolina, Toots's home town. She'd been a heart attack waiting to happen when Toots rescued her, and, yes, that was exactly what Toots had done, rescued her. If she hadn't, Mavis would probably be six feet under this very moment. Under the guidance provided by Toots and a personal trainer, Mavis lost over one hundred pounds and exercised daily as though her life depended on it, which it almost undoubtedly likely did.

Ida, a native New Yorker high-society snob, had been a complete and total nutcase. Recently widowed when Toots contacted her inviting her to join her in Charleston, the former elegant photographer suffered with OCD, obsessive-compulsive disorder, a debilitating fixation on germs. Thomas, her spouse of more than thirty years, was thought to have died from the bacterium, *e-coli* found in a tainted piece of meat Ida had purchased from her favorite butcher shop. Circumstances being what they were, Ida's psychological disorder had caused her to become a total shut-in. Her world of Clorox and sanitizing had quickly ended when Toots sent her to a famous doctor in California who specialized in treating her disorder. Not only had she been cured of her compulsion in a matter of weeks, but she became romantically involved with her savior, who turned out to be no doctor at all but an imposter. He'd almost bilked Ida out of $3 million to boot. To see her now, minus her cleaning kit, was a true miracle.

Sophie, also a native New Yorker, an RN and a former pediatric nurse, had been recently widowed as well. Walter, her abusive alcoholic husband, died from cirrhosis of the liver. No big surprise there. Planning ahead and looking forward to the day he died, Sophie had taken out a five-million-dollar life insurance policy on him before it was too late and was now quite comfortable. Toots, an expert at planning funerals, having had a great deal of practice over the years, or *events* as she liked to think of them, helped Sophie arrange a quick *event* for Walter. Toots sang an off-key, "*Ave Maria*," they said their *Hail Mary's*, baked Walter's remains, then spent the rest of the day shopping before jetting back to Los Angeles, where Toots had fulfilled a secret lifelong dream when she purchased *The Informer,* a tabloid newspaper where her daughter, Abby, was working as a reporter.

Two years later Abby, now editor-in-chief of the tabloid, still had no clue her mother was the real power behind LAT Enterprises, the corporation that owned the paper. Abby seemed content to accept her new bosses' preference for communication—e-mail and FedEx—so until Toots had a darn good reason, she had no intention of revealing her own involvement with the corporate owner of *The Informer* to Abby.

Knowing she'd have to stay in close contact with her daughter, Toots purchased a beautiful three-story hillside minimansion in Malibu. It had been inhabited by a former pop star, whose idea of decorating was hot pink and purple. One of the guest bathrooms actually had a mirror in the shape of a guitar with blue rhinestones on the baseboards. Toots guessed this was a sad tribute to the King himself, dearly departed Elvis.

Prior to the pop star, the house had belonged to Desi Arnaz and Lucille Ball. Toots, along with her dear friends, had moved into the Malibu beach house while it was being remodeled. It was during the remodeling that Toots experienced a paranormal phenomenon in her own bedroom.

She remembered that night as being the most frightening of her life.

Awakened by a pounding heart and an eerie chill in the horrid purple bedroom she'd referred to as a hooker haven and paralyzed by a fear unlike anything she'd ever experienced, Toots had been unable to move from her bed. Next, still had difficulties believing this, what seemed to be four clouds, in an eerie, translucent shade of blue, clustered around her bed.

Inside the cloudlike puffs were faces. Yes, she knew how insane it sounded, but she'd seen it with her own two eyes and it was what it was. Afterward, she remembered thinking she could've had hallucinations from a bad case of indigestion or, perish the thought, even a brain tumor. She had read somewhere about tumors on the brain causing pressure that gave rise to hallucinations. But it had been nothing like that at all.

Recalling the faces, she realized that they were familiar to her, but in her traumatized state, she was unable to identify them. In a matter of seconds, the foglike clouds disappeared. Scared and shaken, she'd told Sophie what she'd experienced. Having had a lifelong interest in the paranormal, Sophie hadn't been shocked when Toots told her what had happened. Of course, now they knew that the remodeling had stirred up the spirits of famous movie moguls Aaron Spelling and Bing Crosby, who in life had an ongoing feud over a piece of land. Sophie had suggested a séance. Successful in her attempts to contact and communicate with the dead, Sophie had become a celebrity in the world of paranormal events and ghosts. So there they were, flying in a private jet on their way to the governor's mansion to assist California's first lady with her recurring nightmares.

Toots reclined in the luxurious leather seat, content with her life and that of Abby's three godmothers. Since the girls had temporarily relocated to California and South Carolina—temporarily being two years—their lives as senior citizens had been one big roller-coaster ride. A few rough spots along the way, but thrilling nonetheless.

Toots glanced at each of her friends, who were really more like sisters. Abby's three godmothers were quiet, each lost in her own private world. They had been friends for more than fifty years. She treasured her friendship with each woman. Unique and individual in their own right, Toots could only hope they'd have another fifty years together.

The copilot's deep voice came over the intercom, announcing they were about to begin their descent into Sacramento International Airport. "Ladies, I'm going to have to ask you all to buckle up. The ceiling is down to two hundred feet with some fog and light rain. We'll be making an ILS approach, so it could get bumpy. Please secure any open containers and that little dog."

Ida, an uncomfortable flier on a good day, turned ten shades of white. "What does that mean? I knew I should've taken a commercial flight. I hate these small planes."

"Private jets have the same stupid-ass rules as the commercial airlines," Sophie said as she adjusted her seat belt.

Mavis put Coco in her carrier and placed it beneath the seat. The little pooch growled, then went into a series of earsplitting barks before settling down. "She just hates that crate, but we have to follow the rules. They're for our own protection," Mavis said, darting a glance at Sophie.

"Oh crap, Mavis, I know that, I just like to complain," Sophie added. "At least we didn't have to go through security and get felt off. I bet Ida wouldn't mind going through security, would you?" Sophie said, trying to distract Ida.

When Ida didn't respond to her teasing, Sophie continued. "Ida, clear something up for me. Is it felt off or felt up? I've heard both, but I'm not sure which one to use."

Toots cackled, Mavis smiled, and Ida answered Sophie, her voice trembling with fear. "Either. Personally, I like to think of it as getting 'felt off.' I'm surprised at you Sophie, with your infinite well of useless information that you would even ask such a question." To her credit, Ida didn't react to Sophie's tormenting her as she would have a year ago. She was learning to be a true Southern smart-ass.

"It certainly has been in the news a lot lately, those perverts trying to cop a feel. People have no respect for one another anymore," Toots said disgustedly.

Suddenly, the plane lurched to the left. Ida shrieked. "What's happening?" Unlike a commercial jet, a private plane did not have the closed cockpit rule. Ida strained to see into the cockpit and gasped when she saw nothing but clouds rushing past the windscreen. "Oh my God, how are they going to land this plane? The windshield is covered with clouds! I should have stayed home." Ida bowed from the waist, closed her eyes, and held on tight.

Toots observed Ida, whose normally composed face was etched with fear, fingernails digging into the expensive leather armrest. She knew full well that there was nothing to fear, as one of her eight husbands, she couldn't remember exactly which one in the sequence, had been a pilot. To take Ida's mind off her fear, she said, "I remember doing this many times; it really isn't as dangerous as you think. See all of those little gauges?" She pointed to the instrument panel, which was clearly visible from their seats. "One of those little round things has two needles on it. One goes up and down, and the other moves left and right. As the pilot approaches the airport, the needles will begin to intersect each other. Keeping them centered—it's somewhat similar to the crosshairs on the scope of a rifle—will align the plane directly on the center of the runway at exactly the right height and allow the pilot to make a normal landing even though he can't see."

Incredulous, Sophie asked, "How in the hell do you know that? Or is that something you're just making up so Ida won't be afraid?"

"Trust me, when you've been in a plane that's even smaller than this one, a four-seater, and you're in the copilot seat and cannot even see the wings of the plane, you remember stuff like that. Plus, I think it was Joe, number four or five, anyway, he was obsessed with flying and explained everything to me when we flew together. I listened, too, just in case he kicked the bucket. By then, I was already quite experienced in the widow department."

Suddenly, the turbulence ended as quickly as it had begun. Below was the view of a beautiful runway lit up like a festively decorated tree on Christmas morning. Seconds later, the wheels screeched, and they were safely on the ground.

The copilot announced their arrival, and within minutes the cabin door was opening and the automatic stairs descending for their immediate exit.

"Now this sure beats commercial flying. I always hate when the passengers jump up like pigs running to a feeding trough. Not to mention all the offending body odors you have to endure."

"You're disgusting, Sophie," Toots said.

Their arrival was met with all the pomp and circumstance afforded visiting dignitaries, complete with a meticulously placed red carpet leading to a sleek black limousine.

The chauffeur was retrieving their luggage from the baggage compartment when a well-dressed woman in her mid-thirties emerged from the limo. She greeted the quartet as they approached the vehicle. "I'm Cynthia Johnson, the first lady's personal assistant. How was your flight?"

Returning to her role of society snob, Ida was the first to speak. "It was perfect from takeoff to landing. It was so kind of the governor to send his jet for us."

Sophie looked at Toots and Mavis, rolling her eyes. "Is this the same woman who left fingernail marks on the armrest five minutes ago?"

Ida shot her a shut-up-or-die look.

"I'm not the biggest fan of flying myself," Cynthia said to Ida. "Sophia?"

She shook hands with the woman. "That would be me," Sophie said. "These are my friends, Toots, and Mavis."

"I'm glad you all could accompany Sophie. I'm sure you will enjoy the amenities at the Sterling Hotel. You all have carte blanche, courtesy of the governor." She looked at her slim gold wristwatch. "We'd better get going."

Half an hour later, when they arrived at the hotel, they were greeted by the governor himself.